The WORST WEDDING Date

USA TODAY BESTSELLING AUTHOR

PIPPA GRANT

Editing by Jessica Snyder
Proofreading by Emily Laughridge & Jodi Duggan
Cover Design by Qamber Designs

This book is dedicated to anyone who's ever struggled with perfectionism and learning to break the rules that don't matter.

And also to anyone who lives with loud sneezers. I know you know what I'm talking about. And we love them anyway.

DELANEY KINGSTON, AKA A BRIDESMAID WHO WILL DO ANYTHING for her best friend, no matter how terrible it is

AH, smell that?

That salty, fresh breeze with a hint of passion fruit and a golden sunset layered over the ocean surf?

That's the scent of *happily ever after*.

After years and years and *years* of my best friend waiting for her boyfriend to pop the question, then *another* forever of planning, we are *finally* here.

Their wedding week.

Emma's getting her dream destination wedding, and I haven't stopped smiling—no, *beaming* since my plane touched down in Hawaii two hours ago.

Everything is love. The gentle wind softening the humid air. The fragrant flowers. The giant coconut trees. The gecko watching me from the shorter tropical palm tree. Emma's shampoo as she hugs me outside the entrance to the Midnight Orchid Club Resort barely a minute after I texted her that my driver was pulling into the parking lot.

"Laney! You're here!"

"Happy wedding week, you beautiful bride, you." I hug her back like we weren't watching the January snow fall while we had coffee together at Bean & Nugget Café back home in Snaggletooth Creek four days ago. "Are you nervous? Are you eating enough? Did you have dinner?"

She laughs as she pulls back, but it's higher-pitched than it should be. "Hawaiian feast. You saw the schedule, right? Of course you saw it. You live by schedules."

Her stomach grumbles like she did not, in fact, partake in the Hawaiian feast.

It's an instinctive reaction to reach into my purse and whip out a protein bar for her. "Em? Everything okay?"

Her eyes go impossibly wider and she shake-nods her head too fast and insistently. "Of course."

For the first time since I boarded the plane to catch up to the rest of the wedding party after having to delay a day for an unfortunate work emergency, I'm not smiling. "Talk to me. What's up?"

She has three inches on me, so I have to look up to study her. Her blond hair is pulled back in a ponytail. Her sharp cheekbones are undeniably sharper. And I don't think the tinge of hysteria in her brown eyes is a trick of the fading evening light.

"Wedding stress. That's all. This is normal. How was your flight? Are you exhausted? Here. I have your, erm, room key. We checked in the whole wedding party yesterday. Come on. Everyone's at the pool. Here. Leave your luggage." She turns her Emma charm on the bellhop, a young man with brown skin and a bright Hawaiian shirt. "Can you please get my friend's luggage taken to the Plumeria Bungalow?"

"Of course, ma'am."

"Thank you so much!" she says too brightly as she slips him a tip.

She grabs me by the elbow and tugs me inside the lobby

of the resort entrance, past the unmanned check-in desk and dying potted tropical plants and large beach landscape paintings. At the open-air atrium where three paths split off, she pauses for just a second.

"This way!" she says, even brighter still.

Emma's a happy person.

But this is *too* happy. Even for her.

And there it is.

The nibble on her thumbnail as we head down the tiki-torch-lit walkway on the left.

She has the protein bar in the same hand. She's practically shoving the wrapper up her nose to nibble on her nail.

"Em?" I say.

She jerks her hand down and once again treats me to a smile, but this one feels so fake that I have to blink to make sure travel fatigue isn't making me see things.

"This way," she repeats.

We're surrounded by flowering shrubs and palm trees beyond the walkway. The light wind off the ocean rustles the bright red-and-green leaves on a shorter tree, and upbeat island music trills somewhere in the distance.

Sure, a few of the tiki torches have gone out. And there are some dead palm fronds littering the grass under a tree or two.

But this place is a tropical paradise.

My best friend shouldn't be stressed here. Especially not a few days before she finally marries the love of her life at the resort she's told everyone she'll be getting married at since the day she pulled a photo of it out of a travel catalog when we were little.

I draw to a stop, grab her arms, and look up at her. "Em. What's wrong?"

"Nothing."

Emma's been one of my two best friends for over twenty years. I know when she's lying. I know when she's trying hard to convince me she's not lying. And I know when she's

3

on the edge of a breakdown and is lying as a last resort to convince herself that nothing's wrong.

Which is exactly where we are now.

"Okay. Let's start with some deep breaths. Whatever it is, we'll fix it."

"Laney," she whispers, a plaintive plea full of hope, "I don't know if you can."

"Gotta talk to me first. Tell me what's going on. Everything okay with you and Chandler?"

She winces.

I tilt my head and wait.

"Chandler and I are fine," she says. "The wedding is fine. Everything's fine."

She doesn't *sound* fine.

She sounds like she's a hair's breadth from hopping a passing freighter and running away from her life.

I add a brow lift and wait for more.

"It's not like that time we almost broke up three years ago," she finally says in a rush. "We're *fine*. Both thrilled to be here and finally getting married. It's...neither one of us."

No lies detected, but there's still so much stress making her expression tight and her breath too shallow.

I nod and squeeze her arms. "Okay. So what is it?"

She pulls away and starts down the path again. A hint of the sunset comes into view between two bushes, and *oh my god*.

That's gorgeous.

Oranges and pinks swirled together behind a row of coconut trees.

Whatever—or *whoever*—is ruining this for Emma is going *down*. She should be out on the beach with Chandler, watching this show.

But the sunset disappears behind a tall, flowered bush while I follow her along the winding, cracked sidewalk.

"Emma?"

She uses her teeth to rip open the protein bar package, then gnaws off a huge corner, chews three times, and swallows. "Oh. Cookies and cream. That's my favorite."

"I know. What's wrong? How do I make the bride of the hour as happy as she can be?"

She slides a look at me before attacking the protein bar with a bite that demolishes half of what's left.

Uh-oh.

"Ah nee a vava," she says with a full mouth.

"You need a favor?"

She nods and doesn't look at me while we keep walking.

"*Emma*. You know I'm here for anything you need this week. *Anything*. Name it. *Oh. My. God*." I drop my voice to a whisper. "Are you pregnant? Do you need—"

"No!"

"Okay. Okay."

She visibly swallows and winces again. "I wish I was pregnant," she grumbles. "But no. This is bad, Laney. I should've known, but I didn't, so now I'll deal with it, except I'm tired. I'm *so* tired. And I hate to ask this, but you're the only one I can count on."

"Name it. I'm here for you."

The bushes open up, and she pauses while the music gets louder and the view of the sunset widens beyond a kidney-shaped pool where roughly a dozen people are gathered about, either in the water or on loungers or at the tables at the edge of the deck.

This time, she lets herself fully nibble on her thumb when she could be nibbling on the rest of the protein bar, and she stares at the pool. And it's not a distant, unfocused, *I'm thinking hard about something* stare.

This is an *I'm staring at the problem* stare that's accompanied by the deepest sigh I've ever heard her sigh in my life.

Emma's closest sorority sister from college, Claire, who's her third bridesmaid, has claimed a pool lounge. She's one of my favorites of Emma's college friends. Her hair and her bright swimsuit are wet like she's recently gotten out of the water. There's not enough sun left to soak up any rays, but there's something else clearly keeping her there.

A very distinctive something else.

She's leaning forward at the edge of her lounger, smiling and flirting with a man in a—*what*?

Why is that server wearing an inflatable ride-on flamingo costume?

It's like one of those blow-up tyrannosaurus rex costumes, except it's a giant blow-up flamingo, and his shirtless top half is out. The flamingo costume has inflated legs across its back to make it look like the man's riding the flamingo, and it would be funny if it wasn't so unexpected here.

He's offering a tray of pineapples with drink umbrellas and straws to Claire, who is eating it all up.

Good for her.

I glance at Emma, who is definitely staring at the server.

He's *ripped*. And tattooed. With surfer hair. And I can't see his face, but I can tell Claire is charmed.

Charmed charmed.

Drooling, even.

Oh, god.

Emma also has a crush on a resort pool boy and is having second thoughts.

I mean, I get it. Chandler's a catch in Snaggletooth Creek, but he's not *built, tatted surfer* hot. Do you *see* those broad shoulders? And those back dimples above his, erm, flamingo butt?

I angle closer to her and slip an arm around her waist. "Um, Em? Tell me you're not—"

She cuts me off with a half-sob. "Uncle Owen dared him to wear the costume, and then the bar was understaffed, so he just picked up a tray and started…helping."

I squint up at her. I'm missing something. "Your uncle dared—"

"And I don't know what happened while they were all deep-sea fishing this morning, but they came back and Chandler was *so* mad at him, and he was pretending he wasn't even though I know he was, and I don't get it. I mean, I do. I know he's a total ass sometimes, but he's never an ass *on purpose*. And really, he's almost never an ass at all anymore. It's more like he sees a toy, he goes after it, and sometimes things just...happen...when that happens."

I am so confused. "Chandler isn't an ass, sweetie."

Chandler can totally be an ass, but in all of the years that they've dated, he's never been an ass to Emma, and on the off chance that he gets close to ass territory, he tends to make it up to her with big, ridiculous gifts.

Also, if Emma's considering calling off this wedding because she's attracted to one of the hotel staff, I will defend Chandler to the end.

Marrying Chandler is what she wants.

She's said so approximately forty-three billion times since their first date in high school. We forgave him for not proposing then—we were all way too young, and then they broke up in college—but since they got back together after college seven years ago, the rest of us have gotten pretty tired of waiting too.

In my opinionated opinion, he should've popped the question at least four years ago. It's not like there was ever any doubt where their relationship was going. Even during that little break-up three years ago. And I know Emma dropped hints. Might've even proposed to him once or twice.

But much like he didn't listen to any hints or outright frank discussions until about this time last year, she's not listening to me right now. She's charging ahead with getting everything out, which means she's fixated.

I'll ask questions later.

"And then there was that thing on the plane ride here," she's saying, "and now Chandler's all hung up on what happened at Thanksgiving, and I hate to ask this. I know it's awful. But we're *this close* to getting married, and I know he doesn't mean to put that in danger, but I feel like he is, and can you just... God, I can't believe I'm saying these words, but can you babysit him?"

I gape at her.

I know she's not talking about Chandler.

"Okay, *babysit* is a harsh word. More like...be a buffer. Yes. Can you be a buffer between him and Chandler? Just for a couple days?"

"You need me to babysit the pool boy?"

She finally looks at me, and her whole face crinkles in confusion. "The pool boy?"

I point to the guy in the ride-on flamingo costume, who's clearly telling Claire something hilarious because she's doubled over laughing and fawning all over him at the same time.

I can't blame her.

He's hot. And undeniably funny. Who wears a costume like that to work at a resort?

"That's who you're talking about? The drink server?"

Emma squeaks, and when I look back at her, I realize her face has gone three shades past horrified. "Laney. That's—that's—that's not a *drink server*. That's *Theo*."

I gape across the breezeway at the pool again while the server turns his head so I can see his wide grin, and *oh my god*.

She's right.

That's her brother.

I mean, of course she knows her brother.

But *that does not look like her brother*.

Not the version of him I've known and been irritated by most of my life.

But I look closer, and *oh my god* again.

Theo Monroe, the boy who nicknamed me, Emma, and our friend Sabrina the *ugly heiresses* in third grade, who once got suspended from high school for recreating a scene from *Braveheart* in the school kitchen with a bunch of their dad's taxidermy animals, who nearly took out the town's prized statue of our founder on a dare a few months after high school graduation, and who ordered something so obscene I can't even talk about it from my family's print-on-demand company and then wore it all over Snaggletooth Creek not long after I got back to town after getting my master's degree, accidentally made me drool over him.

Ew.

Ew.

This is jet lag. Or the humidity. Or *something*.

How did I not see that that's *Theo*?

Snaggletooth Creek—*the Tooth* to us locals—is small, but it's not so small that you run into everyone every time you turn around. Especially when I live on the east side of town, where my family's company's world headquarters are located, and last I heard, Theo lives in a single-wide at the edge of his dad's property just beyond the western boundaries of our little mountain town. While I'll go have lunch or coffee downtown, Theo spends his off-time rock climbing or snowboarding or kayaking anywhere *but* the heart of the Tooth. Or so I gather from hearing Emma talk about him occasionally. I don't think I've seen him in person in four or five years. And definitely not shirtless. And definitely not grinning at me the way he's grinning at Claire.

Ew.

This is mortifying.

"Oh, god, Laney, you were my last hope," Emma whispers. "Please don't fall for the Theo glow-up."

I blink, shake my head, and school my expression while I look back at her. "Does he still have the same personality?"

She cracks up, and this is such a real, genuine amusement that my shoulders relax.

"Yes," she says firmly. "*So much yes.*"

"I think we're clear then." Except as I'm saying it, the rest of our conversation catches up with me and clicks into place.

Oh, no.

Oh, no no no.

"So you'll do it?" she says. "You'll baby—erm, be the wall between Chandler and Theo?"

I'm all the way around the pool from Chandler, where he's sitting with his triplet cousins who are serving as his grooms-men. They're at a far table with a great view of the sunset, and even from here, I can see his lip curl in irritation while he, too, watches Theo. He's tapping something that looks like a tennis racket against the edge of the table while he scowls.

This wedding? A week of sun, fun, and being a tourist with her family and best friends while everything's cold and snowy in the mountains back home?

This is Emma's *dream*.

She grew up in a crumbling cabin just outside of town limits. When we were little, my parents ran a local T-shirt shop and her dad owned a small taxidermy business.

With the internet age, our families' businesses have both expanded.

But hers doesn't have quite the same level of respectability around town that mine does.

Never has. Not even when her mom was alive and driving our bus to school.

And I know it bothers her that she's celebrated back home as *that Monroe girl who overcame her humble beginnings to make something of herself.*

Making something of herself was coming home with an accounting degree and starting an accounting firm that now does taxes for half the town. And she loves it.

Marrying Chandler and starting a family?

This is the final cherry on Emma's dream life sundae.

"Of course I'll do it," I say with what I hope is all the conviction I need to believe myself too.

Theo can be a dick, and he wouldn't know responsibility if it did a striptease for him on top of Ol' Snaggletooth, the gold miner statue in front of city hall back home. Emma's quit fretting that she'll have to support him in old age, but I suspect it's more out of loyalty to family and not wanting to talk bad about him to anyone than it is that she no longer worries about him. But he *is* known for having fun.

So the flamingo costume? The flirting? The drinks?

It's all perfectly *Theo*.

"I'd ask Sabrina, but she's been making these faces at him—" Emma starts.

"Awesome," I sigh before I can stop myself.

"—and I'm sure it's just loyalty to Chandler since he's her cousin and they work together and everything, and Chandler was *really* mad this afternoon because he's stressed—"

"Everyone wants everything to go right the week of your wedding."

"And as for Claire—" She drops her head in her hands and sighs, smearing the last bite of cookies and cream protein bar over her forehead as she mumbles something.

I take the bar from her and wipe her forehead. "What was that, sweetie?"

"He'd seduce her before the night's over, and then I'd have to deal with her broken heart too because she doesn't know he's totally a love-'em-and-leave-'em guy," she whispers. "And any other time, that would be absolutely fine, but she's super vulnerable right now after a horrible break-up and I just don't want to put this on her and leave her worse than she got here."

I don't think she's wrong.

Theo's drawing Claire's attention like he's a sea nymph and she's a love-starved sailor who's been lost for weeks, which isn't exactly the Claire I remember. The Claire I remember is fun and put-together and wouldn't flirt with *Theo*. And she's not the only woman at the pool giving him their undivided attention.

Although Chandler's Great-Aunt Brenda might be glaring. Hard to tell the difference between her glare face and her swoon face sometimes.

I swallow hard. "Don't worry, Em. I'm on it."

"It's just for a couple days. I swear, once Chandler has some space from Theo and gets to just hang out on the beach and play a round or two of golf, he'll be fine, and Theo being Theo won't bother him so much anymore."

"Absolutely. No problem."

"And maybe talk to Sabrina and find out why she's mad at him too?"

"*Emma*. Bare minimum here. Of course. I've got this."

"And there's one more thing."

I look at her.

She doesn't look back at me. "We're short one bungalow so I put you in his," she says on a rush.

Don't twitch, Delaney. You are a Kingston. You are one of Emma's very best friends. You are here for her. This is her week. This is for her wedding. The wedding of her dreams. Do. Not. Twitch.

It's not working.

I'm twitching.

And then I think about what my parents will say—they are *not* fans of Theo and would have an absolute fit if they saw me going into his bungalow—and I twitch all over again.

They've also made subtle comments about how lovely it is that *Emma* is getting married when I declined a proposal from their perfect choice for me a year ago, and they're *concerned* that I'll end up a lonely old maid without any good prospects if I don't start considering the men my mother keeps introducing me to.

"It's a big bungalow," she assures me too enthusiastically. "With two bedrooms. All of the bungalows have at least two bedrooms. And I'm working *every day*—no, every *hour*—with the staff here to get you into your own as soon as it opens—I know you were planning to share with your parents, so we'll have a space for them before they arrive for sure without having to put them in the overflow hotel, and I know you'd be fine sharing with Claire and Sabrina and there are pullout sofas and all, but I realized..." She pauses, sighs while she eyes Theo again. "It'll be easier for you to keep him out of Chandler's way for a couple days if you're with him all the time," she finishes with a whisper.

I am definitely going to need four of whatever's in those pineapples that Theo's handing out. "Oh my god, Em, this is the *least* I can do for you."

I'm squeaking.

She can hear it.

She knows this is the *worst* thing she could ask any of us to do.

But it's just for a day or two. Just until space opens up somewhere else and tensions die down and everything goes back to normal. I can do this for a day or two.

Probably not three—my parents get here in three days—but I can absolutely help tensions die down by keeping Theo away from Chandler until then.

I pat her back and stifle a frown at how sharp her shoulder blades are. She's always struggled to keep weight on. Stress isn't good for her.

And while my parents abhor Theo, they love Emma.

The girl who rose above being raised solo by a taxidermist after her mom tragically passed while we were in middle school to become a respectable accountant who pays her own bills and socializes with the *right* people in the Tooth.

They'd want me to do whatever it takes to keep her happy and healthy. "Don't you worry. I'm on the job. Five years from

13

now, we'll all look back on this while your babies are opening their birthday presents and laugh and laugh at how silly we all were this week and how amazing it all turned out in the end. Everything's under control. I've got this."

She tackles me in a hug. "Thank you."

"Em, it's your wedding. Of course."

"I know it's an awful thing to ask—"

"It's not. Awful would be asking me to monitor who your uncle's flirting with."

She laughs.

I laugh.

We both sound like desperate fools.

"Em. You're marrying Chandler, and then after a week in Hawaii, you're going to *Fiji*. You've waited your whole life for this. Even the years when you were on a break in college. Waiting for that doofus to propose counts as double, right?"

She laughs again as she pulls out of the hug, and this time, she sounds more normal. "You're the best, Laney. Truly."

I smile at her. "Just wait until I ask you for a favor for my wedding."

"Oh, god, tell me you're not dating that banker your mother introduced you to last week."

And this is why I love Emma. "No, but I'm starting to think about dating someone completely inappropriate just to freak them out," I joke, even though it's not as much of a joke as it would've been a year ago.

She looks at me.

Then at Theo.

Then back at me.

"No," I say.

She snickers.

It's still a little hysterical.

"Not yet, anyway," I say quickly. "Maybe…later. *After* they've signed the company over to me and can't go back on it."

Which is supposed to happen in the next five years so that they can retire and enjoy the rest of their lives.

I love my job. I love our mission and our purpose, and I'm so excited to continue expanding what I watched them build as I was growing up.

I just wish it didn't come with quite so many expectations for *all* aspects of my life. It wasn't like this when I was little.

But as Kingston Photo Gifts has expanded, my parents have gotten stiffer and pickier about everything. Mostly about who's *worthy*. And believe me, some days I think they still question if I am.

I glance at Theo again.

He doesn't have any expectations to live up to. And so he gets to go to a destination wedding in Hawaii and be a total screwball.

"What's he doing right now?" I whisper to her. "Like, for real. Do I need some background on the costume?"

"The costume—it's Theo." She rolls her eyes. "He and Uncle Owen saw it in the window of a thrift store. Uncle Owen dared him to wear it. And like I said, the resort is a little short-staffed, so he decided to help pass out drinks. And it *is* kinda funny. Isn't it?"

"You want me to make sure he doesn't wear it to breakfast tomorrow?

"That would be amazing. But when you talk to him, don't—"

"Em. I think I know how to handle your brother and at least what *not* to say." Probably.

Mostly.

I haven't actively avoided Theo since I got home from college, but I haven't been sad that our paths have rarely crossed.

She sags in relief while Chandler swings the tennis racket at something.

"What—" I start but stop myself when *her* eyelid starts twitching.

"The bugs here really like Chandler," she whispers. "This is maybe not his ideal wedding spot."

"That's...?"

"An electrified tennis racket bug zapper. Theo got it for him and he was super annoyed at first, but now he's using it all the time. So. You ready?"

Right.

Ready.

For my job. The *one thing* that will make my best friend happiest during her wedding week.

Theo's circling the pool closer to the groom's table. His shaggy light brown hair lifts in the breeze as he holds a tray with a final pineapple drink in one hand and the flamingo reins in his other. His hair isn't *long*. More due for a haircut, which is a big change from the days that he kept it buzzed close to his scalp, which was a direct result of an incident with a match and fermented apple juice in the middle school cafeteria. And if he wasn't *Theo*, I might be gawking at his tattooed chest too, like Claire is.

But it's Theo.

And he's definitely headed toward Chandler, which is the one thing I've been asked to make sure doesn't happen.

"I'm on it," I say.

Did *not* see this coming, but I probably should've.

Why would Theo be anyone but himself even here in paradise? And who else can Emma trust to make him behave beyond her biggest wet blanket of a friend?

I stifle a sigh. When do *I* get to have fun?

Not when your best friend needs you to make sure she gets the wedding of her dreams.

"I swear, I'll get you another room before your parents get here," she says. "Them too if we can't get another bungalow."

"Don't worry about it. I'll take care of that too." We've

been besties for a *long* time. It's pretty normal for her to know I don't want my parents knowing I'll be spending a lot of time with Theo.

Just like I can tell you she's having nerves but knows this is what she wants, and once she gets through making sure her wedding week goes great, everything will be amazing and they'll start a family soon and she'll be the happiest Emma to ever Emma in the history of Emmas.

Theo pauses next to Chandler's table and offers the table a pineapple with the paper umbrella.

And then it happens.

As he's standing there extending the tray of drinks, Theo sneezes.

And I don't actually mean *sneezes*.

Normal people?

Normal people sneeze.

Theo, however, has a full-body, full-lung, full-nose, full-vocal-cord seizure that sounds like a freight train slamming its brakes and honking its horn at full speed.

He is one of *those* sneeezers.

It's sudden.

It's loud.

And it's so startling that Chandler yelps, *"Jesus Christ!"* and swings his bug zapper tennis racket in the direction of the danger, which just so happens to be Theo.

But he doesn't hit Theo.

Oh, no.

He hits something *far* worse.

A paper drink umbrella.

There's a *zzzzzzzip!* that echoes across the pool as the zapper connects with the drink sloshing in Theo's hand.

It's immediately followed by a very distinct *poof!*

And accompanied by a spark of flame.

"Oh my god." I drop my purse. I drop the leftover protein bar. And I take off at a dead run.

The drink umbrella has lit up on fire.

It's on fire.

And it's too close to Theo's costume.

Way too close.

"In the pool!" I yell as I get halfway around the pool. "Theo! *Jump in the pool!*"

The Sullivan triplets scatter, one closer to get pictures, the other two to clear the older people out of the way of the fire, while Chandler gapes at Theo.

Theo twists his head at me *while his costume ignites*. The flamingo head is on fire.

It's on fire.

We're mountain people. We don't screw around with fire.

Especially flaming flamingo head fires.

But Theo's giving me a look I've seen so many times, I *hear* him in my head. *Oh, good, Princess Plainy-Laney is here.*

I'm still in sneakers. Practical for plane rides, practical for sprinting around a pool, and I'm closing in fast. "You're on *fire!*" I shriek at him.

Finally—*finally*—he looks down.

And then the dumbass *grins*. "Aww, are you worried about me, Laney?"

"*You're. On. Fire,*" I yell again. So close. *So close.*

"What the *hell*, ass—idiot—*Theo*," Chandler snaps.

"Theo. *Theo!* Jump in the pool!" Chandler's mom yells from behind the triplet who's trying to get her out of harm's way.

I'm finally right on top of him.

He has me by at least six inches and probably fifty to sixty pounds of solid muscle, but I won't let a little thing like his size and his strength stop me.

He's about to be *on fire* himself.

There's only one thing to do here.

I angle in my dash toward him, feel the heat growing as I

get right up next to him, and I use all of my momentum to shove him into the water.

Unfortunately though, that's not where my momentum ends.

And when his eyes go wide and he realizes he's falling backward, he reaches for the nearest thing.

Me.

And that's how I, too, end up tumbling into the pool.

2

THEO MONROE, AKA A GUY WHO DOES HIS BEST TO NOT GET himself into these situations when it's important, but who generally has zero regrets

UNCLE OWEN'S dares aren't usually quite so lit. They're normally more low-key, like the time we left a bunch of mice all over the park.

Taxidermy mice. Just so we're clear on that.

Once people were done freaking out, we went viral on Instagram as the Colorado mouse town. Even had those national news people in to interview everyone, who pretended they had no idea where so many taxidermy mice would've come from.

This one could end with similar attention. Decker Sullivan was recording it.

Not that setting a flamingo costume on fire and being shoved into the pool by my sister's straight-laced best friend was my *intention*.

Funny shit happens when I'm around.

It's pretty awesome being me.

Or so I'm thinking as I surface.

And then I shake the water out of my eyes, slick my hair back, and spot the look of utter grief on Emma's face as she tries to nudge Chandler further away from the pool. And me.

Fuck.

Lucky Sullivan, another of the Sullivan triplets, is apparently oblivious to the bride and groom's reactions. He's grinning while he offers me a hand to help me out of the pool. "Can't just set yourself on fire, can you? Have to get yourself rescued by the last person I'd ever guess would go into a pool fully clothed to help your ass. Classic, man. Classic."

I grin back at him, actively choosing to ignore the horrified looks from everyone behind him. It's not just Em now. It's pretty much everyone in Chandler's extended family who are down here with us. "What can I say? Trouble likes me."

He snorts.

I grin bigger and almost fall back in the pool while I try to pull myself out.

This blow-up costume's awkward when it's wet. Who knew?

"Careful next time," Jack Sullivan, triplet number three, is saying as he pulls Delaney Kingston out of the pool a few feet away. "That thing's battery-operated. Not enough juice in a couple double-A's to shock the pool, but you definitely don't want to take a chance with electricity and water."

"Well, when my options were electrocution with double-A batteries or watching Emma's brother explode in flames, I went with the lower risk."

"Stick in the mud," Lucky mutters.

"Which one?" I reply.

He chokes on another laugh while I drag the rest of my flat, dead costume out of the pool.

I start to chuckle too, but then I catch sight of Emma again.

Tossing another frustrated frown my way like this is one

more thing I've done on purpose to make her fiancé miserable.

Like I was supposed to know he'd get seasick when I offered to take everyone deep-sea fishing this morning. Or that his video screen was broken on the plane and he spent the entire flight watching the movies I picked since he was behind me, and that I apparently spoiled the ending of the latest *Avengers* movie for him.

Lucky glances their way and sighs too. "Don't get it, dude," he says. "Chandler's not usually tighter than an inflamed sphincter, yet here we are, in paradise…"

"Not hearing this," I reply. Last thing any of us need is Chandler's groomsmen turning on him. Dude has issues. Needs some wingmen this week. But not me. Definitely not me. "Go be on his side."

"Shouldn't be sides."

"There's always sides. Don't tell Emma." Chandler's not my favorite person in the world, but I'm not marrying him.

Emma is.

Her choice. Her right. He's made her happy more years than not. I'll play nice for her sake.

"Bar later?" Lucky asks.

I sneak another glance at my sister, who's now comforting Chandler like *he* was the one who almost had his face melted off because of a bug zapper and drink umbrella malfunction.

I shake my head at Lucky. "Groomsman duties for you, my friend. We'll hook up next week at home."

"I'll text you if he goes to bed early. There's a karaoke bar down the way."

"Fuck, yeah." I love karaoke.

"If who goes to bed early?" Decker asks as he approaches too. Guess Chandler's mom has recovered from the horror of seeing the flamingo die a flaming death and no longer needs to cling to him while he records everything.

"You," Lucky says. "You're too boring for bars."

Both of them crack up.

I would too—messing around with these guys is generally my thing—but Emma's giving me another look.

The *please just give him space* look.

And she doesn't mean any of the triplets.

That look hits me in a spot that hasn't been super vulnerable since high school. Been a long time since I felt this level of guilt creeping in. But here we are. In paradise, where everything was fine five minutes ago, before Chandler set me on fire with a present I gave him.

So I sneezed.

Everyone sneezes.

Apparently I need to *not* sneeze the rest of this week though.

Time to regroup.

"Have fun tonight," I tell Lucky and Decker while I pull myself to standing, bringing my sopping wet costume with me to cover my underwear.

The triplets all seem to realize we're the only ones enjoying ourselves on the pool deck, and a collective sigh goes up among the three of them.

Identical sighs, much like they're all brown-haired, white-skinned, blue-eyed identical triplets. Pretty easy to tell them apart once you get to know their personalities though.

Even Jack's sighing as he finishes pulling Delaney to her feet too.

"Remind me to elope if I ever find the woman of my dreams," Lucky says. "This wedding stuff is dumb stress."

"Like anyone would have you," Decker says.

"Fuck, yeah, they would. I'm the pretty one of the three of us."

I'd normally laugh at that.

They would too. Instead, both of them sigh again.

"You going out anywhere for real?" Decker asks me.

"Nope." I am definitely hitting a bar somewhere tonight.

But I'm not taking them along.

Might make Chandler sad to get jilted by his groomsmen.

Can't have that.

I give Em a tiny salute of *I'll get out of your hair*, then nod to Delaney. "Thanks for the save. Owe you one next time you catch on fire."

Her nostrils twitch. "Happy to help."

Total teacher's pet answer.

As expected.

She starts to say something else, but I head around the pool like I didn't notice.

If Chandler's sphincter's too tight this week, Delaney Kingston's has been too tight since before she was born.

Not her fault. Probably. But it will be my fault if I hang out here and annoy her more after taking her for a fully-clothed dunk in the pool. Nothing like getting on the groom's *and* the bridesmaid's bad sides.

So the best I can do is make myself scarce.

Claire, Em's blonde sorority friend and another bridesmaid, lifts her brows and smiles at me as I pass her. "Nothing's boring when you're around, is it?"

I wink. "Boring's for other people."

She smiles wider and opens her mouth like she's about to ask if we can be *not boring* together.

I remember Emma's *disappointed* in me, and I continue on my way.

This week's weird. Not that I don't put Emma first on a regular basis, but this week is *extra*. And apparently I haven't toned myself down enough yet to make the couple of the hour happy.

"Okay, son?" my dad asks as I hit the edge of the pool area.

"Barely singed," I report with a grin.

Uncle Owen cracks up. Dad sighs and shakes his head while I keep going.

He wasn't meant to be a single dad. Definitely not to two middle schoolers and then high schoolers. But he does his best, and that's all we can ask.

And I know he adores Emma as much as I do.

She's such a genuinely good person that you can't help but be happy for her when she's happy, even if you don't understand things like how Chandler Sullivan makes her happy.

You still want to stand in her glow. You want to be the reason she's glowing, because the brighter she glows, the more the world is a better place.

Not my time to be in her glow though. This is my time to give her space.

Sucks, honestly.

She's one of my favorite people in the entire world.

And this week, I am *not* hers.

Feels way too much like being in high school again.

I'm trying to shake it off, reminding myself weddings are stupidly stressful and life will go back to normal next week as I head down the coconut-tree-lined path to my bungalow.

"So that was a nice, refreshing dip," Delaney Kingston says when I'm nearly there.

Ah.

So that's who's huffing along behind me.

Her bungalow must be this way too.

And I probably owe her an apology for her unexpected pool dip, courtesy of me.

Don't want to give it to her though.

"Hey, Princess Plainy-Laney." I grin at her over my shoulder like she's not the only other person from back home besides Chandler who can make me twitch today. "Like your shoes. They squeak real nice."

"Bonus feature. They're supportive *and* musical."

Huh.

That's an unexpected response.

Would've thought I'd get an eye roll and a lecture on not taking paper umbrellas near electrified bug zappers. You want a rule followed, a problem solved, or a lecture about how the world is supposed to work, you go to Laney.

You don't go to Laney for jokes. She's the type who wouldn't know fun if it landed on her desk in a brown manila envelope clearly labeled *fun*. Once saw her refuse to go sledding because there weren't nets at the bottom of the hill. Was voted in high school as the most likely to live to a hundred and six because she flosses every day.

No heart disease taking her out early due to inflamed gums.

I have not missed seeing Delaney Kingston since she quit showing up to parties on my side of town and I quit dropping into bars and restaurants on her side of town.

She's one of Emma's best friends though, so I'll be nice if it kills me. I grin back at her again. Add a wink. "You need help carrying your bag to your room?"

"That's so kind, but I can see you already have your hands full, and it's just a purse."

"Just a purse? That's a purse the size of a suitcase. Wouldn't take anything at all to drop this costume and carry that for you."

"While I'm sure that wouldn't be a hardship for you, Emma really doesn't need you to get thrown out of the resort for public indecency, so I'll carry my own bag. Thank you though. That's a kind offer."

Emma would be so disappointed if you fuck up again.

Fucking guilt.

I hate the guilt. Worked really hard the last decade or so to get over it and live my life in the sunshine, but here she is, tossing it around like confetti for Emma's wedding week.

I keep smiling as I approach my bungalow, ignoring the twitch under my skin that I tell myself is an allergic reaction to being near a wet blanket.

I stop and face her at my doorway. "Good to see you, Princess Plainy. Maybe next time you shove me in a pool, you can be in a bikini." I wink again.

She winks right back.

Delaney Kingston.

Winking right back.

This is High School Theo wet dream material, and yeah, I've worked really hard to forget *that* too.

What the fuck is going on?

"Wouldn't that be fun?" she says. "Oh, good. We're here. Thank you so much for showing me to my bungalow."

I look around.

Then look around again.

Nearest other bungalow is a whole building's length away, and Laney's trying to step around me to my porch. "If you'll just excuse me—"

"You lost?"

"No, this is my bungalow."

"Don't think so."

"The Plumeria Bungalow. Says so right here on my key card envelope."

She flashes the little paper envelope holding her key card, and *no.*

That's what it says.

But *no.*

I cross my arms, letting my dripping, half-melted flamingo costume fall off my hips and leaving me standing there in nothing but my black briefs, which is a dangerous place to be.

My brain is slowly catching up to the fact that Laney's hot as fuck right now in ways that she shouldn't be. And not just because the strength she put into shoving me into the pool would've been a turn-on had any other woman done it.

But now she's strong-hot *and* wet-hot at the same time.

Brown mousy hair all messed up. Expensive shirt sticking

27

to her skin. Nipples puckered under the performance fabric, the clean outline of her plain-Jane bra visible too. Linen pants clinging to her hips and showing off her panty line. Dark lashes clumped together over bright blue eyes. And her sneakers still squeaking.

"While I don't mind sharing my room with a pretty lady," I drawl, ordering my dick to not have a reaction to this wet woman standing in front of me, "I also don't think I'm the kind of roommate you'd be into."

"Guess you're wrong," she chirps in response as she side-steps me and bounces up the three stairs to the porch. "Because this is my bungalow too."

I blink.

Then blink again.

Then I get pissed, and getting pissed makes me more pissed since I hate being pissed.

Hate being pissed.

Make it a life rule to avoid it, in fact.

But Delaney Kingston is an annoying, insufferable, rule-following, Prudy McSnooterson who would *never* lower herself to sharing a room with a guy whose favorite Saturday night activity is pulling harmless pranks with friends that sometimes end with all of us a little too happy to *make good decisions.*

Trust me.

I'd know.

Spent too many years wishing she *would* lower herself. Wanting to see what she looked like with her hair down and her inhibitions gone.

And she just said *my bungalow too.*

Like she *knows* this is my bungalow.

And if she knows this is my bungalow—*fuck.*

Happy Theo has left the whole damn Pacific Ocean. Everything is suddenly clicking into place.

"I don't need a babysitter," I grit out, tripping up the steps myself to block her and sounding more like the fuckup I was in high school than the man I am today.

"I'm not a *babysitter*. Think of me more like a buffer. You don't really want Chandler accidentally setting more of your clothes on fire, do you? Wait. No. Don't answer that."

I reach the doorframe and slide in front of her to block her. This is the worst possible thing Emma could've done.

I love my sister. I adore my sister. The two of us have been through some shit and come out on the other side, and I would do anything for her.

Doing way more for her this week than she even knows, and I legit don't care if she never finds out. Just want her to be happy, even if I don't understand what makes her happy all the time.

But *sending Laney to babysit me*?

This is cruel.

And it's not happening. It's a step too far. "You ever have fun, Princess Plainy-Laney?"

"Yes, sometimes I stay up late at night doing puzzles while adding a little dollop of brandy to my chamomile. But just a dollop. Much more than that, and it might give me *dirty* dreams."

I'm momentarily speechless.

Mostly because I can't decide if she's serious or if she's fucking with me.

She smiles brighter, blue eyes almost dancing. And while I'm unscrambling my brains after having *Delaney Kingston* mock herself to my face, she ducks around me and presses her keycard to the lock mechanism on my hotel door.

There's a click, and she strolls into my bungalow.

And then she lets the door slam in my face.

Fuck.

Fuck.

Do I care where I sleep? No.

But am I letting this woman loose all on her own inside

my hotel room when I know what's in the spare bedroom and she doesn't?

Fuck fuck fuck.

Rule-following Delaney Kingston *cannot* be in my bungalow unsupervised.

She absolutely cannot.

I reach for my pocket, remember I'm in nothing but my briefs, and then dive for the sopping, mutilated costume on the bungalow porch. It takes too long to find my keycard in the interior pocket, and when I do, I half hope it doesn't work.

Let me be lost. Let me be lost. Let me be lost.

But it clicks open just like it did for her a moment ago.

And when I walk inside—yes, after tripping over my costume and kicking it off—Delaney's there.

I rub my eyes.

Blink a few times.

Hope a whole lot.

Doesn't work.

She's still here, halfway across the tropical-patterned rug in the living room on her way to the first bedroom, pulling along a god-awful floral-print suitcase.

"That's my room," I say.

She redirects as only Ms. Know-it-all can, heading instead to the closed bedroom door on the other side of the spacious sitting area with a kitchenette along the wall nearest me.

"That's mine too," I say.

"You're using *both* bedrooms." Not a question. A statement like she's pointing out that I'm ridiculous.

I'm an easygoing guy. Love having fun. Love helping the people around me have fun. I can handle a lot.

I *cause* a lot.

Almost always a harmless lot these days, but a lot.

But sharing a room with Princess Plainy-Laney so that she can *babysit me*?

No.

One of us has to go.

Any other day, any other place, with anything else hiding in that second bedroom, I'd volunteer to be the one to go.

But that's not an option.

"Yes," I say like she's the one being dumb, even though I know she isn't, "I'm using both rooms."

Her face twitches just like you'd expect. "Emma's working with management to find me my own bungalow or an open room in the overflow hotel, but really, this won't be so bad until she does. I *know* you're not using both bedrooms."

She's annoying as hell when she *knows* things.

And why didn't Emma tell me herself? "You can have the pullout bed. The bedrooms are mine."

"Theo. You *cannot sleep in two beds at once.*"

"Maybe I just don't want you here."

It's been a long while since we spent any significant time together. Most of our adult lives, in fact, and I have zero doubt she's expecting high school turd-waffle Theo instead of grown-up has-his-shit-together Theo.

Her expectations are making me fall back into old habits that I got over a long time ago and don't like.

"I'm an easy roommate," she says flatly with a giant fake smile plastered on her face. She's probably unhappy with this arrangement too. "Promise. Very quiet. You won't even know I'm here."

In all of my school years, she was the only classmate I was never able to win over. Finally swore to myself I'd quit trying, no matter how much it killed me on the inside to know how very, very much I wanted to win her over. So Emma asking *her* to *babysit* me?

This is insult to fucking injury. "You haven't stopped talking since you walked in the door."

"Just getting out all of the words so that I can be quiet later. Unless you want me to talk more?"

"No." *Shit.* I don't know if I'm supposed to reverse psychology her or be honest.

"Works for me. I don't know that I want to talk to you a whole lot more either."

"Not mincing words, are you, Princess Plainy?"

She shrugs like she's deflecting the nickname out the balcony doors and off into the darkness over the Pacific as she heads once more for the closed door. "Not much of a point when we both know we'll never be close friends. At least we know where we stand with each other, right? This is for Emma. I would do *anything* for Emma."

I wiggle my brows at her. Can't help myself. Easiest path to annoying her. "What if Emma wanted you to strip down with me too?"

She crosses her arms and stares me dead in the eye. "*Anything* she asks me to."

Alarm bells go off in my head.

To be fair, that's only like, two of them, because that's all the alarm bells I have, but both at once is cause for concern.

"Are you fucking with me?" I ask her.

She doesn't answer.

But a very loud yowl does from behind that closed bedroom door.

I imitate it while I yawn. "Tired. Go away. I need my beauty nap before I go party all night."

She stares at me.

Then at the door, where four tiny mews carry through the wood.

"*Out*," I repeat, pointing to the exit while I stalk across the decorative rug to keep her from opening that door.

She's no longer smiling. "Tell me you're not collecting animals for your dad."

My temper, which generally exists about as much as alarm bells, roars to life like someone stuck it with a hot poker. "Get. The fuck. Out. Of my room."

She ignores me and marches to the door of my spare bedroom.

I ignore her ignoring me and cut her off, standing between her and the doorknob.

Every last kitten inside that room decides to find their vocal cords at once, which is impressive considering how small they are.

"Theo," she says.

Just my name.

Like she's a goddamn teacher and I'm in trouble for bringing a wounded baby chipmunk into the classroom.

Not so I could wait for it to perish and present it to my dad for stuffing like my teacher assumed that day too.

"The only reason I'm not tossing you off my balcony right now is that it would ruin Emma's day," I force out through gritted teeth.

"Plus we're basically at sea level in here, so I'd have a pretty soft landing," she says. "That would ruin *your* day to go to all that effort for a small impact, I'm sure. And I'm no cowering weakling, as you might've noticed when I saved you from a fire a few minutes ago. Wouldn't want me to turn my muscles on you twice in one day, would you?"

Who *is* this woman?

It's certainly not the Laney from middle school who would've informed me that if I didn't stop bouncing a tennis ball against the wall when we were supposed to be having quiet indoor recess, she would tell the teacher. "You can have the pullout bed. Because it'll make *Emma* happy. But don't open that door. If you open that door, I will fucking ruin the rest of your life, no matter what kind of crazy *muscles* skills you think you have. Stay out of my bedroom too."

Her blue eyes waver and she takes a half-step back. "I realize this isn't convenient for either of us," she says softly, "but I'm confident we can both manage this for Emma's sake.

And you can surely see that it's unexpected at the least to hear what sounds like a herd of cats in your spare bedroom."

"I can only sleep if there's a separate room with a closed door and the nature channel playing on the TV inside."

She opens her mouth.

Closes it like she's deciding she doesn't want to know if that's the truth.

Sweeps her gaze down my body like she's just now realizing I'm standing here in nothing but my underwear.

Good news—her personality has once again destroyed any desire my dick might have to pop a boner.

I lean back against the bedroom door. "Sabrina's two bungalows down. Go stay with her."

Her gaze snaps up to mine. "No."

"You don't have a lot of negotiation room here, Princess Plainy."

"Emma wants me to stay here."

The kittens mew softly behind me. I need to check on them. See how they're doing. Determine if I need to have that vet come out tomorrow and examine them again. But I don't want to do it while she's standing here.

Or while I'm mostly naked, which doesn't bother *me*, but would bother *Emma* if it caused an incident here.

I could argue that Laney's lying about Emma wanting her to keep an eye on me, but I know she's not lying.

One, there's no reason for her to lie. Her mother once cornered me at a high school dance and informed me that *Delaney's no-no box is off-limits to the likes of you.* Completely unnecessary, considering I've never been under any delusions that Delaney Kingston might ever look at me as anything other than a waste of oxygen, no matter how I might've felt about her once upon a time, but she still did it.

And Laney reinforced that she agreed with her mother's opinion more times than I care to remember.

But worse—Emma's stressed to the max and Chandler's

being a dick at every opportunity.

Usually, we both make an effort to get along for Emma's sake.

But this trip—this trip isn't normal. And he's the groom, which means he's *special*.

He doesn't get a babysitter.

I do.

Em won't ask her sorority sister. Not when she's told me not to flirt with Claire, who doesn't need more drama from men right now. She'll probably think I was flirting just by offering Claire a drink, but I wasn't. I was merely being a nice guy. Promise.

Won't ask Sabrina either, and not just because Sabrina's Chandler's cousin and therefore obligated to be on his side. Sabrina's pissed at me for her own reasons, and while she's fucking Fort Knox when she has a secret she doesn't want you to know, she also doesn't get pissed at you without the whole world becoming aware that you have crossed her.

And for the record—I didn't cross her.

I just didn't tell her what she wanted to hear.

Emma also won't ask the triplets. They'd toss me off a balcony—one higher than sea level—at the first opportunity to teach me a lesson.

For fun.

And with something soft to land on underneath.

And then we'd all have beers together and crack up at how funny it was, because we hang out and do stupid stuff like that all the time.

Basically, they'd be useless as babysitters and that would piss off Chandler more.

Laney's the best choice.

Can't really blame Emma here for making a smart decision. It's what she's done her whole life.

"He fucking started it," I mutter like a toddler.

Laney's whole body seems to deflate. "I'm sorry. It must

be difficult to not get along with your sister's fiancé."

Wary doesn't even touch how I'm feeling as I study her.

I'm used to the Delaney that looks at me with as much disdain as her mother does. So her giving me any credit and considering my feelings?

This is cause for suspicion.

She hitches a shoulder. "He wasn't exactly innocent in you getting set on fire. And I'm sure it's unpleasant to know you're stuck with me now."

"Is this a trick?"

"This is me wanting to take a shower and climb into pajamas and bed. It's been a long day. But I need to trust that you'll stay here while I do, because while I know you love your sister and won't intentionally do anything else to stress her out, she believes things *happen* when you're around no matter your intentions, so she asked me to be a buffer, and that's what I intend to do. For *all* of your sakes."

Mama cat meows loudly in my second bedroom.

Delaney doesn't flinch.

It's like she's trying to telegraph *you can trust me — I'm not asking why you have cats in your second bedroom anymore.*

That means one thing.

The minute I turn my back, she'll be getting into this room and letting the cats out.

End of the world?

Fucking might be. Those kittens aren't old enough to be wandering around the island unsupervised. And I'm not one to worry about anyone being *unsupervised*.

And don't tell me feral cats have been surviving on this island for decades.

I don't. Want. To fucking. Hear it.

For one, I'm certain their mama is domesticated. And for two, these are *my* kittens now—along with their mama—and I will protect them to the end.

And also not let Emma know that I'm keeping them here

36

for fear she'll freak out about me getting tossed from the resort.

Laney's right.

Things *happen* when I'm involved. I'm not having anything *happen* to my kittens.

I point to the bathroom just outside of the room I'm sleeping in. "Shower's there."

Delaney doesn't turn to look.

Instead, she keeps staring up at me. "How do I know you won't leave while I'm showering?"

"You don't."

I stare at her.

She stares back.

And then she does the last thing I expect her to do. *Again.*

She turns and heads toward the bathroom, pulling her luggage behind her, like she trusts me.

The Delaney Kingston I remember from school would've stood there and stared at me all night to make sure I *behaved myself.*

But this Delaney?

She's on babysitting duty, and she's leaving me unsupervised.

Like she trusts me.

I trust me. But I don't trust that *she* trusts me.

"I'm going to hang with the triplets," I call to her through the closed door.

"Awesome. Emma will love that," she calls back.

Fuck.

She got me.

I'm grounded.

And not because I sneezed wrong and got myself set on fire at the pool.

After Thanksgiving, and the plane, and then fishing this afternoon, not to mention that favor Chandler asked, and hated that he had to ask, this was inevitable.

LANEY

I AM DOING this for Emma. I am doing this for Emma. I am doing this for Emma.

If I repeat it enough, knowing my *why* will make this tolerable.

In the meantime, the minute the bathroom door shuts behind me, I drop to the floor and peer under the crack between the door and the tile.

Theo's standing there in his underwear, frowning—no, *scowling*—at the bathroom door, looking like Theo, but also looking like a grown man who could crush a rock with his bare hands and then use that intense gaze to will it to put itself back together again.

I hold my breath.

Or try to.

He stares at the door for a *long* time. Is he waiting for the water to turn on? Can he see me peeking at him from under the crack? What's he doing? Why isn't he moving?

Is he actually a robot?

Does he need some sort of restart?

I'm about to leave the bathroom with some lame excuse that I need a cup of water from the small galley kitchen in the white-walled suite when he finally turns around, casts one last glance back at the bathroom where I'm starting to get a crick in my neck from watching him under the door, and then he twists the knob on the second bedroom and slips inside.

Finally.

I leap to my feet, creak open the bathroom door as softly as possible, and go against every inclination inside me as I creep across the living area to the extra bedroom.

Ignoring someone's specific instructions and requests is relatively foreign to me. Especially when it matters as much as it apparently matters to Theo.

But if he has cats in this suite, and the resort doesn't know, he could get thrown out.

Theo getting in trouble would be another damper on Emma's wedding week.

I'm reaching for the door when I hear it.

Not just the soft mewing of cats, but Theo's voice. And *that* is what has me stopping in my tracks.

"Who's a good kitten?" he croons softly. "Who's such a good kitten?"

Oh. My. God.

That is possibly the sexiest thing I've heard in *ages*.

I squinch up my nose. *Assuming* he's talking to a kitten. And not some woman he has in there and is screwing around with.

Yep.

More likely.

Has to be. If he truly has kittens in there, I might melt, and *I cannot do that.*

It's *Theo*. I don't care that I noticed he has a tattoo of his mom's name in the midst of a field of roses on one bicep, or how intriguing the *you are enough* in script on his other bicep amidst a field of thorns is. I don't care that I was mistakenly intrigued by him before I realized who he was at the pool.

And I don't care if he's saving every stray cat on this island himself.

For Emma's sake, I need to leave my feelings out of it and see what's going on in this room. Figure out how to solve it. Make sure Theo doesn't get caught by the resort staff with animals in his room.

I don't know how he got them in here. Or why. But it doesn't matter.

The point is that *he cannot get caught with animals here.*

I probably owe it to Emma to investigate, but I'm reasonably certain the reaction my ovaries are having to listening to Theo baby-talk kittens—no matter how much I'd rather that was a woman so that I could dislike him—puts my own self-preservation momentarily higher.

I dart back across the tropical rug and past the worn ivory couch and chair set in the living room to the bathroom just outside the first bedroom.

And yes, my eyes totally snag on the bag of knitting next to the rumpled bed inside that bedroom.

And the ring light stand.

And the ridiculously large present wrapped in silver bell wedding paper. And by ridiculous, I do mean *ridiculous*. At least two feet on every side.

Theo's voice is muffled by the other door, but I can still hear the soft tones, and it's causing definite issues for me in the lower belly area.

But who *wouldn't* be a little soft toward a guy who'd baby-talk kittens? And those were *definitely* kitten sounds.

Unless he's screwing with me.

Dammit.

He is.

He's screwing with me. And I almost fell for it.

Like I'll let on that I fell for it.

I dive back into the bathroom, go against every bit of training I've gotten since I was old enough to remember the phrase *we're in a drought, Delaney, don't waste water*, and turn on the water full-force while I grab my phone and open my texts.

Talking to Emma is out of the question.

But talking to Sabrina?

This is a must.

> Hey. You around? I have…a situation.

SABRINA

> Join the club, hon. Where are you?

> Theo's bathroom.

SABRINA

> WHAT?

> Not like that. Em asked me to babysit and staying in his bungalow is the most efficient way to do it. Bigger question—she said you're mad at him. What's up?

SABRINA

> Are you serious? Which one of us has held a deep-seated grudge against him since the Ugly Heiress incident? Which one of us got drunk to recover from the suspicion that his naked boob blanket-cape that he wore all over town was ordered from her parents' company? Which one of us still talks about how her only fender-bender in her entire life was courtesy of Theo and his old beater truck? And YOU are asking ME if there's a reason I'm mad at Theo?

> That's the most avoidy response to a question in the history of avoidy responses.

41

SABRINA

Em asked you to babysit him? That sucks.
What are you going to tell your parents?

I'm just a BUFFER for a couple days. It'll all
be cleared up before they land. If you won't
tell me why you're mad, can you at least
hang out at the door here to make sure he
doesn't leave while I'm taking a shower? I
don't want to let Em down my first hour on
the job.

SABRINA

Considering you saved him from becoming
toast at the pool…

YOU WERE THERE? I wanted to hug you
and say hi.

SABRINA

I was NOT there. Sullivan cousin text chain
activated. I mean, we kept Chandler out of it,
but then, we were talking about him… If it
helps, 95% of the family agrees that we also
need to do all that we can to keep Chandler
and Theo separated until Em's finally part of
the family, but the triplets definitely can't
hang with Theo and also stay on Chandler's
good side.

I figured. Too bad none of your aunts and
uncles are spry enough to keep up with him
anymore.

SABRINA

I hate that you're the best person for the job. And at the same time, I love that Em has you to ask so that she can breathe easier. How's the bungalow? Does it smell? Has he clearly had female guests? Is he walking around naked to try to make you uncomfortable so you'll leave?

Is that what he did to you to make you mad at him?

SABRINA

Hello, avoidy yourself.

Seriously. Why are you mad at him? What can I do to help make this better?

SABRINA

Laney, I love you. I ADORE you. And I know you could fix Hell itself if you had the chance. But this one... This one, I need you to sit out.

Oh my god. How bad is it?

SABRINA

I'll put on my big girl panties and play nice and tag in to babysit him for a while, okay? Here. Look. I'm right outside your bungalow now. He's not escaping while you shower.

SABRINA

picture of the door of the Plumeria Bungalow, complete with the saggy flamingo costume on the porch

THANK YOU. Also, I'm totally getting you drunk on mai tais later so that you'll tell me whatever's going on.

SABRINA

Priority here is getting Emma hitched to my cousin. I can't wait until she's legit my family legally too. You can get me drunk once we're home.

Promise?

SABRINA

By the time we get home, it's far more likely you'll want ME to get YOU drunk to forget babysitting Theo.

It's just for a couple days. Just until Chandler cools down. And until another space for me opens up.

SABRINA

And now I'm seriously debating if Drunk Laney would do a better job babysitting Theo than sober Laney... You might be a little too optimistic here.

Stop. This is fine. It's a small favor for Emma in the grand scheme of things. Theo's so mad that I'm invading his space that I think he'll avoid Chandler on his own so that I can come stay with you and Claire instead until more rooms open up.

SABRINA

This is not a small favor.

No, it is. What's a couple days of my life in exchange for one of my favorite people in the world having less stress for her wedding week?

SABRINA

Okay, Saint Laney.

You'd do the same for me. So would Emma.

SABRINA

Except you have no weird family members that your parents would let you invite to your wedding, and one has to DATE in order to have a reason to GET MARRIED, and we all know how that's going since Christopher the Boring.

Maybe I'll use one of those dating apps and find a hottie here in Hawaii.

SABRINA

During babysitting duty for Theo? He's not the troublemaker he was in high school anymore, but he'll still be a handful. Your optimism truly knows no bounds.

Last question, and then I really need to get in the shower before I waste too much water—do you know if Theo has...an animal...problem?

SABRINA

bulging eyes emoji Was that autocorrect, or did you just ask me if Theo has an animal problem?

I haven't seen him much in years, and I get the impression that he...likes...animals.

SABRINA

I'm breaking this door down.

> NO! Do NOT cause problems for Emma. DO NOT! I just need to know if it's normal for him to do things with animals everywhere he goes. Like, is this a project for his dad? Or is he just screwing with me to try to chase me out of here?

SABRINA

Laney. Theo has literally not ventured more than two hours from home for like four years. There is no "everywhere he goes." And no, he does not DO THINGS WITH ANIMALS at home. What the HELL is going on in that room?

> Never mind. I'm realizing just how stupid of a question that is. Theo's screwing with me. He loves to screw with people. I'm sure it's just the TV in the other room making weird noises.

SABRINA

Theo doesn't screw with people.

> Yes, he does.

SABRINA

No, he doesn't. He has two main goals in life: Have fun and don't get caught. He does not go out of his way, ever, to screw with people. Not like this.

> Even people who have moved into his bungalow for his sister's wedding week?

SABRINA

Tell me he has geckos in your room and not the feral GOATS that roam this island.

I swear on my reputation as a Kingston that he does not have goats in this room. And I think he's screwing with me so that I get out of his way and leave him alone.

SABRINA

I'm going to chalk up that assumption to your long travel day. Go take a shower. I'm not letting Theo out of this room, and if he does come out, I promise to not murder him. For Emma's sake. I don't promise to not invade the room and figure out what the hell he's doing in there, but I do promise to not murder him. Okay?

We need to talk in person soon instead of texting from ten feet apart.

SABRINA

Agreed. Go shower. I'll be here.

4

THEO

LANEY TAKES a million hours in the shower, and when she finally emerges, she's in shorts and a tank top.

No bra.

And the shorts are *short*, which show off the slender legs hiding under her ass.

I'm staring at her ass—swear to god, even her *ass* is sophisticated—as she heads to the main door of my suite, opens it, and pulls Sabrina Sullivan inside.

If Emma's the smart one of the trio they formed when Em skipped second grade and joined us in third grade when the rest of us were eight, Delaney's the perfect one, and Sabrina's the green-eyed, red-haired fun one.

Sabrina's also the biggest gossip in all of Snaggletooth Creek.

She knows things she shouldn't.

But she can also keep a secret. Most of the time. Unless it's beneficial for her to *not* keep the secret.

Which is what has me on edge as she surveys me with a cool glance. "Theo. Lovely to see you and your underwear."

I have a babysitter, and now I have the town gossip way too close to my kittens.

I'm in paradise and it fucking sucks. "Sabrina. Missed you at the pool."

Her nose lifts a quarter-inch in the air. "I was having my own fun."

Yep.

She's still pissed at me.

She'll get over it. Or she won't. But since helping with her problem would make bigger problems for me, she's gonna have to find another solution.

"We're going out for a little dinner," Laney says, clearly avoiding looking at me and my underwear. "Back in a bit." She gives me a finger wave, grabs Sabrina, and the two of them slip out the door.

I give it a minute, head to the door, and look out the peephole.

Yep.

They're whispering right outside.

Perfect.

I leap into action. Have to hide my recording equipment under the bed. Shove my knitting under my underwear and swim trunks in my duffel bag. Unplug my computer and stash it behind the wedding gift that Chandler will hate and Emma will laugh and laugh and laugh over.

And then I peek out the peephole again.

The women are still there.

I could leave off the deck on the ocean side of the bungalow, but that would put the kittens at risk of discovery when Laney goes snooping, and right now, I don't have a better place to keep them or a way to get them there without being spotted and questioned by my guard at the front door.

I'm trapped.

I hate feeling trapped.

Hate. It.

Reminds me of school.

Rather be back at the pool. Hanging out. Drinking tropical drinks. Flirting with a few ladies. Eating fish.

Eating.

Just eating.

But instead of wallowing in self-pity, I indulge in kitten therapy. Miss Doodles—yes, that's mama cat, and no, I have no regrets about her name—isn't as hostile as she could be, but she's still a scratch risk while she's being protective of her kittens, which I'm guessing are about a month old. Eyes are open. Ears are up. They're playing with each other. Using the litter box. Attacking the toys I picked up yesterday after I found them.

And still nursing off of Miss Doodles, whom I'm working to fully win over.

If I could move in here and close the kittens inside the ginormous bathroom in this primary bedroom, I would. But I can't.

This bedroom is an open-concept suite. A half-wall separates the bed from the tub. Two sinks are opposite the wide shower, and the closet has no door. I'd have to trap them in the throne room, and I'm not doing that to the kittens. And putting them in the other bedroom wasn't an option. Not when cleaning up their messes requires access to water.

The kittens have clearly had an eventful day exploring in here. It's not long before they get tired of me and pile on each other to sleep next to their mama, so I leave them to rest. I'm back in the main living area flipping through channels between sit-ups and push-ups and burpees—never have sat still well—feeling more like myself, more like I can handle *being babysat*, when Delaney lets herself back into the room. I brace for impact, waiting for her to freak out on me over my side hustle since I'm assuming Sabrina would've told her how best to manipulate me into behaving, but she doesn't say a word.

Just leans against the door and looks at me like she's tired and doesn't want to be here.

I'm not a sigher. Prefer to spend my time and energy living, having fun, building up everyone around me the way my mom used to build me up instead of grumbling.

But a weighty sigh leaks out of me right now.

"Take the bedroom," I grunt.

"I don't mind sleeping on—"

"Take. The fucking. Bedroom." She has a bigger job than I do this week. Not only is she *in* the wedding, but she has to make sure Chandler isn't pissed at me for breathing.

That's a Chandler problem.

Not a me problem.

I know he's not pissed that I'm breathing. He's pissed for other reasons.

But no matter why Chandler needs a buffer from me, Emma thinks he does, and Emma thinks Laney's the person for the job. So Laney should have a real bed.

And that's why I'm staring down the Tooth's original Little Miss Perfect and giving up the fight against having a babysitter.

To make my sister happy.

No matter how pissed I am that I went from being my normal happy-go-lucky, mischief-loving self an hour ago to being *a problem* who needs a *solution* in the form of Delaney Kingston as my babysitter now.

This is so much like high school I want to check the date on my phone to make sure I haven't been sucked into a time machine. And I don't want to talk about what it's doing to my mental health.

Her whole body sags, and she glances down at her own bare feet before looking up to meet my gaze again. "Thank you. We can trade off. I don't mind. I can—"

"Stop at *thank you* next time." Fuck, I hate being grumpy. But when it comes to Laney, there's rarely another way.

Call it self-preservation.

She eyes me for way too long, then looks way too long again at the closed door to the other bedroom.

"Okay," she finally says. "Thank you. I'll be quiet when I get up in the morning. If you want me to bring something in for breakfast—"

"Go to bed, Laney."

Thank fuck, she listens.

As soon as the bedroom door closes behind her, I poke my head out of the bungalow.

Sabrina lifts a single brow at me. She's standing at the edge of the porch like she has Theo radar, arms crossed, taller than genetics made her thanks to her chunky sandals.

Don't take on a five-foot-two redhead who knows all the dirt on you.

Just don't do it.

"Hey, Sabrina." I grin at her like I'm not agitated as fuck over how far down the toilet this day has been flushed. "Like your shoes. That flower between your toes is a nice touch for the tropics."

"If you're going to sneak out, you should put on pants first." She snaps a quick photo of me, then pockets her phone. Blackmail material. Awesome. "Emma would appreciate it."

I like Sabrina.

She never judged me for being a crappy student. Occasionally has a drink with me. Sometimes slips a little hint about who I should or shouldn't piss off or help out.

You want to know what's going on in the Tooth, she's your person. Provided she deems you worthy of the information.

And right now, I want more information. Because the bomb she dropped on me yesterday is still sitting heavy, even if I have no intention of being the one to bail her out.

Plenty of people around town would do what she asked me to do.

For instance— "Why didn't you ask Laney what you asked me?"

"Reconsidering?"

"Nobody's giving me a loan to hand over to you and you know it."

"You don't need a loan, and *you* know it."

I shrug.

While she's not wrong—my side hustle brings in a pretty penny—I don't like that she knows it.

And she probably doesn't like that I have dirt on her now.

Not that I'd use it. That's not my thing.

Won't catch me holding it over her that Bean & Nugget is overextended after expanding into neighboring communities that weren't as interested in Snaggletooth Creek coffee. Or that they're two years behind on taxes. Or that they're at risk of shutting down.

Sabrina wants help bailing the shop out.

And she came to me.

Wonder if she knows I'm paying for the wedding this week too. At Chandler's request. Which I doubt Emma knows.

And yeah, his damn *pride* over that is the reason I have a babysitter and he doesn't. Working hard to not be pissed about that.

Not there yet.

But I'm not refusing to help Sabrina because I'm a dick, or because I want Bean & Nugget to fail.

I know she can get the money. She has friends like Laney, whose family could bail out the café without hardly blinking. Kingston Photo Gifts has done fucking awesome for themselves.

The Kingstons might not be my favorite people in the

world, but I can't deny they've been successful, and they've done a lot of good things for the town and the people in it.

And they're not the only people who could afford to help Bean & Nugget.

Much as I love my hometown and the people in it, I don't want them knowing anything about my side hustle or what it's done for me. The minute people find out you got yourself something of a windfall, it's no longer *let's go hang pickles off the tree in the park and see how long it takes people to figure out it was us.*

Then, it's *hey, wanna get a box at the Avs game?* Or *you need a financial planner, because I'd love to help you make your money make more money for you.* Or *yo, Theo, we should hit Vegas and see if we can get into the high-roller rooms.* Or, *can I borrow a fuckton of cash because my family's café shouldn't have expanded to more locations that we can't support and now we're in debt up to our eyeballs?*

Add in *how* I make my money with my side hustle, and there are even bigger problems.

I spent the first twenty or so years of my life as the problem child of Snaggletooth Creek before I found where I fit and what I love. Now, when I hit a bar with the triplets, I know they're with me because they like hanging with me, not because they're hoping I'll pick up the tab on some high-end whiskey.

When I'm on a job with the construction crew I've worked with for about five years now, my coworkers aren't nice to me because they're hoping I'll drop off random sacks of money outside their house at Christmas, and the boss doesn't ask my opinion because he's hoping I'll buy out the owner or give him tips on how he can get himself a side hustle to make him some dough too.

I don't keep my day job as a cover. I keep it because *I like it*. It makes a difference in the community.

I make a difference in the community.

Having something physical to do where I'm improving something around town matters to me. Makes me feel good.

And I do care that Bean & Nugget is in trouble.

It affects Emma. It affects her friends. It affects the whole town.

"Why didn't you ask Laney?" I repeat.

Sabrina sighs and rubs her palms into her eye sockets. "Already did."

"You know your lip does this funny thing every time you lie?"

"No, it doesn't."

It doesn't. But I'm not telling her what her actual tell is. And she is definitely lying. "Can't help you if you don't tell me."

"You're not going to help me anyway. Even though it would be helping Emma too."

"If Emma wanted my help, she'd ask for it herself."

Sabrina pulls another face and looks off toward the lights of the other bungalows glowing in the darkness down the way.

I bite my tongue to keep from asking if Emma knows.

She knows Chandler.

She knows what she's getting herself into. Says all the time that they don't keep secrets. Which means she probably doesn't want to tell me because she knows I don't like him, no matter how much I try to hide it. Or, if he's keeping secrets from her, I'm still the bad guy if I let it slip.

Just when I think Sabrina's gonna mutter something about finding someone else to loan her the money to get Bean & Nugget back in the black, she makes eye contact with me and scowls. "I *can't* ask Laney because my family won't take things from her family. That's all you need to know. But if I have the cash to save the company, I can buy it off of Chandler and *fix this*."

My dad runs a taxidermy empire that's grown in the

digital age, much to Emma's credit for getting Dad on the internet and managing his sales and advertising. But it doesn't have the same impact in the community as Bean & Nugget.

If Rocky Roadkill went under, no one would care. They've never really cared. Why would they?

But if Bean & Nugget goes under, the Tooth loses one of its primary hangouts. A bunch of people lose their jobs. Em would deal with the stress since Chandler would be dealing with it, even if she can support herself with her own accounting business.

She can support him too.

But she can't dig the café out from its debt. She doesn't have that kind of cash.

"We have maybe two months, Theo," Sabrina says. "Think of the wedding gift this would be to Emma."

And the gift it would be for Sabrina too. It's her life, even though her mom sold her share in the café to Chandler's parents so she could send Sabrina to college. The triplets' parents sold their share to Chandler's parents too. And they handed the reins to him not long after Grandma Sullivan passed away.

"If Emma wanted my help—" I start.

"She wouldn't ask you for it, because she knows you don't want anyone to know you can afford it, she knows you don't want people knowing *why* you can afford it, and she knows how much Chandler would hate knowing you're the reason he's no longer in debt."

I feel like I'm about to crawl out of my skin.

If Bean & Nugget's time came to an end, some other enterprising person in Snaggletooth Creek would open a new shop.

We wouldn't be without coffee. People would get jobs back. There'd be a new kind of hangout.

Some people hate change.

I love it. It has a scent of possibility. Of surprises. Of fun.

But I don't like knowing that change hurts in the middle of it. Especially when it could hurt my sister.

And I don't like feeling trapped and blackmailed.

One more checkmark in why I don't want people knowing my bank account—the one *not* kept at the Tooth's local bank —is as large as it is.

"You gonna sit out here all night?" I ask Sabrina.

"For Emma and Laney? Yep. Also, I scattered broken glass on the ground under your porch on the other side, so if you're thinking of going out the back way, I'd advise you to reconsider."

I know she knows that I know she's lying, but I also know if I leave here and run into Chandler and anything goes wrong again, she'll probably do worse. I grunt a noncommittal noise and turn back to my bungalow door.

I can handle being trapped inside for one night, even if it makes me testy as hell.

Chandler will get his head out of his ass for Emma's sake —much as I don't like him, I can admit that he treats my sister right and gets along with me for her sake too—and tomorrow will be fine.

"And go easy on Laney," she adds softly. "She will fix *anything* to make sure Emma has the wedding of her dreams. It'll be easier on everyone if you just avoid Chandler until after the wedding. No matter how unfair it is that you don't get to enjoy this week the way you should."

Hell. Does she know I paid for the wedding too?

"Do *not* tell Emma," I say.

She scowls, but she doesn't tell me I can buy her silence by saving her family's café.

Two points to Sabrina. We might stay friends beyond this week after all. And not because she's borderline blackmailing me for money.

"And I'll think about it," I mutter.

Two months.

I don't have to decide today.

The café has two months. Emma can get back from her honeymoon. We can sit down and talk. Clear the air. I can ask her what she wants me to do.

How to do whatever she wants me to do.

Or if she wants me to do nothing at all.

I tell Sabrina goodnight and let myself back into the bungalow. Both bedroom doors are still closed. The balcony doors off the living room are open though, letting in the sound of the surf and the scent of the ocean through the screens.

Not a bad way to sleep.

And I'm honestly ready for sleep.

Run hard during the day.

Crash hard at night.

It's crash time.

I head to the couch and toss the cushions aside to pull out the hide-a-bed.

Or try to.

I get the thing halfway out, and it sticks.

Totally, completely frozen.

I tug.

It doesn't move.

Tug again.

Still doesn't move.

It's just hanging out, sticking out of the couch at a forty-five-degree angle.

So I push it back in, except that doesn't work either.

Try unfolding the lower half of the bed.

No dice.

No matter how I push, pull, tug, lift, or do anything else, the damn thing *will not move.*

"Are you kidding me?" I mutter to it.

I don't go looking for trouble.

I don't.

Not anymore.

But it's apparently finding me this week in all kinds of inconvenient places.

Mama cat meows loudly inside the primary bedroom.

"You're right, Miss Doodles," I answer, knowing it's not an invitation from the cats to join them. They'd scratch me all to hell, Emma would notice, Laney would notice, Laney would turn me in for the cats, and then everything will go to hell. Better to let them decide they like me before risking them eating my face off in the middle of the night. "I *am* paying for this place."

Mind made up.

I have three beds in this suite, and I'm sleeping in *one* of them.

No matter how much it's going to suck.

5

LANEY

A NOISE PULLS me out of a sleep so hard and deep that I barely remember lying down at all or where I am.

"I fixed the naked man!" I gasp.

"Must've been a sight," a deep voice replies.

Hawaii.

Emma's wedding.

And *Theo*. Looming in the doorframe, backlit by the soft glow of a night-light somewhere beyond my room, shirtless, pants-less, and definitely broader and harder than I remember him.

More tattooed too, though I can't see them in the dark. It's just the memory of the ink all over his chest and stomach and arms.

And *what the hell am I doing*, thinking about Theo's body and tats?

"A large corporation ordered three thousand mugs with their logo and the artwork got switched and they were sent three thousand mugs of a guy with a Santa hat covering his

—" *Shut up, Laney. He doesn't care why you were delayed getting here. Or that you're dreaming about work. Or rambling because your baser instincts are overruling your better sense.* I clear my throat. "What are you doing?"

"Scoot over," he replies.

"Scoot...what?"

"Over. I get this side."

"You...huh?" I am one hundred percent fully awake now, but his orders have scrambled my brain and made actual sentences impossible.

"The fucking couch broke. It's a king-size bed. Scoot. Over. Or go sleep on the floor."

No is on the tip of my tongue, but it won't come out. "I'll fix the couch," I stutter.

"Knock yourself out."

His answer puts my teeth on edge.

I'm trying *so hard* to be nice to him. And he's being an utter ass.

I should be glad he's being an ass. His personality should compensate for my hormonal reaction to his body and his voice.

Except it doesn't.

My nipples are hard and there's a frantic anticipation deep in my belly at the idea that I might have to sleep in the same bed as Theo.

It's been over a year since I broke my parents' hearts when I declined Christopher's proposal, which means it's been over a year since I've realized that their image of what my life should be and what I want for my life don't line up.

Work is fine. Work is *great*, in fact. I'm fully in step with what they want for the company professionally, and honestly honored that they're letting me prove I can do what it takes to run things when they retire.

Not because I want to please them with what I think, but

because I believe they're taking it in the right direction to continue growing and thriving.

It's outside work hours that things get tense. They *really* want me to get back into the dating world with someone safe. Someone respectable. Someone with good genes for making the next generation of Kingston babies, preferably two or three in case the first one isn't a perfect clone of me.

So, basically, they want me to live a gender-reversed Victorian-era dream.

Instead, I'm nearly thirty and finally hitting my teenage rebellion stage.

Which is a bad time to have my hormones reacting to Theo Monroe.

There's a difference between dating someone I meet at a bar and become infatuated with and telling my parents that I've been sleeping in the same bed as Theo.

I flop out of bed, realize I'm only in my tank top and panties, squeak, and lunge for the neatly folded pajama shorts I left on the nightstand. "Turn around."

"Seen naked women before, Laney."

"Turn. Around."

You know what's most aggravating about Theo Monroe?

When we both surfaced in the pool, he was wearing the biggest grin known to man. I remember that from high school. He was *always* smiling. He was always having fun. Even when he was in trouble, he'd find a reason to smile about it. Clearly still does. Which must be really nice.

But he never smiles at me.

Not then.

And only briefly today before he realized my job here is to make him miserable.

Or at least, that's how I assume he classifies my task of being a buffer between him and Chandler.

I hide behind the bed and yank my pajama shorts on. "I am doing my *very damn best* to make the most of this situation. Would it utterly kill you to acknowledge that I'm doing your sister a favor, and *you too* for that matter? That I'm not trying to make your life hell? Is it that hard to be as pleasant as you can be about this too?"

He doesn't answer, and instead, flings himself onto the left side of the bed, face down in the pillow, and mutters something.

I take a deep breath and sigh loudly out of my nose.

He mutters something else in his pillow.

Forget this.

I march out to the living room. If I can't sleep, I might as well sleep on the couch.

He's left the folded bedframe half out of the couch, sticking up at a weird angle.

I roll my eyes and tug on the bar at the top, but it doesn't budge.

I tug harder.

Still not a bit of movement. "C'mon. You can do it. Good couch," I murmur supportively.

Shockingly, that doesn't work either.

I tug. I pull. I try different bars on the contraption. I push. I tug and pull and heft all of my weight into it, but the only thing I succeed in doing is making the couch thump and bump across the floor.

And now I'm sweating.

I eyeball the closed bedroom door for the second bedroom.

Something hisses inside.

So that's a *nope*. And also a problem for tomorrow.

I can't get the couch fully open into the hide-a-bed, or fully closed so I can sleep on it. I don't have the tools to take the hinges apart and investigate this further.

And I need to sleep so that I can be on top of my game for doing everything in my power to keep Theo separated from Chandler for the next few days, which is honestly obnoxious when I consider that I'm positive they were friends in high school.

Crap.

Dammit.

Best way to keep an eye on Theo?

Share a damn bed with him.

I won't sleep well, but at least I'll know if he tries to get up in the middle of the night.

Deep breath, Delaney. Deep, deep breath.

This will be okay.

I can do this.

It's only for a couple nights. Just until Chandler is back in his happy place and Theo's so tired of me that he finds a way to voluntarily avoid Chandler on his own.

I trudge back to the bedroom. Don't look at the Theo-shaped lump on the left side of the bed. Climb delicately into the right side of the bed, leaving my shorts on.

Close my eyes.

And immediately wonder if I snore and don't know it. Or if Theo snores. Or if he sneezes in his sleep. Or if he's a thrasher.

I know I don't toss and turn in my sleep. I lay down on my back, close my eyes, fall asleep, and wake up in the morning on my back.

The only time my covers are a mess is when I'm sick.

God, I'm boring.

I clear my throat. "Good night."

He grunts.

"We'll call maintenance tomorrow about the couch. If they can't fix it, they can probably—"

"Good night, Delaney."

Well.

That was a very direct and pointed *shut up* if I've ever heard one.

I sigh again.

Scoot closer to the edge of the bed. Just in case.

Readjust my pillow.

Close my eyes.

And I feel someone staring at me.

Nope. He's definitely not staring at me. *Definitely* not. He's completely uninterested in anything I'm doing, and it's all a figment of my imagination that I feel the weight of his gaze on me.

If I open my eyes and glance at his side of the bed, I'll see that his head is still buried in his pillow and he's not staring at me and my imagination is running wild because Sabrina has snuck me one too many romance novels that my mother doesn't know I read with a very similar but *entirely different* situation here.

Those always involve two people who secretly like each other.

I *do not* like my best friend's brother.

And he most definitely does *not* like me. He's made that abundantly clear.

Dammit.

I can't fall asleep.

Brain. Will. Not. Shut. Off.

I need to turn on a meditation app or something, but I don't want to hear about it from Theo.

I pop one eye open.

Aim it in his direction.

Crap.

It's just bright enough in here thanks to the moonlight streaming in the window that I can see him. And he is totally staring at me.

I roll onto my side and face the wall.

Tell yourself a story, Laney. Tell yourself a story.

As if that's going to work.

This is going to be a very, very, very long night.

6

THEO

SO THIS IS UNEXPECTED.

Thought I'd wake up on the floor. Tied up so I can't go anywhere. Possibly under a pile of clothes, since while most women would toss you out in nothing but your underwear when you annoy them, Laney is not that kind of woman. She'd want me to put my clothes *on* before she forcibly removed me from her presence.

Instead, I'm waking up with her hand wrapped around my cock.

She's curled up right next to me, breathing on my shoulder, with a limp grip under my briefs and on my very hard dick.

Any other woman, I'd be leaning into this opportunity.

But Laney?

Pretty quick she's gonna figure out she's making my balls sweat.

And that's not a good sign for today getting back on the right track.

I don't know if Emma knows she made the worst possible choice in asking Laney to be my *buffer* from Chandler. Probably does.

And that stings.

No, it more than stings. It fucking *sucks*.

Sometime between freshman and senior years, I noticed that Laney's a girl. A know-it-all, straight-A, silver-spooned pain-in-the-ass, but still a girl.

And a girl who made me feel warm inside every time I looked at her, watched her laughing with my sister, saw her talking to my dad anytime she'd come visit Emma like it wasn't weird that he was always surrounded by taxidermy animals that he sometimes talked to more than he talked to Em and me.

And then, after being so nice to everyone else, Laney would make me feel like the world's biggest fuckup whenever I talked to her.

I didn't want to like her. Why would I? To her, I was her best friend's lazy, C-average, going-nowhere, waste-of-oxygen brother.

She was always polite. Of course she was. Even in a small town like Snaggletooth Creek, we have folks of *good breeding*, and the richer her parents got, the more *good breeding* they insisted they had.

But back then, I was beneath her and I knew it.

I might be able to financially take care of myself—and more—now, but I'm still *that guy*. The guy who'll call in sick to work when there's fresh powder for snowboarding. The guy who'll randomly put potatoes with googly eyes glued onto them on every bench in the park in the middle of the night. The guy who's never met a dare he wouldn't take, whose presence somehow inspires bigger bets and bolder fun at the bars, who doesn't really care what fork is for what course, or why meals have to have courses.

And while having her hand on my raging hard-on is wet

dream territory for my inner teenager, she's still the last person who'll follow through when she wakes up and realizes what she's been using as a handlebar in her sleep.

Fuck.

Not just my balls that are sweating now. My dick is too.

She's gripping my sweating cock. She's gonna wake up with my sweaty cock in her hands, think I jizzed all over both of us, and it'll be game over for me.

I don't get easily embarrassed.

Spent too much time the past decade coming to terms with who I am, what I want, where I've fucked up, and where I fit in the world now to worry about little stuff like what judgy people that I'll never please think about me.

But waking up in this bed with her hands all over me? Getting a feel of everything that teenage me fantasized about for years while pretending I was completely unaffected by her presence, and knowing that she'd reject me all over again?

This is different.

And don't get me started on what it's doing to me that she's sleeping with her face smushed against my shoulder after tossing and turning half the night.

Drooling a little on my skin, even.

Fucking adorable.

No.

No.

Not adorable.

Annoying. I need to wash Delaney drool off me now.

She's cute, that backstabbing asshole in the back of my head whispers.

Time to move.

I shift a millimeter, and she bolts straight upright, her tank top riding up and showing off the smooth skin on her soft belly.

Higher, an instinctive part of me that I have no control

over mentally orders her shirt. *Go higher. Give me the thrill of my life and show me a Laney nipple.*

"Oh my god, who am I?" she gasps.

"My dick wants to know the answer to that question too." *Jesus.* I fucking *hate* being the grumpy asshole.

Why does she bring this out in me?

Because she makes you feel fifteen again, and fifteen sucks, the rational part of my brain answers for me.

She yanks the sheet up to her chin and stares at me.

While she's still gripping my cock.

With what's apparently her third hand.

Wait.

Wait.

"Please leave your unmentionables out of all of our conversations," she says almost as stiffly as my cock's standing up under her hand.

But it's not her hand.

Can't be her hand.

I can see both of her hands.

Now *all* of me is sweating.

Who's gripping my dick? Someone is. Aren't they?

I give him a little wiggle with my hips.

Oh, yeah. Someone is *definitely* holding onto my cock.

Her brows furrow. "Theo?"

"Did someone sneak in here and put a fake hand around my woody?" I whisper.

Not outside the realm of possibility here. I've seen weirder shit.

I might've been involved in doing weirder shit a time or two.

Her lip curls. "What are you *talking* about?"

"Show me both of your hands."

She doesn't break eye contact while she shows me her hands, one at a time so she can keep the sheet covering her breasts. I don't tell her I can still see all of the exposed skin on

69

her back from her shirt riding up, and it's making me harder, despite Inner Sex Freak Theo's disappointment that she's not laid out like a morning buffet for me to feast on.

Fucking morning hormones.

"Someone's holding my dick," I say.

"Very funny."

"*They are.*"

She huffs. "Look, I understand men have *needs*, but can you please *not* jerk off *in the same damn bed as me*?"

"I'm not fucking—are we alone?"

"Yes, Theo, we're alone."

"*Someone is holding my dick.*"

"It's clearly not me, so it must be you."

"I think I'd know if I was holding my own dick."

She sucks in a deep breath through her nose, closing her eyes as she does it, and when her entire body lets that breath out, she opens her eyes and stares at me exactly the same way she did every single day in high school.

Like I'm *a problem.*

And one more time for the peanut gallery, *I do not want my hormones to be attracted to this woman.*

I had no idea my sister hated me so much. Yet here we are.

"So lift up the sheet," she grits out, "and *look.*"

Huh.

Not a bad idea.

Probably should've thought of that myself, but I was so flustered at the idea that Laney was gripping me for dear life that my brain short-circuited.

And fine. *Gripping me for dear life* is probably an exaggeration, but the point is still that she wanted to touch my pee-pee, which she once told me was the most disgusting thing on the planet when she caught me taking a leak behind a tree.

But I'm not holding my dick.

She's not holding my dick.

So who's holding my dick?

She lifts her brows. Doesn't have to say a word, and it doesn't matter that it's been years since I voluntarily talked to her before yesterday.

Easy to see what she's running through her brain.

If you think stalling will make me look under that sheet, you're dead wrong. I know a setup for a flashing when I see one.

But it's not a setup.

Someone's holding my dick.

I snort out a grunt and push back the sheet. And yeah, I'm pushing it back far enough for her to see, no matter where she sits on the bed or in the room, because I'm going to fucking prove to her that *someone is in this room with us.*

I look down.

And I see—

Oh.

Huh.

Fuck.

That's *my* hand.

Unless someone else got tats identical to mine down their forearm and has that same scar under the knuckle on their index finger that I got during that incident involving a marmot, a mountain bike, and a raccoon jawbone.

So that's my hand holding my dick. Even though it doesn't *feel* like my hand is holding my dick.

"Are you kidding me?" she mutters.

"I don't know how it got there."

I move it, except it doesn't work.

Try again.

Nothing.

My gaze flies to Laney. "It won't move."

I get a dead-faced stare back. "Very funny, Theo. News flash: exposing yourself to me won't make me any less effective as your babysitter today."

"*It won't move.* It—"

Oh. Oh, *there* we go. The tingles. I'm getting the tingles in my fingertips. "It—it fell asleep," I stutter. "I couldn't—I didn't—look."

I pry my hand off my dick with my other hand, lift the dead arm, and drop it on my stomach. "It fell asleep. I couldn't feel it. That's why I thought—"

"So glad we got that sorted out."

"I wasn't flashing you—"

"Okay."

"And I wasn't choking the chicken—"

"Whatever."

Yeah, me with my hands down my underwear in my sleep is definitely a point in my favor. "*My hand fell asleep.*"

"Sure."

She's walking out the door, showing off her short, silky pajama bottoms that are giving her a wedgie in that sophisticated ass of hers, and *fuck me*.

"I don't do this on purpose," I call after her while I yank my briefs back up with my awake hand. "Things *happen* to me. It's what makes life *fun*. One day you're gonna realize just how much joy and fun and laughter you've missed out on because of the stick perpetually wedged up your ass."

Delaney Kingston, snooty proper princess of Snaggletooth Creek, responds with one stiff middle finger.

"Nice job," I mutter to my hand and my dick.

My left hand responds by tingling a little more.

Fucking hurts.

But not as much as the ego I didn't realize could still be bruised.

7

LANEY

I AM DOING this for Emma.

I am *happy* to do this for Emma.

But I still scrub my face way longer than necessary to try to wash out the image of Theo in all of his naked glory on the bed, holding his thick erection against the backdrop of miles of muscles and tattooed skin.

He's an objectively attractive man.

I can admit that.

I can also very firmly know that I will *never* act on any kind of attraction to Theo. *Who jerks off in the same bed as someone they're not even friends with?*

And don't tell me that's not what he was doing.

Theo Monroe has taken perverse joy in tormenting me—or at least making sure I knew he thought I was *no fun*—for as long as I can remember. And while I can appreciate that a grown man wouldn't want a babysitter, I *cannot* appreciate that he'd masturbate *in the same freaking bed*.

I cannot get clean enough.

And also *why* am I wondering if he knows how to use his equipment for the benefit of someone else?

It's because he's so very wrong for me, and it's been too long since I've dated, and I'm getting tired of my mother throwing businessmen from Denver at me and talking about *suitable matches* and *continuing the family line* like we're some kind of Manhattan socialites instead of a small family who worked hard in the right business at the right time with the right plan.

And because he looked so *fun* when he was smiling at the pool yesterday.

So fun.

Oh, god.

I will not have my rebellion moment at my best friend's wedding. I will not have my rebellion moment at my best friend's wedding. I will not have my rebellion moment at my best friend's wedding.

I can wait a freaking week, and *then* I can have my rebellion moment.

Okay.

Now that I've reminded myself what this is, and now that I have my rebellion mentally scheduled on my calendar for a more convenient day, my entire outlook on life is significantly improved.

And it only took forty-eight minutes in the shower to get here.

With the door locked.

And several minutes of self-talk about how I did *not* need to work out any frustrations by touching any of my own erogenous zones because *I do not masturbate to thoughts of Theo Monroe.*

My mother would be horrified.

Not that I talk to her about who I think about while I'm masturbating—or that I masturbate at all.

She'd be horrified at the idea that I own a vibrator.

Vaginas are *no-no boxes*. Penises are *danger sticks*. And sex will ruin your life with babies you can't take care of after the man who put his cooties in your no-no box leaves you without child support.

Yet here I am, with fresh images of Theo Monroe's penis in my head.

"*Stop it stop it stop it*," I mutter to my reflection in the bathroom mirror.

Or really, in the general vicinity of where my reflection should be.

That was one steamy shower.

Theo takes steamy showers.

I stifle a frustrated groan and turn around to grab my luggage, only to remember I didn't bring it in here with me.

I didn't.

Bring.

My luggage.

Into.

The bathroom.

Every nerve ending in my body ices over, and I get that sinking feeling in my chest at knowing if I had my own hotel room, I could dash out into the bedroom in a towel and no one would see me or care.

But while Theo might be perfectly comfortable letting it all hang out—or point out—I am *not*.

Too many years of being told it's up to me to not tempt men into impregnating me with scandalous looks. Too many years of being told I have to be a model citizen. To be perfect. That if I'm going to take over Kingston Photo Gifts one day, I need to make sure there are no questionable pictures of me in existence.

Breaking up with Christopher and realizing that while my parents want a *safe* life for me, I want to *live*, has made me reconsider a lot of what I tell myself about work and fun. And sex. And life.

I've gotten way more comfortable in my own skin in the past year, but showing Theo my skin is way different from being comfortable in my own skin.

Not that there's any danger of me sleeping with Theo. In the *having sex* kind of way.

But I still get to choose who sees me nearly naked. I did *not* want him seeing me in the only pajamas I brought last night, and I have no intention of letting him see me in them again. Unfortunately, I have nothing else in here to wrap myself in. It's either the pajamas or a towel.

Or is it? a voice I barely recognize whispers deep inside me.

Do you want to live, Laney? Or do you want to be a prude who's afraid of letting anyone see your body for your entire life?

Oh my god.

I twirl to look at myself in the mirror, not quite believing that I'm honestly considering giving Theo a taste of his own medicine by walking out of this door completely naked, but I still can't see myself.

Too much steam in the already humid room.

But seriously.

Why *can't* I walk out of here naked?

Why *shouldn't* I own the skin I was born in?

This is what I've been trying to tell myself for a year now, isn't it? *Your body isn't bad. Skin isn't shameful. Casual sex won't ruin your life. You get to live.*

And here I am, cowering in the bathroom instead of freaking *owning it* in front of my biggest nemesis.

I'm talking myself into giving a big ol' *fuck it* and walking out of this bathroom naked just to prove that I can when I hear the bungalow door close.

Theo's either coming or going.

Neither's good.

I hastily wrap myself in a towel, wrench the bathroom door open, and peek out into the suite.

No Theo.

No Theo in the living room.

No Theo in the bedroom.

The second bedroom, though, the one with the closed door and the cat noises—that one has a very clear sign posted on it.

This room is being used for something that it's best you don't know about, and yes, it involves nudity and pornographic noises. If you open this door, a security camera will notify me, and photographic evidence that you're carrying my secret love child will be sent to your parents.

I gape.

And gape some more.

He's screwing with me.

He has to be screwing with me.

I put my hand on the doorknob. This is stupid. I'm finding out what's in there once and for all, and then I'll deal with it.

Right?

Right?

Crap.

Do I really want to know if he's making porn?

Crap again.

While I'm gaping, Theo's wandering out there somewhere in the resort, possibly dressed, possibly not, and I can't be a buffer between him and Chandler if I don't know where he is.

Which means I need to get dressed and deal with this room later.

I turn away from the door, and three soft *mew*s carry from behind it.

Those are kittens.

Those are *definitely* kittens.

He's not—he's *not* using kittens to make porn, is he?

He's not.

He can't be.

Except it's Theo.

And he looks like *that*.

He could be making porn.

Oh my god. He *could* be making porn. And right now, he's on the loose.

I dash through getting dressed, then take off out the door.

Where am I going?

No idea.

Where would I go if I were Theo and I wanted to get away from *me*?

I'm striding toward the lobby and the gift shop, wishing I had a better idea, when I hear my name.

"*Laney!*"

I spin. "Sabrina. Thank god."

Sabrina Sullivan is the embodiment of a caffeinated squirrel, and I adore her. She's about four inches shorter than me, has a dog back home that's even bigger than she is, and perpetually wears heels or chunky boots so that we almost line up eye to eye, though we both still look up to Emma. Sabrina and I made fast friends in kindergarten when Annabelle Fitzsimmons refused to let either of us play with *her* favorite doll.

Sabrina set us up a play coffee bar instead—she was born in the kitchen of the original Bean & Nugget, unintentionally, of course, but that's so on brand for Sabrina—and as soon as she gave me my first sip of imaginary cappuccino, we were bonded for life.

She tackles me in a hug and I get a mouthful of curly red hair as I hug her back tightly like we didn't see each other just last night.

Pretty sure we both feel like we're headed into battle, though I don't know why *she* feels that way.

"Sleep okay?" she asks me.

"We had to *share a bed*," I whisper. "And I woke up and he was all, *quit touching my thing*, and I was like, *I'm not touching your thing*, and it was just a cover for him jerking off. He says his hand fell asleep, but honestly, *who believes that*?"

Her jaw flaps a bit before she finally finds words. "Was the bed shaking?"

Now it's my turn to do the jaw flap.

Was it?

I don't think it was, but— "Well, *something* woke me up."

"Why did you have to share a bed?"

My eyelid twitches. "He broke the pullout sofa and he won't let me in the other bedroom and I don't know why and I don't believe the reasons he's telling me."

Sabrina knows *everything*. I won't say she's a gossip since my mother frowns on gossiping, but I will say she has a gift of knowing when there's a story, sniffing it out, and sharing it where it needs to be shared for the greater good of all humanity.

So when she wrinkles her nose at me and asks, "What's in the room?", I know she doesn't know either.

Yet.

And honestly? I don't want to tell her what I think is in the room.

I want to have a secret.

"I don't know. I heard him leave while I was finishing up in the shower and I figured it was more important to find him before I make him show me whatever's in the room. And I need to stop by the front desk and ask for maintenance to come straighten out the pullout sofa. But where would he even go? Where's Chandler?"

"If you can't guess where Chandler would be, we have even bigger problems than Theo rocking the boat to wake you up this morning."

"Golf."

She nods. "Golf."

"Does Theo golf?"

"I wouldn't expect in the traditional sense, no."

"I don't want to know what the *nontraditional sense* would be, do I?"

"You probably do in the interest of finally being the *fun Laney* you keep talking about being, but not today. So. Wanna split up and see if we can track him down?"

"Are you still mad at him?"

"Let it go, Laney. You don't want this."

Secrets. *Secrets.* We all have secrets, don't we? This is *not* how Emma's wedding week is supposed to go.

She points to the gift shop. "I'll start there. You head to the desk in the lobby and get everything fixed with your room. Emma's having some secret sorority wedding ritual that she's super excited about with Claire and a few of their sorority friends who got here last night too. Kinda nice that they have more people since it got moved from yesterday when the kitchen staff didn't show up."

I frown. *"The kitchen staff didn't show up?"*

"It's—*argh*. I think the resort is having some, erm, growing pains. But with all of us on the job, everything will be fine. Take care of you first. Find Theo second. I'll shoot you an updated calendar. And then we can have lunch."

I *hope* we can do lunch.

That'll depend on Theo. And possibly his cats.

And on what Theo did to make Sabrina mad, and if they can put it all aside for Emma's sake.

I *think* Sabrina can.

But Theo?

Theo's unpredictable chaos.

And I have no idea how I'll keep him contained.

8

THEO

I KNOW WHAT EMMA WANTS.

Emma wants a peaceful, joyful wedding week.

And that means I need to leave her and Chandler alone.

After the hand incident, I'm not too keen on being stuck with Laney all day, so once I check on the kittens and get them fresh food, water, and litter, then ping Lucky to verify Chandler is golfing and nowhere near this side of the resort, I head to the beach for a long swim.

Sitting still has never been one of my talents. If I went and found Dad and Uncle Owen, they'd be lounging by the pool debating which tropical drink to try next, or hanging out at a restaurant arguing over the quality of the taxidermy tropical fish on the walls.

Love them both, but no thanks.

Not today.

Today, I'd rather push myself, get my head back on straight, and work up a sweat in the salty ocean water protected from the bigger swells by a sea wall.

Eventually, I wade back out and find a good spot on the beach for making a sandcastle, which is more of a sand mountain. Great place for building a sand mountain range. The golden sand is interrupted with black lava rocks of all shapes and sizes, which means the terrain's already there. I'm just helping it along.

Three kids wander over to help me—all of them under seven, I'd guess, with the youngest wearing inflatables on his arms—while their parents keep a close eye on us.

One mom's staring too close.

Wouldn't bother me back home.

But back home, I don't have a lot of reason to strip down and run around in just swim trunks.

Most of the time.

And even then, they're used to me. And they trust me with their kids because they all know me.

I actively ignore the curious mom while we all keep playing in the sand and more and more kids join us.

This? Playing with a bunch of kids and helping them work together to build something with their imaginations, where we're all on even ground and no one's bad and no one's perfect and everyone's having fun?

This is my freaking heaven.

Our sand mountains are rapidly turning into sand volcanoes which are threatening to destroy our pretend dinosaurs, which are all of the kids' beach toys. Even the beach toys that aren't dinosaurs get repurposed as dinosaurs. So do a few lava rocks. Snorkels. Shovels. If we can call it a dinosaur, we call it a dinosaur.

And that's where Delaney finds me. Helping what's grown to be a group of a dozen kids defend the dinosaurs against blow-up flamingo floaties of death and imminently erupting sand volcanoes.

I *feel* her the minute she steps on the beach. It's this mix of judgment, irritation, and curiosity that invades my senses and has me casting covert looks around to spot her while I dash around the beach flying the floatie of death.

And there she is.

Wearing a wide-brimmed straw hat, sunglasses, a tank top that shows zero cleavage, and a long tropical skirt. Settling down on a flat lava rock where the resort grass meets the sand beach. Pulling her phone out of that annoying alligator purse like she has nothing better to do than work while she's in paradise.

She annoys the fuck out of me.

"*Ahh!*"

Oh, hell.

I just ran over a kid and knocked her down because I was paying attention to my *babysitter* instead of watching where I was going.

"Oh, no," I cry. "The Flamingo of Death got Briley!"

"Death to the flamingo!" a little boy named Xavier yells. He lets out a Tarzan cry—seriously, you'd think he'd go *Braveheart*, but this kid is all in with the Tarzan impression instead—and then he leaps onto the flamingo floatie and pours lava—aka water—on it. "Take that, Flamingo of Death!"

And while he's taking on the floatie, I squat down to the poor girl who got caught in my distraction. "Sorry about that. Forget I'm not a little kid too some days. You okay?"

Her nose twitches and she blinks fast before she nods. But I still feel like an ass until she follows it with a grin. "Death to the Flamingo of Death!" she cries.

The kids all rally around her and Xavier, celebrating them as heroes.

But it kills the mood.

At least for the parents.

Two moms call their kids back for *snack time*.

A third declares they're going to be late for their hiking trip.

83

They all file away after that, taking their toys and leaving me with a bunch of destroyed sand volcanoes and the watchful eyes of my *babysitter* on me.

"You gonna sit there all day and pretend you're not watching me?" I say to the ocean while I try to rebuild a volcano.

Don't expect her to answer. Waves aren't quiet, and I'm facing away.

But she's right behind me, and she definitely heard. "No, I thought I'd join you and help smooth out the sand again."

I twist around to look at her. *Smooth out the sand?* "Or we can build a sandcastle."

She stares at me like I've just lost the last of my marbles.

And I double down.

If I have to have a babysitter, I'm setting the terms, and these are my terms.

"It's called *fun*," I prompt. "Playing in the sand? Building something? Using your imagination? C'mon. Let's build a sandcastle."

Her nose twitches and she studies me like there's some kind of hidden message in my invitation to make a sandcastle.

Or maybe like she thinks I'm acting like a child and doesn't want to say it out loud.

"Sandcastles aren't just for kids," I say.

"I didn't say they were."

"You sure?"

"*Yes.*"

She doesn't sound sure.

She sounds like she just can't handle the idea of me being right.

Forget this. I can have fun another way. I sigh and scrub my hand over my face. "Can you please consider, for one minute, that—*ow*."

Fuck.

My eyeball suddenly hurts.

I blink. Stare down and blink some more while my eye waters and burns.

I lift my hand to swipe at it, but Delaney grabs it before I can make contact.

"Did you just get sand in your eye?"

"No." Yes.

"Let me see."

"No."

"*Theo.*"

"I've got this." Ow ow *ow*. Fuck. *Fuck*. My eyeball hurts. Not as much as my pride at the moment, though, which is a sure sign the swim and a morning playing with kids is *still* not enough to make me get over my reactions to Laney whenever she's around.

"You're covered in sand. Here. Look up. I have eye drops in my purse."

"Of course you do."

She growls.

Delaney.

She *growls*.

And fuck me if that noise doesn't have a direct impact on my dick while I'm sitting here with sand in my eyeball.

"It's just sand," I mutter. "I can handle this without you treating me like you're my fucking *babysitter*. And *my hand was asleep.*"

She sighs. "Okay. Fine. Your hand was asleep. Can you *please* let me help you before you end up wearing a pirate patch to your sister's wedding?"

I glare at her, but lifting my eyes is a bad idea right now.

Is there sand in both?

Fantastic. I have sand in *both* of my eyes now.

I stare down and blink a lot again. Sun's bright off the water.

Sand is officially a bigger nemesis than Delaney now.

"I'd wear a pirate patch to her wedding if she asked me to," I say.

"And if she sees you like this, she'll freak out, because even *small* things are *big* things to her right now."

"Believe it or not, I'm not causing problems on purpose."

"What's done is done. All we can do now is fix it and make sure it doesn't happen again."

"You sound like your mother."

The beach freezes over. Frost. All over the sand. Waves stop rolling because they've been hit by a blast from the ice queen and the entire ocean is officially glaciers now.

This?

This is the sound of *well, Theo, you really stuck your foot in it now.*

Of course I did.

This is Laney.

It was inevitable.

"Tilt. Your fucking. Head," Delaney says.

One, holy shit. She said *fuck.*

Two, this *I'm speaking through a clenched jaw and if you weren't in danger of losing your eyeballs right now, I would be pulling that same move I pulled on you to shove you into the pool yesterday except this time I'd hold your head underwater until you weren't my problem anymore* thing that she's doing is hot.

Hello, my name is Theo, and I am irrepressibly turned on by judgmental Little Miss Perfects who won't make sandcastles with me, and *I don't know why.*

I tilt my head.

She grabs the skin around my eye socket—the one that's worse—including my eyelid, forcibly separates it, and squirts a whole purse-size bottle of eye drops into it.

Hurts.

Hurts like a motherfucking hemorrhoid has exploded into flames in my eyeball.

But I don't flinch.

Or whimper.

No matter how much I want to.

This is my medicine, and I will take it like someone who needs to be stoic in the face of imminent death.

It's like she wants me to be able to see her before she kills me.

I probably owe her that.

Have a lot of respect for it, actually.

That's hardcore.

I like it.

But also, when she's drained the entire bottle into my eye, there's still gritty sand in it.

"Better?" she demands.

Sounds a little like she's ordering me to be better so she can be done with me, to be honest.

"Yep," I lie.

She grabs me by the face and peers into my eyeballs, which I can tell less because I can see anything clearly right now and more because there's a humanoid-shaped thing looming close and it smells like that shampoo that she left in the bathroom last night.

It's not fruity or flowery or baked goods-y.

Reminds me of being little and going with my mom to her once-a-year pamper-herself haircut at the fancy salon that she'd get back home before she passed.

"Did you bring anything out here with you? Where are your shoes?" Laney asks.

"Came barefoot."

"Get up. We're taking you to urgent care."

"I don't—"

"*You are not losing your goddamn eyes on my watch*. Okay? Get up. Move. March. Now."

I hate authority.

Always have. Always will.

But as I'm stumbling after her, I swear I hear her mutter,

"So much for the sandcastle."

Like she *wanted* to build it, and didn't know how to say yes.

For the first time in my life, I realize much like I'm not who Laney expects me to be, she might not be exactly who I always thought she was either.

9

LANEY

I'M SUPPOSED to be at a late lunch with Emma and Sabrina, but instead, I'm helping Theo check out of the urgent care clinic across town from the resort after getting his eyes washed out.

And he's flirting shamelessly with the receptionist.

There are grins. Swollen winks. Leaning on the desk to be closer to her, but acting like he needs it for support.

Just like he was flirting with Claire yesterday, and just like he was laughing with the triplets after I put the fire out on his costume.

"Point again where I need to sign?" he says to the receptionist. "Can't see all that well yet."

I throw up in my mouth.

She steers his hand to the line he needs to sign on, studies his tattooed forearm longer than necessary, then beams at him like he's the love child of Pele the Volcano Goddess and Ryan Reynolds. "Are you sure you've never been here?"

"First time on the island."

She looks at his arm again. "You just seem *so* familiar."

Is he—is Theo *blushing*?

Does he *like* her?

Of course he does. Theo likes everyone. Everyone except me. And no matter how many times I try to tell myself I don't care, *I do.*

I'm not mean. I don't burn down people's houses or steal their animals or cheat at board games.

Good god, I'm boring.

No wonder Mr. Fun doesn't like me.

"Must have one of those faces," he says.

She squints at him. "I don't think I recognize you, but I feel like we've talked before. Is that weird?"

"If you're done, honey, we really need to get to dinner," I interject perkily. I fake a smile at the receptionist. "Wedding plans."

"Not our wedding, and she only calls me honey because she's my sister," Theo says to the receptionist.

I hate him.

Officially.

I hate him. If I never see Theo Monroe again after this week, it will be too soon.

Because now I'm embarrassed on top of being irritated.

"Anything else, darlin'?" he says to the receptionist.

She smiles at him like she wants to ask for his phone number. "Not from us. Do *you* need anything else?"

He has red, swollen eye sockets and bloodshot eyeballs. Like, *bad* bloodshot eyeballs. His shirt isn't buttoned straight, or even all the way up. His hair's sticking up all over the place, with sand visible in it, and she's *flustered* because he called her darlin'.

I quit life.

I do. I quit.

I'm a nice, respectable, successful, moderately attractive woman, and I don't turn heads the way Theo turns heads when he looks like an extra in a redneck zombie movie.

"We need to go," I say crisply.

He winks at the receptionist once more, even though it looks like it takes supreme effort to make his swollen eyelids move like that. "Tell the doc I'm mighty obliged for saving my sight. You too. Couldn't have done it without you."

"It's our pleasure, Theo."

I get him out the door only to remember that neither of us has a car. Time to book a rideshare ride.

But he beats me to it. "I got this, sweetheart."

"Can you even see to operate the app?" Yes, I'm cranky. But this is far better than the *don't call me sweetheart* I want to yell at him.

He asked me to make a sandcastle with him.

He asked me to make a sandcastle.

Me.

The woman he calls *Plainy-Laney*. He wanted to have fun with *me*.

And I didn't say yes fast enough because I was so surprised at the invitation that I thought it was somehow a trap, and now we're here, and I will never figure out how to not be boring.

He pulls his phone closer to his face and...*are you serious*? His phone case is an exact replica of the interwoven tattoos on his arm, like he took a picture of them and had his case custom-made to match his tats.

"Is that phone case one of ours?" I blurt before I can help myself.

He doesn't look at me. "Probably your competitor's."

I twitch.

I don't *want* to—can he really get worse than *you sound like your mother?*—but I do.

I twitch.

And once more, I bite my tongue.

When I texted Emma that I couldn't make lunch because I had to "do something" with Theo, she texted back that Chandler was having a better day and she was sure it wouldn't be necessary for me to do this much longer, but she sincerely appreciated that they were separated today.

And also that she's so sorry, but management says they still don't have a room or an open bungalow for me.

Sabrina texted that Em's in the best mood she's been in all week. That she's *floating* today. That she looks like the bride in paradise who's fully embracing living out her dream of getting married at the Midnight Orchid Club Resort even if the front desk staff is regularly missing and half the orders were delivered wrong at lunch because of a staffing issue.

I cross my arms and stand at the edge of the parking lot, *this close* to calling my own ride and letting Theo loose on the world for a few hours, when he brushes my arm as he walks past me, striding to a white Subaru pulling into the parking lot.

"Ride's here."

"It's been *a minute*," I mutter.

"Good ride karma."

"I'll walk."

He looks back at me, and just when I think he's going to rub his eyes in frustration again, he looks at the hand halfway to his face, grimaces, and drops it. "I'll walk. You take the car."

"If you walk, you'll somehow find a way to hitch a ride with a surfer who takes you across the island, you two will leap into the ocean to go swimming at some magical secret swimming hole, and get stung by jellyfish. He'll offer you weed to take the edge off the bite, which will make you strip down and flash the exact wrong person, and the two of you will end up in jail, and I'll be bailing your ass out instead of enjoying dinner with the wedding party tonight."

To my utter surprise, he doesn't argue.

Instead, his lips quirk up in a grin. "You forgot the part where we'd try to crack coconuts without remembering we don't know how to use machetes and end up at the emergency room again."

I reach deep for a little more patience and a little less irritation. What would my life be like if I could be that lackadaisical about having *fun*? If I could let my hair down, rip my bra off, throw caution to the wind and see how much life I could squeeze into one day like I've been working myself up to believing I can do for a year now?

I *want* to.

Why *can't* I?

"Please get in the car." Nope. Still not fun.

"Yes, Laney. Whatever you say, Laney."

He's grinning while he climbs in. Red, swollen eyes and all.

I join him under silent protest, telling myself I'm only in the car to make sure he doesn't go somewhere he shouldn't, and distinctly remembering why I've always disliked him.

He makes me feel like I'm doing life all wrong. Like I'm too *serious*. Like my priorities are backward. Like he knows this immense secret about life, and I'm not worthy of being included in the grapevine, and *I want in*. I do.

But Emma's having a better day today *without* me.

And I know she's having a better day *because* of me, but I'm not there. I'm not with her.

And really, Theo didn't need me today.

I screwed up.

He was having a grand time with a bunch of kids, far away from Chandler, and it was honestly utterly adorable, and I wanted to join them but didn't know how because I feel so awkward about doing all the things he was doing.

I don't know how to fly a bucket around a beach and pretend it's a dinosaur, and even if I did, I wouldn't look nearly as hot as Theo with his shaggy hair and killer smile and tight, tatted body.

And when he asked me to build a sandcastle, I froze,

because I couldn't believe *Theo Monroe* was inviting me to have fun with him.

I feel very, very alone and left out right now. And it's probably at least partially my own fault.

Theo chats with the driver the entire ride.

I pretend I'm not listening during the whole ten-minute ride about where to rent the best surfboards. About the best calamari on the island. About if it's worth it to drive up to the volcano park at night. Where to find secret waterfalls. How the driver's cousin runs a parasailing company, and Theo should drop his name to get a discount.

They trade numbers when we get out.

Meanwhile, I feel like the frumpy wet blanket. Again. I hate feeling like the frumpy wet blanket.

Worse?

Theo's eyes are practically clear already.

When his uncle turns the corner as we're strolling back into the resort lobby, he doesn't say a thing about the lingering redness.

But would he?

"Theo," he hisses, "want in on a secret?"

I bite my tongue—*hard*—to keep from answering for him.

And it's not because I feel like whatever the secret is will cause trouble for Emma and her wedding.

It's because I want to know.

Sabrina won't tell me why she's mad at Theo. Theo won't tell me *anything*. And I know there's more to the story of why Emma wants me to be a buffer between Theo and Chandler than she's telling me.

I also know when they don't tell me secrets, it's sometimes to protect me, but it's more often because they need time to solve their issues on their own without me.

There's a distinct possibility I've annoyed half of Snaggletooth Creek at one point or another with my suggestions for how to fix something.

But I want to know a secret, dammit.

"Maybe later," Theo says.

His uncle rocks back on his heels and flashes that Monroe grin. "It's a *good* one."

"Bet it is. Gives me joy to think you get to hang on to it a while longer."

"You don't want to know at all?"

"I have to wear nice clothes tonight. Need something else to look forward to at dinner."

"You can tell me," I interject.

Uncle Owen doesn't even look at me. Just cackles and walks away. "Your loss," he tosses over his shoulder to Theo.

No, my loss. *My loss.*

As if I'd ever admit that out loud.

Kingstons don't gossip.

The number of times I've heard my mother say that...

Theo heads deeper into the resort. Much like yesterday, I tag along.

All the way down the walkway to his bungalow.

Our bungalow? His bungalow?

The place my luggage currently calls home. That place.

I suck in a deep breath through my nose.

Time for a perspective check.

I'm in paradise. I can hear the ocean. I can smell the salty breeze. The flowers here are brightly colored, smell amazing, they're gorgeous, and there are *so many types.* There was an adorable bouquet of knitted hearts in one of the glasses on the sink in the bathroom this morning. Emma's happy. I'm off work and *not* checking email, which is hard but also amazing. Theo didn't go blind. I have a bed to sleep in and I can order room service, since I'm not sure I've eaten anything yet today.

Have I?

Have I eaten?

Did I have a protein bar today, or was that yesterday?

Theo keys into the bungalow and holds the door for me.

"Thank you," I say automatically.

He eyes me.

And then he sighs like *I* usually do, *again*, which is the last sound I ever hear Theo make around *anyone else*.

It's just me.

I make even the *funnest* of fun people *sigh*.

He mutters something to himself, and crosses the living area to the closed bedroom door.

The hide-a-bed is still sticking out of the couch at an odd angle. The gauzy curtains on either side of the balcony door sway in the breeze since I forgot to close the main door when I left. And Theo's looking at me like I'm once again holding him back.

"You coming?"

Just like that. *You coming?* No actual invitation. No suggestion that something's changed since I got out of the shower this morning and saw that note that if I went in this room, my parents would be sent a picture of me sleeping with him and told that I'm carrying his love child. Just *you coming?* like it's assumed I *want* to go wherever he goes.

He winces.

My face must be telegraphing just how much I'd like to toss him into a volcano while we're here.

"C'mon, Laney. Come see. It'll make you feel better."

"Food and going back to life without you will make me feel better."

He scratches his chest under the gaping side of his shirt, not the least bit visibly offended. "Consider it an apology. And a thank you for saving my eyesight."

I feel like I'm about to walk into a trap.

But curiosity is bigger than the fear.

If I can find out what's behind that door, I can find out how to fix it so I don't have to keep sharing a bed with Theo.

Because one thing's crystal clear.

He's not letting anyone from maintenance at the resort in

here to look at that hide-a-bed while he has a big secret hidden in the primary bedroom in the suite.

"Do you truly have a camera set up behind that door with a filter that'll put my head on a naked body and auto-email my parents to tell them I'm having an orgy here too?"

He doesn't react, doesn't cringe or blush or look even the slightest bit called out, despite this feeling I have that he's embarrassed about the note. I can't tell you *why* I feel it.

I just *do*.

But he grins at me like he's having fun with *me* now. Not *making fun* of me. *Having fun* with me. "Yeah," he says, "but it's worth it to see what else is inside."

"I honest to god have no idea why Emma loves you as much as she does."

He shrugs like it's one more insult that doesn't penetrate his tattoo shield. "She has to."

I close my eyes. "Apologies. That was rude."

Is it hard to say? Yes. But was it rude? Also yes. And this will be much easier if the two of us can get along.

"C'mon, Laney. Come see what's behind door number two. Gonna make you forget just how big of a pain in the ass I am. Promise."

I am absolutely walking into a trap.

But curiosity and that overwhelming desire to *fix it*, whatever it is, win out.

Right along with that desperate need to be in on some fun. *Any* fun. No matter what it is or how much I'll regret it later.

Time to see what's behind door number two.

10

THEO

THERE ARE about a million things I know to be true about Delaney Kingston. One of the biggest is that she doesn't do dares. She doesn't wander into danger. She's the most rule-following-est boring person I've ever known.

And I say that as a man who's had stretches of unreasonable attraction to her *despite* how boring she is.

I also know I'm taking an enormous risk in letting her in on my secret.

But she's had a shitty day, and whether it's my fault or not, I don't like seeing people have shitty days.

Even Laney.

Maybe especially Laney.

She's letting me push her first into the second bedroom like she's given up the will to fight. Like I've broken her in two days. Not even two *full* days at that. Actually, not even twenty-four hours.

Jesus.

I'm known in some circles as the guy who makes people feel better about themselves.

Not the guy who tears them down.

But there I went, falling into old habits and waving around my dick for fun.

No more.

I'm better than that. Have been for a lot of years now.

Time to remember it and quit fighting this.

"Go quick so they don't get out," I murmur into her hair, which now smells like a salon in the sunshine, as I open the door and put my hand on her lower back to steer her inside quickly.

She does.

I slip in behind her and close the door in time to hear her soft gasp.

Miss Doodles, the gray tabby mama cat, looks over at us from her perch on the bathroom sink in the open-plan primary bedroom and sizes Laney up while one of the kittens nurses.

"Oh, god. It really is cats and not porn," Delaney whispers.

All of my muscles tighten, but I make myself focus on what I know she knows. "You don't like cats? What about kittens? Kittens are awesome."

"My parents say cats are the devil."

"Your parents are judgmental nutjobs. Cats are *awesome*."

She side-eyes me.

But there's something about that suspicious look that doesn't fully feel suspicious.

It feels *wounded*.

"I do a lot of stupid shit, but I don't lie," I tell her. "No reason to when you live without regrets. So when I say cats are fucking awesome, it's the truth."

"You just called my parents *nutjobs*."

Shit.

But if I'm pushing things, I'll push things. And I'll do it with a smile. "Again, no lies detected."

She's not amused.

Be better, Theo. Be fucking better.

My eyeballs still sting, so I catch myself once again before I rub them in utter frustration at the complete lack of belief in her body language, reach deep, and pull out an even bigger megawatt Theo Monroe smile. "Your parents are lovely human beings who are mistaken about cats. And cats are awesome for useless, hell-bound demon-spawn like me. We fit. Great companions. Cut from the same cloth."

Even with the smile, she takes me seriously. She wrinkles her nose, and while she doesn't tell me I'm not a hell-bound demon-spawn, the next words out of her mouth still surprise me.

"That's what they always said when I'd ask for a cat. That cats were the devil."

Fuck me.

She doesn't believe them.

She was *hurt* by them.

I'm bent over in an instant, making a soft little clucking noise to call the friendliest of the kitten bunch, because I'm gonna do for Delaney what her parents never did.

Mind made up.

I don't care who she is. I don't care what our history is. I don't care how much it's gonna hurt like hell if seeing her with a kitten makes all of those old repressed feelings roar back to life.

A girl should have a cat if she fucking wants a cat.

"Jellybean, c'mere," I say to the gray kitten who fell asleep in my hand two nights ago.

And when the tiny, barely-one-pound ball of fluff comes boingy-boingy-running to me with her little tail pointed in the air and her blue eyes open wide and her big ears fully up and curious, I scoop her right up.

Then I grab Laney's hand and deposit the cat into her palm.

Laney squeaks.

Jellybean mews.

And then the very worst thing in the entire world happens, just like I knew it would.

Laney Kingston melts over that kitten in front of my eyes.

"Oh, you are *precious*," she whispers as she lifts Jellybean until they're almost nose-to-nose while the two of them stare at each other, blue eyes lined up with blue eyes.

I lift my hands, fully intending to grip Laney by the shoulders and guide her to the chair in the corner to sit and enjoy the kitten—or maybe all of the kittens—but I'm terrified to touch her again.

Compliant Delaney? Kitten-deprived Delaney? *Hurt* Delaney?

She's inspiring instinctive caveman tendencies that I haven't let myself feel for her since I couldn't control it in high school.

"You're so soft," Laney whispers. "How are you so soft?"

Jellybean meows at her.

"Oh, look at your eyes. And your *ears*. They're so big for your head. And your paws. Oh my god, how are your paws so tiny?"

Fuck me again. I need to get out of here, but I also need to make sure they have fresh water and enough food, and I need to make sure she won't tell anyone they're here.

Get me in trouble? I don't care.

Hurt my kittens?

Don't. You. Fucking. Dare.

She carries Jellybean past the bed to the wicker chair in the corner beside the closed balcony doors all on her own, carefully stepping around the other kittens swarming her as she goes.

All except Fred.

Fred does *not* like people, so he's not swarming.

I poke my head under the bed and verify that he is, in fact, still hovering back there. The black-spotted tabby shrinks back at the sight of me.

I grab a toy mouse and settle it as deep under the bed as I can get it without disturbing him in case he wants to play, then head to the bathroom area behind the half-wall separating the bedroom from the sink, tub, and shower.

"What are you doing?" Delaney says, prompting a round of adorable baby meows from the kittens, when I step into the open shower.

The fact that she's not doing baby talk clues me in to the fact that she's talking to me. "Cat litter doesn't change itself," I answer.

Once again, I'm getting the *what kind of alien freak am I stuck with?* look from her.

Probably shocked that I'd change cat litter. Wasn't exactly the type the last time she saw me on a regular basis.

But that's not me anymore.

And I have no idea how much she's changed since high school either, so I shouldn't be an ass for history's sake.

"Treats are next to you," I say. "They like the ones in the purple pouch best."

"Where did you get kittens?"

"Heard them crying in a dumpster the day I got here."

"*Oh my god.* Someone threw them away?"

I shrug. "Don't know. Lots of strays around here. Miss Doodles might've just picked a bad place to have kittens. But she loves people."

Her brows furrow. "Is it normal for stray cats to love people?"

"Here? Guess it depends on how much people feed 'em. Suppose they get pampered at a resort by all the people missing their cats back home."

Do I think someone threw them away?

Yeah. Yeah, I do. The stray resort cats will come close, but not the way Miss Doodles does.

Miss Doodles was absolutely someone's pet.

But will I tell Laney that?

Nope.

Not when she'd probably insist we figure out who Miss Doodles belongs to and get justice.

Not doing that. Not a fucking chance.

Justice happens when my cats have a good home. Not by making someone else pay for what they did.

Far as I'm concerned, they did me a favor.

"You're not supposed to have a room full of cats in the resort, are you?"

"I will fucking burn this place down before I let them make me kick these kittens and their mama out into the street."

Her jaw drops a moment, then she visibly swallows.

Is that a trick of the light, or are her eyes going dark?

Did I just arouse the Queen of the Rules by telling her the rules could go to hell?

"What are you going to do with them?" she asks in a husky voice that makes my nuts tight.

"Taking them home."

She blinks once.

Then blinks again.

"Finders keepers. They're mine now, and they're gonna get a fucking awesome life."

"I'm not hearing any of this."

"It's not illegal."

"But it's—it's—"

"Just fine," I finish for her. "Play with the kittens and enjoy it for what it is. Tell Emma I'm keeping cats in my room, and I really will send your parents the selfie I snapped of us sleeping together last night."

She scowls.

I grin.

Can't help it.

It is *so* easy to push her buttons.

Plus, scowling Laney relieves a lot of the pressure building in my balls.

Reminds me she's a killjoy.

Mostly.

I think I trust her to keep the secret about the cats. And if I can't, I'll still win.

Don't always care if I win or lose—it's more about the journey and the fun—but I will do *anything* to win in this case.

Once I slip into the shower to clean out the litter boxes, I can't see her anymore. She's behind the shower wall. But I can hear her.

"That's my shoelace, you silly goose! Oh my gosh, how are you allowed to be this cute? Where did you come from? Ohhhh, hi, you must be mama. You're beautiful. Miss Doodles? That's such a silly name. You look more like Cleopatra. Or we can just call you The Empress, can't we?"

If her parents taught her that cats are the devil, the lesson didn't stick. Either that, or she's been secretly volunteering at cat shelters to get her fix.

Nope. Nope nope nope.

Not gonna picture her going behind her parents' backs to help lonely cats find homes.

Do *not* need that mental image.

I finish up and shove the new bags of cat litter into the complicated diaper pail I bought so that no one will smell them in here and so I don't have to carry bags of litter across the resort twice a day. And then I step back out of the shower to a sight that threatens to break me.

Miss Doodles is in Delaney's lap. Laney's petting her and cooing softly while the cat purrs loudly enough to be heard across the room.

Three kittens are climbing all over her and the chair.

She hasn't once yelped over their sharp little claws, though I'd bet she's wanted to.

Kitties *do* have sharp claws and I haven't wanted to terrify them by trimming their nails until they're more used to me.

But Laney seems to be in utter heaven. Smiling. No, not just smiling.

Lighting up the entire damn island.

We're in paradise. Takes a lot to improve on what nature already put here.

But she's doing it. That smile makes me feel warm and gooey inside, like she's put all of the pieces of me together and now I'm a fresh-baked chocolate chip cookie whose entire purpose is to make the world a better place.

"I liked you in high school." The words slip out of my mouth before I can stop them. She's scrambled my brains. And my tongue. "And you were always too good for me, but I still liked you, so I was an asshole because it was easier to push you away than to face the fact that you would forever be better than me and never give me a chance. So it's easy to just be an asshole to you. It's habit. I'm sorry. I'll do better."

Her lips part and her hand stills. "Are you—" She stops herself.

Licks her lips.

Makes my cock half-hard at the sight of her pink tongue.

Shakes her head.

And starts again. "Are you making fun of me?" she whispers.

"How would that be making fun of you?"

"Because we are *nothing* alike, and there's *zero* reason for someone like you to like someone like me."

"I know," I rasp out.

"This isn't funny."

My face is getting hot.

So are my balls. "It's really not."

"You made me feel like I was unattractive and annoying and wrong for just existing. You *still do*."

"I didn't mean—I didn't know. That's not what I—"

"And all the while, you were always having *so much fun*. So much fun. Whereas I—do you have any idea how hard it is to exist in a world where you want to have fun but it's *bad* or *forbidden* or *dangerous* or *something for people who don't have a future*? When you have to be perfect even when you know it's an impossible standard, but you know you have to keep trying because maybe, *just maybe*, one day you'll be the exception to the *nobody's perfect* rule? And then to be treated like dirt by the very people you're so very, very jealous of because they don't have to live up to that? Not even *close*."

Four kittens yowl in distress.

One more darts into the shower.

"I—I can imagine," I force out. *Stop talking, Theo. Stop. Fucking. Talking. Now.*

I'm usually good in these situations. I'm the guy the rest of the construction crew comes to when they need advice, because they know I'm fun, but they also know I've learned a lot of lessons about life and am happy to share. The Sullivan triplets and I goof off together a lot, but when one of them's down and his brothers aren't around, he shows up at my door for a beer and a pep talk.

I'm not the fuckup I was in high school. I took all of those lessons and I turned them around and I put them out into the world to help other people never, ever feel like the fuckup I believed myself to be for most of my life.

But here I am, both feeling like a fuckup myself and feeling like I'm hurting Laney too.

"I sincerely doubt you have any idea how I've ever felt," she says stiffly. "Thank you for the kitten relief. I won't tell anyone. They're clearly happy here, and that's what matters." She rises, causing Miss Doodles to leap away in disgust while Laney awkwardly disentangles herself from the kittens who are clawing her clothes in various places and trying to climb on her to keep her there as their personal jungle gym. "If you'll excuse me, I need to go find some food. I'll be back before we have to leave for dinner. Don't go without me."

"Laney—"

"If I'm going to help Emma have the wedding of her dreams, I need a break right now."

She doesn't tell me to stay put.

Doesn't offer any advice to keep the kittens a secret in the resort.

Doesn't say when she'll be back or where she's going.

She just slips quietly out the door, making sure Jellybean doesn't follow her.

Miss Doodles looks at me.

"I was trying to do the right thing," I tell her.

She blinks at me.

Swear to god, that blink says, *For you, or for her?*

And you know what?

I don't know the answer to that question.

11

LANEY

HE *LIKED* ME?

That's absurd.

I have no idea if he thinks he can wash away years of being an utter turd by telling me *I only pulled your ponytails because I liked you*, but I cannot process this right now.

Nor do I appreciate it.

Fun and *subjecting myself to being treated like crap under the bullshit excuse of he liked me* are two very, very different things.

I grab my credit card and ID out of my purse, tuck them into the pocket of my skirt—I love this thing—and head out my door, only to nearly crash into Sabrina on the porch.

"You're back." She squeezes me in a quick hug. "What's wrong?"

"I need a mai tai."

She looks at the door.

I grimace. "If he leaves, I will personally strap him to that half-open pullout sofa with unbreakable ties and leave him there for the rest of the weekend once we find him, and I can nearly certainly promise you he knows it."

"Mai tais it is," Sabrina says.

Twenty minutes later, we're at the pool. I'm not in my swimsuit. I left it in the room. But I have a mai tai in one hand, a plate of shrimp skewers in the other hand, my straw hat and sunglasses on, and Sabrina right next to me.

"This goes in the vault and we will *never* speak of it again," I tell her, and then I catch her up on most of my entire day.

Whispering.

Because the bushes behind us might have ears.

Also, I tiptoe around the part about the kittens. I don't mention it at all, in fact.

Loyalty to the cats. I swear that's all it is. Not me holding a grudge and wanting to have a secret when everyone else around me is keeping secrets.

When I get to the part where Theo told me he *liked* me, she doesn't react at all.

Like, *at all*.

"Hello?" I whisper. "A gasp? A *what the hell*? Maybe a *that's so mean of him to lie about thinking you were attractive in high school to wipe away his bad behavior*?"

Her expression is completely and totally blank. "Hm."

"Do *not* poker-face me on this one."

"Laney."

I shove a shrimp in my mouth and feel like Emma with her protein bar yesterday. Was that seriously just yesterday? "And *do not* say my name in that *I'm about to tell you something you don't want to hear, but you need to hear it, so I'm going to say it anyway* tone. I cannot handle that tone right now."

"Here. Have more mai tai."

I gulp.

Give her the *do not tell me what I don't want to hear* eyeball.

The *there is not enough alcohol in the world for whatever it is, and I have barely had a teaspoon of it* eyeball.

And she ignores me. "Emma told me our freshman year that Theo had a huge crush on you, but she made me swear not to tell because he was super embarrassed about it."

"So it's embarrassing to like me."

She shoves a piece of shrimp in my mouth. "Your parents made sure to tell him he wasn't good enough for you, and he was embarrassed because he thought they were right."

"Abagabbagoo?"

"Don't talk with shrimp in your mouth. Here. Eat another one."

I bat the second shrimp away. "*Sabrina.* That's *awful.*"

"Theo in high school wasn't good for *anyone.* He had all of his wild but none of his sense."

"What does that mean?"

"Remember when he got suspended for...actually, pick a time he got suspended. Any of them."

I grimace, recall the time he sat on a copy machine at school after hours and scanned his ass, which he then labeled as the principal's ass and hung ten thousand copies of all over town, and take another swig of mai tai. Good thing it's super weak. For the number of mai tais I want right now, I wouldn't be able to walk later if they weren't.

God, I'm boring.

"He crossed lines he won't cross now," Sabrina says, "because he finally figured out the consequences got bigger once he was old enough to understand how much he didn't want to spend time in jail. And he has...a job...now, and—"

"What does he do?"

"What do you mean, what does he do?"

"You hesitated when you said *a job.* What does he do? For money? For rent and food and cloth—no, wait, he doesn't wear clothes anymore apparently, but I assume he has a car, so he needs money for gas and insurance too. And possibly a coat and boots for back home."

Sabrina grins at me from under her straw hat, which matches mine since we went shopping for them together two weeks ago. "Even on mai tais, you are so very *Delaney*."

"What does that mean?"

"I just love that you worry about how anyone pays for car insurance. Did you know you reminded me to pay my insurance bill just now? Hold on. Let me pull up my phone and do that before I forget."

"Your insurance bill auto-pays, and you're trying to distract me."

"I am not," she lies. With a massive grin. "Oh, hey, look. I got a picture of my puppy from the dog sitter. Want to see my cutie-pie?"

"*Distraction!*"

She grins bigger. "Laney. I'm offended."

She is not.

But fine.

Fine. "You know what? You're right. It doesn't matter."

"Okay, okay. If you must know, he works—" she starts, but before she can finish her sentence, a giant splash from the pool blasts both of us.

I gasp and stutter, then whimper as I realize my shrimp skewers are now coated in pool water.

Theo surfaces fifteen feet away, out in the pool.

"Afternoon, ladies," he calls. "Just reporting for being-babysat duties."

The old Theo is back.

Acting like he didn't drop the bombshell of all bombshells on me an hour ago.

And is it a bombshell?

Yeah.

Yeah, it is.

Because *I liked him too*, but I never, ever, *ever* would've said it out loud. I could barely admit it to myself.

He was forbidden. He was *fun*. He was dangerous.

And *I craved that*.

I knew better. Clearly. I had—*have* a big future at my family's company. In high school, that meant my immediate future was defined by getting good grades so I could get into a good college and get a good education that would lay the foundation to one day step into my parents' shoes and run Kingston Photo Gifts.

There was an element of obligation that I'd continue what they started, but I *wanted* to do it.

I still do.

There's pride in being a part of continuing what my parents built. I love that we make products that bring so much joy to families and friends and people connected in so many other ways.

But there are other expectations to being a Kingston too.

Expectations that I don't want anymore. But I still haven't shed them.

Not entirely.

Nor have I tried as much as I've been telling myself I want to since I broke up with Christopher.

"You owe Laney a new plate of shrimp," Sabrina calls to Theo.

"Put it on my tab," he calls back.

And then he's gone, swimming like he was born in the ocean instead of in a dry-as-dry-can-be Colorado mountain town.

"He's still wild and unpredictable," Sabrina says, continuing like he didn't interrupt us, "but he takes ownership now, and he pays for his mistakes."

"*Oh my god.* Are you trying to make me like him?" I hiss.

"It would be nice if you two could at least be friends." She shrugs. "Em's gone out of her way to avoid making plans with either of you that would have both of you in the same place at the same time with her, because she knew he'd be a dick and you'd get all stuffy about it, which you rightfully should, but I figure if you know *why* he's a dick, maybe that'll help you tolerate him better."

"I don't like dicks."

Theo coughs and sputters at the edge of the pool.

But it's the way his face goes a deep burgundy before he pushes off and glides through the water to the full opposite side of the pool that has me dropping my head to my knees on my lounge chair. "Tell me he's not going to walk around the rest of the weekend telling people I'm not into men."

"I'll handle that," Sabrina assures me. "I know where he keeps his dirt."

"You terrify me and I love you." I sigh and lean back in my chair. "You know the worst part of this?"

"That he's unfortunately super easy on the eyes?"

I roll my eyes like that's not true, even though it is. But it's not the worst. "I feel like I've missed all of my fun years and it's too late to start now because it's too ingrained in me to be a *good girl.*"

She doesn't answer right away.

"I have, haven't I?" I glance at her, knowing if anyone else were studying me that closely, I'd be super uncomfortable. But Sabrina, Emma, and I have been through too much together for her to intentionally hurt me with the truth. "I've put so much effort into doing the right thing and being the right person that I've missed out on so many opportunities to have fun."

"How drunk are you?"

I lift my glass, which is still half full, and not merely because Theo splashed more water into it.

"Good. C'mon. We're going shopping."

I look back at the pool.

113

Theo's Uncle Owen isn't around, so there's little chance he'll goad Theo into another dare.

Claire's approaching from the beach side with a few of her and Emma's sorority sisters who are here for the wedding but not *in* the wedding. She'll *definitely* stick around once she realizes Theo's in the pool.

And I don't say that because I think she wants to throw herself at him or introduce him to the rest of the women.

It's more that I'm certain she knows Emma's stressed over his behavior too. Claire's always been great whenever I've seen her. I know she wants Emma to have a good wedding week too.

She'll help.

"Where's Chandler?" I ask Sabrina.

"Golfing. Again."

"Emma?"

"Shopping with the moms. They all want souvenirs and to see the town a little. She'll be back for dinner. Come *on*. We're going to get you some fun."

"What kind of fun?"

"The kind that requires you to buy a brand-new bikini at the overpriced tourist store and go cannonball the hell out of the pool."

My stomach freezes over.

And I know she knows it.

I scowl down at it myself. She's right.

I should do it.

"Your parents aren't here, Laney," she says softly. "And you deserve to see what it feels like to have half the wedding party flirting with you when you show up in a bikini."

She's so full of crap.

Compared to her redheaded bombshellness and Emma's bright glow in the world, I'm the frumpy, flat-bottomed mouse.

But I'm also the one who wants to break out. The one who

wants to take more risks. The one who's in a safe place with people who love me and trust me and who won't let me do something stupid if I've had more of this mai tai than I think I have.

I glance at Theo, out there splashing away as he catches the eye of every single freaking person around the pool.

Then I look back at Sabrina. "Okay. Let's do this."

12

Laney

THIS BIKINI IS SO small it's making me glad that I waxed last week. My stomach is a little poochy. My thighs are white enough that they're practically translucent. I have *cleavage* courtesy of the two postage-stamp-sized pieces of tropical flower fabric held together with dental floss. And I think my right ass cheek is a little bigger than the other because I can't tug the bikini bottoms far enough over to cover it fully no matter how I shimmy or tighten my glute muscles.

"Nope, can't do it," I tell Sabrina through the stall door. I'm changing in a small bathroom near the pool so that I have less time to chicken out. Which is clearly working *so well*. "Bikini, yes. But this one might be too much."

"Okay," Sabrina replies.

"*Okay?*"

"Your journey, your pace."

"Please talk me into this."

"You sure?"

"No."

"Are you dressed?"

"Indecently so."

"Open the door."

She knows I won't argue when she uses the *you will obey me or I will scale the stall door just like that gecko on the wall who's watching you and judging you for putting your skin on display to tempt the men.*

I sigh and open the door.

When I'm being judged by the geckos, it's probably time to either cut back on the mai tais or have more. I'm not sure which.

Sabrina looks me up and down while I try to not look at myself in the mirror. "What don't you like about it?"

I point to my rack. "It gives me *cleavage.*"

She points to her own cleavage artfully displayed beneath a white tank top. "Do you consider me a whore for showing my boob crack?"

"*Sabrina.*"

She grabs me by the cheeks and pulls my face down to hers. "You are smart, you are strong, you are beautiful, and you get to enjoy the body that you live in. If any single piece of shit out there at the pool tries to embarrass you for being a hot-ass goddess with confidence issues because of too many years of being told you have to live up to unrealistic puritan-ical ideals whose entire life would be destroyed if you touched a boy's danger stick, I will *destroy* them. So tell me what you want for *you.* Do you want to wear this bikini and go out there and jump in the pool as a step in your journey of having fun? There is no incorrect answer except for the one you tell me because it's what you think anyone else in this world would want to hear."

Rule number one of being Sabrina's friend: Don't ask her opinion if you don't want to hear it.

"Thank you for not mincing words."

"This is what you pay me for."

I stare at her for a second, and then I burst into laughter.

She grins.

I square my shoulders and look past her to my reflection in the bathroom mirror. I don't know who that woman is. Her cheeks have a pink flush that's creeping down her neck and over her chest. She *does* have a nice chest. Full boobs that are attention-getters without causing back problems. The bikini bottoms cover enough to almost make her hips cute. And her arms are toned and slender.

Maybe I'll pretend I'm her with a little more confidence for an hour or so.

And if my parents see pictures… I flinch a little.

Easier to say *I'll remind them that I'm a grown woman who can have responsible fun on vacation* than it is to fully believe I'm capable of such a sentence.

But I *need* to be capable of it if I'm going to fully embrace this idea of living my life for me.

"It's so much harder when your parents are your bosses at a job you love," I whisper.

Sabrina hooks her arm around my waist and lays her head against my arm, studying me in the mirror too. "I know, sweetie."

"Okay. Let's do this. Gotta have a story to tell my grand-kids about the time I scandalized the family by wearing a bikini one time."

"Oh, Laney," she says on a laugh. "Only you."

"Can I have another mai tai?"

She grabs hers from the marble sink and hands it to me.

I take a big gulp, and yep.

I can do this.

Who knew?

I walk out of the bathroom with my head held high, pretending I'm Sabrina instead of *Princess Plainy-Laney*. Helps that I've slipped my sunglasses back on so that no one can see straight through to the insecurities lining my soul.

I admire the hell out of women who are confident enough to wear bikinis at the pool, so why am I calling myself all kinds of horrible names in my head?

Out, voices, I order. *You lie. Be gone.*

Sorta works.

But not fully.

Not when I realize everyone around and in the pool is turning to stare at me, including the Sullivan triplets, who were *not* here when I left to go shopping.

And now the voices are getting louder.

Laney's having a breakdown. Laney's out of control. What will Laney's parents say?

How old is old enough to no longer worry about what people say about you? Not asking for a friend.

"They are totally checking you out," Sabrina whispers beside me.

"Are you sure they don't think I've lost my mind?"

"The men are all idiots thinking you've done this for them and it's their lucky day. Claire's proud of you and cheering you on, even if she doesn't know exactly why. And Theo is shitting himself right now realizing he's been an ass to the sexiest woman in Snaggletooth Creek for the past twenty years."

"Eww. I don't want to swim in a shitted-in pool."

Sabrina laughs so hard a little snort slips out.

I smile and the tension in my neck eases. There's nothing like making one of your best friends honestly snort-laugh to make you feel all kinds of better when you're afraid you're nothing more than Ms. Frumpy McBoringPants.

"Oh, yeah, Laney, the triplets are *totally* checking you out," she whispers, still giggling. "If you need help telling them apart, don't worry. I've got you."

"I think I can tell your triplet cousins apart," I whisper.

"Really? Which one's checking you out the most?"

"Not fair. Your most and my most are way different."

"*Laney*. Jack just let an entire piece of calamari fall out of his mouth."

"I thought that was a French fry."

She chuckles.

I giggle too.

But what I'm really doing is *not* looking at the pool. At Theo at the edge of the pool near Claire, who is a total actual bombshell just like Sabrina.

"I'm not doing this for Theo," I whisper to Sabrina.

"You're wearing the bikini for you. How's it feel?"

"Naked."

"I can confirm neither of your nipples and none of your vagina are hanging out."

Lucky Sullivan misses his mouth and smears his hamburger across his cheek while he stares at me, and Decker spills his tropical drink.

"Please tell me that's a sign of attraction and not horror. But not too much attraction."

"Laney?"

"I know, I know, get out of my head and enjoy the feel of sunshine on every square inch of my skin."

She grins. "Feels good, doesn't it?"

"Oh my god, it does. It really does. Do you think I might have a vitamin D deficiency?"

"*Delaney*. Go do a cannonball and have some *fun*."

"I didn't grab—"

"I will get you all the towels you want when you get out of the pool. Now go. Shoo. *Have fun*. For you."

Right.

Fun.

Are my arms a little jiggly? What about my thighs? Will the triplets think I want to have sex with all of them because I'm showing skin at the pool?

"Laney," Sabrina whispers, "sex is normal and healthy and *fun*."

"Oh, god, did I say that out loud?"

"You and mai tais are a combination for the ages."

"I need you in the pool with me to make me stop talking. And those mai tais barely have any alcohol in them."

"No regrets today. Today is your day off of expectations. You've earned it."

We've reached the edge of the pool. I can jump in. Dive in. Cannonball in.

Sit on the edge and slowly lower myself in while I get used to the temperature.

"You know how to swim, Laney, or do you need a float-ie?" Theo calls.

The taunt is all it takes.

Did he know? Did he know that's what I needed to hear?

Or is he just an ass?

His smile says he's not being an ass. His smile says *you can trust me, I'm goading you to remind you who I used to be, but I'm not him anymore, and I know you'll do a great cannonball.*

Or possibly that's also the mai tai talking.

Doesn't matter though. What matters is action.

I take seven giant steps back from the pool. Then three more. And then I take off at a dead run, leap as I reach the edge of the pool, and do my very best to tuck my knees up as I hit the water. "Cannon—"

I misjudge and am yelling *ball!* as I go underwater, fully aware that this was the weakest of weak cannonballs.

There wasn't enough splash.

I can *feel* it.

And that's not some sense of needing to make a bigger splash than Theo talking.

Not completely, anyway.

It's more that I can't even *cannonball* right enough to have fun with it.

Also?

I totally swallowed a mouthful of water. Which I will *not* complain about, by the way.

It's part of the *fun*.

I kick to the surface, feeling weird in the bikini. Like, even weirder than I thought I would.

And as I surface, I realize why.

I shriek.

I cross my arms over my breasts and cover them, which makes me dip below the surface.

And I consider staying here.

I do.

Bikini?

It's a stretch, but I'll do it.

Losing my bikini top after a cannonball that didn't even make a splash?

Take me now, pool. Just take me now.

I kick back to the surface and do my best to cover my breasts while I half-swim to the edge, looking desperately around for my bikini top. It has to be in the pool.

How am I going to get it without baring my breasts?

"I see it!" Decker yells from the side of the pool.

There's a tremendous splash—almost as big as the splash Theo made, but not quite—and then Decker swims past me, in his khaki shorts and Hawaiian shirt, and snags something off the bottom of the pool.

Sabrina squats beside me at the edge of the pool, her face a study in not laughing when you want to. "I am *so sorry*," she whispers. "I should've double-checked the tie."

Decker surfaces next to me with a gasp. "Here you go, Laney. Your sunglasses."

Sabrina plucks them from him. "Thank you."

He looks down at my breasts, which I'm covering as much as I can with my arm.

Then at my face.

Then back at my breasts.

And then *his* face goes a deep purple.

"Out you go before I tell everyone what you were doing in the clubhouse bathroom yesterday," Sabrina sing-songs.

Decker takes one more look at my arm covering my breasts, then scrambles out of the pool.

And then the very worst thing in the history of worst things happens.

Theo speaks.

He's on my other side. "Lose this too, Laney?"

My face goes so hot that it could make this entire pool boil in under ten seconds. But I turn my head to look at him with my bikini top dangling from his fingers.

Sabrina doesn't snatch it from him.

She doesn't threaten to tell his secrets if he doesn't hand it over right now.

She just squats there next to the pool, silent, soaking it all in.

"I d-did." My teeth chatter even though the pool's warm.

"Need help putting it back on?"

"S-sabrina can get it."

His dark eyes bore into mine, right there in broad daylight for everyone to see, no sunglasses to shield me from staring straight back.

I liked you in high school.

We liked *each other* in high school.

And we both knew we shouldn't. And neither of us ever acknowledged it. Me especially, even to myself.

Until now.

Here.

In a place that's foreign but so warm and welcoming that it makes me want to do things that I've *craved* but denied for a very long time.

After an eternity, he shrugs and plops the soaking-wet top onto the pool deck. "Don't say I didn't offer."

When the pool starts boiling, it won't be from the heat of my face.

It'll be from the heat of the tension in our gazes.

He breaks eye contact and heads across the pool, not looking back. When he surfaces, he's right next to Claire and the other sorority women again.

He says something I can't hear, and they all laugh.

I look back at Sabrina.

She's gone poker-faced again. "You want me to put that back on you, or do you want a towel?"

"Can I take option C and just die right here in this pool?"

"Not after that. That, my friend, was the biggest you've lived in a long, *long* time."

Dammit.

I was afraid that was what she'd say.

And honestly?

I don't think I want to die of mortification in this pool. My teeth chatter one more time.

I order them to stop.

And they do.

"Sabrina?" I whisper.

"Yeah?"

"Tomorrow I'll think this was fun."

She cracks up. "Good," she says. "Even better if you think it's fun today. You didn't do anything wrong, and you don't have anything to be ashamed of. You get to *live*, Laney. You get to have fun in the moment too."

"You keep saying those words, and I keep *wanting* to believe them."

"You will. One day. It just takes practice." She lowers her voice. "Also, you made a grown man dive into a pool fully clothed to rescue your…sunglasses."

I stare at her.

She stares back.

And then we *both* crack up.

13

THEO

THE WORLD IS a beautiful place with a few people I'd like to punch.

Beautiful? Laney in a bikini. Even if it gave me a boner that I couldn't hide behind a mountain and that's still half-hard a couple hours later.

People I'd like to punch?

The Sullivan triplets.

All three of them.

Yes, they're my friends. Some of my favorite friends, in fact.

But *they fucking looked at Laney in a bikini.*

Didn't think Decker would be the one who thought she lost her *sunglasses* and not her *top*, but he's only alive because he did.

And I'm only able to walk next to Laney on the way to dinner tonight because I'm making myself think about how dead Sabrina would make me if I asked Laney if she wants help with her cannonball later.

Sabrina wouldn't believe I was only worried about Laney's form.

She'd probably be right to believe that.

And so I'm battling a woody again as Laney and I meet Emma right off the lanai where we're having dinner tonight. Chandler's not here.

Don't care why. I'm just grateful I don't have to worry about looking at him wrong in front of Emma.

Em's all smiles and light and joy, as always, while she squeals and hugs Laney and asks how her day was.

Laney says nothing about trips to the hospital or kittens or losing her bikini top. It's only *such a beautiful place* and *I'm so glad we're here* and *I can't believe you're finally getting married*.

Is this—is this the two of us being on the same side?

No. No way.

Not getting my hopes up there again.

"Aww, who's the prettiest baby sister in the history of pretty?" I say when it's my turn to hug Emma.

"Stop, you goof."

"But you are."

She beams at me. And it's not a regular beam. It's a *this is all finally coming together the way I've dreamed it would since I was nine years old when I decided I wanted to one day get married at this Hawaiian resort that I saw in a magazine.*

It's a nut-punch kind of beam. I've stayed away from her all day, and she's having the best damn day of her life.

Knock it off, I tell myself. *This isn't about you. Just be happy for her. Be happy for you having a good day too.*

And it was a good day.

In retrospect, waking up holding my own dick and not knowing it because my hand was asleep is a story for the ages. Gonna have to use that next time I make a video. Watching Laney with the kittens was good. And I don't regret telling her I liked her in high school.

Who can't use the lift of knowing they're attractive?

Even if we need to work on her not believing me. Never would've guessed Laney Kingston had self-esteem issues.

But clearing the air is clearing the air, and I had to tell her if we're going to move on.

"You're not so bad yourself," Emma says to me. "I heard you were quite the superstar with the younger crowd on the beach this morning."

"Just found where my maturity level fit."

She rolls her eyes and hugs me again. "Thank you for avoiding Chandler and not being mad at me," she whispers.

"I ran over a kid at the beach, got sand in my eyes, and had to be taken to the doctor so I wouldn't go blind," I whisper back.

She laughs.

But only until she cuts her laugh off, jerks back, and stares at me in horror. "Oh my god, you're serious. *That's* why you missed lunch?"

She looks between me and Delaney, and when Laney winces and makes the *he's not lying but we handled it and all is fine* face, Em squeaks like I've just deflated her joy balloon.

"Nobody died, and I can still see." I smile at my sister and fling an arm around Delaney's shoulders. "Brilliant of you to give me a keeper who can handle it all so effortlessly."

Em flushes. "Theo, I—"

"*Theo, you're right,*" I interject in a falsetto. "*I'm brilliant, which goes without saying, and Delaney's much prettier than Chandler's ancient Aunt Brenda, and I'm glad you recognize what a giant favor I've done for you with your date this week.*"

"If all he has is that I'm prettier than Chandler's ancient aunt with the permanent scowl on her face, then I'm doing my job right," Delaney quips.

"What's that, you little whore?" Aunt Brenda says behind us.

Emma jumps. Delaney jumps and gasps and her face morphs into a tomato.

I slowly turn to frown at Aunt Brenda.

She's technically Chandler's great-aunt, but she's really the entire town's cranky old aunt.

And she has about ten seconds to take back the name before Ugly Theo enters the conversation. "Hey, Auntie No-No. Insulting my date? Tsk, tsk, Auntie No-No. So rude. What would your mother think?"

Laney makes a strangled noise.

The old bag of crankiness peers at me. "What would *your* mother think?"

"Of you tossing out insults to my sister and her wedding guests?"

"Of *you*."

I grin and wink at her, even though she's on my shit list. "She'd probably be glad I went for someone my own age instead of succumbing to all the flirting you've done with me over the years."

Laney makes another noise, but this one's definitely more amused.

Emma slides between us. "You're sitting with my parents and my cousin and some of your nieces and nephews, Aunt Brenda. You remember my cousin Sandor? He loves hearing how many bra-burners you arrested back in the day."

Sandor, the poor dude with horrible timing, flashes Emma a horrified look as he stops behind Aunt Brenda.

"Immodest hippies," Aunt Brenda grumbles.

Laney flinches.

And I get a flashback to her cannonball and the results of it at the pool.

It was a minus five on a ten-point scale as far as cannonballs go.

And I'm trying very, very hard to remember that instead of letting my mind speculate on the show I missed under the water when her top came off and how much I'd love to sneak her down to the pool late tonight to help her with her form.

"Ah, and here's Sandor now." Emma smiles at him. "He's in *banking*. You should ask him if he's ever seen any fraud."

Aunt Brenda is still eyeing me. "She's too good for you, and you know it."

"Who?" I ask.

"This woman you claim is your date."

"Didn't you just call her a very unflattering name?"

"Whores are too good for you."

"Doesn't mean I can't have fun until she figures that out for herself." I wink at her again. "Name-callers go to hell, Auntie No-No."

She points at me and looks at Emma. "I want to sit with him. He needs someone to keep him on his best behavior."

Emma gives me The Look.

It's basically the only look that isn't Emma being a perpetually optimistic, believe-the-best-of-everyone ray of sunshine.

Too bad, really. There's little I love more than pushing Auntie No-No until she cracks.

In irritation or laughter, I generally don't care. If Aunt Brenda wants to be miserable her whole life, that's her business. Can't fix that kind of determination.

But if Emma doesn't want me making a scene, I won't make a scene.

At least, not much more of a scene.

"I have really bad gas," I tell Aunt Brenda. "It's loud. And it smells. I wouldn't want to sit with me if I were you."

I belatedly remember that when she wasn't arresting hippie bra-burners, she was a middle school gym teacher. Probably had all her sniffer sensors burned off already.

Which might account for why she's always cranky. I would be too if I couldn't smell coffee or cookies or flowers or Laney's shampoo.

Stop it, dumbass. Not Laney's shampoo.

But it was probably the wrong tactic.

Aunt Brenda's scowl gets deeper.

It was definitely the wrong tactic.

She grabs Sandor by the arm. "Flatulence jokes are for people without two brain cells to rub together. Back in my day, we never would've discussed it with our elders either. Come, young man. You don't have flatulence, do you?"

"N-no," Sandor stammers while Aunt Brenda drags him onto the lanai where we're having luau food and dance lessons tonight.

"*Theo*." Emma's full-on glaring and hissing at me as Auntie No-No marches away. "She's had serious digestive issues that have caused a few horrifically embarrassing moments in public the past few years."

I open my mouth.

Close it again.

Whoops. "Sorry, Em. I'll stick to sports and babies and the unstoppable forces of physics as my only conversation topics at dinner. Cross my heart."

"We'll go find seats," Delaney interjects in a strangled voice. She hugs Emma again. "Don't worry, sweetie. They all know who you're related to and no one holds you accountable for that."

"Yeah. You're related to *awesome* people," I say. "The best of the best. And you're even bester than the rest of us."

Delaney grabs my arm and tugs.

I follow like a freaking dog.

But four more steps down the small, tropical-flowery-bush-lined corridor toward the lanai for tonight's private family dinner, she makes a noise that almost sounds like a stifled laugh.

I shoot a glance at her.

Is she—holy fuck.

She is.

She's *laughing*.

"You like fart jokes?" I ask her in my most seductive voice.

"Because if you love fart jokes, there are way more where that came from."

Can't help myself.

My hormones have decided it's time to win Delaney over. There's no *try your normal tactics* on her either.

This is go big or go home.

Be so ridiculous that when she doesn't take my interest in her seriously, I know it's my own fault.

Is this self-preservation? Or is this me really wanting to see that Delaney who whispered that she wanted to make a sandcastle this morning?

Fuck.

It's definitely me wanting to see the Laney who'd make a sandcastle.

She makes a muffled, high-pitched noise despite pinching her lips together, and then she does the most un-Delaney-like thing ever, and after a quick glance behind us, she yanks me off the boardwalk and into the bushes.

She looks toward the ocean, then tightens her grip and pulls me even farther into a dimly lit tropical alcove between the resort buildings, the beach, and the lanai.

Yessss, my dick says.

I tell it to shut up.

She probably wants to make sure we're too far away to be overheard.

When she finally stops, we're beneath a coconut tree. I peer up. *Way* up.

Is it likely one of those coconuts will fall on us?

The breeze makes the palms sway above us, and I push Laney over to a shorter, non-coconut-bearing tree.

She looks up like she's just noticing the coconut tree.

Her eyes flare wide.

She squeaks. Takes a long step farther from the coconut tree.

And then she doubles over as something *thunk*s behind me.

Are you kidding me?

There's a new coconut on the ground where we were just standing.

And she's *laughing*.

Laney.

Laney Kingston.

Princess Plainy-Laney. Prim and proper rule-follower who left me with an aching boner in the pool by showing up in a bikini and almost made me come in the pool in the aftermath of a terrible cannonball.

She's doubled over laughing at fart jokes and nearly dying by falling coconut.

Laney laughing?

This is ten levels beyond Laney playing with kittens.

I am not the guy who *had a crush* on this woman in high school.

I'm the idiot who still does.

Emma's sunshine. Sabrina's fun.

But Laney?

Laney's like this secret castle. She's a mystery. An enigma. I always wanted to believe she's hiding something magical and special and out of this world behind that mansion-on-the-hill exterior.

And now I want to believe I can be the guy who helps her find what she probably doesn't even know she has inside of her.

Because of moments like this.

Moments when she's completely unguarded. Letting go and letting herself enjoy the lighter side of life.

I want inside her castle.

I want to find where that *fun* part of her is, where the *adventurous* part of her is, and I want to help her let it out.

And right now, I get to watch her just *be*. And enjoy

herself just *being*. And laugh like nothing else in the world matters.

And know that she trusts me to be the guy she shares this moment with.

"We can't go to dinner," she gasps between peals of laughter.

That's the best idea I've heard all day. But when she says it, I can't help the way I brace myself like this is a trap.

Liking Laney has never ended well for me. And no amount of telling myself that I'm so much better for her today than I was in high school can alleviate the instinctive fear that letting myself like her again will end just as badly. "Why?"

"God, Theo, things just *happen* when you're around. They'll probably serve peach flambé for dessert, and just because you're in the room, the flames will go too high and set the banana trees on fire."

I swallow.

Once in high school, late enough that I had access to a car and could drive, Emma had a fancy dinner for some honors thing that everyone's families went to. It was all of the *good* kids, the *smart* kids, the *right* kids, and then there was me.

And then there was Delaney.

She had looked like she'd just been informed every college in the nation had rejected her because grades weren't real, and her entire life was upside down.

I knew why.

Her preppy boyfriend had just dumped her because they *wanted different things out of life*.

And what I wanted was to throw her over my shoulder, blow off the dinner, and take her up to Marmot Cliff to look at the stars and show her how much all of the fancy shit and the stuffy shit and the assholes didn't matter when you could see the Milky Way, but I knew she'd tell me that *wasn't proper*.

So I blew off the dinner and took myself up there.

And I didn't enjoy it at all.

My head was back there where Laney was upset, and I was pissed at myself for caring enough to let it ruin a great night up on the cliff, and pissed at myself for not having the courage to offer it to her anyway.

So having her suggest we blow off a family dinner where I'd have to avoid Chandler and avoid Aunt Brenda and avoid making subtle threats to the Sullivan triplets about looking at Laney wrong?

Chandler's obnoxious laugh drifts through the air, and every muscle in my back tightens.

But then I look at Laney, who's wiping tears from her eyes, she's laughing so hard.

And then I glance at the sun sinking low on the horizon between the lanai where family dinner is supposed to be and the black-rock-covered beach closer to where I want to be.

Banana leaves are full of water. Doubt they burn easily.

But she's not wrong.

If I go in there and something goes wrong, it'll be my fault, and if there's one thing I want more than anything for my sister, it's for her to be happy.

With or without me around.

I nod once and take her by the elbow, ignoring the shiver that races up my arm at the feel of her soft skin beneath my fingertips. "I'll drive."

14

LANEY

I SHOULD NOT BE FOLLOWING Theo out of the resort, but I am so tired of *should*s.

Why *can't* I have fun?

Why *can't* I be irresponsible?

I hate missing Emma. *Hate* it. This is her week and I want to be here for her and see her for more than five minutes at a time. But there are forty people coming to dinner tonight. *Forty.* Parents, grandparents, the bridal party, aunts, cousins… It might be a family dinner, but it's still a lot of people.

I tell myself I'm helping Theo stay away from Chandler, which is better for Emma, whom I see *all the time*. That she had a *great* day today *because* I handled all things Theo-related.

But I also feel an utter thrill at knowing I'm doing something I shouldn't do. Something *forbidden*. Something *dangerous*.

Something with potentially life-altering consequences bigger than me losing my bikini top in a pool.

Something that would give my mother a heart attack and a half.

And that makes it all the more appealing.

Not because I want her to suffer. But because *I want to live*. And I can't live in the fear of the world that I was raised to cower in.

It's happening.

I'm having my rebellion. And now that it's started, I can't stop it.

Nor do I want to. This can't wait until next week.

It has to happen *now*.

Theo stops next to a red convertible. "Climb in."

"Are you serious?"

He dangles the keys.

My jaw is on the pavement. A *convertible*? "When did you get—"

"Airport. When I landed."

"But we took—"

"Ride share to and from the clinic? Even I won't drive when I can't see, and no way was I letting you behind the wheel of this baby."

He says it with the same flirty grin he was aiming at Claire earlier.

The one that reminds me of the smile he aimed my way when he nudged me into doing my cannonball.

"Because I have a horrible driving record?" I say like *old* Laney, and I immediately want to take it back.

But he grins wider. "No, because she's built for *speed*. None of that granny driving you do."

I look at the car again. Red. Shiny. Top down. A feral black cat peering at me from the passenger seat's foot well.

And then I look at Theo again.

"I didn't steal the car," he says.

There's cheek in his words, there's something else too. Like he expects *did you steal the car* is the top question in my head right now, because it's the first thing I would've asked him in high school.

But he's *not* high school Theo. And I'm not high school Laney.

I swallow. "I didn't say you had."

"And I didn't say I've *never* stolen a car. Just not this one."

Oh, god. I'm running away with a bad boy.

Oh, god. I'm running away with a *bad boy.*

Maybe not the same kind of bad boy he was in high school, but still someone well outside my normal dating circles.

This is going to be fabulous.

I hesitate only the briefest moment before I open the door, shoo out the stray cat—he has *enough* cats, and this one has a clipped ear, indicating it's wild and fixed—and slide in.

Theo doesn't open his door.

He pulls a movie-star move and swings his legs over the side of the car, slides into the driver's seat, takes a minute to unbutton his Hawaiian shirt all the way before buckling his seat belt over his dark jeans, and then punches the button to start the motor.

The car roars to life and makes my clit tingle.

Not. Good.

But I can ignore this.

I text Emma quickly. *Turns out Theo actually DOES have gas. Have fun dancing! I've got this under control.*

Theo looks at me. "Did you just tell my sister that I have gas?"

"Yes."

Why is he aiming the flirt grin at me again? "Good. She knows how bad I can stink. Add that I had sardines for lunch."

And then he's tucking his arm around the back of my seat while he looks behind us and backs the car out.

Like there's not a backup camera right there in the dash.

A thrill zings through the rest of me.

I'm being a bad girl tonight.

For just one night.

For good reasons.

I am absolutely going to be that person I've always been told I shouldn't want to be, but that person that I've wanted more and more to explore every single day of the past year.

"Where are we going?" I ask over the engine as Theo heads out of the parking lot.

"Does it matter?"

The question shouldn't stump me, but it does.

And not because I don't know the right answer. *No* is clearly the right answer here.

But how often do I ever do things in my own life without purpose?

Never.

And that's not *wrong*. But maybe it's not *enough*.

"I want fish tacos," I tell Theo.

It's what pops into my head. I'm hungry. Fish tacos sound good.

No overthinking.

I just want fish tacos.

Fifteen minutes later, I have a bag of fish tacos in hand courtesy of a local drive-through place, and Theo's driving us out of town.

I don't ask where we're going again, or why he didn't get anything for himself.

Instead, I eat fish tacos and watch the sun dip lower in the horizon until he steers us up a road going inland, putting the sunset behind us.

Going nowhere.

Or maybe somewhere specific, and it's a surprise.

Theo's quiet. It's an unusual side of him from what I expect. Almost like he can turn down the chaos dial sometimes and just be chill.

I want to ask him what he does for work, but that's too *Laney* of me. So instead, I finish licking all of the delicious fish taco sauce off my fingers, then I pick a quite possibly more dangerous topic.

"Are you enjoying Emma's wedding week?"

His gaze shifts to mine briefly, and I swear he knows it was on the tip of my tongue to ask him how he supports himself. "Could be worse," he replies finally with that smile dialed up again. "Aunt Brenda could be babysitting me."

Good thing I'm done eating, or I'd be choking on a fish taco right now. "I'm sure she wouldn't have minded at all if you woke up with your hand asleep."

"When you wake up with *your* hand asleep tomorrow, I'm going to laugh my ass off."

"I don't wake up with my appendages asleep."

"Of course not."

"I'm a good sleeper." *Shut up, Delaney. Shut. Up.*

His lips twist in bigger amusement. "Was today your first time going skinny dipping?"

"*I was not*—ahem. Excuse me. No. No, it was not."

The car swerves. Like, *actually* swerves as Theo jerks the wheel while he glances at me as we leave behind the black lava rock landscape and head into a more desert-like area of the inner part of the island. I hope I get to see the tropical rainforest side while we're here too. I want to see all of it.

"When was the other time?" he asks.

Is that my imagination, or did his voice go a little hoarse?

My imagination, I decide. Or a side effect of the wind whipping around the open top of the car.

But I smile at him like his voice *did* go hoarse. "Much like Sabrina, I am a steel trap. Fish tacos cannot buy this secret out of me." And yes, I'll be paying him back for buying my food.

I didn't grab my wallet before dinner. I have no credit card and no ID on me. I'm living *on the edge*.

"Ah," Theo says. "You quickly pulled your suit down during senior dare night in the pool in the dark."

"*No.*" Okay, yes. I did that too. But I don't count it.

I didn't pull my suit all the way off. And it was like, half a second. I didn't want to be the one with my suit down if we got busted. My parents would've died.

Bad enough I was *there*.

But *I should've done it all the way*.

"Being naked in your own bathtub doesn't count," he tells me with a grin.

"Just how often do you think about me naked?"

"Pretty much every day."

My nipples tingle. I tell them to stop because this is *not* the kind of fun we're having tonight, but they don't listen. And my mouth doesn't get the message either. "Like, once a day? Or is it breakfast-lunch-dinner, *time to think about naked people time* several times a day? Do you just flip through your contact list and picture everyone naked, or only certain people?"

"Only certain people. Usually several times an hour."

"Do you say that to make me uncomfortable or because it's true?"

"Do you really want to know the answer to that?"

Do I?

Usually, no.

Today?

"I want to know."

He glances at me again. "Are you going to call me a dick if you don't like my answer?"

"Yes. It's my defense mechanism so I don't notice you have very nice abs."

Oh my god. I said that out loud.

I said that out loud, and now he's flexing his abs.

The man *is flexing his abs.*

For me.

Today's been a weird day. *So* weird. From the *very* unexpected wake-up with his personal problem looming between us, to watching him playing with a bunch of kids on the beach, to worrying over his eyes, to the kittens he rescued in secret and his confession that he used to like me, to the bikini mishap in the pool, to running away with him now—

He puts himself out there.

For *everything.*

"What's it like to not care what anyone thinks of you?" I ask before I can stop myself.

"Who says I don't care?"

"If you cared, you wouldn't be so…"

"Stupid?" he supplies.

"No, I was going to say whatever the word is for *willing to jump into potentially dangerous and often unwise things without thinking them all the way through,* but then I realized that sounds like Frumpy Dumpy Delaney, and I'm not her tonight, so please erase the question from your brain. It doesn't exist."

"You think I don't care what anyone thinks of me because I'm *spontaneous.*"

"I think you're forty-six steps beyond spontaneous. I also think you care what Emma thinks of you or we wouldn't be in this car running away from her wedding together. You would've ditched me."

"Maybe that's my plan."

I gasp.

Like, *actually* gasp.

He laughs but then stops as he seems to realize I'm taking him halfway seriously. "I'm not dumping you in the middle of the island."

"But I know about your kittens. I could make life *horrible* for you."

"I have way bigger secrets than *kittens.*"

"Like what?"

He cuts another look at me and chuckles again. "Dream on, Laney."

"Maybe I'll tell everyone about your kittens if you don't." I totally won't. But I feel like I'm *flirting*.

Like I'm having *fun*.

Like I don't have to watch everything that comes out of my mouth to make sure it's living up to the expectations that I've been told the world has for me.

And he hasn't kicked me out of the car. He's not slowing down. The sunset is so lovely that it's even lighting up the clouds looming to the east with a gorgeous pink-orange hue again.

I love the sunrise and sunset back home over the mountains, but this sunset is special too.

"You won't tell anyone about my kittens," he says.

His confidence annoys me. "Why won't I?"

"Because if you do, I'll launch a *save the kittens so Theo can take them home* campaign, go viral, get thousands of dollars in donations from around the world, have half the women at the resort fawning over me, and you'll be *that woman* who turned in the internet's new favorite son."

I don't gasp this time.

I squeak.

He's the type of person that could happen to. I swear he is.

Can this car maybe swallow me whole? I'm trying to be fun, and instead, I already feel like the horrible person who'd sacrifice the future of a litter of kittens for the sake of learning a secret.

Theo cuts another look at me. "Laney. If you were going to tell anyone, you would've done it already. Crazy rule-breaker, you."

"I can have fun."

He doesn't answer.

"*I can*. It's just hard when there's so much pressure to

always do the right thing and look the right way so that you don't mess up your future."

"Ask you a question?"

The correct answer here is *no*. Every instinct inside of me is hollering for me to say no.

I ignore it. Tonight's about ignoring what I've been taught and leaning into being someone else. "Sure."

"How long's it gonna take for you to get to that magical future you want to live in, and do you really think you'll like it when you get there?"

My brain breaks. Splinters and shatters and cracks wide open. "I—I—I mean, I'm living it right now, but I also have to think about how that impacts next year, and next decade, and—"

"You really enjoying it?"

Once again, I know the correct answer. *Yes. Yes, this is what I want and it makes me happy.*

But instead of answering, I'm frozen.

I love my job. I love the fulfillment. But there's still pressure.

One day, Delaney will take over Kingston Photo Gifts. She's so good there. We might retire early. No worries at all. The company will be in the best hands. All she needs now is the perfect husband to run it by her side.

Theo doesn't call me on my silence.

To his credit, he's not smirking either. Not making fun of me for being *boring Princess Plainy-Laney.*

I take a deep breath, fully intending to find it inside me to tell him that I love my job but yes, I'm unfulfilled in my private life and working on that—*boring, Laney, boring*—when something else entirely comes out of my mouth.

"Deer. Deer. *Deer!*"

There are no deer in Hawaii. Not like at home. But there's an animal running into the road and I don't know what it is and I know I'm supposed to say *right bumper* or something else to tell him *where* the animal is, but instead, he swerves off the road and slams on the brakes as a *thump* and a *crunch* come from the front of the car, and then there's a sudden white explosion as the airbags deploy.

"*Oh my god*," I gasp as I rock in my seat in the aftermath of the crash.

"Well, that's a new one," Theo says.

"Your car. Rental car. Did you take the extra insurance?" *Dammit*. Can I *not* be that person for *one damn hour*?

Theo unbuckles, then flings his door open and steps out.

I scurry out my side too, cringing. He's going to be so pissed. I hurry around the front of the car, bracing myself for images of him kicking the tire and cussing and yelling at me for freaking out and yelling at the animal we hit for running across the road, but instead—

Instead, I find Theo tilting his head and staring at a barrel-shaped black animal about a third as long as the convertible is wide with a thoughtful expression on his face.

"What...what is that?" I whisper.

He whips his phone out of his pocket and aims it at the dead animal like he's taking its picture. "Pig, looks like."

And he wants a souvenir photo.

Of course he does, Laney. Insurance will require it. He doesn't keep pictures of dead animals as souvenirs.

I glance at the front bumper, which is totally crushed. The light is crushed. The pretty red hood is crushed. The fender is crushed.

Can we drive this?

Will it even start?

"I'm sorry," I blurt. "I should've said something sooner. Or clearer. It came out of nowhere. I'm sorry."

"Not your fault."

"But I saw it before I found words. I should've spoken up sooner."

He looks up at me and studies me like he's perplexed. "You're not responsible for the whole world, Laney."

"No, but I—"

"Wasn't driving," he prompts.

"But I saw it and you—"

"Also saw it. And tried to avoid it. And failed. You still alive?"

"Yes, but—"

"You hurt?"

"No, I—"

"Not at all?"

"No, not at all. I'm fine."

He studies me longer than absolutely necessary, and then he does the last thing I expect, which honestly should've been the *first* thing I'd expect, given that this is Theo.

He cracks a grin. "Think we can load it in the car so my pops can stuff it?"

"*What?*"

"The pig. Don't think he's ever done a stuffed Hawaiian pig before."

"Are you—*are you serious right now?*"

His smile gets broader and impossibly more attractive. "It's a feral pig. You were gonna eat it anyway tonight if we'd stayed at the resort. And this is just a car. Piece of metal. Replaceable. I'm fine. You're fine. Now find your muscles and help me get this thing in the trunk."

"Absolutely not. And *not* because I'm a stuck-up rule-follower. There is *zero* good that will come of us putting that thing in the trunk."

"You'd deny my dad the chance to work on a new species?"

"Is that even legal?"

Yep. That came out of my mouth.

Theo's lips curve up into a dirty, naughty grin. "I never realized just how much I like it when you get all rule-follower. It's a challenge. I like a challenge. You challenge me, Laney. Thank you."

My stomach dips low and my mouth goes dry. "Are you seriously pretending to flirt with me over a dead pig?"

"Not pretending. C'mon. Help me get this thing in the trunk."

"We should call someone. The sheriff's office. Is there a sheriff on the island? Or is it the police? Who's in charge of roadkill here? Will the car move? Are we going to need a tow truck? Oh, god. Emma. She's going to be so upset." I whip out my phone, and—

No signal.

"Em's fine. We're not hurt. And in case you forgot, *Rocky Roadkill* put food on our table and clothes on our backs our entire childhood. She knows about the circle of life."

He squats next to the pig and takes a selfie.

A selfie.

I stifle another squeak.

"Makes more once it's stuffed if you know where it came from," he says like it's the most reasonable thing in the world. "Rest well, little piggie. Didn't mean to kill you. But I promise we'll find your body a forever home where you'll be loved and revered."

"I can't get a signal. We can't call for help if I can't get a signal."

"Someone will come along. People were hitting animals on the road long before cell phones, and they survived to tell the tale."

"We'll walk. Can't be far to find a signal."

"Pig in the trunk first."

"*I am not helping you—*"

I don't finish.

I can't.

Not when the dead animal suddenly squeals the unholiest, loudest squeal in the history of undead squeals, shoots to its feet like it took a hot poker up its ass, and charges Theo.

"*Zombie pig!*" I yell. "Duck! Dive! Run! *Zombie pig!*"

Theo gets the full force of the pig right to the chest and goes sprawling back onto the pavement.

I shriek and dash for him.

But that's the exact wrong move because the zombie pig is *pissed*, and now I'm his new target.

"Holy fuck, it's alive," Theo gasps.

It flares its snout at me. There's murder in its eye. It paws the ground once, snorts, and then charges me.

I scream and scramble onto the hood of the car.

Or try to.

Really, I'm grasping for purchase on the slick surface while the pig *rams the car*.

"Hey! Get! Stop!" Theo bellows at it as he jumps back to his feet, staggering only a little as he runs at the pig.

Did he hit his head?

Does he have a concussion?

The pig does a fast turn and hurtles its barrel body back toward Theo, who takes off around the car. "That's right, fucker! Chase someone with your own kind of stubbornness and innate good looks and solid muscle structure!"

I'm trying to climb up the car so I can dive over the windshield and inside, and I'm trying not to laugh at his ridiculousness at the same time. "Get in the car, Theo! *Get in the car!*"

He dives.

The car shakes and my bottom half goes sliding to the edge of the hood.

There's a *thump* as the pig slams into the car and connects with the door right where Theo just went over inside the convertible.

"Can it jump?" I shriek. "Is it going to eat us?"

"Pigs can't jump." Theo climbs to his feet on the front seat and reaches over the windshield to grab my arm.

"Are you sure?"

"No. Get in. We're getting out of here before we find out otherwise."

He pulls me over the windshield while I try to clamber up too, but I've never climbed a convertible windshield before.

Especially not while the car is being repeatedly head-butted by the most solid pig in the existence of wild, terrifying pigs.

I finally get the rest of the way up the windshield with Theo's help, but that's where the very worst thing in the history of terrible things happens.

I lose my balance.

Do I fall out of the car and get trampled by the very angry feral pig?

No.

That would be better.

Instead, I trip and fall headfirst onto Theo.

And he loses *his* balance.

And then the two of us are splayed together in the passenger seat, which has collapsed beneath us, both of us panting, our noses barely an inch apart, every inch of his solid body lined up against mine.

Belly to belly.

My breasts squished against his broad chest.

My thighs spread across his pelvis.

Our eyes locked.

It's the locked eyes that are the worst.

Maybe.

The growing bulge against my pubic bone might be the very worst.

Okay, not the very worst. It's definitely worse when the pig rams the car again, making the whole thing rock, which rocks my nipples against his chest while also rocking his

148

erection against a spot *soooo* close to my clit, but not *quite* there.

And I want it to be there.

It's raw, primal instinct. I haven't had a date in months. Okay, over a year.

God help me, this is the closest thing to sex I've had in over a year.

And it's *with Theo*.

The pig flings itself against the side of the car with an ungodly squeal. My leg slips and opens me up so that my clit is rubbing against Theo's shaft while the car jolts around us.

Accident.

I swear.

Just trying to hang on. If it happens to take clamping my legs around his hips for purchase, then I guess that's the price I have to pay.

Theo's eyes bore into mine, his pupils getting larger and his lids getting lower. He licks his lips. Visibly swallows. "That thing's pissed," he says while the animal hits the convertible once more.

"Y-you would be t-too." Oh, god, his cock feels good against my clit. *Sinfully* good.

It shouldn't.

But it does.

And isn't this fun? a little voice that sounds like a long-forgotten me whispers deep inside my head.

The car rocks. Theo's erection shamelessly rubs my clit. I stifle a moan at the sheer pleasure flowing through my body and pretend I'm whimpering in terror.

What would life be like if I could just *enjoy* this? If I didn't feel that sense of fear, that feeling that I'm disappointing my parents every time I want sex that won't lead to babies?

What if I just let go?

What if I stripped naked and had sex with Theo right here, in the middle of a road, while a wild pig attacks our car?

"It needs to stop." Theo's voice is thick. He closes his eyes, the tendons in his neck straining. "It's going to hurt itself."

Is he saying *I* need to stop?

I don't want to stop.

This feels good.

It feels reckless. Daring. Adventurous. Wrong, but in the *best* way.

I bite my lower lip as a particularly hard ram from the pig makes the car bounce harder. The motion sends a spiraling sensation of need deep within my vagina, and I want to let go.

I want to let myself come.

Right here.

"Do you think it'll get tired soon?" *My* voice is thick. And it hitches on the last word as the sway of the car makes my clit rub particularly deliciously against Theo's hard length.

"Don't—know—stamina of a—pig."

Oh, god.

He's turned on too.

He is *so* turned on.

The pig hits the car.

Crap. *Crap.* Crap fuck no no no no—*yes*.

That last jostle is pushing me over the edge and I'm coming.

I'm coming.

I'm having a freaking orgasm on top of Theo and his breathing is labored and I think he's coming too.

I do.

I think I have just rubbed one out for him through our clothes by riding the waves of a wild pig shaking this wrecked convertible.

You wanted to live, Laney, that voice of temptation and sin whispers deep inside me while little earthquakes rock my core.

Yes.

Yes, I want to live.

But this is *not* how I saw *living* going when I got up this morning.

Theo stifles another noise deep in his throat as I realize the car is no longer moving beneath us.

The pig is gone.

The freaking pig prompted both of us to come, and now it's freaking gone.

Neither of us says anything for a long, loooong time.

We just lie there, me splayed across Theo, him catching his breath beneath me, in a wrecked car in the middle of a road to nowhere, eventually working up the nerve to stare at each other.

And when I look at Theo, it's like I'm seeing someone completely different.

Like we have no history. No animosity. No complications.

In this moment, we're simply two people supporting each other through an unexpectedly erotic experience brought on by a wild animal in paradise.

"Are you okay?" he finally says.

"Yeah. You?" I pant.

"Why did you think I'd be mad at you?"

It takes a hot minute for me to understand the question, and when I realize he's talking about me freaking out over not warning him fast enough about the pig, I flinch and realize I need to move.

I need to get off him.

We're *in the middle of the road* with the light fading rapidly. We could get hit by a passing car. Or a wild goat could decide it wants to crash the party too, and goats *can* jump.

But Theo grips me by the waist and holds me tight when I start to squirm off. "It is not your fault I hit a pig. I know you were trying to warn me the best way you could."

If you'd told me two days ago that Theo Monroe would hit a tender spot inside of me that needed to be told *this mistake is not your fault,* I would've laughed until I choked and then choked until I passed out from a lack of oxygen.

Yet here we are, with him soothing a wound I didn't even know I had.

"Stop talking," I whisper.

"We're not so different, are we? Both of us living in the direction of the world's expectations of us."

My whole world stops spinning. Gravity ceases to work, and my entire existence floats out of my body, spiraling and spinning out of control to compensate for the fact that the world as I thought it was is not the world that actually is.

Theo's trapped.

He's trapped by *low* expectations just as much as I'm trapped by *high* expectations.

He's right.

We're basically the same.

And that changes *everything*.

I will never—*ever*—see him as a simple troublemaker again.

15

THEO

I BELIEVE I've mentioned that there's not a lot that embarrasses me.

I'd happily be a nudist if I lived in a place where my dick wouldn't be at risk of frostbite over half the year. I've spent time in jail and won't hide it. Never had any hesitation in telling a buddy they'd have to pick up the tab for my beer if they wanted me to go out with them when my bank account was low. I knew I'd make it up to them in other ways later.

How the world works.

Everything evens out if you do your best.

It's something my mom told me a long time ago that's held true throughout my life.

But there is no evening out the fact that Laney Kingston and a feral pig made me blow my load in my pants.

Take Laney out of the equation, and I'd be less embarrassed.

I don't know if she knows.

But if I know *anything* about Laney, it's that it won't be

long before she has regrets. And regrets will mean that she keeps *babysitting* me while pretending nothing happened and nothing's changed when for me, nothing will ever be the same again.

So I don't wait for the regrets.

Instead, as soon as Laney throws herself at Emma and Sabrina when we arrive at the karaoke bar down the street from the resort where the dinner after-party is happening after the luau dancers apparently didn't show up for the lessons after dinner like they were supposed to, I bail and head out into the night.

I *love* karaoke.

But there's no way I'm staying tonight. I need to get a grip on my emotions. Play with my kittens. Knit.

Hell, it's a good night to get some work in on my side hustle. Really feeling in the mood right now. And I'm a tad overdue on my next *assignment*.

As it were.

But instead, I dash up to the room just long enough to change my pants, and then I head to the beach.

Need a little peace and solitude. Meditation time. Be one with nature. Get my head back on straight and a little less embarrassed before I bombard myself with the kitten brigade.

Don't want them to know what I did.

They'd be the wrong kind of nice about it.

Remind me how much Laney fell in love with them this afternoon.

Make me wish she was there so I could kiss her. Pull her into the bedroom and show her I'm not some green buck who only comes in his pants.

Jesus.

Last time that happened?

Never.

Never's the last time.

Don't know how long I walk. How long I sit when I find

the perfect sitting rock and tune in to the sounds of the ocean while I watch the occasional light of a passing ship.

I do know I'm grateful for the moon lighting the beach, even if the moon being so high and bright means no Milky Way viewings this week. Grateful for the small knitting needles that I can tuck into my pocket with an equally small ball of yarn too.

Don't knock the knitting.

It's meditative.

Important, even.

Plus, it reminds me of my mom. She taught me to knit in the hopes it would be enough of *something* to fidget with during the times when I needed to sit still.

Not that I was ever brave enough to take it to school, where it would've probably helped me the most.

Didn't want other kids making fun of me.

Ironic that it's one of the things my fans and followers in my side hustle seem to love most about me now.

Eventually, I find my inner peace again. I'm totally zen as I start my walk back.

Harmonious with all that has happened tonight.

Yeah, I blew my load in my pants. But Laney's a woman. An attractive woman that I've always had a secret thing for who was rubbing her pussy all over me. Of course I got hard and lost all of my control. Who wouldn't have?

Plus, it's been a while since my last hookup.

Guess I'm getting pickier.

Pickier?

More insecure?

Fuck.

Both.

Wouldn't think it, would you?

Yeah, I know I look good. Spent a lot of time bulking up the past few years, and not just naturally through all the construction work.

But you don't grow up knowing people judge you by everything on the outside without knowing you want someone attracted to who you are on the inside.

And this body?

Won't last. Still gonna get old eventually. And I can't keep this diet up forever. I fucking *hate* this diet.

Laney's tacos almost broke me. Smelled *so* damn good.

But so long as my side hustle needs me to look like this, I don't eat fried fish tacos covered in whatever that magic sauce was that Laney licked off her fingers like it was the best food she's ever eaten in her entire life.

And I'm done thinking about tacos.

Done thinking about how even if Laney doesn't have immediate regrets, she will when she finds out what's been funding most of my bank account.

And my side hustle's important.

It makes a difference. Unconventionally so, but that's why I'm so fucking good at it. It doesn't follow the rules.

I don't follow the rules.

And that's okay.

I'm not hungry.

I am at peace.

I am—*dammit*.

I am almost back to the path that leads from the beach up to the resort buildings when I hear Chandler.

"Yeah, of course. We've got a bungalow saved just for you, waiting for whenever you want to get here, and—no. No, of course. Nobody will know. You're just an old friend, you know? Totally get where you're coming from, man. Completely. One hundred percent."

Fuck me.

I didn't hear that.

I did *not* hear that.

There's subtext and context and a story that I don't want

to know, but the biggest thing—*I don't want Laney moving out of my room.*

There.

I said it.

If there's an open bungalow, Laney could move in to it, and I don't want her to.

There's the not-so-subtle sound of a bug zapper zapping a bug, and I flinch.

He's still using the damn fire starter.

"Yeah, man. I mean, we're family. So we act like it. The *good* kind of family. Couldn't buy a better one. Heh. Joking. But like, not, considering you just—anyway. Come on out. You'll see, and I won't tell them who you are. Not unless you want me to. Honestly, I'd rather the announcement not come until *after* I'm on my honeymoon. But don't worry. You'll win them all over. I mean, it's you or shutting down. Can't argue with this, can they?"

Yep. Heard enough. Don't need to stay here. Not my drama.

Won't make it my drama.

Learned a long time ago that no good comes of telling Emma anything Chandler's done that makes him look like anything less than a god.

She doesn't want to hear it from me. She doesn't like it when we don't get along. She loves us both, even if we can't stand each other, and she insists they don't have secrets so she knows it all anyway.

And you know what?

I'm glad it sounds like Chandler found a way to fix the café's money problems.

Glad to know he'll give her the family and the life she wants, and that they're starting the married part of their life without his business in debt.

At least, not the kind that'll get the shop shut down imminently.

He's what she wants.

I do an abrupt about-face, intending to head to my room the long way so I don't have to see Chandler—or so he doesn't have to see me—but instead, I almost run over a woman who's standing there holding up a hand like she was about to tap me on the shoulder.

She leaps back with a shrieked "*Ack!*" then puts her hand to her heart. "Sweet baby Jesus in heaven, you scared the ever-lovin' shit out of me."

"I get that reaction a lot."

She giggles, and recognition hits me.

Saw her this morning. One of the kids' moms.

And now she's looking me up and down like she's considering having a snack.

Specifically, a Theo one-night-stand snack.

"You were out there buildin' all those sandcastles with my son this mornin'," she says in a thick Southern accent.

I nod, angling toward my escape. "Kid at heart. That's me."

"I just wanted to say thank you. My Elijah doesn't have a daddy in his life, or any good menfolk to set the kind of example you want good menfolk to set, so that was incredibly special to me."

"My pleasure." Any other night, I'd stay and chat. But not tonight.

"I've been thinking all day that you just seem so darn familiar. You ever been to Goat's Tit, Alabama?"

My whole body flushes hot, and I wish I could rip off my shirt and fan myself with it. This is the only part of the side hustle that ever makes me squirm. And it shouldn't. They shouldn't recognize me.

Guess my tats are distinctive.

Or my voice.

"Haven't had the pleasure," I say.

"You sure?"

"Never been to Alabama at all. But if I ever do, I'm starting with a town called *Goat's Tit*."

A hand claps down hard on my shoulder, and it's not hers.

It's the second half of what I was hoping to avoid the minute I realized this woman wanted to talk.

"Ol' Theo here's never left the state of Colorado until this week," Chandler says. "Parole conditions."

I know my sister loves him, but his small dick energy has been the only part of his personality growing in the past year or two.

And knowing that he's being a dick because he doesn't like that I'm paying for the wedding doesn't help.

Dude should be fucking grateful. Not threatening to tell the whole town where I got the money if I breathe a word about covering everything here.

Which I wouldn't do anyway.

I grit my teeth while I force a smile at the woman. "Only time I was ever on parole was for joyriding a go-kart down Main Street at three in the morning in my underwear when I was nineteen."

Chandler stiffens.

"Too much snow," I continue. "Crashed into the revered statue of Snaggletooth the Gold Miner and put a chip in his pickax."

Fun night. Sneaking beers with all of my friends, some back in town after their first semester of college, the rest of us enjoying a Friday night off after long work weeks at minimum wage jobs that our parents all hoped were temporary until we found something bigger to do with our lives.

Chandler was there.

Right up in the thick of it.

Right up in the thick of ratting everyone out to the cops too. Always assumed he thought the rest of us were too drunk to remember what really happened.

But I remembered. I wasn't too drunk.

Not that the cops believed me.

Why would they? It's the rules. Your family's standing in the community makes a difference in how you're treated and how much you're believed, and Chandler's family brewed the juice that made Snaggletooth Creek run, while my family collected roadkill for taxidermy during the lean times when hunters weren't bringing in deer and elk and bears and lions.

Didn't break my heart when Emma and Chandler split up not long after they went back to their respective colleges after that winter break.

And jail wasn't so bad.

Did me a favor in the end, honestly.

Still would've preferred if Emma hadn't gotten right back together with Chandler when they both moved home after college though.

The woman glances between us, one of her eyes crinkling a little more than the other.

Or maybe it's a trick of the lamps.

"I—I must be thinking of someone else," she finally says in her thick twangy accent. "Thank you for your time."

"Enjoy your night," I call after her rapidly retreating backside.

Not the first time Chandler's cock-blocked me.

Don't mind being cock-blocked, truth be told.

Not really interested in the Southern single mom.

My dick's too hung up on someone *else*.

But I do care that Chandler's rounding on me and glaring like I'm the problem.

I know I'm not the problem, and if he thinks he can channel making me feel like a high school fuckup, he's dead wrong.

"What did you hear?" he growls.

Okay, *tries* to growl. Dude's got a weak growl. Goes higher-pitched than he means to. It hasn't worked on me since about fifth grade, when I asked him if the llama from *The Emperor's New Groove* was his daddy.

Got suspended for fighting after that. Chandler got a lollipop and a broken nose and the gift of everyone's amnesia about him starting it.

I let it go because it was easier than holding a grudge. "Heard the pretty lady flirting with me."

"Before that."

"Ocean. Night bugs. Music. Tourists."

He keeps staring at me like he's trying to decide if I'm fucking with him.

I rock back on my heels and give him the *what?* look.

"You better be as dumb as you pretend to be." He's going for the growl again. And I'm wondering just how big his dick must be for my very intelligent sister to truly want to marry this guy. "If you repeat a single fucking word, I'll destroy you."

Yep.

This is what my sister wants to marry. A guy who doesn't want me at his wedding but knows he can't object because that would make his bride unhappy. "Sure Em would love that," I say.

His face twitches.

I nod to him. "Better get back to my babysitter. Have fun being you."

I walk away without reminding him who's paying the bills here. No point in it, and he'd take the opportunity to remind me he could spill my biggest secret.

That one's *mine* to leak on *my* terms.

Not because I'm embarrassed.

But because I know *other* people will be. They'd think I need to be saved from it. That there's something wrong with how I choose to make a difference in the world.

Chandler follows me to my room.

I pretend I don't know he's behind me.

161

For Emma's sake.

It's always for Emma's sake. She's the one who'd come to my bedroom door every single time I stepped in major shit while we were growing up, knock softly and whisper, "I know it wasn't all your fault, Theo, and I still love you, and you're still the best brother in the world."

Therefore, I will do anything for her.

I can't count the number of times she told me she knew it wasn't my fault.

Especially after Mom died.

I know she knows all the shit with Chandler isn't entirely my fault. And I know she's allowed to love a guy who will never be my best friend.

So long as he truly makes her happy in every other aspect of her life, who am I to object?

The minute I'm inside my suite, I pull out my phone. Delaney would say I need to call the rental car company and get paperwork started, but I have other things I want—and need—to do.

I don't call anyone. Instead, I text Emma.

Gotta work tomorrow morning. You can have Delaney back for a few hours. Overnight, even. Won't leave my room. Promise.

I don't expect an immediate text back, but there it is.

Um…speaking of…we're headed your way. Laney's a little… happy…and would like to go to bed. In her bed. She keeps saying you have something that will make it all better but that she's not telling what since she can keep secrets too. And this is NOT me asking if what you have that will make her feel better is any part of your body.

She doesn't threaten to disembowel me if I use my penis to make Laney feel better.

But she wouldn't.

We have a deal.

We don't interfere with each other's private lives unless we think it's a toxic situation.

I still know better than to take this as permission. Especially this week.

Got it, I text back.

I'll take her for breakfast so you can work tomorrow, Em adds.

I glance at the pullout bed, still stuck halfway out because I'm tipping maintenance to stay away.

Not that I think it's necessary.

Haven't seen housekeeping in the time we've been here. Gift shop was closed right before dinner, despite the posted hours saying it would be open until eight. Heard a rumor the restaurants aren't running well.

Seems Emma picked a falling-down resort for her wedding.

But if she's happy, I'm happy.

Happy as can be with Laney heading back my way though.

Good thing she's drunk.

I don't freaking touch drunk women.

Hopefully she'll pass out quickly. And snore. And drool. And maybe puke.

Not because I wish puking on her, but because it might make her less attractive.

I wince.

Let's be honest. It probably wouldn't.

It would probably make her even more real and relatable. And that's something I'll just have to deal with.

16

LANEY

PIÑA COLADAS ARE *WAAAAAAY* MORE fun when they're not mai tais and when your friend bribes the bartender to put extra rum on top of the extra pineapple on top of the extra rum and when they're *delicious* and when they make you make a *fool* of yourself.

Ha-*ha!* Delaney Kingston is making a fool of herself! Take that, expectations!

But walking up stairs is *not* fun.

"Why are they so *big*?" I moan while I lift my thigh with my hands to make it lift high high *high* in the air to put my foot on the first step of the porch.

Sabrina laughs next to me. "You want 'em big, sweetie."

"But not too big," Emma adds.

"How would you know?" Sabrina shoots back. "You're marrying *Chandler*, and he's practically the only guy you've ever slept with."

"I've tried bigger dildos when he's been away on work trips," Emma replies.

I crack up.

Like, crack up so hard that I can't see straight.

Am I standing?

I don't know if I'm standing.

Or sitting.

"I can't feel my butt!" I shriek.

Something touches it. "Still there," Sabrina declares.

"Is it still flat and ugly?"

Emma gasps. "*Laney*. Your butt is *not* flat and ugly. It's trim and adorable."

"Do you have any idea how many times I've wanted your butt?" Sabrina adds.

"It's like this perfect little dream butt that the rest of us have envied for years," Emma continues.

Sabrina grips me tighter while we make one more step up. "You never have problems with jeans gaping in back."

"Or falling off of you."

"And men stare at it all the time."

"It's truly the perfect butt."

"Best booty in the business."

"Is this when I chime in or when I leave?" Theo asks.

Theo.

Freaking *Theo*.

"Be quiet," Sabrina orders.

Emma makes one of her cute Emma noises that means she agrees. "You're on standby in case we need you to carry Laney inside."

"Or to *my* bungalow," Sabrina adds, "which is where I think we should be going."

"No, I'm thoing to Geo's gunbalow," I remind them. "*Because of the secret*. Ha! I have a secret *tooooooooooo*."

I'm not telling them the secret.

My lips are sealed.

It's important.

I don't remember why, but when I keep a secret, I keep a secret.

There aren't enough piña coladas in the world to ruin this secret. Not when *I get to keep a secret*.

Am I singing that?

I stop with my hand under my thigh for the last gigantuan step—and yes, that's a word, because the piña colada says so —and I test my mouth.

I think I was singing that out loud.

Time to stop.

Instead, I look up at Theo. And his chest with all of those tattoos. And his arms. And his face.

He has a nice face.

I like his face. It's so *facey*. And bad boy-ey. And it has secrets too.

I wink at him, and the world goes dark. But he's still there when it lights up again. Did I wink? Or did I do a double-blink?

Not important.

"I didn't tell," I assure him.

"Good job," he replies dryly, his lips wobbling like he's trying not to laugh at me.

"*Not* a good job," I reply. "It's a *bad* secret. It could get you in *trouble*. And I kept it. I am part of the *problem*. I'm a bad, *bad* girl."

Sabrina snickers.

Emma chokes.

And Theo—freaking *Theo*—gives up and smiles at me.

Wow.

Wow.

He has a pretty smile.

No, not pretty.

Heavenly.

It's a tropical heaven smile.

I scrunch my nose at him while Sabrina and Emma

support me on the porch. "Put that away. I don't like it."

He looks down at his shorts.

Then back up at me. "It's not out."

"Your *schmile*, you foogus. Put your *schmile* away."

"I feel like we shouldn't leave her alone with you," Emma says.

"I'm going in with them," Sabrina informs her. "You go find your groom. Be all—no, I can't say that to you. He's still my cousin. Just go—go do bride stuff."

"You're drunk too."

"I'm *happy*. I can hold my mai tais."

"I had twenty-eight piña coladas because I like coconuts," I tell Theo. "You can't touch me in bed. It's against the rules."

Emma chokes again.

"As I said," Sabrina says, "I'm going in with them."

"Shhhhh," I say. "You can't. You'll know the *secret*."

"Laney, sweetie, have we met? I know all the secrets."

"*I knew it first.*"

"In we go." Theo pushes the door open so both Sabrinas can help me inside.

Uh-oh.

Two Sabrinas is a bad sign.

I don't think I've ever seen two Sabrinas, and I once did three shots of Jägermeister in an hour.

But only once, because it was irresponsible of me.

"I'm so boring," I blurt.

"You are *not* boring," the front Sabrina replies. "Here. Come sit on—well. Not the couch."

The couch looks like a giant mouth trying to eat the rest of the living room, and it makes me snortle.

Snortles are so unsophisticated.

They're full-up snort-giggles that come out my nose and make me burp piña colada.

Ew.

That tasted way better going down than burping back up.

Who invented burps?

They should be put in time-out.

"Night, Em," I hear Theo say. "Love you. Go have fun. We've got her."

"I know. You're the best."

I squint at all of the Sabrinas.

"Did you always know Theo's a nice guy?" I whisper.

"No," she replies. "Why didn't maintenance come fix your couch today?"

"Really wanna ask that?" Theo says.

Sabrina sighs.

I don't like the sigh.

It's *frustration*. I don't like *frustration*. I like *other* f-words.

Dirty f-words.

And also fun f-words.

Like felish—felitten—*feline*.

Feline.

I like felines.

"Go away," I tell Sabrina. "I love you. You're my favorite. But you have to go away. I'm gonna have fun in secret."

"I am *not* taking her clothes off or doing anything if she takes them off herself," Theo says.

There's only one of him.

I wonder if that's because he's so unique. Like all of the extra Theos that are special are on the inside instead of the outside.

We're the same, but opposite.

My brain is still wrapping around that.

It's a lot. Especially on this much coconut rum.

"What's behind the closed door?" Sabrina asks.

"All of his extra pussy. Go away," I reply.

And then I snortle again.

"I am definitely *not* going away," my other very best friend in the entire world replies.

"If you love me, you'll go away," I tell her.

She laughs at me. "Not a chance, sweetie."

"I'll give you a cookie."

"Tell me a secret, and maybe I'll go away."

Ha. I can do that. "A pig attacked Theo's car. Go away."

"Told us that one at the bar already," she replies.

"Whoops."

I don't look at Theo.

Even under the influence of a thousand piña margaritas, I know I told that secret.

"Was Emma mad?" I whisper.

"Was the pig named Chandler?"

"Now it is."

All of the Sabrinas double over laughing.

"Chandler has the staff holding an open bungalow for someone," Theo says.

The Sabrinas stop laughing.

"Why's that not funny?" I ask.

Not that I care.

I want to go live in a pile of kittens.

Shh.

That's the secret. That Theo has kittens. And I want to love on all of them.

I want to *steal* one. Take it home so I can have a kitten too.

All I ever wanted when I was little was kittens.

"Say you heard it from me, and you know what I'll do," he adds.

I try to creep to the second bedroom door while all of the Sabrinas are whispering something to Theo, but a chair leaps out of nowhere and trips me.

"Not that she should be alone tonight," I hear Theo add.

I flip him off.

I think.

Do my fingers work?

Which one is my flipping-off finger?

"That's your pinky, Laney," he says.

His voice in my name makes me fuzzy and warm inside.

Wait.

Is that my name in his voice?

Did I think that right?

I didn't.

Doh.

I lift my hand and make fourteen of my five fingers sit down right, until only one is left up.

"Pointer, Laney," Theo says.

Someone starts singing.

It sounds scary.

Scary enough to make Sabrina say things that would make my mother wash her soap out with mouth.

Who's singing?

I'm not singing.

And if I *am* singing, I'm not singing *that* song. It sounds like a real party in here.

Why are they—*ooooooh.*

That's Sabrina's *ringer phone.*

Ringer phone?

Phone ringer?

I blink hard at the chair that tripped me while Sabrina answers her phone. "Did I think that right too?" I ask it after I've flopped around arguing with it with my body for a bit.

It doesn't answer.

Stupid chair.

One of the Sabrinas hauls me to my feet and then holds my face to hers like it's important that I pay attention to what-ever she's saying.

I can do that.

She's talking.

Unlike the chair.

"Laney, sweetie, that was Aunt Lisa calling me. Aunt Brenda's a little tipsy too, but unlike you, who is absolutely perfect when you're tipsy, she's throwing bar stools at the limited staff left here. The triplets have disappeared, so I need to go run interference. But I'll be back, okay?"

"Fart at her," I say.

Theo laughs.

He laughs.

Like a full-on, surprised but happy laugh.

"I *will* be back," Sabrina repeats.

"*I'll be back*," I echo back in my best Arnold Schwarzenegger impression.

"Emma won't threaten you, but you damn well know I will," Sabrina says.

Oh, god.

Oh god oh god oh god.

I'm a problem.

I'm a problem because I'm not in control of myself and that means that I might make Theo take advantage of me and get in trouble with Emma.

I thought I was just having fun and stress relief, and instead, *I'm a problem.*

I burst into tears. "I didn't drunk to get mean," I sob. "I'm sorry. I won't do it again. I won't be the problem."

"Oh, Laney, honey, we know you didn't mean to get drunk." Sabrina gives me a quick hug. "And you are one hundred percent allowed to get as drunk as you want in safe places with your friends around you after having a bad day. *You are not the problem.* You are amazing and perfect and I love you. We all do. I was threatening to cut Theo's balls off if he doesn't take the utmost care of you while I'm gone."

"He's a nice guy," I sob. "He does nice guy things."

"He's about to have to prove it. Go to bed soon, sweetie. Love you. You're okay. *You are not a problem.* Having fun is *not* a problem. I *have* to go. I'm so sorry."

I blink, and she's gone, and the chair has moved and is between me and the door to the kittens again, and *I just want to hug a kitten.*

Theo angles into view.

He's blurry, but I'm pretty sure he's a deer in the head-lights. And god knows I've seen deer in headlights.

And now pigs in headlights.

"I cry when I'm too drunk," I sob. "I'm okay. I'm fine. I'll be okay when I sober up. *Tomorrrrroooooooowwww.*"

"You wanna hold a kitten?"

"*Yeesssssssss.*"

"Do you need me to carry you there?"

I am not drunk enough to give him the incorrect answer, but I hear it come out of my mouth on another sob anyway. "*Yeeesssss.*"

Okay.

Maybe I'm that drunk.

This has happened maybe four times in my life. Because I'm *boring*.

I can't see Blurry Theo well enough to know if he's still watching me like I'm a wounded mountain lion or if he's looking forward to touching me again.

"I want to be fun like you," I wail. "I want to drink without crying. I want to *live*. I don't want to feel dirty and wrong and in trouble because I had a reaction to your body in the car."

He doesn't say anything while he lifts my arm and puts it behind his neck.

I can't see him at all. He's just a big blob of light brown hair and sun-kissed white skin. And solid warmth lifting me like I'm a china doll.

"Am I over your shoulder?" I ask.

"No."

"I feel like I'm upside down."

"That's because your underwear is always too tight. Push the door handle if you want to see the kittens."

He's carrying me.

Theo Monroe, the bane of my existence in my school

years, is carrying me into a room of kittens because I'm crying because I'm drunk.

"Why are you nice?"

"Because I like to like myself."

He kicks the door shut behind us while a chorus of teeny-tiny meows goes up.

"They're so cute," I cry.

My eyes won't open wide enough to let me see them. No matter how hard I try, I can't pry my eyelids open far enough to see all the cuteness. Plus, Theo keeps making noises like I'm not supposed to squirm.

I can *feel* them against my chest. It's like a nipple-tickling rumble.

But only one nipple.

Just the nipple closest to him.

"Why are you attractive?" I ask.

"Because I'm secretly a god sent down from Mount Olympus to test all of the women to see who'll look past this awesome exterior to the super cool dude inside."

I pry my eyelids wider apart and almost poke myself in the eye as I start to laugh while I'm still crying. "*I can't see.*"

He heaves a sigh, sets me down, and then suddenly lightning flashes in all corners of the room.

"*Stop,*" I cry. "No thunderstorms! Make it—oh. *Oh.*"

He turned on the lights.

That's why I couldn't see. The lights were off.

It wasn't my eyeballs.

"I'm so dumb," I wail.

Theo takes my hand, turns it palm-up, and deposits a soft, fluffy, furry body into it before walking away.

I hiccup.

I am *never* drinking again. This is mortifying.

And if it's mortifying while I'm drunk, I cannot even imagine how I'll feel in the morning.

"Hi, kitty," I whisper unevenly through the sobs that I'm desperately trying to stop.

"That's Snaggleclaw," he says from somewhere else in the room.

"*You named him after Snaggletooth?*"

"She named herself."

This one.

I am stealing *this* kitty. She's purring in my hand and her name is Snaggleclaw and I just dropped a tear into her fur, so she's mine.

Theo returns and squats in front of me.

"More kitties?" I whisper.

He doesn't answer.

Instead, he wipes my face with a soft, damp cloth.

My whole face puckers. "Don't be nice to me."

"Been here a few times myself, Laney. You'll pull through."

"I said, don't be nice to me."

"If you want Asshole Theo, I wrestled him mostly into submission a few years back. Nice Theo is all that's left. Personality flaw. Apologies, princess."

He wipes the cloth over my cheeks again. It's warm but not too warm. I can smell him too. Clean soap with a touch of salt and mystery.

"I liked you too but I wasn't allowed to," I whisper from behind closed eyelids.

"You're a grown-ass woman. You can do anything you want."

"No, I can't."

"Yes, you can."

"I want to but I don't know *hoooooow.*"

Snaggleclaw squirms in my hand, digging her little claws into my palm like pinpricks that startle me back to exactly where I am and exactly what I'm doing.

"Oh, god," I whisper. "I made trouble for Emma."

"Emma enjoyed the hell out of watching you have fun."

My head hurts, and my dress is falling off.

My dress is falling off.

"That's not how you do it, Jellybean." Theo stops wiping my face. There's another tug on my skirt, and then I have two kittens in my hands and my dress is no longer falling off. "Pet the kitties, Laney. They need you."

"They need me."

"Yep. They need you."

He brushes the washcloth over my face one last time, and I close my eyes and lean into the cool sensation. My sobs are finally subsiding.

Yep.

Gonna be mortified tomorrow.

But not right now.

Right now, I just feel heavy. Rooted to this chair, but also light on top.

Clear.

Free.

Clean.

Happy.

It's the alcohol. I shouldn't drink. I shouldn't drink *ever*.

But maybe it's not all the alcohol.

Maybe it's Theo too.

The kittens. His smile. His gentle touch.

Why can't I be happy?

Why can't I just choose to be happy?

"Can't sleep in here," he says quietly. "They'll keep you up all night, and you'll have to explain a bunch of scratches to Emma."

"I'm not sleeping."

"Laney."

"Shh. This is just a dream. A very, very bad dream."

"What makes it a bad dream?"

"Emma's marrying Chandler and they think you're the bad guy."

"What's wrong with Emma marrying Chandler?"

"She deserves somebody who asked her five years ago."

"Who asked her five years ago?"

"Nobody. But he should've. And he didn't. He doesn't have balls."

"You have photographic evidence of that?"

I smile behind my eyelids.

Theo is funny.

"Why did he make her wait so long?" I ask Theo.

"No idea."

"Does he make her happy?"

"Fucking better."

"Fucking better," I agree.

Theo chuckles.

It's warm and rumbly and it makes my belly tingle. And that's not just the kitty cats on my lap.

They're warm and rumbly and making my thighs tingle.

Not my belly.

Only Theo's chuckle makes my belly tingle.

"Kitty time's over, Laney," Theo says quietly. "C'mon. I'll put you to bed."

"That's dangerous."

"Why?"

"Because drunk Laney likes you."

"Sober Theo will keep his distance."

"Drunk Laney doesn't want you to."

"Drunk Laney will thank me in the morning."

17

THEO

You know what makes for a long night?

Tossing and turning for what feels like days, trying to fall asleep on the floor so you don't give in to temptation and pull your sister's best friend into your arms because she's so fucking irresistible, only to have her fall out of the bed and on top of you five minutes after you finally fall asleep.

Worst part?

She barely wakes up.

Even through me getting her back to bed.

When the soft mumbles in her sleep tell me she's getting close to the edge of the bed again, I get up before she can succeed at falling out a second time and scoot her closer to the center.

But when she loops an arm around my arm, snuggles it, and sighs contentedly?

Fuck me.

I do the thing I know I shouldn't do, and I crawl into the bed with her.

Just as her wall so she doesn't fall out of bed again, I tell myself.

Drunk Laney is a mess.

And I like it. Because the Laney I grew up with, the Laney I've always known, she's so put together it makes everyone else feel inferior.

Drunk Laney? Messy Laney?

Less-than-perfect Laney?

Coming-apart-at-the-seams Laney?

It's not that I enjoy her suffering.

It's that I've been let behind the curtain.

Trusted to see the cracks.

Asked to help.

Me. The guy who would've been voted least likely to *ever* have a chance with Laney Kingston in high school.

She wanted to come to my room instead of staying with Sabrina.

I know it was for the kittens.

But as soon as she flings an arm across my stomach and mushes her cheek up against my shoulder, she stops mumbling in her sleep.

She gives that heavy, contented sigh once more, and then the only sound in the room is her slow, deep, rhythmic breathing.

I tell myself this doesn't mean she needs me. Doesn't mean she even *wants* me.

I'm just the closest warm body to make her feel like she's not alone.

And isn't that what we all want? To not feel alone?

Fuck knows I've felt alone too much in my life. I assume most people have at some point. Some more often than others.

But Laney always seemed above problems. Her biggest issues in school were getting too close to that line between an A and a B. Which dress to wear to prom. Which college to choose among the fourteen that accepted her. If she'd start running her parents' company before she was thirty, or if she'd be forty before they retired.

If she liked a guy, she'd date him. When she got tired of him, she'd dump him. If he dumped her first, he was shunned and she was loved.

She was first on the list for special programs that got her excused from school, but still had the perfect attendance award, which was the dumbest award in the history of dumb awards.

And now we're all pushing thirty, and she's the one cracking up at fart jokes at Chandler's Aunt Brenda's expense and riding me in a convertible while a wild pig attacks it and snuggling me in the moonlight coming through the open window so that she can sleep.

I want to stroke her hair.

I want to wrap my arms around her and hold her closer, no matter how hot it makes me.

I want to climb into the shower with her and wash her hair and kiss her until I can't breathe and fuck her against the wall.

And all I can do is lie here in the dark being a wall so she doesn't hurt herself, knowing all too well she'll regret me in the morning.

I fall asleep with a hard-on to hallucinations of Laney waking me up with kisses, stripping off her shirt to let me see her breasts, and riding me into oblivion.

It's so real that when a shriek and a moan pull me back to full consciousness in a bedroom flooded with morning light, the first thing I do is check to see if I'm still in my shorts.

"Oh, god, turn the light off," Laney groans.

Yep.

Still wearing clothes.

So's she.

Still have a raging hard-on too.

Don't think she'll notice. Or want to do anything about it.

"It's the sun, Laney." I test both hands—both fully awake today—and realize the arm Laney was sleeping on is cold and wet.

She drooled on me again.

No matter what happens the rest of my life, I will forever know that Laney drools in her sleep, and I will forever like that about her.

"What did I do last night and where did my arm go?" Her voice is husky enough that the whimpering makes my cock even harder.

"Which arm?" I ask.

"The one I can't move."

"Which one can you move?"

"This one."

There's no movement.

None.

Her eyes are squeezed shut. Her hair's a tangled bird's nest against the white pillow. Her skin's pale, almost green.

I shift on the bed to face her, stifling a grin that I'm sure she wouldn't appreciate.

She whimpers. "I want off the boat."

"Feel your arms yet?"

"They're gone. The elf stole them."

And I have officially lost the battle and am full-up smiling now. "What elf?"

"The elf that made me drink last night."

"Good news. Elf's gone, and your arm's still here. I can see it." I touch her bicep lightly, pretending I'm not enjoying the feel of her skin beneath the shirtsleeve of her dress that rode up overnight.

She squeals and then grumbles.

"Just me, Laney."

"*Tickles,*" she gasps.

"Huh. Tickles. Weird. Is it like…your arm fell asleep?"

She whimpers. Squeezes her eyes shut.

I stroke a single finger down her bicep.

A strangled noise slips out of her throat.

She doesn't tell me to stop.

"So weird," I say, unable to keep from teasing her. "Just yesterday, I was in the company of a woman who claimed her appendages never fell asleep."

"This is me not telling you I hate you right now."

Wish I could say I didn't hate myself a little right now. But I'm in that spot where I love where I am and know I'm setting myself up for a *colossal* fall when I get home and she goes back to her normal life.

I could tell myself this is closure on an old crush, but that's a stretch.

There's nothing *old* about how I'm starting to feel about her after yesterday.

"What time is it?" she asks. "Where are we supposed to be?"

"It's seven-thirty."

"*At night?*"

"In the morning. Why are you awake? First rule of hang-overs: Sleep until at least noon the next day."

"My body won't *let* me."

"Your arm's still asleep. Clearly parts of you are capable."

She moves her head to the side and pries one eyeball open with another whimper. "Was I a total idiot last night?"

"You were fun."

"Oh, no. Did I cry? I did. Oh, god, I cried. I was fine if I did. I swear. It's like—"

I cut her off with a finger to her lips. "You're so repressed that the only time emotion comes out of you is when alcohol lowers all of your inhibitions enough to let you?"

She cringes. And then cringes again like cringing hurts. "What are you, a therapist?"

"Sure. Let's go with that."

"I'm sorry I cried. I didn't mean to put that on you. Or to drink that much. It was...a long and unexpected day. I'll be much better today."

I stare at her.

She watches me out of one eye for a minute, and then she closes it again.

It's like we're playing *if I can't see you, then you can't see me*.

"The world won't fall apart if you're not perfect, Laney."

"It's so easy for you to say that when *perfect* has never been your standard."

I should roll out of bed. Shower. Go in search of coffee and other hangover foods. Bet fried poi balls would be fascinating on a hangover stomach.

But instead, I lie in that bed while she scrunches her eyelids tightly shut.

"Believe it or not," I tell her quietly, "living down to expectations sucks too."

One lid cracks open a smidge. "How?"

"World sees what it wants to see, even when you try. So when you quit trying, when you give in to the belief that you might as well play the nobody they expect, you start to believe you *are* the nobody. You, however, have always known you're somebody. Even if it's not the somebody you want to be either."

Both eyelids are cracked now. "This is a lot on a hangover," she whispers.

Understatement of the year.

"Ask you something?"

"The last time you asked me that, you threw my entire world off-balance."

I ignore the implied *no*. "You have fun yesterday?"

Her face does all of the answering for her. *Yes. And it was worth it. Until now, when I'm having doubts and regrets and if I squeeze my eyes shut tightly enough again, I won't have to think about the answer to that question and the consequences of what it means.*

Fair enough.

I shove up and off the bed, shaking it as little as possible. "What do you take for a hangover?"

"I don't know. I—I've only been hungover maybe two other times."

My phone has a text from Emma. Looks like she texted both of us, and she's looking forward to brunch with Laney at ten. "Go back to sleep. Don't have to be anywhere for a few hours. I'll be back."

"But—"

"And I'll stay out of trouble," I add dryly.

"I know," she whispers. "You don't look for it. It looks for you."

"I'll watch out for it and avoid it if I see it coming."

A deep sigh comes out of her as her body sags back into the mattress. One of her legs is kicked out from beneath the sheet, and I can see a small bruise forming on her other shoulder.

Probably from where she fell out of bed last night.

"I'm sorry I didn't believe you about your hand yesterday," she adds, even more softly. "It *hurts* to have your arms wake back up."

I smile.

And then I duck out of the bungalow, chuckling to myself.

This won't last. I'll never be the guy a woman like Laney needs in her life, no matter how satisfied I am with myself and my own life.

But I'll make the most of it in the meantime.

18

LANEY

THERE ARE NOT dark enough sunglasses in the world to erase everything that happened in the last twelve hours or so.

Or to block out the sun effectively enough.

"I'm so sorry I made such a fool of myself during your wedding week," I tell Emma as we get settled at a cute little beach bistro overlooking the ocean for a late breakfast. The open windows let in a soft ocean breeze, and beach paintings line the walls behind us. The table's a little wobbly, but there's a pretty fishbowl in the center with more of those knitted hearts in it. Must be a resort theme.

She laughs. "Laney. Seeing you having fun was a *gift*. I'm just sorry you're hurting today."

I grimace.

It *was* fun.

But I feel like an absolute idiot.

"Did Theo behave himself?" Sabrina asks.

She, too, is in dark sunglasses. A lot about last night is

relatively hazy, but I remember she had to go. Something about her Aunt Brenda.

And I'd rather think about that than about how much of a mess I was last night. And how understanding Theo was about it this morning.

"Theo's a pro at handling hangovers," Emma says. "I'm guessing he brought donuts, French fries, fried poi balls because they're handy here and he's always curious, coffee, Diet Coke, and..."

"Fresh-baked cookies," I supply.

Sabrina gasp-moans. "Fresh-baked cookies? How fresh?"

"They were still warm."

"Oh, god. Were they amazing?"

"*Soo* good." Like *let me rethink all of my life choices so that I can now make choices that result in Theo bringing me chocolate chip cookies* good.

Which, naturally, I didn't say to him.

Not that he gave me much of a chance.

He showed up with cookies, dropped three on the bed, and before I could take a single bite, he told me he was going to check on the kittens and disappeared.

Leaving me alone with the knowledge that my moment of rebellion last night led to him having *zero* interest now, despite my growing crush on him.

Growing?

Renewed?

I'm a disaster.

Emma blinks at me. "Fresh-baked cookies?"

"Unless I'm still having drunken hallucinations."

She's frowning. "Chocolate chip?"

"With a dusting of salt on top. And they tasted like melted caramel."

Her frown goes deeper as she reaches for her phone, then shakes her head and drops it back into her purse.

"What's your beef with chocolate chip cookies?" Sabrina asks.

Emma shakes her head. "Nothing. It's nothing."

Sabrina and I share a look.

Clearly not nothing.

"You think he robbed a bakery?" Sabrina asks.

Emma chokes on her water. "*Stop.* He didn't rob a bakery. Laney, I need to hear more about this pig incident yesterday. You didn't make a lot of sense last night."

I reach into my own bag, desperate to move on from talking about Theo.

Do I like him?

Yes.

Do I like him enough that I want to get to know him more?

Yes.

Can I handle that right now?

No. No, I cannot. Because I feel like an idiot. Like a failure at having fun. Like *I'm* the trouble. Like I'm high-maintenance.

Whereas he was nothing but sweet and kind and gentle in ways I didn't expect and can't help craving. "No stories until we're drinking right."

I plop three iridescent insulated wine tumblers onto the table and wait.

And the reaction is worth it.

"*You didn't!*" Emma squeals, which honestly hurts my head a little, but I don't care.

Sabrina bursts out laughing. "Oh my god, *you did.*"

"Seemed appropriate," I say with a grin.

Emma picks up the nearest insulated wine tumbler and lifts it into the sunlight to examine the logo more clearly. "Remember our *Ugly Heiress Society* clubhouse?"

Not long after Theo dubbed us the *ugly heiresses of the Tooth*—Sabrina as an heiress to Bean & Nugget, me to

Kingston Photo Gifts, and Emma to Rocky Roadkill—Sabrina found an old treehouse on her grandparents' property within walking distance from the school. The three of us decided we'd own the crap out of the nickname, make ourselves a fancy club with our rickety new clubhouse, and we'd go there all the time after the bell rang and before we had to get home.

I nod. "We were so lucky that thing didn't fall apart."

"Hey, we don't do rickety treehouses in my family unless we know they're sturdy," Sabrina says.

"Is it still there?" Emma asks.

Sabrina shakes her head. "Aunt Lisa had it torn down after Grandma couldn't make it out to the yard to see if it was still there anymore."

Emma wrinkles her nose, but she doesn't say a bad word about her future mother-in-law. "I guess that was probably the safe choice."

Sabrina grabs her mug and inspects the inscription too. "I can't believe you remembered and did this."

"I can," Emma says softly.

My cheeks get hot. Also, here I go again, fixating on the one man I am absolutely positive has been cured of whatever crush he might've ever had on me. "In retrospect, I shouldn't have taken it so personally when Theo called us that. There's a solid chance one of us—probably me—upset him and he was lashing back, and just based on everything I remember from childhood, it most likely came right on the heels of my mother telling me I needed to learn to dress because my face would never be what found me the right man."

"Oh, honey," Emma whispers.

I wave a hand. "I know she meant well. Like, tempering my expectations, you know?"

"Except you're gorgeous," Sabrina says.

"Not next to you two."

"Are you serious right now?" Emma points to her arm. "Do you *see* the freckles? And that's *with* seven thousand

187

gallons of SPF 100 applied hourly. And let's not talk about how I look like a walking stick with a pointy nose and a pointy chin and *elf ears*. I look *sick*. No matter how much I eat."

"*You* are also gorgeous," Sabrina tells her.

"You have to say that because I'm the bride."

"I choose to say that because I'm your friend who sees all of your beauty. And also who knows you eat all the good things, see your doctor regularly, that your metabolism isn't your fault, and that your face is utterly charming and captivating and you *rock* it."

"And you're easily the most beautiful of the three of us on the inside," I chime in.

"Agreed. I'm a total bitch on the inside." Sabrina grins.

"Me too," I say.

My two best friends find that hilarious.

"I really think I am," I insist. "At least…to some people."

"Those people have provoked you your entire life," Sabrina says dryly.

"But that doesn't mean I have to rise to the occasion and provoke back." I wave my hand. "And back to Emma. How's your wedding week? Is it everything you hoped it would be? What's missing? What else do you need?"

She smiles.

It's one of those glowy smiles that makes her eyes light up, even if they're pinched at the edges. "It's a good week. I have my family. I have my friends. I have my groom. We're in paradise. I have everything."

"But…?" Sabrina says.

"No buts."

There are totally *buts*. "C'mon, Em. What's wrong?" I prod.

She opens her mouth. Closes it again. Then glances around the bistro like she's afraid someone's going to overhear her. "Have you noticed that everything's really…slow?"

"Like island time slow?" Sabrina says, which is complete and total baloney.

"No, like...even slower. Like half the staff isn't here or something. I thought that first day was a glitch, but now I'm getting worried. Chandler was complaining last night that there's only been one day when the bar was open at the pool, and it was thirty minutes past his tee time yesterday before the clubhouse opened so he could get his golf cart. And like... we're almost the only party here, but they still don't have a room for you, Laney. And—"

"Aw, Em, a few staff shortages won't ruin your wedding. You still get to be Mrs. Sullivan by the end of the week." I reach over to squeeze her hand. When I asked what she needed, I thought I'd be calling a cab to run out to a store and pick up a load of candles for her wedding night.

Not that she'd be stressing that the resort isn't living up to expectations.

And did I hear—

I cut off my own thoughts as Sabrina glares at me with the *do not say what I'm afraid you're about to say* look.

Right.

I was drunk last night.

Even if I heard what I think I heard about open bunga-lows, I don't have the full story.

And honestly?

I don't know that I *want* to move rooms.

Nothing to do with Theo, I tell myself, though even I think I'm lying. But I'm not lying about the sadness that would happen if I had less kitten time.

I feel very complicated right now.

"It's just so different to *dream* about your wedding and have these expectations than it is to *live* it," Emma says. "Like, I thought meeting my perfect man would be a fairytale, but being in a relationship is a lot of work. And I thought I'd feel this magical sense of being a princess all week, but instead,

I'm worrying about if my dad and uncle are getting along okay with all of Chandler's family, and why there aren't enough rooms, and if there will be enough food at all the meals, and if Chandler's really having a good time or if he's lying to me for my sake, and if Theo's having fun or if he's starting to feel…well, just if he's enjoying this week too."

"You are officially off worrying duty and hereby ordered to spend the rest of the day at the beach," Sabrina says. "No relatives. No future in-laws. I mean, except me, but I was yours before Chandler was yours, so I don't count as a future in-law, and who counts cousins-in-law anyway? We've already been family forever."

"I'll check in again with the desk about extra rooms," I offer. "And I'll follow up with catering too."

"But you have too much else to do because you're *babysitting my brother*." Emma cringes. "That came out wrong."

"No, no, that came out right," Sabrina says with a smile.

None of us laugh though.

Me chiefly because I have no idea what my face is about to do. "Em, you know I've never been Theo's biggest fan, so when I say I don't think he's causing trouble on purpose, or even that it would *be* trouble if it wasn't your wedding week, that has to count for something, right? Things just *happen* when he's around. Let's be real here. Who sneezes at just the right time to prompt himself getting caught on fire? And who has a collision with a feral pig and then has to hide in the car and wait for a local to rescue you because the *one pig* on the entire island that's rabid is the *one pig* that you hit?"

And who liked it?

This girl.

This good girl right here who had an orgasm that she is *not* telling her best friends about because she's still processing that too.

Along with processing that it was fun.

Nobody died. Not even the pig.

My parents' business didn't fall apart.

Thunderclouds didn't gather and strike us with lightning, and I didn't get pregnant by having a solo orgasm caused by a rocking car and Theo's incredible erection.

' If anything, I got a glimpse at what's possible when I let myself go and have fun.

Which has to be the lamest fun Theo and his penis have ever had in their lives.

Emma frowns. "Do you think they'll catch it and put it down?"

I start.

The pig, Laney. She's not talking about putting Theo's penis down.

"I hope so," Sabrina says. "And then I hope they send it to your dad so the stuffed feral pig can be a first-anniversary gift to Chandler if he doesn't do everything in his power to make you the happiest wife in the whole entire world."

Emma smiles and rolls her eyes. "He's never taxidermied a Hawaiian pig. And he does love checking new animals off his list."

"Theo said the same thing while he was taking pictures of it last night," I report, hoping they can't tell I'm thinking about his penis.

She grins. "Did he ask you to help him put it in the trunk?"

"*Yes.*"

"Did you say no?" Sabrina asks.

"There was literally no other answer. And can you imagine if we'd put it in the trunk before it came to?"

Before *it came.*

I came.

Sabrina giggles.

Emma tries to stifle a laugh and ends up snorting.

"I was trying to be *fun*, but even fun has its limits," I tell them.

I'm sweating. They don't know I'm sweating because I'm thinking about coming on Theo's penis, right?

Sabrina giggles harder.

Emma snorts twice more.

"You wouldn't be laughing if we'd been murdered by an angry pig," I mutter, hoping my brain is tracking the out-loud conversation right. "Hey, where *is* the staff? We need water."

"Coffee and mimosas," Sabrina corrects, still giggling.

"*I* need water. *You* can have a mimosa and all the coffee your caffeinated heart desires."

"We're not taking joy in your suffering, Laney, I promise," Emma says. "It's just the image of the pig chasing Theo all over the inside of that convertible…"

"The glow of happiness at the idea of him shrieking for his life…" Sabrina agrees.

"Nowhere in that equation is you getting hurt."

"Or needing to drink that heavily over anything else the rest of the week."

I wave them both off as I rise. "I'm going in search of beverages to fill our cups. It's fine. All good. If it makes you happy, Em, then that's what I'm here for."

"You both make me happy," she tells us.

But as I head away, I hear her whisper to Sabrina, "You don't think there's any chance he's pulling his charm routine on Laney, do you?"

"Absolutely not," Sabrina whispers back. "He wouldn't cross that line."

I stiffen, but I keep walking like I didn't hear.

I *do* feel like Theo's more than I gave him credit for.

And after what happened in the car last night—which I will definitely not be discussing with them now, for sure, or possibly ever—and then how he took care of me while I was drunk, and then waking up plastered all over him, I thought maybe we were finding some common ground.

Especially after his confession that he's always had to live down to expectations as much as I've had to live up to expectations.

But once he left and took forever to come back, and then disappeared to play with the kittens when I didn't have time to do much more than throw on clothes to come meet Emma for the first event of her wedding that I've been to?

I think he's giving me space to get back to being me.

Or whoever it is I'm trying to become.

Weird stuff happens on vacation.

That's all.

When we get home, everything will go back to normal.

But I don't think that's honestly what I want.

I think what I want is to ask Theo to show me how to have more fun.

And I don't know yet how to handle that.

Or ask for it.

19

THEO

I MOSTLY KEEP myself hidden away in my room until it's time for the joint bachelor-bachelorette party to start later this afternoon. Not in my nature to stand still, do nothing, go nowhere, but the kittens and their mama are good company, and I catch up on some work.

Like my side hustle. That helps. So does being able to do it anywhere.

But I don't talk about it.

Certainly not here. Not now.

Here and now, I'm strolling past the pool on my way to tonight's events, contemplating Laney losing her top yesterday and getting half-hard.

I shouldn't be falling for her again.

But when have I ever listened to *shouldn't*?

"Hi, Theo," Claire pops out from the walkway to the gift shop area. "You weren't at the pool today."

I smile. "Sure I was. You didn't see me? Must've been that stealthy."

She laughs. "You're hilarious."

"It's a curse."

"So you're coming to the bachelorette party?"

Yeah.

The bachelorette party.

It's a dual bachelor-bachelorette party, which I'm fine with.

Better than fine, actually. No interest in going to hang out with my sister's fiancé at a strip club, drinking beer and smoking cigars and pretending like I won't kill him if he touches one of the dancers.

Pretty sure he wouldn't cheat on Emma. That he's not the dick he's playing this week. Or even the better part of this past year.

I mostly tolerated him fine from the time they hooked back up after college until he proposed.

Or maybe he tolerated me until he proposed.

Or until I made a fuck ton of money while he was running his family's business into the ground.

Doesn't take a genius to know that bothers the shit out of him.

Not like I'm rubbing it in his face. He came to me. Not the other way around. And yeah, I'm not really happy that he knows I have a pile of cash.

Em swears she didn't tell him on purpose, that he found out by accident while she was working on my taxes last year, but they also have this *no secrets* rule.

Which apparently doesn't extend to Chandler telling her how her dream wedding's being paid off.

I nod to Claire. "Looks like. You been to one of these before?"

Small talk is where it's at. Easy to pay attention while keeping an eye out for the rest of the wedding party.

Like one of the other bridesmaids who didn't come back to our room at all today, even though I know she should've been done with brunch with Emma and Sabrina hours ago.

Was one of the triplets flirting with her?

Were *multiple* of the triplets flirting with her?

Fuck.

I hope she's not embarrassed.

I should've told her I've also gotten so drunk I cried a time or two.

Shouldn't have taken so long to get back to the room with hangover food.

But I couldn't go back without the cookies.

Couldn't do it.

I wanted Laney to have those cookies.

"You wore a veil with penises on it too?" Claire is staring at me like she doesn't know what to think of me.

I replay the last few bits of our conversation that I wasn't paying attention to, and yep.

She said something like *but you've probably never worn a penis veil to a bachelorette party*, and I said *sure have*, because that's my default.

Yep. I've done that. Name it. I've done it.

I grin and wink at her. "Why not? Made everyone happy."

"What made everyone happy?" Sabrina asks.

She and Laney are lurking behind an enormous hibiscus bush that needs to be trimmed back from the sidewalk.

Laney's poker-faced.

Fuuuuck.

Did she see me wink at Claire?

I'm an idiot. I'm officially an idiot who needs to get his wink under control.

"Theo was just telling me he crashed a bachelorette party in a penis veil once," Claire says.

"I didn't hear about that," Sabrina says.

Code for *if I didn't hear it, it didn't happen.*

I hit her with some solid eye contact. "You don't hear *everything*."

Yep.

That one landed.

Her lip curls while she narrows her eyes at me.

"Are you seriously going to let him get your goat?" Laney asks her. She doesn't wait for an answer and instead grabs me by the elbow. "Theo. Come on. We're sitting at the *back* of the room for instructions."

She's stiff as Princess Plainy-Laney used to be in high school.

And I feel every bit as uncoordinated and dumb as I did back then in the height of my crush-on-her days.

Especially since the feel of her hand on my elbow is giving me goosebumps.

The *good* kind of goosebumps.

And she can probably feel them.

"I had a twitch in my eyelid," I tell her as I hustle to keep up, hoping she's just embarrassed about last night and trying to hide it. "I wasn't winking at Claire."

Laney's quickly becoming one of the highlights of my week.

Don't really want to lose it when I'm dreading this wedding more by the day.

"Mm-hmm. Leftover effect of all of that sand in your eye yesterday?" she asks.

"Must be."

She doesn't believe me.

And she's pissed that I was smiling and winking at another woman.

My dick high-fives my nuts. *She likes us.*

"Fun brunch with Em and Sabrina?" I ask.

"Yep."

"Went long, huh? You left me unsupervised."

"I was supervising *Chandler* instead."

"Ew."

She slides me a look. Her lips twitch, and I grin in triumph.

Made her smile. Or at least *want* to smile. And suppress it.

And for the record—*this* grin that I'm giving Laney?

This one's my best. None of the showboat grin that Claire got.

"Guess babysitting me doesn't look so bad after that, does it?" I nudge her with my elbow.

Her lips twitch more. She makes a sigh-harrumph that I tell myself is her way of getting her face back under control so I don't know that I'm amusing her.

But as she's settling her expression, her gaze wanders to my chest.

I puff it out.

Just a little. Not enough to be obvious, but enough to show off what I've done with my body.

"Why is your shirt always unbuttoned?" she asks me, like that's the reason she's staring.

"It's hot here. You should try it."

"You wish."

"I do. It's freeing. I want you to feel free."

She slides me another look. This one comes with pinkening cheeks and makes me smile harder.

"Ah, fuck, your parents got here, didn't they?" The words fly out of my mouth before I can stop them.

And I should've stopped them.

Because now she's scowling. "No, Theo, my parents are not here yet."

"I didn't mean—"

"It's fine."

"—anything by that. Except that—nope. Nothing. Didn't mean anything at all." Except that her parents are prudish nightmares who taught Laney that fun is bad and duty is all that matters.

"Emma has requested that you and I be a team for the scavenger hunt, and she gave me all of the clues and answers, which I will *not* be sharing with you, so that we can make sure you avoid Chandler."

Already got the clues and answers elsewhere a few hours ago, which I don't really need to tell her. "I haven't seen—fuck. I did see Chandler."

She pauses and looks at me, and then, for the second time in two days, Laney hauls me through the bushes to a more secluded area as the sounds of the voices get louder and closer. She shoots a look up at the sky and pushes me past where we rendezvoused last night to a spot even farther from the lanai and the wedding party, with no coconut trees overhead threatening to drop fruit on us.

Yes, my body crows. *We're having fun in the bushes.*

But, unfortunately, Laney's all business. She keeps her distance while she launches into the inquisition. "What happened?"

I shrug. "I barely overheard a phone conversation, he realized I was there, and he got pissy. Story of my life with Chandler. He sees me—he gets pissy."

If I were Laney, I'd be pulling out a *you have that effect on people*.

Or maybe that's what I expect of her after a lifetime of us picking at each other.

Instead, she's frowning deeper. "What was he talking about?"

"I don't know. Didn't care enough to pay attention."

"Theo."

"Don't know," I repeat. "You know something I don't?"

She opens her mouth.

Closes it.

And then goes pink in the cheeks again.

I start to smile.

She doesn't care that I saw Chandler.

199

She just wanted an excuse to pull me into the bushes.

And look at us, standing inches apart, her leaning into me, me leaning into her...

"I just feel like everyone's keeping secrets and I don't like it," she finally says. "It makes all of this feel *wrong*. And I don't want to feel wrong about Emma's wedding."

My face accidentally agrees with her before I can stop it.

"You feel it too." She angles closer, hesitates like she realizes what she's doing, but then takes a bold step all the way into my space bubble. "You feel like something's wrong here too. What is it? What's going on?"

I have so many secrets right now, I can't even count them. "Laney, this one's not yours to fix."

She frowns. "That's the same thing Sabrina said. But why *can't* it be? This is Emma's *life* that we're talking about, and I feel like I've been asked to sit on the sidelines, and it makes me feel—it makes me feel like I've failed her as a friend," she finishes on a whisper.

"It's not you."

"Isn't it?"

Fuuuuuck. "It's me."

"Theo."

"Not just saying it. It's me. Chandler's issue is with me. The secret is me."

And now I sound like a damn egomaniac.

"How are you the secret?"

Dammit.

Dammit.

Have to give her something. Anything. Preferably something that won't make her recoil in horror. I tilt my head up to look at the sky.

Can I do it?

Can I tell her?

"Theo. I was dead-ass drunk last night and still didn't tell anyone about *you know what*. Why do you think you can't trust me when I'm never, ever, ever drinking again?"

"Because you're perfect—"

She snorts. "I am *so* far from perfect. Want proof? Ask my parents."

"Your parents are dicks." *Shut. The fuck. Up. Theo. Shut the fuck up.*

She sighs. "Why does Chandler have a problem with you?"

Well, Laney, I started making faceless videos of myself knitting with my woody hanging out while telling women that they should have higher standards, somehow became the most popular creator on GrippaPeen.com, and he doesn't like it that my dick makes more money in a week than his brain could lose in a year.

Nope.

Not telling her that.

Besides, if that was the only problem, then it would be *his* problem. Not mine. "Reverse it, princess."

"Fine. Why do you hate Chandler?"

I should not tell her this.

I shouldn't.

It's mine to bear. Not hers.

But it's an easier secret than telling her I have a side hustle as an online adult entertainment star. And I've been *bearing* this other secret all by myself since Emma and Chandler hooked up again when they both moved home after college. Everyone thinks they're so perfect and cute, the over-achieving daughter of the town taxidermist and the chosen son who's taking over running Bean & Nugget.

Laney won't stop asking until she has a reason.

So I'll give her one.

I suck in a deep breath and make myself look her in the eye. "You remember the Snaggletooth statue go-kart incident?"

She nods once.

"Chandler was driving. He told everyone it was me."

She gasps.

Like literally gasps out loud. "He was—"

"*Shh*." I put a finger to her mouth and immediately wish I hadn't.

Jesus, her lips are soft. And plump. And pink. And hot.

"Theo," she whispers, "*you went to jail for that.*"

"My word against his. Who's gonna believe me?"

"But—"

"It was years ago. And I came out of it with a better understanding of what I did and didn't want for my life. Who cares now?"

"*You* care."

I shrug. "Shouldn't. Changed my life for the better."

"It was *jail*."

"It was a wake-up call."

"But *he lied*. And *you paid the consequences*."

"Wasn't fully innocent. I was there. I dared him. And you know what they say. *So much potential. Learned his lesson.* And now he's the CEO of a budding café empire in the middle of the mountains, and I happen to really like where my life has taken me since. So it turned out all right from where I'm standing."

She flinches so hard I feel it in my own chest.

Or maybe that's the weight of all of the exaggerations that just came out of my mouth making my heart heavy.

"You still shouldn't have paid for his mistake," she whispers. "That's not fair."

And now my chest is feeling something else.

Warmth. Comfort. Relief.

She believes me.

She believes me.

"Long time ago," I repeat.

"Does Emma know?"

"You know she and Chandler don't keep secrets." I keep

my face as straight as I can so as not to clue Laney in to the fact that I believe *Emma* doesn't keep secrets from *Chandler*, but I'm not sure it goes the other way.

"Does *Sabrina* know?"

"What doesn't Sabrina know?"

"But she never—of course she didn't. Why would she tell me? But why didn't she—"

"Laney. Long time ago. Let it go."

She studies me like she's looking for what I'm not saying. For the parts of the story I'm leaving out.

None of those parts really matter though.

Not to me.

"You want me to let it go, but it's bothering you enough to cause problems between you and Chandler."

Dammit. I hate logic. "You believe me," I say instead of making more excuses about why Chandler would be on my shit list now.

That is what matters to me.

That she believes me.

She flinches. "I'm sorry if I ever gave you the impression I wouldn't."

"Wasn't the most reliable guy for a lot of years." It's true. Hiding from who I was back then won't change it.

"But you *own* what you do. *I didn't do it* isn't a phrase in your vocabulary. So if you say you didn't do it, why wouldn't I believe you?"

"Because I don't want my sister to marry a douchebag."

Fuck.

Fuck fuck *fuck*.

That definitely wasn't supposed to come out of my mouth.

"I don't mean—" I start, but she cuts me off.

"Honestly, if they'd started dating in the last year, he wouldn't be who I would've picked for her either, but then, there aren't many people I'd pick for Emma. She's just too *good*. He makes her happy, though. He has for a long time. I know he loves her, and you know she can't wait to start a family with him, and this is *her* choice. Not ours."

Ours.

I like when she says *ours*.

She wrinkles her nose again. "And really, in the Tooth, she could do a lot worse."

"I'd rather be alone than do worse."

She studies me again, and once again, entirely too closely. "Have you told her how you feel? That it still bothers you?"

"Tensions are high. Weddings are hard. I probably pushed some shit too much in the past few years and did things to him I don't even remember now. Probably just as much my fault as anyone's. I won't ruin this for her because I'm having a wallow fest. I'll get over it." I hold out a hand before she can object or use some more logic and reason to tell me that I should say something to Emma. "C'mon, forced date. Let's go kick ass in this scavenger hunt."

"You're right," she says slowly. "Weddings are hard."

She slips her hand in mine, her face a study in *something is broken and I can't fix it*, and I feel it again.

Warmth. But not the bad kind that makes me want to shed all of my clothes to get comfortable.

The *good* kind.

It *also* makes me want to strip off all of my clothes, but for an entirely different reason. And *this* good kind comes with feeling like I don't need to strip.

Like I'm okay however I am.

I know it's a lie. It's a temporary thing. A vacation fluke that'll end the minute she finds out what I do in my spare time.

But for this moment, it's real.

20

LANEY

THE LAST TIME my life was normal, I was on an airplane, blissfully ignorant of exactly how many complications my best friend's dream wedding week would bring.

And I should be happy for her—for *them*—finally being here.

I should be.

But I can't quite dig deep enough to force it right now.

Emma's beaming. She's *glowing*. I'm not sure I've ever seen her so happy as she hugs family and friends on the tiki-torch-lined lanai while she and Chandler make the rounds of greeting everyone.

She was born to be a bride.

And she'll do great as a wife and a mother too. Having a big family is basically all she's ever wanted for as long as I've known her.

But I wish I didn't know what Theo just told me.

I can't believe *Theo went to jail for Chandler*.

My mind is blown.

It's blown over something both men—and my best friends —have known for over a decade. Something they all got over —mostly—a long time ago. I need to let it go.

It would be easier, though, if Chandler didn't look like he's carrying the weight of a thousand moons, which isn't something I've noticed about him before, but now I'm wondering if weddings stress him out, like Theo said, or if he's always been like this and I had blinders on because I knew how much Emma adored him.

And he's never made me mad the way Theo did.

I know Emma's complained about him more this past year, but that felt pretty normal. Don't all couples fight more when they're planning a wedding?

I've been on enough phone calls at work with happily engaged couples breaking down over misplaced expectations with their custom orders to have a firm belief that planning a wedding is the true test of a couple's commitment to each other.

But should I have looked closer?

I'm struggling to smile through hugging Emma and Chandler as they reach us when I'd rather be hugging Theo and telling him that he's not a bad person, and that I'm sorry for every time I acted like a stuck-up snot-bucket to him, that I wish I could've removed my *good people do good things and bad people do bad things* black-and-white opinions years ago.

Decades ago.

"Could've saved a lot of money if we just hugged everyone every time we saw them back home," Chandler says to Emma, who laughs and hushes him.

Theo's cheek twitches.

The two men don't hug.

Or shake hands.

Or acknowledge each other at all, which is frankly weird.

Theo's smiled at *everyone* this week. Me. Sabrina. Claire. His dad and uncle. The triplets. The resort staff.

He even smiled at Aunt Brenda while he was taking her down a notch last night.

"Any hints on what's at the end of the scavenger hunt?" I ask Emma, hoping to distract her from the tension between her fiancé and her brother.

"I don't even know," she tells me. "It was an option from the resort. They put it all together. Oh, honey, look—Cecelia made it!"

They dash off to greet their newest arrival, and I look at Theo.

Not because Emma was clearly trying to find any excuse to not have the two men stand together a minute longer, but because *the resort put it together.*

"Do you have a bad feeling about this?" I whisper.

"It's fine."

He doesn't elaborate while he scans the room.

I look around too, wondering exactly what he's looking for.

"Theo, I don't know if you've noticed this, but—"

"I noticed. Took care of it."

"You—"

"Scavenger hunt's set."

"It—"

"I checked."

I stare at him.

He lifts his brows.

"You know I kinda have a thing about fixing problems," I say.

He grins. "Kinda noticed."

"It's really…attractive…when other people do it first."

He holds eye contact for a solid fourteen years while I silently beg him not to mock me for calling him attractive.

This is hard.

It's so hard.

But he is. He's attractive. And if I don't tell him so, he'll flirt with other women and wink at them and make me feel like a frumpy, jealous asshole again.

Or maybe he'll still flirt with other women.

Maybe he doesn't care that I think he's attractive.

But I need to take this leap.

I need to be brave. I need to be bold. I need to be *fun*.

His mouth twitches up in one corner, and I want to kiss it.

Oh, *god*, do I want to kiss it.

He angles closer to me, that grin morphing into a smoldery smile. "Laney Kingston, are you admitting that my secret competence might turn you on?"

"Yes," I whisper.

His grin gets bigger.

But then it freezes.

"Be right back," he murmurs.

"But—"

"*Laney*. Oh my god, Laney Kingston?" Addison Hunter steps in front of me and smothers me in a hug while I gape at Theo's retreating back. "I can't believe it's you! I haven't seen you since high school."

Freaking Theo.

Where is he going?

Why is he leaving *now*?

We were having a moment. Weren't we?

"I heard you're taking over for your parents as one of the youngest next CEOs in the country," Addison gushes. "That's so crazy. I remember when they just printed shirts for our soccer teams. And now they practically own the photo gift industry."

"Yeah. It's pretty cool." Where did he go? There's Sabrina. Does she know where he went?

Nope. She's not paying attention to me or Theo.

Not that Theo's anywhere that someone could pay attention to him. He has totally and completely disappeared.

"Laney?" Addison says.

"I'm so sorry," I say quickly. "I think I just started my period and I need to find the bathroom."

Liar, I yell at myself internally.

My mother's cringing back home, and she doesn't know why. But I know she is.

I can feel it.

We don't talk about periods. They are *private* matters and we all pretend for my father's sake that they don't exist.

But it's the perfect excuse to dash away from the lanai and see where Theo went.

Yes. Yes, I'm *that woman*, running after a guy who ran away when I told him I thought he was attractive.

Doesn't take me long to realize it's futile.

Of course I can't find him.

It's Theo.

His brain works in ways I can't possibly understand.

No matter how much I want to.

But I still look all over. The gift shop. The alcove where I keep pulling him aside to talk. The beach. Our bungalow.

I do it all quickly, fully aware that I'm chasing a man who just disappeared because I awkwardly told him he was *attractive*.

And I should just face the fact that this isn't where I'm supposed to aim my attraction.

Spending time with Theo is giving me the courage to leap out of my box. But I shouldn't consider it a long-term thing or anything.

That would probably end poorly for me.

How fast would he get bored?

So fast.

I head back toward the lanai, feeling like a total and complete idiot, and *freaking Theo is waiting for me there*.

Not just waiting for me.

Slipping an arm around my waist like we're dating or something.

"Where *were* you?" I whisper. *God*, this feels good to have him holding me against him. And the view under his open shirt—*hello*, chest tattoos. Oh, *look*. That's a mountain lion peeking over the summit of the mountain we can see from Marmot Cliff back home amidst the landscape of his other tattoos. And it's *gorgeous*.

Whoever did his ink did an amazing job.

I'm no longer tempted to ask him why he doesn't button his shirts.

I don't want to button his shirt.

"Checking the catering," he replies.

"Catering's fine. I stopped by the front desk this afternoon and confirmed it myself."

He smiles and shakes his head. "Heard you got your period."

Ocean, swallow me now. *Hi, you're attractive. Let me tell you about how I'm bleeding out of my no-no box.* "Oh, god. I forgot. *I forgot.*"

"You forgot you got your period?"

"I forgot Addison's as big of a gossip as Sabrina except Sabrina knows when to just *gather* the gossip and *not share it*."

"You need a painkiller or anything? Heating pad? Shoulder to cry on? Axes to throw?"

Is he serious?

He shrugs at my expression. "Mom wasn't around when Em started hers, and Dad didn't know what to do, so I figured I might as well do *something* right as a big brother."

Yep.

I totally and completely have a crush on this man. "I remember that," I whisper. Then I shake my head. "But I did *not* start my period. I used it as an excuse to look for you."

"Nobody else here knows it was an excuse," he assures me. "We could beg off. Say you're not feeling well. At least two-thirds of the groom's family is already uncomfortable being in the same room as a woman who would dare to bleed out of her no-no box."

I choke on air.

Is he reading my mind? Does he know I literally just thought that?

Are we on a wavelength?

Oh my god.

The *only* reason he'd say *no-no box* is if...is if...is if my mother said it to him.

She's the only person in all of the Tooth who calls vaginas *no-no boxes*.

"We are *not* leaving *one more* wedding event," I say like the frumpy, flat-bottomed hag that I'm trying so desperately to *not* be.

He grins and presses a kiss to my temple like he's *actually* my date.

And I kinda like it.

Until I remember my parents are arriving tomorrow and this is *not* what they need to see.

Not yet.

Shut the fuck up, Laney, I order myself.

Yes, with the *fuck* and all.

Theo's a decent guy. I shouldn't have judged him, and my parents shouldn't either. And even if he *did* place an order with us a few years ago for a blanket with boobs on it to use as a cape, I don't think that should define him. And definitely not as the miscreant my parents have always labeled him as.

"Did my mother ever talk to you about no-no boxes?" I ask.

"I like being stuck on the subject of your no-no box. And the word *vagina* doesn't bother me either."

I can't tell if I'm turned on or embarrassed, but I know which one I *want* to be. "Are you making fun of me?" I whisper.

He squeezes me tighter. "I'm trying to have fun with you, but if it's making you uncomfortable, I'll stop."

"I *want* to have fun."

"All different kinds of fun. Don't have to like them all."

I peer up at him.

He's watching the room around us like he's waiting for something, but I don't get the feeling he's unengaged.

Is he *too* engaged?

Is *he* trying to play it cool with offering to show me fun?

Addison isn't watching us. She's chatting with Theo's dad and uncle and cousin. Sabrina and Decker are whispering furiously. Most of Chandler's family is fawning over Emma.

Everything seems pretty normal.

Lucky stands and clinks a spoon against his glass before I can figure out the answers to all of my questions. "Ladies and gentlemen, thank you all for coming to Chandler and Emma's bachelor-bachelorette party. In just a minute here, we're gonna be handing out clues for you to scurry off into the night on a scavenger hunt to find the world's most epic bridal shower gift. You don't get to keep it, but you do get to give it to the happy couple. You ready for this?"

There are probably sixty people here now, and they all erupt in cheers.

"A'right! That's what I love to hear. Party people finding the presents! Yeah! Let's *do this!* My brothers, roll out the clues."

Theo adjusts himself so he's looping his arm around my shoulders, his hand hanging casually over my collarbone.

And it's a thrill.

A serious, *a sexy man is touching me* thrill.

I know this is just Theo. He flirts with anything that moves. He puts fun above all else. And this is *fun*.

But it's also making me warm and fuzzy and more than a little turned on inside.

I tell myself it's because I'm basically playing besties with the baddest bad boy to ever *bad boy* in the Tooth. That it's the thrill of rebelling against the idea that he's off-limits to a woman from a proper upper-middle-class family running, as Addison said, the biggest photo gift business in the country.

But thinking about him being not good enough for me makes me want to hit something at the same time.

He's *not* a bad guy. Sabrina's right. Since he discovered legal boundaries, he's mostly harmless fun.

Who apparently solved an issue with the scavenger hunt before I ever thought to wonder if there was a problem with it. "When you say *you fixed this*," I say quietly as Jack approaches us with a basket full of clues, "what exactly do you mean?"

"In the interest of your innocence when everything goes to shit, as it inevitably will since I have done a good deed, I'm not telling. But before everything goes to shit, you should know that I did the best I could with what I had when the resort didn't do what they're fucking being paid to do."

Jack stops in front of us. He looks at Theo, then at me, and then at Theo's arm. "Ooooh, somebody's parents are gonna have a shit fit," he says.

"I know," Theo says. "Dad was hoping I'd go for a chick with a motorcycle and more tats than me, maybe a longer rap sheet too, but here we are."

Jack chortles. "Here, Laney. Bet you figure this out faster than he does. Good luck and don't cheat." He points two fingers to his own eyes, then at Theo, then back to his own eyes. "I'm watching you."

"Not as close as I'm watching you."

They both grin and do a complicated handshake, then Jack moves on to the next couple.

"Doesn't that bother you?" I ask Theo.

"That Jack, Lucky, and Decker think you're worth protecting?"

"That they have to tear you down to say something nice about someone else."

"I've dragged all of their asses out of the bar one too many nights for me to take any of them seriously. And the day any of those dudes finds a classy-ass woman who takes him down a billion pegs will be the day I'm standing in line to say the same, then beat the shit out of anyone else who insults him the way I get to."

We're following everyone else off the lanai, even though Theo and I both apparently know where all of the clues will take us. The staff is supposed to lay out food while we're scavenger hunting, and then we'll have fun again.

"You sound like you're their brother," I say.

"Brothers of the heart. Sullivan triplets are fun." He grins, then takes the clue, holds it up, and reads it. *"You will be very lucky tonight. In bed."*

"That is *not* what our clue says. Hey. You're holding it upside down. And backwards."

"You sure?"

"Theo."

"Wanna do something bad, Laney?"

A thrill zings through me from my nose to my vagina. "It's Emma's wedding week," I whisper.

He steers me off the path behind the cute little resort bistro on the beach where Sabrina, Emma, and I had a very, *very* long brunch today—all fun, most of it waiting longer than I've ever waited for a pastry before in my life—and then he does something that makes me squeak in horror.

He twists the handle on the back door, the door marked *staff only*, and pulls me inside.

"Oh my god, we can't be here," I whisper in the dark.

"You know what this is?"

"It's the bistro kitchen. We're not staff. We can't—shut up. I know what you're thinking. *Rule-following Plainy-Laney can't have any fun.* But *this will get us kicked out,* Theo. We're not supposed to be here."

"You know who *is* supposed to be here?"

"*Not. Us.*"

"The staff making dinner for Emma's bachelorette party."

"What?"

He flicks on a light.

I wince.

"The staff, Laney. The kitchen staff. The wait staff. The staff that the front desk told you would be here? *They're not here.*"

Oh, no. Oh, no no no.

"So. You wanna have some fun and help me solve another problem, or you wanna stand here talking about how we're not supposed to be here?"

My brain is breaking even as it's lighting up at the idea of solving a problem.

Pretty sure he knows this is like talking dirty to me.

"Why isn't the staff here?"

"Not the most immediate concern, princess."

"Okay. Okay." I blow out a slow breath. "Right. Problem. Let's fix this. Is there food? I can't cook. I mean, I can cook, but I can't cook for—"

"Were those tacos good last night?" he asks.

I blink at him.

"Laney. *Were the tacos good last night?*"

"They were until they made us hit a wild pig."

He grins. "That's the spirit. You in? Or are you gonna let Emma freak out when there's no food for her guests in an hour?"

When he puts it that way, is there any other choice for a solution?

I fling my arms around him and impulsively kiss his cheek. "Are you kidding? You know I'm in. Let's do this."

21

THEO

NOTHING INSPIRES fast action like telling Laney there's a problem. She's on the phone ordering enough tacos for a hundred before we make it to the parking lot, even though we have sixty people at most to feed.

It's hot as hell.

"Oh, crap," she says suddenly. "How are we picking them up?"

I pull a set of keys out of my pocket and unlock the Jeep three spaces down.

She looks at the Jeep.

Then at me.

Then back at the Jeep.

Then back at me.

"How—what—when—"

She's cute when she's surprised. "Some of us can adult even when we don't want to."

"You rented another car?"

I shrug. "Don't like being trapped. Think that many tacos

will fit in this thing?"

Better question is if the restaurant can whip up that many tacos and fixin's in the next hour.

And the next question after that is if she'll throw herself at me again.

Hope so.

I can still feel those lips on my cheek, and I want more. Hurting later? Don't care. Closure? Whatever.

All I care about is that this is my chance with Laney, and I don't want to fuck it up.

"I don't want to know what your credit card bill will look like when this is over," she mutters. "And I'm getting dinner. *No arguments.*"

"Whatever makes you happy. Hop in. This one has pig radar."

She laughs even as she side-eyes me while I open the door for her. You can see the question on her face. *What do you do that you can afford this, and if you can't afford this, just how soon will you be filing for bankruptcy?*

But she doesn't ask.

And I want to kiss her.

I want to pretend she wouldn't be horrified if she knew my naked junk was paying off my credit cards, and I want to kiss her. Right here against the side of the Jeep. I want to kiss her until she can't think straight, until she's yanking my shirt off and running her hands all over my body and begging me to make her feel good everywhere.

I want to mess up her hair. Her makeup. Leave her so satisfied she can't remember her own name.

"Theo?"

Fuck me.

When she says my name like that, when she looks at me with her eyes going dark and darting to my mouth, I think she wants it too.

Like that wasn't just an excited *you gave me one of my favorite things to do* kiss on the cheek.

I clear my throat and gesture for her to climb in.

She licks her lips.

My dick goes full salute.

"I *really* like being on a team with you," she whispers.

And then, thank fuck, she climbs into the Jeep.

I take my time walking around it to get into the driver's seat, doing some deep breathing and ordering my dick to get himself under control.

She likes *this* Theo.

She likes what I let her see.

Would she still like me if she knew I've spent the past three years making videos of my woody for anyone with twenty bucks a month to see?

And that thought—that she'd judge me if she knew *all* of who I am—is what keeps me from pulling the Jeep to the side of the road and testing that theory that she wants to kiss me too.

She steers the conversation on the drive and while we wait, sticking to safe topics like rollercoasters and if tacos or hamburgers are better food.

Rollercoasters are overrated.

And talking about hamburgers makes me hungrier than talking about tacos, but both make me want to gnaw my own arm off.

I might not show my face in my videos, but I show off my six-pack. Not risking losing it so long as I'm making a difference in the world.

Which I don't share with Laney.

I'm a complicated inspirational porn star isn't at the top of the list of things I discuss with women when I don't see us having a future.

Not that I've seen myself having a future with *any* woman since my channel took off. Didn't expect relationship paranoia would come with financial success, but here we are.

The restaurant pulls off a miracle, and Laney and I are back at the resort unloading tacos before most of the scavenger hunters have returned.

Sabrina's first.

Naturally.

And her eyes almost bug out of her head when she sees us rolling in carts of tacos. "What... No, you know what? I don't want to know. What I *do* want to know is what's in this big-ass box that was at the end of the treasure hunt and who in the ever-loving hell thought it would be a good idea to give a couple something this huge for a *destination wedding gift*, but I'm not asking that either."

She and Decker, her scavenger hunt partner, jump in to help us unpack everything before Emma gets back.

Yeah, fine, before her *beloved* gets back too.

I didn't do this for him though.

Sabrina mutters something to Laney about this resort seriously not living up to the dreams Emma's had since she was little, but everyone's all smiles by the time the rest of the wedding guests trickle back onto the lanai.

Uncle Owen sees me, makes the finger guns, then cackles and walks over to the buffet to help himself to a taco as Emma and her groom return. Dad was paired with Aunt Brenda, and he looks like he needs a stiff drink and a few stuffed elk heads to talk to for him to get over it when he gets back. And he's not much of a drinker.

Though he's totally a talker when it comes to talking to his art.

"Oh my gosh, *what* is that thing?" Emma points to the very large wrapped package sitting at the head table.

And by *very large wrapped package*, I mean it takes up most of the table, and Sabrina and Decker probably needed a hand cart to get it back here once they found it.

Laney's eyeing me.

I know she knows where it came from.

Been sitting in our room for the past few days. And she's not one to miss things.

"It's your present," Sabrina says.

Emma's eyes flare wide. "I really hope that's a box in a box in a box."

"Whoever bought it, ships it, babe," Chandler says.

She smiles indulgently at him.

I look away.

Don't want to see it.

His interference in my conversation with that single mom last night changed something.

Or maybe Laney's reaction to a decade-old truth changed something.

Either way, it's harder to watch him with my sister today. Harder to accept that someone so important in my life wants to spend hers with someone who can regularly be such a dick.

"Is everyone back?" Em asks. "Oh my gosh, everyone, eat. We have...tacos?"

"Looks like," Sabrina says.

There's a flash of confusion before she smiles hard, like it's taking effort. "Great! Awesome. We have tacos! Eat, please, while they're hot."

Emma loves tacos.

I know she loves tacos.

So why—

"I don't like tacos," Chandler says to Emma.

It's not loud.

But it's loud enough to explain why Em's not thrilled.

It's also loud enough that Laney's back snaps straight and a glower ignites her face.

Shouldn't have told her.

Should *not* have told her.

"Let it go," I mutter.

"You freaking *saved dinner*."

"Technically, you did."

She growls.

And yet again, I'm half-hard in public because of this woman.

"I don't know why they swapped out tacos," Emma's saying to Chandler. "I'll go find someone and ask."

Sabrina slides up to my sister. "I'll go ask," she says. "You eat. Enjoy. And then I want to know what's in this massive present."

Laney shoots me another look and pulls me farther from the bride and groom. "What's in the present?" she asks.

"Why would I know?"

"*Theo.*"

I grin and wink. "You think I know because big's my style."

She pins me with a look featuring dilated pupils, that soft spot fluttering quickly in her neck, and yeah.

I need to sit down.

Not because having a woody embarrasses me.

More because I don't want to cause a scene.

For Emma's sake.

"Is it fun?" Laney whispers as she sinks into the chair next to me.

Takes a minute to catch up to the fact that she's asking about the present and not the toy in my pants. "I think so."

She smiles. But it's accompanied by stress lines on her forehead.

I scoot my chair closer to hers. "It's not that bad," I tell her. "Other people will think it's funny too."

"No, I'm sure it's funny. I was just thinking that if the resort didn't *make the dinner she paid for*, after telling me everything was under control, what else are they going to miss? Will *the wedding* be ready? Who's providing the officiant? Who's setting up the chairs? The decorations? The catering and the music and the cake for the reception? *All of it?*"

I open my mouth, then shut it again.

"I'm camping out at the front desk all night to talk to management if I have to," she adds.

I don't just want to kiss those stress lines in her forehead.

I want *all* of it.

I want to feel even a fraction of the love this woman has for my sister aimed at me.

And that's always been my fascination with Laney.

She cares. She's invested. She might follow the rules and be a stickler, but she loves, and she loves *big*.

There's not much she wouldn't do for the people she loves.

She agreed to babysit *me*, didn't she? And I know that's the last thing she wanted to do when she got here.

But now?

"Oh my god, you *two*." Addison drops into the seat next to us with a plate loaded down with tacos and tortilla chips. "I would *not* have called this. But I should've. Opposites attract, right? You're adorable. For real. Are your parents shitting total bricks over this?"

Laney doesn't flinch or rear back or choke on air.

She simply shifts that frown to Addison. "Why would my parents be upset about choices I make as the fully-grown, competent, rational adult that they raised me to be?"

My stomach grumbles in the silence that is Addison freezing in confusion with her taco halfway to her mouth.

She's not wrong. Laney's parents *hate* me.

Probably should confess to being responsible for that graffiti on their car not long after the *leave Delaney's no-no box alone* conversation in high school before her parents arrive.

But I'm pretty stunned myself at Laney's response, honestly. She's *always* worried what her parents will think.

Swear I overheard her whispering something about that to Sabrina in the last two days.

"I—you know parents," Addison stutters. "They never let us go."

"That's their problem then, isn't it?"

My stomach grumbles again. I ignore it.

Does she mean it?

Would she honestly, fully, truly tell her parents to fuck off if they weren't willing to accept her choices?

Would she tell them to fuck off for *me*?

Laney frowns at me. "When's the last time you ate? C'mon. Taco time."

"I'm good."

The frown turns into a full-on *I will eviscerate you if you don't stand up and get me the hell away from Addison immediately*.

And it makes me smile like smiling is the only thing that matters.

"Yep. You're right. I'm hungry." I order my dick to get down, which works better when I pair the instruction with thinking about Aunt Brenda getting it on with my Uncle Owen, and I rise from the table and follow Laney to the line for tacos.

"I haven't seen you eat at all in the past two days," she muses.

"You're not the only one with ninja skills."

She meets my eyes, then looks down at where my shirt is gaping open.

"Don't," I mutter.

"You're not eating."

"I'm eating."

"Why aren't you eating?"

"*I'm eating.*"

"What are you eating?"

I force a smile. "If you give a Laney a bone…"

"This isn't about me making sure you don't pass out in the

middle of Emma's wedding and it's not about me being *right* and it's not about *rules*. This is about the fact that *human beings need to eat*, and you're—you're—" she waves a hand over my gaping shirt "—you're *this*, and that takes diet and exercise no matter how much all of those ripped guys on TikTok pretend it's just natural and that men don't have body issues."

"I—" I cut myself off, not at all sure what to say in response.

"You're a human being with needs that too many people around you overlook," she finishes.

I'm stunned.

Utterly. Fucking. Stunned.

High School Theo would hit back. Make her feel like shit for suggesting I'm a fuckup that no one cares enough about to worry over my basic well-being.

But hungry Theo who's been hung up on this woman for longer than I can remember, even when I didn't want to be? Hungry Theo, who *doesn't* eat enough because I know what I have going now won't last forever, so I need to look my best for as long as I can?

Especially since the entire package of me—my dick, my abs, my knitting, my stories—have me getting more validation in the comments of my videos than I've gotten in my own real life in ages.

Possibly ever.

Yeah, that Theo, the one getting *validation* from *comments on the internet* has a few issues.

And Emma hasn't noticed my diet. My dad hasn't noticed my diet. My buddies on the construction crew haven't noticed my diet.

But Laney has.

I swallow hard. "Okay."

She studies me too closely.

Way too closely.

Like she knows I'm terrified I'll lose my six-pack. That strangers won't tell me I inspired them or comforted them or lifted them up so much the day my body isn't hard and tight.

The GrippaPeen thing was an accident, but it's the best accident of my life.

And the worst at the same time.

Laney doesn't say anything else while we make our way to the front of the line.

My stomach growls harder while the scent of tacos gets stronger.

We're almost to the front of the line when Chandler's voice makes my face twitch.

"What the hell?" he says.

Emma makes a noise. "*Chandler*. I told you. No peeking."

"It's a fucking *human hamster ball*," he hisses.

"It is *not*."

"It *is*. Look." He rips the fancy wrapping paper off the box at the head table, and Emma's face goes through about forty-six different emotions while she studies the box.

Laney angles closer to me. "Is it really a human hamster ball?"

"Two," I murmur back. "Blow-up style. For working out their frustrations after an argument."

She stifles a noise, then double-stifles it with a hand thrown over her mouth.

"Are you laughing or crying?" I ask.

Her eyes answer for her.

She's laughing.

Jackpot.

And she's not the only one.

Giggles and chuckles cascade over the lanai.

"When do we get to come over for game night at your place?" Jack asks.

"Dude, I only want in if they're not doing freaky

newlywed stuff in those. Like, I need to see it bleached before I climb in," Decker calls.

"Isn't your yard pretty hilly, Chandler?" Lucky chimes in.

"Oh my god, they're the perfect size for my dog too!" Sabrina says.

"Why?" Laney whispers to me, her voice strangled like she's trying not to laugh still.

"Who doesn't need a set?" I whisper back with a conspiratorial grin.

She muffles another laugh behind her palm.

Home fucking run.

Except for the part where Chandler's turning a glacial glare on me.

He doesn't say anything.

Doesn't have to.

Emma looks at me too, and she winces.

Dammit.

Just *dammit.*

When does she take *my* side?

She told me she wanted a set. Dad had a paper sitting out at Thanksgiving with all of the holiday shopping ads in it, and we were looking through it before Chandler got his panties in a bunch, and she pointed to the human hamster balls and cracked up and said they'd be fun.

"Where's the real present?" Chandler asks.

"Honey, we're getting married in paradise," Emma says. "It doesn't matter."

"*He stole my real present.* He swapped my dinner, and he stole the real present."

Laney snaps straight.

"Don't—" I start, but it's too late.

"The tacos are my doing," she announces. "Resort catering goofed. There wasn't food. I got tacos. And that's an *awesome* present. If you don't want it, I'll take it back. The resort goofed there too. It was a glitchy day. You're in *fucking paradise*. Quit being a baby."

"…do that," I finish.

Chandler gapes at her.

Emma's face has twisted into such utter confusion that she probably can't see straight.

"But—but—but you don't do funny shit," Chandler says.

Emma winces harder. "Chandler—"

"And you know I hate tacos," he adds.

"Emma loves them." The deadly calm in Laney's voice has such a high degree of warning in it that my balls should be shriveling into cold, dead, dried-out walnuts.

Instead, having her defend me—and make no mistake, everyone on this lanai knows that's what she's doing—is making me want her.

Badly.

Not for closure.

Not for a vacation fling.

For *everything*.

Time to go.

I can't do this.

I want her too much.

I can't want Laney this much while knowing that even stepping-out-of-her-box Laney wouldn't appreciate finding out she's flirting with an adult entertainment star.

That's too far.

While chatter starts up again about who brought the present and if it's funny or tasteless and who still wants to play and who loves tacos, I angle back until I'm at the edge of the lanai.

And then I disappear.

If I don't—if I wait for Laney—I'll do far worse.

And on a day when I already feel like I'm on the verge of losing my sister, my heart isn't up for the pain of having one more dream dashed.

22

LANEY

THEO'S MISSING.

Again.

And this time, I'm not slipping out of the party to look for him because I promised Emma I'd make sure he didn't cause problems for Chandler.

This time, I'm slipping out of the party because I'm worried about him.

If everything Emma touches turns to gold—and it truly does—then everything Theo touches apparently turns to dust.

And that's not fair.

Not when he's trying as hard as I am to help Emma have the wedding of her dreams.

Don't tell me he's not.

I have zero doubt if I'd told Chandler that I had to substitute in a gift at the end of the scavenger hunt, he would've laughed.

It's like he *wants* to be mad at Theo.

And that's irritating the *shit* out of me.

I check the beach first. No sign of Theo. Our bungalow is next. Also not there.

Not even with the kittens and their mama.

The rental Jeep is still in the parking lot, so if he went somewhere, it's on foot.

He could've gone any direction, and he could be anywhere.

I check the party one more time—no Theo, no surprise—and then text Sabrina for his number while I head back toward our room one more time.

But as I'm passing the bistro, I realize there's a light on in the kitchen.

And I smell something sweet.

I start to think *he wouldn't*, remember this is Theo we're talking about, and I circle the building.

When I poke my head in the back door, I'm both surprised and also not to see him inside.

He's stripped off his shirt and only flipped on a single light in the white-and-steel kitchen. The prep table is a mess of flour and sugar, butter, eggs, chocolate chips, and dirty spoons and bowls. He's pulling a tray of cookies out of the oven.

And it smells like heaven.

Also like my hangover cure this morning.

Emma knew. She knew he found a place to make home-made cookies.

I slip in the back door and let it close behind me.

His shoulders bunch like he heard me.

"Cross my heart, I won't freak out about rules," I say quietly. "Those smell too good."

"You missed dinner."

"Eh. I had tacos yesterday. *You* missed dinner."

"Shouldn't be here."

"Me? You? Both of us?"

"You."

"It shouldn't be only your responsibility to play nice with your sister's fiancé. He should've said thank you. You've done a lot for them this week, and I don't care what his reason might be, it's not right that he's being an ass about it."

"Go away, Laney."

His gruff dismissal is a cannonball to the heart, which is the last thing I'd expect.

Theo has been a pain in my ass for years. But I'm realizing I've misjudged him. Or at least never taken the time to look at the man he's grown into instead of the boy I assumed he'd stay his whole life.

Never thought about *why* he does what he does.

What matters to him. The things that he's been through that no one talks about. That he's allowed to live his life on his own terms, but even when you're happy with where you're at and happy with what you're doing, people will judge you for it.

And they shouldn't.

I shouldn't.

That's on me. That's my bad.

He won't look at *me* differently if I never give him a chance to do it either.

And honestly? I think he's making me look at myself differently too.

Not all rules are necessary. People change. Being *good* isn't necessarily *better*.

Not when it makes me feel like I'm not *living*.

I've known for over a year that I'm missing something in my life. But it wasn't until this trip that I realized how much I'm still standing in my own way with all of the rules I'm subconsciously following that shouldn't be rules at all.

"Do people ever tell you it's not your fault? Do people ever tell you you're right and someone else is wrong?" I ask.

He doesn't look at me while he flings more dough balls

onto a cookie sheet. "Get plenty of validation in plenty of places."

I swallow my next argument. *But here? Are you validated here? Your sister gave you a babysitter. How is that validation?*

No point in saying it out loud.

That much is clear.

He doesn't want to hear it from me. And no matter how much we both adore Emma, she shouldn't have asked me to babysit Theo.

Chandler should own his part in this. And she's marrying him in two days.

Because he's truly her soulmate?

Or because she's wanted a family for so long that she can't fathom starting over with someone she doesn't know as well, even if that someone could be better for her?

I've known Emma for a long time, and I hate the conclusion I can't help but draw right now, and that it's taken me until *two days* before her wedding to question it at all.

"I appreciate what you did tonight, for whatever that's worth," I tell Theo.

"*Go. Away.*"

"Why?"

He drops the tray of cookies on the prep table, oven gaping open behind him, and finally looks at me.

There's an uncharacteristic intensity in his normally easy-going, but currently piercing gaze that makes me stumble back half a step.

It's not anger.

It's not frustration.

It's—

Oh my god.

It's *desire.*

Theo *wants* me.

"Because if you don't," he says, low and gravelly, "I'm going to pin you to the nearest wall and kiss the ever-loving fuck out of you, and if I start kissing you, I won't stop until we're both bare-ass naked and completely spent on this floor."

I suck in a quick breath as my breasts tighten and my clit tingles, and it's not enough air.

Theo's always been off-limits. The *bad boy*. The rule-breaker. The guy all the girls would whisper about in the hallway in high school, the one they wanted to lose their virginity to, the one rumored to know more about sex than any high school boy should.

And that was over a decade ago.

When he was scrawny and wild and unpredictable.

He still has a wild side.

He's still unpredictable.

But he's *more*. It's like he has all of the chaos harnessed deep inside of him, and he knows when to unleash it for maximum advantage.

He's also *fun*. Good fun.

And he has Emma's sunshine, which I never noticed before, but it's unmistakable. Aside from the moment he realized he was stuck with me, he's been cheerful and upbeat no matter the obstacles in his way.

And realizing he *cares*—and that he's utterly irresistible in how much he cares—is making this all the worse.

I want him.

I do.

I want him.

He gives me one last withering glare that makes me feel more like he's mentally stripping me than that he hates me. "Please go away."

I lick my lips. "Do you want me because I'm convenient or because you want *me*?"

"You are *not* convenient."

That wasn't complimentary. Don't think he meant it to be.

I don't want to want you, but I can't help myself. This is part of the chaos that I can't control.

He splays his hands wide on the table like he's using it as a buffer between us. The scents of vanilla, sugar, and melted chocolate float through the air, made more potent by the tension hanging between us.

I could do this.

I could have raw, wild, uninhibited sex with Theo in a kitchen he broke into and is using to make chocolate chip cookies.

Because he's not already attractive enough.

"You won't like all of me, Laney," he says, low and tight.

"You made my hangover cookies," I whisper. "That's why it took so long. You broke in here and made fresh cookies."

"If you don't leave, I'll ruin you."

I know exactly what he's saying. *You will never want sex with another man after you get a taste of what I can give you.*

I shiver. It's a *good* shiver. A forbidden shiver. A *fun* shiver. "What am I, a governess in the eighteen hundreds?"

"If you don't leave, you'll ruin *me*." I've never heard his voice like this. Desperate. Anguished. Vulnerable.

"I don't want to ruin you," I whisper. "I want to *know* you."

"You really don't."

"I really do." I reach behind me, make sure the door is fully closed, and flip the lock.

His brown eyes, already dark, go fully midnight. "You shouldn't do that."

"I like you," I whisper while my feet carry me around the prep table.

He watches me like he's a trapped, wounded mountain lion. "You shouldn't."

"You're a good person."

"You have no idea who all I am."

"You save kittens and rescue your sister in ways she doesn't even know and you take care of me when I'm drunk."

He visibly swallows. "I won't be some plaything you can dabble with today and throw away when your parents get here."

I shut the oven door, knowing full well that my face is flushing for more reasons than just the heat coming from the appliance. "I'm tired of playing the good girl for everyone else."

"Tonight."

"*All the damn time.*"

I stop next to him. He's still bracing himself on the table, his head turned to look at me, pupils fully dilated, his breath coming short and fast.

Kiss me.

I want to say it, but a lifetime of being told sex will ruin my life makes it hard.

I can barely bring myself to make the first move to touch him.

But I force myself to do it.

To put a hand on his shoulder, the heat of his skin searing my palm while I push him back from where he's braced himself.

"You have no idea what you're doing," he murmurs thickly.

"I broke up with the *perfect man* a year ago because it didn't feel right and I'm finally understanding why."

"Because he was a fucking boring-ass piece of shit?"

"Yes."

He grips my hips hard. "So I'm a plaything."

"No."

"Say it. *You're a plaything, Theo. You're a walk on the wild side. You're a fuck-you to my parents.*"

"You're living your own life on your own terms without apology and *I want that.*"

"Fucking around with me isn't a shortcut to changing who you are and you won't like me when you know all of who I am."

"Brutal honesty is such a turn-on."

He's glowering at me.

Glowering.

Theo. The guy who smiled through hitting a wild pig.

Also a turn-on.

There's no *you're so pretty* lip service. No lies. No forcing anything. No faking it.

Just a guy who wants me despite not *wanting* to want me.

Pure hormonal instincts making his searing-hot gaze dip to my lips while his fingers hold my hips tightly enough to bruise.

I want you even though I don't want to want you.

I feel more like a woman, like a goddess, for knowing how much he can't resist me than I've ever felt from roses and fancy dinners and champagne as foreplay.

"I will ruin you for any other man, ever, and I won't apologize for that," he growls as he steps closer, pressing his hard erection against my belly.

"Promise?" I whisper.

A feral noise emanates low in his throat, and then there's nothing else but the feel of his lips crushing mine, his arm wrapping around my waist to pull me tighter while he flexes his hips to grind his thick erection harder against me.

A thrill washes over me. A thrill, and a throbbing in my vagina, and a heavy longing in my breasts, and a desperate, deep need for *more*.

More of his punishing kisses. Deeper kisses. His tongue.

Oh, *god*, his tongue.

It's delicious.

And his hair.

It's surprisingly silky. Long enough to grip and lose my fingers in.

But his ass.

Oh my god, his ass.

It's a round, solid bubble of *I cannot get enough of this*, and when I squeeze it tighter, his erection pulses against my stomach, making my lonely clit beg for what he gave us last night in the car.

"Last chance, Laney," he gasps as he breaks the kiss. "Last chance before we can't take it back."

"Strip my clothes off."

His eyes are so dark, I could fall into them and never find the bottom. His breath comes in short pants, lips parted and moist from our kiss. Everything about him screams *coiled snake, danger, danger*, but *god*, I want this.

I want *him*.

And not for *fun*. Not to *take a walk on the wild side*.

I want him because he's *life*. I feel like I'm taking a full breath of fresh air after living underwater. I feel electric. *Alive*.

"I don't regret last night," I whisper. "Any of it. And I remember *everything*."

I don't know how he does it, but in one smooth motion, he's stripped me of my dress.

It's somewhere in the kitchen that is not on my body.

Humid air touches my skin, and then *Theo* touches my skin.

He skims his hands down my ribs. Slips his thumbs just barely under the waistband of my bikini briefs and circles my hips, not dipping low enough to touch my clit or my butt crack before he leaves my panties on and glides his hands back up my ribs.

Watching me.

Watching my every inhalation. Every soft gasp. Every stifled moan for more while I squirm in his hands, wanting him to touch me everywhere all at once.

"Don't hold back now, princess," he murmurs as he dips his head to my shoulder and bites me in the crook of my neck.

A garbled *oh, god* leaves my lips.

He hooks a hand under one of my legs, turns, and *oh god yes yes yes there*.

There.

Right there.

With his cock pressed against my clit, him rotating his hips to rub me *so so so* right.

His free hand moves up my back, and then my bra's gone too, unhooked so the cups fall off and the straps slide down my arms.

He shifts twice, and I'm standing in this kitchen grinding my clit against Theo's erection in nothing but my panties and strappy sandals.

There's no time to get self-conscious though.

Not when he pinches my nipple and makes me cry out in sheer thrilling pleasure.

"Again," I gasp.

He rolls it between his thumb and forefinger.

My hips thrust out of control against his thick length.

"Touch my cock," he orders.

I don't think. Don't hesitate.

I just shove his pants down, reach between us, and grip the hot, silky skin of his erection.

"*Fuck, yes*," he hisses. "Stroke me, Laney."

I grip him harder and stroke him root to tip, brushing the bead of moisture at the tip of his length around his head.

"Good girl." His voice is strangled.

And his words piss me off. So I squeeze his dick harder.

He sucks in a breath that I feel deep in my core.

Probably because I want to know what it feels like deep in my core when his cock surges like that.

Holy *hell*. I like his penis.

I like his penis *a lot*.

"I am *not* a good girl," I force out.

"You are such a good girl."

"I am—*ooh god.*"

I am not a good girl.

I'm arching into his touch, because Theo's pushed my panties aside and thrust two fingers up inside me, and he's also playing with my clit, and *oh my god oh my god oh my god*, this feels—

Not good.

Not even *better*.

This is pure, raw, carnal *heaven*.

I drop his penis and grip his shoulders instead, my hips jerking while I bury my face in his neck and breathe in the raw, musky scent of him. "Don't stop," I choke out while need spirals higher and tighter inside of me with every thrust of his fingers and every swirl of his thumb around my clit.

Oh god.

Oh god.

"I want you to sit on my face and I want to eat you until you scream my name and then I want to bury my cock so deep inside your pussy you'll never be able to walk again," he breathes in my ear. "I want to fuck you in this kitchen. On the beach. In a goddamn broom closet at your fancy-ass office. I want you to never look at a cookie again without knowing I give you the best damn cookies of your life."

"*Theo.* Oh god. I—I—I—"

"Say it, Laney."

I'm twisting and writhing in his touch, *right there*, right on the edge of coming.

"Say you want to fuck me too," he breathes while his fingers make me wetter than I've ever been and the tension spiraling inside me gets higher and higher. "Say you want to eat my cock. Say you want me to make you come in the ocean. Say you want to give me a hand job in your old bedroom in your parents' house."

Everything breaks loose inside me, and spasms overtake me. "*Yes*," I gasp.

"Are you coming?"

"*Yes.*"

"Say it, Laney. *Say it.*"

"Oh, god. I'm—I'm—*Theo*. I—"

"Tell me you're coming."

He's still jerking his fingers inside me. Still playing my clit. I'm coming hard and fast and long and deep, so deep I can feel it in the pit of my stomach, so hard I'm almost cramping. "*I'm coming*," I gasp. "*Oh my god, I'm coming.*"

"Yeah, you are, you sexy-ass goddess."

My entire body flushes as the sensations roll through me. "Don't—make fun—"

He swallows the rest of my sentence with a searing kiss while he slows the delicious torture on my spasming inner muscles and my overly sensitive clit.

"Fucking. Goddess," he repeats against my mouth before thrusting his tongue back in.

And I love it.

I do.

Not because I feel like I'm rebelling.

But because I feel *alive*.

And *free*.

And *safe*.

He slips his fingers out of my vagina, and I whimper at the sudden emptiness.

But then he rocks his cock against my clit, and *oh my god*.

Bare skin to bare skin.

His thick, hard, straining length nestles between my slick thighs.

I should ask him if he has a condom.

I should.

But I don't *want* to.

I *want* to take him inside my overworked vagina and do for him what he just did for me.

But then I hear it.

A key.

In a lock.

And cursing. "Which fucking key is it?" someone says outside the door.

My gaze flies to Theo's.

His gaze flies to my nearly naked body.

"Front door," he says.

I don't know how he does it, but he pulls his pants back up over his hard penis, grabs my dress, shoves it over my head, and pockets four cookies in less time than it takes whoever's on the other side of that door to try two more keys.

And then we're darting into the dining area of the bistro, where Theo expertly unlocks the door without hesitation, and then we're dashing off into the night.

I don't know if he has my bra.

I don't know if the kitchen smells like sex.

I don't know who was trying to get in.

But I know that running away from the bistro on shaky legs that haven't recovered from that orgasm, Theo's hand clutching mine while he steers me down the tropical-shrub and tiki-torch-lined path to the back side of our building, feels like utter heaven.

Like I'm finally finding a part of myself that I've been seeking for so long, I forgot who, exactly, I was looking for.

And while *old* Laney would freak out about nearly getting caught, that's not what I do.

I giggle.

I giggle until I snort, and then I laugh so hard we have to stop so I can catch my breath.

And while I lean against the side of a building and laugh until I almost cry, no matter how much I say I'm trying to catch my breath, Theo just watches me.

"So that's all it takes," he says quietly with a soft smile on his lips.

"What's all it takes?" I gasp between peals of laughter.

He doesn't answer.

Just shakes his head and watches me.

But when I've finally pulled myself together enough for us to continue on our way, he does the last thing I expect.

Again.

He wraps an arm around my shoulders, presses a kiss to my temple, and shoves a chocolate chip cookie in my mouth.

This, my heart whispers, even over the sound of my mouth having a full-on foodgasm at the warm, salty toffee-and-chocolate treat on my tongue.

This is the dating we've been missing.

It's not wrong.

Also not wrong?

Theo.

He has absolutely ruined me for any other man. Ever.

My vagina's expectations of sex for the rest of my life have been reset with just his fingers.

Oh my god.

As for the rest of what I want—I'm just this side of shaky at knowing we nearly got caught naked in a restaurant kitchen, but the thrill.

The thrill.

And one very, very delicious chocolate chip cookie on top of it.

"I'm not done with you," I tell him around a mouthful of cookie.

Again, he doesn't answer.

But I catch the way his lips tip up in the corner.

Theo Monroe isn't *trouble*.

He's trouble *and more*.

And I've only just started discovering the *more*.

23

Theo

MY BALLS ARE BLUE. My cock is permanently hard. And Laney Kingston has ruined me for all other women *ever*.

I knew this would happen. I knew I was already at the tipping point of falling for her. I knew it would barely take a nudge before I'd be tumbling head over heels all over again, dreaming, wishing, *hoping* that this will end differently than it would've in high school, even though I know better.

I know I'm a vacation fuck.

I know I'm a moment of breaking free.

I know she'll go back into the cute little perfect box she's supposed to live in the minute her plane touches back down in Denver in a few days, and I know the day she hears what I do for a side hustle, she'll be horrified with herself.

But I'm still mellow as a fucking mushroom as I open the bungalow door for her.

She's happy.

Glowing.

Relaxed.

That's what matters.

Right now, she's happy.

Tomorrow, I'll care that I'm happy too. But a quick shower with a nice little yanky-yanky on the ol' dick will go a long way to fixing my junk, at least.

At least, that's the plan until I look inside the bungalow. "Fuck," I gasp.

The door's open.

The kittens' bedroom door.

It's open.

My heart stops. The bottom of my stomach drops out.

My kittens.

Fuck me, if something happened to my kittens—

Laney is *still* moaning over my cookies and stops mid-noise as she spots it too. "Oh my god, *how*? Where are they? Are they okay? Are they still here?"

She tosses the last cookie on the counter as she speeds into the room almost before I can process that I need to do the same, and I'm no slowpoke.

"Miss Doodles?" she says softly while we enter the main bedroom, me still unable to form words for the horror at the idea that any of my kittens are missing or hurt. "Are you here, Miss Doodles?"

Jellybean meows at us from the bed. She and Snaggleclaw are bouncing over it like they managed to get up but don't know how to get down.

Two.

Two kittens.

Miss Doodles isn't in the bedroom.

Fred is though.

He's still under the bed, cowering.

Three kittens. *Fuck*. Where are the rest?

"Where'd they all go, Fred?" I ask him through the crushing weight of fear in my chest.

He backs up against the wall, arches his little back, and

stares at me like he wants to be a big brave kitty who can defend his barely-one-pound frame all by himself.

"Are they down there?" Laney drops to her knees next to me and peers under, her shoulder touching mine and making my skin flush hot all over my body.

"He's skittish," I tell her. "Move slow."

"Oh, you're beautiful," she croons softly. "Do you want a treat? Here, sweet thing."

"Slow—" I start again, but it's Laney.

Never does anything wrong.

Unless I'm involved, and then she's all-in for sex in a public kitchen before running away and hiding.

Which isn't wrong.

It's just different from what she's used to.

She slowly reaches under the bed and deposits four of the treats from the purple bag as far under as she can, then backs up. "We're gonna go find the rest of your family, sweetie," she says, and the way she touches my arm tells me she's talking to me as much as she is to the kitten. "Don't worry. You're safe. They will be too."

It's crazy in this moment to think of how much her confidence used to annoy me.

After last night and the car accident, I know she doesn't have it all the time. But right now, she's saving me with her belief that everything will be okay.

A dozen needles suddenly plunge into my back.

I stifle a startled squeal of pain but make enough of a grunt that Laney jerks her head to look at me.

"Cat," I say. "Back. Claws."

She straightens, and then she claps in triumph. "Where did you come from, you pretty thing? Up you go. Up on the bed with your siblings. We have *four* kittens in here, Theo. How many are missing?"

"Three and Miss Doodles."

"Great. Let's go find them."

With the kitten off my back, I straighten too.

Laney's already on her feet, holding out a hand like she thinks I need help up.

If half my kittens weren't missing, I'd take that hand, haul her onto the bed, and kiss her until I was sure this was real.

Not just a temporary dream state in paradise before her parents get here, before we all head back home, before reality pulls her back into that safe, predictable, *boring* bottom-line world that she lives in.

Instead, I take her hand and rise slowly, my thumb brushing over the back of her hand, not using her for leverage at all. "Thank you."

"M-my pleasure," she stutters.

"Thank you," I repeat.

She smiles softly at me. "I'm kinda good at fixing problems."

And I've never been more grateful.

"I didn't open the door the last time I was in here," she says as she leads me out of the room. "I promise."

I jiggle the handle while I follow, then close it behind us. "Miss Doodles can probably operate one of these."

Just has to hit it right.

"Oh! Look! Kitten in the sofa."

I flip on the flashlight on my phone and aim it under the hide-a-bed, still sticking halfway up. "Two kittens. Blinky and Panini."

I'm breathing easier with every passing minute.

My kittens are okay.

"Six, then," she says. "Who's missing?"

I head to the back porch to check the door while I answer her. "We have Jellybean, Snaggleclaw, Fred, Blinky, Panini, and Cream Puff. Miss Doodles and Widget are missing. Wait. Correction. Only Miss Doodles is missing."

Widget is climbing the curtains covering the door.

Laney's right on my heels. I untangle Widget, turn, and drop the furry little gray beast into her hand.

Balcony door is locked still.

So Miss Doodles— "Found her," Laney says.

She points to the kitchenette, where I swear there wasn't a cat a minute ago.

But Miss Doodles is there now, sitting on the counter and grooming her butt.

She pauses to look at me—*stupid human, you think I'd give up a cushy place like this with toys and food and clean litter*—then goes back to licking herself.

I've never in my life been so glad to see a cat licking her own butt.

"I'm locking your kittens in the bedroom," I tell her.

She keeps licking, one foot up in the air.

"Oh, that's a relief," Laney says. "I'll look at the door and see if I can figure out how to—"

"Laney."

"Right. Right. You can solve things yourself. Sorry. Habit. Can't help myself."

"Not what I was going to say."

I snag the kitten back from her, then collect the two hiding under the broken-ass couch, and put all three back into the bedroom.

Should go change the litter.

Make sure they have enough food for overnight.

I'll get there.

Right now, though, Laney's watching me like she, too, is afraid I'd rather have reality.

"You're not putting Miss Doodles back in?" she asks.

"You ever know a mama who didn't want a break sometime?"

Her gaze dips to my chest again.

And now that I know my kittens are safe, yeah. That's what I like to see.

Her eyes going dark. Lids getting heavy. Her pink tongue darting out to lick her lips while she drops another quick glance to my torso.

"It's really sexy to watch you save kittens," she whispers while she closes the distance between us.

I swallow hard. "It's really sexy to watch *you* save kittens."

"I want you to kiss me again."

"What if I want you to kiss me?"

She licks her lips again and settles her hands on my shoulders, then slides them up my neck. "I suppose that's only fair."

"Not everything's about fair."

She flinches a little, but she's also sending goosebumps all over my skin as her fingers make their way behind my ears and into my hair.

"I—I want to kiss you," she breathes.

The years—*the years*—that I've wanted to hear those words from her. And here they are. And I don't know if I can keep them.

But fuck it.

We have tonight.

I'll worry about tomorrow when it gets here. "Not so hard, was it?"

"Good girls aren't supposed to."

"Fuck that."

Her lips spread in a wide smile that brings out the subtlest dimple in her right cheek and lights her blue eyes up even as they're smoky and heavy with need, and *fuck me*.

Making Laney smile is a headier rush than anything. And I've done some daredevil shit.

I'm in trouble.

I am in so much fucking trouble with how much I want her.

"Fuck that," she agrees.

She pushes up on her tiptoes while she pulls my head down to her level, and then Laney Kingston, the prim-and-proper buttoned-up princess of Snaggletooth Creek, licks my lips before thrusting her tongue into my mouth.

There's no kissing foreplay.

It's all deep and hard and instant, diving in headfirst without measuring the depth of the creek.

And the hardest thing I've ever had to do in my life is to let her be in charge.

But it's also the hottest thing I've ever done.

Who knew Laney Kingston would be so invested in fucking my mouth with her tongue while gripping my hair and turning us so she can walk me back toward the bedroom with her?

I thought I was hard last night when she was riding me in the car. I thought I was hard just a bit ago in the kitchen when she was stroking my cock in her bare hands.

But having Laney using her body and her hands and her tongue to boss me around is making me so hard it hurts.

In the best fucking way.

"I want to strip you naked," she breathes against my lips.

"Whatever you want, princess."

"We should have a safe word."

There's zero chance I need a safe word with Laney. She saved my kittens. She can do anything she wants to me. "Your choice."

"Rumpelstiltskin."

I crack up.

Can't help it.

"Right." There's barely a blue ring visible around her dark, wide pupils, and her breath is coming in short gasps while she walks me through the doorway to our bedroom. "Too long. Beans. Beans should be our safe word."

"You gonna remember that when I'm ripping your pussy to shreds with my big, thick cock?"

"*Oh my god*. More. Talk more. All the dirty things."

"Kiss me. Earn it."

She whimpers softly, and then she's shoving me down onto the bed, straddling me, and kissing me like she'll drown if she doesn't.

Maybe she will.

Maybe she'll suffocate under the weight of all those fucking expectations, and I'm the only person standing there next to her, urging her to leap for her life.

I'm the difference between living her life for someone else and living her life the way she wants to.

"Touch me, Theo," she gasps between kisses.

"Where?"

She straightens, rips her dress off, getting her hands tangled in the process and giving me the most fabulous view of her bouncing, rosy-tipped breasts.

I want to hold them. Suck on them. Bite them. Worship them. And it takes every ounce of control I don't have to keep my hands on her hips instead of all over her chest.

"Help?" she whimpers.

Fuck it.

I lean up, sliding my hands up her smooth, silky sides, and bury my face between her breasts while I blindly fumble with her dress until it's gone.

"Oh, more, please, *more*," she gasps, gripping my head and holding it nestled between her plump, gorgeous breasts while I taste her.

"More what, Laney?"

"Lick me. Touch me. Strip me. Do everything to me." She shimmies in my lap, and I realize she's trying to pull her panties off.

"Lick you where?"

"My b-breasts. And my n-nipples."

249

"I like your big words."

She gasps out a laugh a moment before I suck one of her nipples into my mouth, and then there's no more laughing.

Only panting. Gasping. Jerking her hips against my hard-on through her panties and my pants. Holding my head to her breast.

I pinch her other nipple, even though she didn't ask, because I can't help myself.

I love hearing her lose control. I love *making* her lose control.

Feeling all of the good things her body can do for her.

"How—didn't—haven't—*more*," she pants.

"More what, Laney?"

"More hands. You need more hands. *Oh god, that's so good.*"

More hands.

Always figured if I ever got naked with Laney, it would be solid hate fucking.

Instead, I'm smiling against her nipple.

I flick it with my tongue, and the unearthly sound of pure pleasure that comes out of her mouth makes my balls ache.

I want inside this woman.

I want—I just *want*.

She reaches between us, her hands dipping under the waistband of my pants. "I want to touch your penis," she says. "I want to hold your penis and be totally naked with you."

"Tell me you want to stroke my dick."

She shudders, and I don't know if it's the thrill of saying something *so dirty*, or if it's terror at the idea of those words on her tongue.

"I want to stroke your dick and then I want you to fuck my pussy until I can't walk," she says.

Jesus.

Fucking.

Hell.

"I want to come all over your big, thick, hot cock," she pants. "I want to come so hard I cut off all circulation to your —your—your meat stick."

I have zero idea what kind of noise is coming out of me. Or that it could be possible to be so fucking turned on that my nuts feel like they're inside out while wanting to laugh at the same time.

"*Meat stick*. Oh my god. I said *meat stick*. And that's not sexy. It's—*mmph!*"

Yeah. Totally silencing her with a kiss.

A long, deep, wet, thorough kiss that has me at the edge of blowing my load in my pants—*again*—while she melts back into my arms.

I squeeze her breasts, then trail my hands down her sides, rolling us when I reach the waistband of her pretty pink panties so that I can pull them off her.

By the time I've rolled on top of her, I have my pants yanked down too.

But not before snagging the condom from my back pocket.

"Theo," she pants. "I want—I want it all."

"Welcome to living, Laney." I push up to my knees to roll the condom on and look down at her while I make quick work of suiting up.

Her pussy is so perfect.

It's Laney. Of course it is.

But I *like* it. The slick wet pink skin hiding beneath her light brown curls. The scent of her. The way she's clearly squirming under my gaze but still parting her thighs to let me see more.

"Can I be on top?" she whispers.

"*Roll over, Theo, I'm in charge*," I whisper back with a smile.

The smile that blossoms on her lips in return is everything. "Roll over, you big lug. I'm the boss of this bed."

"Make me."

Determination lights those dark, dark eyes ringed in blue, and then she has her legs hooked around my hips, and she's twisting, all power and sex goddess, until she's straddling me on the bed again.

But her bare pussy hovers over my straining cock.

This close.

So close.

And I still don't believe I'm the lucky bastard who gets to be inside of her until she grips me and guides herself right over me, then sinks down.

Fuck.

Fuck.

She's hot. Slick. Tight.

And I have to clench my teeth to keep from coming from the simple act of this woman taking me deep inside her.

"Good?" she whispers.

"You're a fucking goddess," I whisper back.

"You're so big." She cringes even as she lifts herself and lowers back onto my dick. "Sorry. That sounded—"

"Perfect," I thrust my hips up to meet her and am rewarded with the sight of one of her eyes sliding shut while the other crosses. "You own me tonight, Laney. Do whatever feels good."

"You feel good. *God*, you feel so good."

Her breasts bounce as she picks up her pace, and *fuck me.*

I have no stamina when it comes to this woman.

I've wanted her too long. *Denied* wanting her too long.

Still don't believe it'll last.

But *she wants me.* And I can't resist being wanted by her.

I'm thrusting up to meet her while she rides me, her breath coming faster and faster, desperate to make this so good for her that she'll want me again.

And again.

And again.

Even knowing it'll end. That we're more alike than either

of us ever could've expected, but I'm still not the kind of guy Delaney Kingston wants or needs for all time.

"You're fucking gorgeous," I tell her while I tease her nipples.

She's braced herself against my shoulders, her fingers digging into my skin while she bounces faster and faster, her breath coming in short pants that match mine, her eyes unfocused, the hottest noises coming from her lips.

"Oh, god, Theo, so good," she pants. "So—so—*so*—"

I can't.

I absolutely, positively cannot hold back a minute longer.

Not with my name on her lips and her pussy clenching my dick and those gorgeous breasts bouncing in my hands.

I've had this dream.

I've had this *wet* dream.

"*Theo*," she gasps, and I am *done*.

Spilling my load. Coming harder than I've ever come in my life. My gut cramps. My balls ache.

And that's before she moans like she's trying to be quiet while her pussy clenches tight and hard around my cock.

"Let it out, Laney." I can hardly talk. "Don't hold back."

"*So good*," she cries. "*Can't stop.*"

"Don't stop."

Fuck. I can't stop either. And every time her sweet pussy clenches and spasms around me, I think I'll die.

Sensations.

Joy.

Relief.

Terror.

I'm coming so hard, I can't feel my toes.

And I don't care.

This? Being buried deep inside Laney, the tendons in her slender neck straining as she presses her pussy down on my hips while she rides out the waves of her own orgasm, and knowing that *I did this*, that she wanted *me*?

Take my toes.

Take my fingers.

Take all of me but my heart and my dick and whatever parts she wants.

I don't need it anymore.

All I need is whatever she wants.

She collapses on top of me with a soft moan, her breath tickling my neck as the last of my own climax finally fades on a string of small spasms.

I can't catch my breath.

Don't care.

Just care that I'm wrapping my arms around her while she gasps for breath too.

"Oh my god," she whispers.

"Not the safe word," I murmur back.

She giggles.

Sucks in another big breath and giggles again.

It makes her pussy tighten around my overly sensitive cock, and for a second, I swear to god it's gonna kill me.

Forget worrying about tomorrow. I won't last that long. I'm gonna die right here, right now, by her pussy squeezing my dick.

I should ask her to take care of my kittens when I'm gone.

"Do you do shower sex?" she asks.

"I'm a fucking god in the shower."

That was seventy percent my dick thinking he can be a superhero and thirty percent the rest of me.

Because the rest of me is pretty sure I'll never move again.

My arms are already sliding off of Laney's back.

They're noodles. Limp spaghetti noodles.

Probably should've had one of those tacos.

But it doesn't matter because Laney's giggling again.

She sounds so young. So carefree. So fucking *perfect*.

But the good kind of perfect.

The *happy* kind of perfect.

"Can we try that tomorrow?" she whispers.

Tomorrow.

Her parents get here tomorrow.

Will she still want me tomorrow?

"We can do anything you want tomorrow, princess. Anything at all."

24

I DON'T KNOW where I am, or possibly even who I am, but as I slowly drift to consciousness, unaware if I've been asleep for five minutes or five hours, I don't care.

I'm content.

Every bit of me.

My body is a giant lump of happy. My brain is whispering peaceful suggestions of beach sunrises with the gentle sounds of the surf. Something is vibrating comfortably on my hip. And I can smell the musky, clean scent of warm man and feel his body lined up behind mine.

Theo.

Oh my god.

I had sex with Theo.

And it was *glorious.*

Magnificent.

Earth-shattering and life-altering.

And he's still in bed with me. In paradise.

And that's a cat curled up on my hip, purring.

This, my soul whispers. *This is what you're missing.*

I never would've expected feeling so much peace and safety *here*. With Theo. But I do.

Fun? I've always envied his ability to find it anywhere. *Always.* And I've thought some extremely unflattering things about his sense of responsibility over the years at the same time that I was craving fun.

But I never realized he could be fun *and* have moments of utter peace. That he ever has moments of rest.

That he can be smiling with the mischief of ten thousand wood sprites one minute and washing my face of tears the next.

And that I'd love to listen to the rhythmic sound of his breath, and that I'd like that he's holding my breast in his sleep, and that I like even more that I'm slowly realizing there's a thick, hard *meat stick* cradled against my butt cheeks.

Meat stick.

Oh my god.

I said that.

"Beans," he murmurs into my hair.

Oh my god again. I told him *beans* was my safe word.

Who uses beans as a safe word?

Worse, why did I think I'd need one when I was in charge? *Tie me up and blindfold me, Theo.*

I am still so boring.

"Beans," he repeats, stronger, and I realize he's *using* the safe word.

"Do—do you want me to leave?" I whisper. There's pale morning light filtering in through the curtains.

"Stop—claws—ow." He moves his hand off my breast and swats at something. "*Beans,* Miss Doodles."

Oh.

The cat.

He's shooing the cat.

I giggle as the cat leaps off the bed.

He *harrumphs* into my hair, readjusts his whole body so his erection is nestled harder against my butt, and resumes holding my breast.

I bite my tongue.

Am I supposed to ask how he slept? Or if he wants me to do something to relieve some pressure in his penis?

Hi, I'm Laney, and I am so lame and bad at dirty talk.

He probably forgot it's me here in bed with him.

This is probably one of those things he does so often that he doesn't really care who he's with.

But is it?

He told me I'm not convenient. Did he change his mind in the ten minutes that he was making me come in the bistro kitchen, or when we had sex?

Or is he pickier about who he dates than I think he is?

"I was this close to getting engaged a year ago," my brain decides I need to blurt out.

Theo yawns. "Guess you're awake."

"And I haven't slept with anyone since," my mouth continues for me.

"The logic logics," he murmurs in my hair.

He's not telling me to shut up.

Not squirming.

Not running for the hills.

"You're right. You ruined me for sex with any other man, so I'm now going to turn into the crazy woman who desperately needs to marry you for your penis."

He snickers, which makes his cock rub more along my butt crack, and *oh my god*, I'm wondering what it would be like if he played with me there.

And I sigh.

I'm not a *can you see if I get turned on if you play with my butt?* kind of girl, nor can I manage to tell him I like him without sounding like a complete doofus.

But then he kisses my shoulder. "Regrets, Laney?"

"No," I whisper. "Not at all."

He doesn't reply.

He doesn't kiss me again either.

Doesn't pinch my nipple, even though I know he could.

"Do you do this all the time?" I cringe, wishing I'd done a better job of hiding the naked vulnerability obvious in the question.

He's not moving, so it's not like he can go more still, but I swear he does. More tense. More something.

Did he quit breathing?

Am I finally freaking him out?

"No," he replies quietly before I can take the question back.

He doesn't elaborate.

I should get up.

Or turn around and stroke his erection and ask if he wants to have morning fun.

Instead, I think I'm ruining this. "Why not?" I whisper.

"Some things matter."

My heart flutters in a slow somersault. "What matters to you?"

"Do you always wake up this talkative?"

"No."

He takes a deep breath and settles closer, pulling me even tighter still, until his chin is resting on my shoulder. I shift too and hold his forearm against me.

And I wait.

Once again, I don't think he'll answer me. But even when he's quiet, even when he's not answering—and let's be real, why should he?—I don't feel like an inconvenience.

I don't feel like I'm annoying.

I don't feel like he's pulling away.

Hard to imagine when he has me tucked so thoroughly against him.

"Why'd you say no?" he asks.

"Not like I have anyone to talk to in the mornings."

"To the proposal."

I cringe.

He tightens his grip.

Not like *I can't breathe* tight.

More like *I've got you, you're safe* tight.

"I didn't like him," I whisper. "I was supposed to, and he was fine—he didn't mistreat me—but I didn't like him. My parents loved him, so I thought there was something wrong with me that I didn't. That if I just got to know him better, I'd find this mystical *thing* that seemed to be missing in our relationship. But when he started talking about getting married…"

Theo doesn't say anything.

Just lies there, quietly breathing behind me.

"When I realized I was more worried about disappointing my parents than I was about if I'd be happy with him, I knew it wasn't the right relationship for me. And I realized I didn't even know if my whole *life* was the life for me."

"Hard thing to face."

"Why is it so easy to tell you this?"

"I've been too much of a shit to judge anyone else."

"I don't think you're a shit."

"Can be."

"Are you being a shit here? Right now?"

"No."

"Would you tell me if you were?"

"Yes."

"Would Sabrina think you're being a shit?"

That earns a soft chuckle. "She always thinks I'm being a shit."

"No, she doesn't."

He shifts behind me, and this time, he pulls away.

But only for a minute before he's pushing me onto my

back and crawling on top of me. It's instinct to spread my legs and cradle his hips and his impressive morning erection.

"Hi," I whisper, like a complete and total dork.

His brown eyes study me. There's no cocky grin. No mocking my awkward *hi* at the first sight of his face this morning. Just an entirely more serious Theo than I ever would've given him credit for being. Even if only in the occasional moment.

"I don't fuck around with women I don't like."

My belly tingles. My nipples tighten. And my overworked vagina decides she's not so tired after all.

"Is this—is this fucking around?"

"I like you, Laney. I have *always* liked you, even when I hated myself for it. This is the scariest shit I have *ever* done."

"I don't want to be scary."

"You were born that way, princess."

"I didn't mean to be."

He squeezes his eyes shut, but there's a smile playing on his lips. "You're my favorite pain in the ass."

I loop my arms around his neck, wanting to lick the patterns of his tattoos from his collarbone down as far as they go. "I like you too."

One eye cracks open, and *oh my heart*.

Is *Theo Monroe* terrified that I'll hurt him? That I'm playing with him? That this is a vacation fling, a walk on the wild side, something to get out of my system so I'll have stories to tell when I go back and marry a total stick in the mud that my parents approve of?

He seems so immune to what anyone thinks about him.

But he *does* care.

He cares what Emma thinks. He cares what his dad thinks.

And I'm slowly realizing he cares what *I* think.

"I've been stuck in this holding pattern for the past year," I tell him, "waiting for something exciting to happen, and that's exactly the problem. I can't *wait* to live. I have to take the step. And I don't know who I'll be when I land, but I can't find out if I don't jump."

"You wanna jump?"

"I've always wanted to jump, but I've never been brave enough to deal with the consequences."

"Feeling brave now?"

I nod while I brush his hair back off his forehead.

"You sure?"

I nod again.

He studies me again like he can see into not just my soul but my future.

I hold my breath.

I don't know why. But it feels necessary.

Like jumping off of one cliff just showed me there are so many more to leap from.

My mom used to say that the only way you go when you jump is down.

But I don't think she's right.

I think jumping is the first step to soaring.

And then Theo's serious face disappears behind the world's largest, most mischievous, most breathtakingly gorgeous grin. "Good." He scoots off me, rising in the morning light without an ounce of modesty or discomfort about being naked. "Let's go."

"Go…where?"

He flings my suitcase up on the bed, bringing with it one of those knitted hearts that are all over the resort, then bends, giving me a view of the most spectacularly chiseled butt cheeks for a mere second before he's pulling briefs up to cover them.

"Time to be brave, Laney."

"But—but—" I can't make the words *aren't we going to have morning sex?* come out of my mouth, so instead, I jerk a hand up and down, demonstrating my bare breasts.

His grin gets grinnier. "Only good girls who face their fears get more orgasms."

My heart pitter-patters.

I could fall for this Theo.

I could fall very, very hard.

And it might hurt when I land, but what if it doesn't?

Only one way to find out.

And that's to be all-in.

25

THEO

"OH MY GOD, WE'RE FLYING!"

I grin at Laney in the seat next to me beneath our parasail as we rise higher and higher above the sea. Her eyes are huge. Her knuckles are white on the bar in front of us. And a split second after her shrieked exclamation, she tosses her head back and laughs. "We're *flying!*"

Beneath us, the ocean's a brilliant blue against miles and miles of beach, with more appearing as we go higher. Palm trees. Black lava rock fields. The volcano watching over the island. Clouds lingering beyond it.

The boat pulling us below cuts a path through the water, leaving white wakes in its trail as we climb to altitude.

And Laney laughs again. "This is insane!"

"This is *fun.*"

She looks at me, eyes sparkling. "This is *insane.*"

"Like it?"

"Depends on the minute."

Her hair whips around her head, but she doesn't let go of

the bar to push it back. "Do you do stuff like this all the time?"

"As often as possible."

"It's so *pretty* up here. You can see forever. Like being on top of a mountain."

"But a little warmer."

She laughs again.

And it's gorgeous.

All of that pink rising high in her cheeks. The wild hair. Swimsuit under her life vest.

That smile.

I want to put that smile on her face every day for the rest of her life.

Not that I'm fooling myself about her place in my future.

Her parents get here later today. No matter where she's at in figuring out she can't live for them, I don't see her picking me over them.

And even if she did, the minute she finds out about my side hustle with GrippaPeen, it'll be *you can't do that and date me. Your side hustle or me, Theo.*

If it's not a flat-out *I cannot believe I slept with a porn star* with a heavy dose of horror.

Either one is a relationship-killer, and a major part of why I've dated less and less the bigger my channel has grown.

But I have today. I have this moment. And I have something I can give her that she won't find anywhere else.

A morning of fun. More orgasms. The full-on, best-of-the-best Theo Monroe treatment.

"*Theo. Look.*" She points down at the water where a huge dark shadow is moving. "Is that a whale?"

I settle an arm around her and lean over into her space as much as I can in our parasailing seat while I look too. "Dunno."

The shadow gets bigger and darker, and then—

"It *is!*" she squeals while a waterspout erupts from the

surface of the ocean. A moment later, we see its tail as it flips and heads back down under. "I've never seen a whale before."

"Never?"

She shakes her head. "Have you?"

"Haven't traveled much."

"We're sharing a first." She smiles at me, then tucks a wild flying lock of hair behind her ear. The ponytail she put in earlier isn't doing much to keep the wispy flyaways out of her eyes. "For all the places I've been in the world, I've never gone off the beaten path. It's always museums and landmarks and *safe* resort tours. But you've probably seen things back home that I can't even dream of."

"Ever go backpacking? Sleep under the stars?"

She shakes her head again.

"Want to?"

"In the snow?"

"We can."

"That's—" She cuts herself off with a laugh. "Very adventurous."

"Crazy?"

"I said *adventurous*."

"Not what you wanted to say."

"Excuse you. If I don't call you crazy, you can't call me boring."

I lean in and kiss that smile.

Can't help myself.

The number of years I've wanted that smile aimed at me, and now there's no mistaking the fact that it's all mine.

There's no one else up here with us to smile at.

And when she cups my cheek and kisses me back, five hundred feet over the ocean, no fear, no worries, no cares—

This.

This is all I've ever wanted.

"Have you ever jumped out of a plane?" she asks.

"Nope."

"*No?*"

"Won't."

"Why not?"

"Emma asked me not to."

She tilts her head and studies me, getting brave enough to take both hands off the bar now. One keeps trying to control her hair.

The other settles on my thigh.

It's nice to not have to explain this one to Laney.

Pretty sure she knows Emma lost a friend to a skydiving accident in college.

"This is different, huh?" she asks.

"Already know the chute works."

"You gonna tell her?"

"If she asks." I settle my hand over Laney's.

She doesn't pull away.

Instead, she flips her hand upside down and intertwines our fingers.

Like this is real.

Like it's a *thing*.

Simmer down, I tell my heart.

Fucker doesn't listen.

Especially when she squeals again. "*Four* whales! Look! *Four* of them!"

"Wanna swim with them?"

"Oh, no, I couldn't. It's their water. Let them have it."

I side-eye her.

She smiles wider. "It's *not* an excuse. It's how I feel. I'd swim with dolphins though."

"What else?"

"Stingrays? Although, we did that once at a resort in the Caribbean. *Stop.* Don't make that face. You know where I come from."

"So what's on your adventure bucket list?"

"Hot-air balloon ride."

Zero hesitation. *None*. "Done," I tell her. "You. Me. Hot-air balloons in Denver. Next week."

"*June*. And don't even try to *that's no fun, Laney, live a little* me about this. I refuse to be terrified *and* freezing *and* subject to unpredictable winter winds that close to the mountains."

She's researched hot-air balloons.

Adorable. I like it. Very Laney of her.

"June," I agree. "What else?"

"Zip lining."

"Added to the list."

"Have you zip-lined?"

"Yep."

She wrinkles her nose. "Of course you have. Probably bungee jumped too. And pretty much anything I can think of except maybe the hot-air balloon. Wait. Have you hot-air ballooned before?"

I laugh. "No. That's one I haven't done."

"What else haven't you done?"

I look out at the ocean. Love the view from up here. Really gives perspective. "Not much."

"But there *is* something left on your list?"

There is.

It's a big one.

"Theo?"

I blow out a breath.

Here I am, giving Laney an adventure of her lifetime, terrified to tell her what's on my own big scary things list.

Can't have that, can we?

"I want to fall in love."

Her eyes widen and her lips form a small *o*, like she wasn't expecting me to go there.

But I have. And now I'm all in. I look her square in the eye. "Not the *happy* kind of love. Not whatever it is Emma has. It's what she wants for her, great. But I want *more*. I want *ecstatic* love. *Purpose* love. I want a love that's the very reason for my existence. I want a love that makes life make sense, and I want a love that makes me want to be better. My *own* kind of better. Fuck *happy*. Fuck *easy*. Fuck *settling*. I want *everything*."

She doesn't blink.

Doesn't look away.

Just stares at me, listening.

Absorbing.

Yearning?

Does she feel it? Does she get it? Does she want *everything* too?

"That sounds terrifying," she whispers.

"That's how I know it's right."

There's a tug at the line.

I look down at the boat and wave.

Captain's pulling us in.

Laney doesn't say anything else on the way down.

She's polite to the captain while he gets us back on the boat and pulls us to shore, then drops us at the dock.

We need to get back to the resort.

I know we do.

More wedding stuff. Bridal shower or something later this morning.

Not that I have a gift left.

Could dash into the gift shop, but I'm not feeling it.

Better to not take anything at all than to take something Chandler will deem wrong.

Laney slips her hand into mine as we leave the dock and head down the street for the half-mile or so walk back to the resort once she's covered up her swimsuit. "You make me want to live more," she whispers.

Here.

She wants to live more *here*.

Could I make her want that at home too though? Is *dating*

an online adult entertainment star something she'd call living? Would she take a leap that big for me?

I squeeze her hand. "You make me want to misbehave."

She laughs.

And then she does the least Laney-like thing I'd ever expect, and she pulls me behind a building and kisses me.

And pulls me deeper behind the building to a small little enclosed garden.

And kisses me more.

And slips her hand down my pants and strokes me.

And then she drops to her knees.

In public.

Where anyone could walk by and see.

And she licks me. Sucks me into her mouth. Strokes me with her tongue and takes me deeper until I'm panting.

Dying.

Coming.

Coming so hard down her throat.

Right here. In public.

Fuck me.

I like this Laney Kingston.

I like her *a lot*.

And it'll hurt like hell when this is over.

26

Is this what being awake feels like?

I'm _exhilarated_.

Not just dreaming about being free but _feeling_ free. Feeling like I'm _enough_. Like I'm understood and accepted and imperfect and _celebrated_ for being imperfect.

Like I finally know what that _thing_ is that I've wanted but have been afraid of putting into words.

I didn't have to put it into words though. Theo did it for me.

And it's not _wrong_. It's so right it hurts but in the best way.

I want my entire purpose on this earth to be loving someone with everything I have. Fuck happy. I want a love that's so much more.

It's so simple, but so _everything_.

Meaning.

I want _meaning_. A purpose. Not just in my work life, but in my _home_ life.

"Here. This way." I pull his hand as we duck back out of

the little alcove where I left him cross-eyed and tug him toward a small restaurant with an *Open* sign in the window. It's adorable, a cute little blue shack with a sign hanging in the window proclaiming it has the island's best bacon.

Theo resists.

I ignore him.

I heard his stomach grumble the minute we stepped off of the boat. Heard it again right before I pulled him off the path. And I hear it now, even as he's resisting.

"Should get back," he says.

"We went *parasailing* and nothing went wrong. We're keeping this streak up, and I'm feeding you bacon, because that will turn me on."

He whimpers.

He actually whimpers.

I pause and turn to face him, and *oh my god*.

I thought he looked at *me* like he was falling in love.

Nope.

Start over, Laney.

You are not a plate of bacon.

I pat his ass. "You earned it. Let's go."

"I *can't*."

"Why not?"

He makes a frustrated noise, then points at his abs while he looks up at the blue, blue sky.

I make quick work of buttoning his shirt, sad to see his skin and tats disappearing behind the bright Hawaiian fabric. "There. Now you're suitable to go inside."

His lips flatten and he tries to glare at me.

I grin.

He's so satisfied that he can't even be mad at me. "I meant I need to *look good*, Laney."

"I'll take a picture of you eating the bacon. You'll look great."

"That is *not*—never mind."

And everything clicks. "Oh my god. *Oh my god*. You're a *model*."

He briefly closes his eyes.

"I mean, I don't care what you do, but it seems like you're not eating enough, and—"

"It's a side thing," he says.

"That makes sense. It's probably a lot like acting, right? Not something you do every day since they have to pick you? What have you—where would I—" I cut myself off with a squeak. Flap my hands. Shake my head. "Never mind. Never mind. The only thing that matters about a job is that it makes you happy. If you want to talk about it, you'll talk about it."

"I don't want to talk about it."

"I can understand that. It's probably something that makes people act—um…like this?"

I am such an idiot and I need to stop talking.

But one corner of his mouth hitches up like he's amused.

Not all the way amused.

But some amused.

The woman at the doctor's office.

Of course.

She recognized him *because he's a model.*

His stomach rumbles again.

I give him a stern librarian look even though I want to google him and see what he's been in. Like, *now.*

"Fuck me, that's hot," he mutters. "Okay. Okay. Let's go have bacon."

I squeal and clap my hands—even models need to eat, don't they?—and ten minutes later, we're having coffee and a plate of bacon while we wait for pineapple pancakes and loco moco, which is apparently a Hawaiian breakfast dish that I declared we both have to try while we're here.

Theo eyes the bacon.

I pick up a piece and bite into it, and *oh my god.*

Is it being in paradise?

Is it the effect of multiple orgasms and parasailing?

Is it being here with Theo?

Or is this the most freaking delicious bacon I've ever had in my life? It's salty and just a little sweet and the perfect kind of crunchy and *oh my god*, I am moving here and living in this kitchen where Theo will make me chocolate chip cookies and the chef here will make me bacon and I will love everyone with everything I have and life will be complete.

"Are you coming over that bacon?" Theo asks.

"Mm-hmm."

If I grab the whole plate and declare it to be mine, will that be enough to spark him to steal a piece?

Wait. Why are there two of him? Even getting drunk off my ass didn't result in *two* of him.

Oh.

Because my eyes are crossed from how perfect this bacon is. "You should definitely not eat this," I tell him. "It's terrible. You'll hate it."

He laughs.

Theo.

Laughing at my awful dad joke.

I grab the plate and wrap my arms around it. "You can have the *rest* of breakfast."

"Mind games?" His eyes are getting warmer. No, *hotter*. And he's working that smile in ways that are guaranteed to make me forget about this bacon.

And this is *fucking awesome* bacon.

"No," I lie. "I want all of this for myself. Sorry. I thought maybe we had something, but I'm going to run away with this bacon instead."

He snickers.

And I smile.

I made Theo laugh. *Again*. Considering how many years he's called me *Princess Plainy-Laney*, it's a sweet triumph to cause any kind of amusement for the man who basically redefined *fun* in our hometown.

I lift a piece and rub it all over my lips, and I'm not pretending much when my eyes slide shut and I moan in appreciation.

"Do it again," Theo croaks.

"Not until you eat a piece and I get to watch you do the same."

"I hate bacon."

"Theo Monroe. You are a lot of things, but you are *not* a liar. Don't start now."

He visibly swallows.

I dart my tongue out to lick the bacon.

Holy hell.

That is *good* bacon.

We're getting another plate. And six more to go.

He growls softly to himself, reaches across the table, snags a piece of bacon, and shoves the whole thing into his mouth.

And then he growls again.

This one's feral and erotic and desperate and *everything*.

"Holy *fuck*," he says.

His eyelids droop, and he chews slower, like he's savoring it.

And I get hot and bothered in every single freaking cell in my body.

My skin is on fire. My vagina is legit throbbing. My clit is heavy. My nipples are tight. My breasts ache. My lips and tongue want to be on him. I can't take my eyes off of him as he whimpers softly, rubbing his mouth like he can make it last longer, or experience it with more parts of himself.

Even my hair roots are turned on.

And watching a hot, tatted god of a man be reduced to a whimpering pile of need by bacon while he reaches across the table to grip my wrist with his free hand after I went down on him *in public*?

I will never, *ever* be the same.

"Don't. Touch. That. Bacon," he orders.

I squeeze my legs together, old Laney whispering *you're going to get thrown out if you both have orgasms right here at the table*, new Laney shoving the prudish poor thing back into a corner.

"This bacon?" I stroke it with my free hand.

He swallows, moans, and then scoots his chair around the square table until he's so close to me that our thighs are lined up. He wraps one arm firmly around my back, then picks up one of the two remaining pieces of bacon. "One bite," he says as he touches it to my lips.

"A *big* bite?" I feel myself talking, but I hear Marilyn Monroe coming out of my mouth.

"A small bite. I'm the only fucking big bite you get today."

So I need to change my panties now.

And I don't really care.

I part my lips and let him feed me the bacon, but I lick the whole underside before I bite the tip off.

"Naughty Laney is my favorite," he says hoarsely. "I need you to know that before this hard-on you and the bacon are giving me kills me."

"Your turn." I grip his hand and guide the bacon to his mouth.

His eyes slide shut while he, too, licks it, then bites off a piece.

A *much* larger piece than I took.

But I don't mind. Not when he's acting like he hasn't had food in months.

"Theo with a hard-on for me and bacon is my favorite," I whisper while I nuzzle his ear with my nose.

"I just came ten minutes ago," he mutters around the bacon.

"I'm aware."

"Fuck me. Who *are* you?"

"I don't know, but I like finding out. Want another nibble?"

His gaze dips to my chest.

Then lower.

He can't see my pussy, but I get another throb deep inside at knowing he's thinking about nibbling on *me*.

"Pancakes and loco moco," our server says, making both of us jump.

"More bacon too," I stutter out.

She smirks.

"Four plates of it," Theo says.

His voice is thick and husky and raw, and our server pauses to squint at him with one eye. "This your first time in here?"

His ears go red.

Not just pink.

Red.

"Yep," he says.

"You're familiar."

Oh my god.

He's famous in Hawaii.

Theo's a famous model in Hawaii.

And he's clearly uncomfortable with it. "One of those faces," he says without looking at her. Or me.

"No, I don't think that's it. But you're *familiar*."

Weird. But also, he's clearly suffering here, so I'll help the poor guy out. "I see him in my dreams all the time," I say.

Theo's eyes flare wide while he whips his head to look at me, and then drops his head, laughs, and attacks breakfast like a starving man.

"He just got out of prison," I add in a whisper. "We were pen pals. Never met before today."

She looks at me.

Then at him.

I stroke his arm. "Not bad for slammer ink, is it?"

He snorts over his pancake, then moans as he shovels it into his mouth.

The server stares at his arm. "Probably right. He must have one of those faces," she finally says. "More coffee?"

"And bacon. Please." I give her my best *good girl* smile.

She nods and heads back to the kitchen, tossing glances back at us as she goes.

"You're ruining me, Laney," Theo says between gulps of pancakes.

"One meal will *not* ruin you, and while I sincerely hate having people tell me what I should and shouldn't eat, I'm still going to tell you that you *do need to eat*, and on top of that, you deserve to enjoy a meal here and there, *especially* with all of the stress this week."

I don't think he hears a word I say while he's shoveling in the pancakes. He pauses, blinks, and then sticks a forkful of pancake in my mouth. "Is that as good as I think it is?"

I chew slowly. And then I give him my best *naughty Laney* grin. "I make better."

"*Fuck me*," he mutters again.

"Come over sometime when we get back. I'll show you."

His gaze lifts to mine.

And holds.

It's not deer-in-the-headlights.

It's *don't fuck with me*.

It's *I've always liked you but never thought this would happen*.

It's *I told you what I want out of a relationship*.

"We can try to break the code on the magic bacon too," I whisper.

He keeps staring like he wasn't the one who said just an hour or so ago that he'd take me on a hot-air balloon ride when we get back home. "There are a lot of parts of me you won't like when we get to know each other better."

"That's a pretty large assumption. I thought I'd been

pretty clear that perfection is bullshit and I don't want to be Princess Plainy-Laney anymore."

He flinches like it hurts *him* to remember he's called me that all his life. "You're not worried about what Emma will say?"

"Emma adores you."

"Or what your parents will say?"

"I can't live for them. And if they expect me to..." Then I have a hard road ahead of me.

But it'll be hard no matter what. I've known that for a year, and I've been sitting on my hands *not living* out of fear.

Screw the fear.

Fuck the fear.

His brown eyes study me like he knows so much more about life than I can even begin to imagine. Like he knows what I'm facing with choosing me over my parents' expectations. Like he can see my future playing out in ways I would never expect, and he could tell me all of his hard-earned wisdom, but he knows I need to face it for myself in the moment for it to truly change me from who I've been to who I want to be.

One corner of his mouth hitches up in a smile. "Good for you."

And once again, I wonder who this man is. Because I don't feel like I'm sitting next to the guy who gave me the orgasm of my life last night.

I feel like I'm sitting next to a life coach. Or a therapist. Or at least someone who understands so much more about the world than my sheltered ass can even begin to comprehend.

He shoves the pancakes in front of me, then snags the plate of loco moco, which is like a breakfast hamburger with eggs and all the trimmings on it.

And he eats.

And moans.

And eats.

And moans.

And feeds me until I'm stuffed.

And eats some more, until he finally collapses back in his chair and lets his eyes slide shut while he rests a hand on his belly.

I squeeze his thigh. "Happy?" I murmur.

"Gonna regret this so much later."

"But are you happy *now*?"

One eye peeks open and aims at me. "Yeah," he says softly. "I'm happy now."

The sentiment lights my whole heart brighter than all of the stars in the universe combined.

But it's short-lived.

Because my phone is suddenly exploding.

Based on the way his face twitches, his might be too.

"Wedding SOS, I'd bet," I say quietly.

He loops a hand behind my neck and pulls me in for a long, deep kiss.

Not the answer I expect to my guess.

But I love it. I want *more* of it.

And I hope I'm not fooling myself in thinking we can continue exploring all of what this is once Emma's happily married and we're all back home.

27

THEO

THERE'S a special kind of living that comes with watching someone else step out of their shell and embrace everything they've been missing.

Watching Laney blossom? Watching her put on a bikini and launch herself into the world's worst—but also best—cannonball? Watching her laugh as she parasails above the ocean? The confidence it took to go down on me *outside,* where anyone could've walked by the little garden? The joy and arousal on her face over the bacon at breakfast?

This is a whole new side of Laney and it makes me like her more than I thought I ever could.

I shouldn't have let her think I was a model.

But I'm not ready for this to end. I still have today. I still have tomorrow.

I can find a way to tell her what I do on the side without scaring her off.

I have to. Every minute I spend with her, I want two more. I'm falling hard. And I don't want to stop.

It's hell to watch her dash off toward Emma's room to deal with a dress emergency that I'm unequipped to help with.

If she wanted it knitted back together, I'd be her guy.

But I know it's lacy and frilly and satiny, and I am *not* the guy for that. Lot more experience ripping those fabrics than putting them back together.

Doesn't mean I'm useless, though.

I promise Laney I'll stay away from the golf course—*for your sake, Theo, because nothing's gone wrong today and you don't deserve to get shit for doing nothing wrong and it's likely Chandler will give you shit just for breathing, which isn't fair*—but I don't promise her I won't provoke trouble in other ways.

And *other ways* is me checking on the kittens, and then leaving the bungalow to stride behind the unmanned front desk of the resort and into the office.

A woman with brown skin and thick black hair pulled up into a bun with a red hibiscus in it looks up at me from digging in one of the drawers. She's in the resort's Hawaiian print pattern, and her nametag says *Kalani*.

"Sir, this area is off-limits for guests. I'll be with you at the desk shortly."

I smile at her and pull up a floral folding chair across from her. "My sister's getting married here tomorrow, and I was hoping you could tell me everything's squared away for it."

"No one's getting married here tomorrow, sir."

"Theo, please. My sister booked a resort wedding. For tomorrow. Here. Got the receipt and everything."

She squeezes her eyes shut. "It's not on the calendar, sir."

Of course it's not. *Dammit.* "So how do we get it on the calendar?"

She stares at me with undisguised suspicion.

I give her a friendly, nonthreatening smile in return.

"Are you a federal agent?" she whispers.

Don't know why I didn't see that coming, but it catches

me so off guard I almost fall off the seat laughing. "Sorry," I sputter. "Sorry. That's—that's never happened before."

She heaves a sigh. "A girl can hope."

"Things aren't so great around here, huh?"

There's more wariness in the look she gives me than I've felt about nearly anything in my life.

I hold up my hands. "Don't need to know. Look, my sister's had posters of this place hanging on her walls since she was about ten years old. If she wants the wedding of her dreams, I'm giving her the wedding of her dreams. Point me to your storage closets and anywhere I can book a minister last minute, and I'll get out of your hair."

"You say you already paid for a wedding."

I shrug. "I'll talk to management later."

"You're being suspiciously nice about this."

"All I want is for my sister to be happy."

And for Laney to be happy. But that's not something I'll find in this office today.

That's something I'll have to fix when I tell her my whole truth.

Eventually.

"Her fiancé is a terrible tipper," Kalani finally says.

Fitting. "Are *you* a fed?" I joke. "Tricking me into saying things I'll regret later?"

That earns me a smile in return. "I wouldn't want my sister marrying a terrible tipper."

"And I won't be the reason her wedding doesn't happen when I have time to fix it. So can you help a guy out?"

"Why not? The new management's wrecked this place so badly, it won't even exist in another week. Here. Take my keys. I have a new job lined up starting tomorrow. Don't even care if I don't get my last paycheck. I'm just—"

The bell dings at the front desk four times, and then a nut-shriveling voice calls, "Hello? Hello, we'd like to check in, please."

The Kingstons.

Laney's parents.

They're here.

Kalani sighs again. "—apparently checking in one last set of guests before I leave this place too." She hands me a set of keys. "There's a storage closet on the back side of the bistro. It should have what you're looking for. And, for your sake, be aware that there are cameras basically on the corner of every building. If you want to...you know...have fun entertaining your girlfriend outside of your bungalow again."

My shoulders hitch.

But Kalani's smiling as she heads out to the front desk. "Lucky girl," she adds.

I pocket the keys and follow her, head down, hoping I won't be noticed, but there it is.

The sniff of disdain.

I glance up, verifying Laney's parents are here, and yep.

I've been spotted.

And I am not a welcome sight.

My entire body flinches.

Can't help it.

Old habit.

You have this, I tell myself. *You know your worth.*

Not talking about my bank account either.

Talking about my basic worth as a human being.

I force myself to make direct eye contact with Gail Kingston. Charles is right behind her. Both of them are in business casual travel clothes that would go well with the getup Laney had on when she arrived the other day.

Charles is slower on the uptake, but when he spots me, his lip curls too.

Like I'm the *riffraff*.

I nod to both of them and turn to continue on my way.

"Dear god, he even has to get a part-time job on vacation," she mutters to him.

He grunts.

Fuck this. I have a wedding to save.

First place I'm heading? Back to the restaurant I just left.

I have a strong suspicion I know why I'm familiar to the server. And I know I can charm the hell out of anyone, and I need someone who can cook a rehearsal dinner.

That's all that matters.

"Oh, lookie, the Kingstons are here," Uncle Owen says as he enters the lobby too. He chuckles. "Came looking for towels, and instead I get Snaggletooth Creek royalty. Good to see you. Em's gonna be so glad you're here. Won't she, Theo?"

"Sure." I step out from behind the desk, jangling the keys in my pocket and telling myself the Kingstons' opinion of me doesn't matter.

Except it does.

Because—

"Theo's been hanging out with Delaney every day," Uncle Owen continues. "Nice to see all the young 'uns getting along, isn't it?"

I turn at that.

Can't help it.

Want to know if it's my imagination or if they're still horrified.

Still horrified.

That's definitely horrified in the way Gail's face has twisted while she *actually clutches her necklace* and Charles's spine snaps straight and his eyes turn into laser beams that threaten to flay me alive if I've so much as thought about his daughter's *no-no box*.

Walk away, Theo. They don't matter.

Except they do.

They're Laney's parents.

I like Laney.

I like Laney *a lot*.

I want to wake up with her in my bed, in my own damn house, and help her make pancakes. I want to experiment with recreating that bacon. I want to take her sledding down Death Hill—over-named, by the way—and listen to her shriek and scream and laugh when we get to the bottom. I want to kiss her while it's snowing. I want to take her on a hot-air balloon ride.

"I'm sure there's a good reason for a bridesmaid to associate with the bride's family," Gail says crisply.

Charles looks like he's debating if anyone would miss me if he skewered me like a shrimp and dumped my ass at sea.

"Vacation Laney's fun," I say. "I like her."

Yep.

Can't help myself.

And you'd think there'd be some satisfaction in their shocked horror, but there's not.

All I have is a creeping feeling of utter worthlessness that I've spent more than a decade trying to get over.

I have worth. I have worth. I have worth.

Laney knows it. Laney knows it. Laney knows it.

Not helping.

Not as much as I want it to.

Especially considering that little bit of *hope* growing in my chest is futile.

Dreaming about Laney back home requires telling Laney that my penis earns a nice big paycheck every month.

It doesn't matter how much she's changed.

That'll be a dealbreaker for her.

No doubt.

No question.

So I'll be the guy showing her a fun time, showing her she *can* be courageous and bold and live the life she wants to live, until I have to tell her.

Which is *not* before Emma's wedding.

No trouble. No upset bridesmaids. No more hiccups for Emma getting what Emma wants.

My phone buzzes in my hand, and my heart leaps in joy when I see it's from Laney.

Dress is going to take a while. Can you double-check that everything's okay for the rehearsal dinner tonight?

Yep.

Even when it's about a disaster, I love seeing her name on my phone.

It's not, but I'm on it. Don't tell Emma, I text back.

And then I get busy fixing what I can.

With the creeping sensation that all too soon, I'll have to face what I can't.

28

LANEY

I DON'T SEE Theo again until I dash onto the lanai a few minutes before the rehearsal dinner is supposed to start, and alarm bells go off in every part of me the minute we make eye contact.

My parents are here.

I don't see them.

I don't hear them.

But I *know* they are, and not just because they're supposed to be, and they texted to let me know they'd landed and gotten checked in.

It's the look on his face—that wary, *did you mean it when you said your parents would have to accept that you can make your own choices?* look on his face—that telegraphs that they're here, they've seen him, and they've passed judgment without him doing a damn thing beyond existing.

I beeline to him without telling Emma or Sabrina or Claire where I'm going.

Pretty sure they all know.

Pretty sure Emma's ecstatic that we're getting along.

Thank goodness.

Someone needs to be.

"Are you cooking?" I whisper to him as he hovers at the edge of the lanai where it's easiest to roll out the food from the bistro kitchen. There's a smear of something on his shirt.

"Got help."

"You are amazing." I want to throw myself at him. Kiss him. Thank him. *Touch* him.

But I know my parents are here, and *dammit dammit dammit*, be bigger than this, Laney.

Be bigger.

Touch him.

"Dress okay?" He stares at something on my left cheek instead of making eye contact.

"Yes. We got the dress fixed. I don't have a clue why it was sent to the cleaners, or what they thought they were doing with it that was most definitely *not* cleaning it, but we have it, and it took most of the day, but it's fixed, and it's fine. Are you okay? What do you need?"

Wary eyes finally look at me full-on. "I'm good."

"You don't *look* good."

"I'm *good*."

"Theo, I—"

"Delaney! Sweetheart, we missed you."

My shoulders tense at the sound of my mother's voice, but I don't turn around to say hi.

Not yet.

First, I lift a brow at Theo. "Did they do something?"

"Gotta go make sure dinner's ready."

"*Theo.*"

"Long day. Up in my head. Working on it."

He doesn't sound like he's *working on it*.

But he is turning around and walking away with a muttered, "They missed you."

"There's my girl." My mom squeezes me in a hug from the side. I glance up in time to see her wrinkle her nose at Theo's backside.

And that's all it takes to make me tense.

When I was little, Mom wore jeans and T-shirts to work. She had long hair that she pulled back in a ponytail, and *girls' day* meant we camped out in her bathroom and painted each other's toenails.

Now, she gets Botox. She also dyes her hair, and she keeps it short and chic. *Girls' day* these days means an all-day adventure to a high-end spa in Denver—yes, that's what counts as an *adventure* in my life back home—and I think the last time she wore jeans was probably fifteen years ago. "Mom. Can you *please* be nice to Theo?"

"I'm being perfectly nice."

"You're making faces at him."

"We ran into Owen. He said you've been very friendly with Emma's brother."

"He's a nice man."

"I know, sweetie, but he has blinders on when it comes to his nephew."

"*Theo* is a nice man, Mom."

Her lips purse again. "What's this frown for? Emma's getting *married*. And we're in Hawaii, and dinner smells fantastic. There's an early morning dolphin cruise. We should go Sunday morning before you have to fly back home."

"Mrs. Kingston! You made it." Emma dashes across the lanai to hug my mom, then waves at my father, who's standing with Chandler's father close to the short walk to the beach.

"Oh, Emma, sweetie, you look beautiful. I can't believe your day is finally *tomorrow*."

Emma's beam is only half-strength. "Me too. It's been *forever*, hasn't it?"

"Good things are worth waiting for. Where's your groom? I haven't seen him yet."

"Still cleaning up after golf. He'll be here soon. Can I borrow Laney for a minute?"

"Of course, sweetheart. Anything you need."

"Thanks, Mrs. Kingston. Oh! Chandler's mom is over at the bar. Have you said hi to her yet? I know she'd love to see you."

My mom heads to the bar.

Emma grabs my elbow in a death grip and hauls me back in the direction I'm usually hauling Theo.

"What's wrong?" I whisper.

"You looked like you were about to bite your mother's head off."

"Em, I—"

She squeals and throws her arms around me. "I knew it! I knew you'd like Theo if you gave him half a chance. What do you need me to do to help handle your parents?"

I gape at her.

Like, I am a fish.

I am *completely* a fish.

"*Laney.* You've spent the past year saying you want to have fun. I know *no one* who's more fun than Theo. And this wasn't a setup. I really did need someone to keep him separated from Chandler. But *you like him*. And he's had a crush on you forever. And this is *the best thing ever*."

"But—but—but you didn't want Claire to babysit him because you were afraid he'd—he'd—"

I cannot say the words *seduce her* to my best friend when we're talking about her brother.

And the fact that I'm having sex with him.

And wanting to see him and date him when I get home too.

She shrugs. "You're a year off your last break-up instead of a week. This is different."

I do a fish imitation for a little bit longer.

"I know, I know," she says. "This might be just a little fling. But you're having *fun*. I can see it all over you. Even if it doesn't last, it won't be any worse than it's been with having you two avoid each other for the past ten years. And if it does last...then I get my two favorite people together all the time. This is the best wedding gift. Seriously."

"Even better than the hamster balls?" I blurt.

Her eyes bulge a little, and then she giggles.

"Chandler was *so pissed*," she whispers.

"But it was *funny*," I whisper back.

"I think it was just timing. You know he would've laughed his ass off if he wasn't so stressed."

I do. "I'm so glad I didn't marry Christopher."

The words leave my mouth, and I realize too late how that sounds. *Christopher would've been an uptight ass during our wedding too.*

Emma winces.

"I didn't mean—" I start, but she squeezes me in a hug before I can finish.

"I know he's difficult sometimes," she whispers, "but I love him. I do. And I know we'll be happy once we get through this."

Oh, god.

That's what I told myself every single bad date with Christopher.

Every. Single. One.

We'll be happy once we get used to each other's quirks. We'll be happy once he gets a promotion. We'll be happy once we're living in the same town. We'll be happy once we get through this.

Have I not been paying attention? Is this what Em's been saying about Chandler for years and I didn't notice? Or is this really just a hard time for them?

"Em—"

"Oh, did you hear that? I think Chandler's back. He's

bringing an old friend from college. One I've never met, if you can believe it. Have to dash. Bride duties and all that." She squeezes me harder. "Be happy, Laney. Just be happy, okay? And all the other stuff—it'll work out. Theo's complicated sometimes, but he has the biggest heart. Love you. And *thank you*. You will never know just how much I appreciate everything you've done this week."

I try to say something else, but she's gone.

I clench my eyes shut and take a deep breath.

Everything feels wrong.

Everything.

Two arms loop around my stomach.

I don't jump. I'm not startled.

I know who it is.

I can smell him. *Sense* him.

And it's so easy to lean back into his arms while he presses a kiss to my shoulder in this quiet little alcove tucked away from everyone else.

"Tomorrow's gonna be a clusterfuck," he says softly.

I doubt he's wrong. I blink my eyes open and study the flowers, the trees, the bushes, the bright green grass all around us as I tilt my head to his. "How do you tell someone you love that you're afraid they're making a huge mistake when it's all they've wanted for *years*?"

"Can't stop people from making mistakes."

"But I *want to*."

"You sure it's a mistake?"

"No," I whisper. "Not when it's what she says she wants. When she says it's all she's ever wanted. But all day, I keep wondering if there are supposed to be so many disasters. If this was my wedding, I'd say it was a sign. But it's Emma, and she'd say—"

"Anything worth having is worth working for," he finishes for me.

I sigh. "What do you think?"

"Doesn't matter."

"If it was your wedding, would you listen to the signs, or would you say it's worth working for?"

He kisses my neck. "I don't care about weddings. I care about people."

So simple.

So Theo.

I close my eyes again and hold his arms while he holds me.

How can this feel *so right* here, but so complicated just a few feet away?

"I told my mom to be nice to you," I whisper.

"I can deal with people not liking me."

"But she's not giving you a chance. And that's wrong."

"One thing at a time. I went back to where we had breakfast. To find a chef for dinner. That's all."

"Oh, that's brilliant. I can't wait to see what they do with dinner."

"You're sitting with the bridesmaids."

"Only physically."

I feel his lips smile against my neck. "I wanted you to know. So you don't think I was flirting with anyone else."

"It's okay. I know you have resting flirt face."

It's not my imagination when his entire body relaxes behind mine. Especially when it's accompanied by that chuckle. "Can't help being born this fabulous."

He's so easy to smile at, which is one more unexpected gift of this week. "If I rub you a little more, think it'll come off on me?"

"We should try it and see."

I laugh. "I know you didn't just say I could be more fabulous."

"Sorry. Thought about you rubbing me, and my brain broke."

The voices on the lanai get louder, and because I'm boring

at every given opportunity, no matter how much I try to fight it, I pull out my phone and check the time.

Nearly there.

"Still staying with me tonight?" The husky hope in his voice doesn't just make my clit tingle.

It also makes my heart tighten. "Yes."

"Even if your parents see?"

I shiver. That won't go over well and I know it. But I *can't* live for them.

And I'm frankly horrified that I ever treated Theo the same way my mom still does. "Even if my parents see."

He presses another kiss to my neck, and this one comes with a gentle suckle that turns my nipples inside out and makes me want to skip dinner entirely.

"Promise me you'll eat," I order.

"I'll eat you."

"*Dinner*, Theo."

"I'll eat you for dinner."

I sigh.

He gives me one last squeeze. "Thank you for worrying about me, Laney."

And then he's gone, heading back to the kitchen where he'll get zero credit for saving the night.

No, that's not true.

I'll give him credit.

I'll give him all the credit in the world.

And I'll be counting the minutes until I can do it in private.

29

THEO

IN THE INTEREST of *not* looking like the guy who's saving the wedding that he doesn't want to happen, I leave the kitchen in the capable hands of the temporary staff and head to the lanai in a fresh Hawaiian shirt.

I hang with the Sullivan triplets across the way from where all of the mothers and bridesmaids are squealing over Emma and each other, and when they ask if I want to get together later to play hot pineapple—aka hot potato, but with pineapples and a lot of alcohol and some truth-or-dare mixed in—I decline.

I want to say yes.

But I don't want to be the reason anything goes wrong. Not this close to Emma's wedding.

She's ushering everyone to their seats so that dinner can be served.

The triplets head to their spot at the front tables with the rest of the wedding party and the parents.

I duck to the back to sit with Uncle Owen and Aunt

Brenda and a few guys I knew from high school who flew in to celebrate the happy couple.

"Wanna bet which one of the triplets throws food first?" Uncle Owen says.

"There will be *no* food-throwing," Aunt Brenda says.

Uncle Owen winks at her.

She blushes.

Go, Uncle Owen, but maybe not in front of me?

I spot my dad up at the head table, looking around.

Probably means he's looking for me. I wave.

He gestures to the seat next to him.

I jerk my head at Chandler.

Dad sighs.

I shrug.

He shrugs.

He doesn't know I'm paying for the wedding. Don't know if he knows about my GrippaPeen stardom. I do know he's picked up on the tension between Chandler and me, and after all we've been through, he probably recognizes that I'm staying out of the way to try to not cause any trouble.

Not like he wasn't there when I caught a flamingo costume on fire by sneezing.

A plate of nut-crusted mahimahi, purple potatoes, and coleslaw appears in front of me.

"I figured it out," the server from this morning whispers in my ear. "I know where I know you from. Your... arms... are very distinctive."

Every ounce of blood in my body drains to my toes.

"I won't tell." She giggles. "I'd be telling on myself, wouldn't I?"

"Speak up, young lady," Aunt Brenda orders.

"He's already got himself a nice girlfriend. We think," Uncle Owen adds. "Okay, we hope. Been a while since he had a girlfriend. Could use someone to make him feel good about himself."

"Thanks, Uncle Owen."

"I got your back, kiddo."

He fist-bumps me.

"What was she whispering to you?" Aunt Brenda demands as the waitstaff I hired for the night passes plates to the rest of them. "Was it inappropriate?"

"Do I ever do anything appropriate?"

She sniffs.

Uncle Owen cackles with utter glee.

I wish I was having a private dinner with Laney anywhere but here. On the beach. In the back of the Jeep while looking up at the stars from the volcano park. In our bungalow while kittens frolic all over both of us.

No parents.

No relatives.

No wedding.

"I heard a secret about Bean & Nugget," Uncle Owen says.

Ah. The secret. Seems I can't avoid this one any longer. "Yeah?"

He leans in. "I heard they started sourcing *unethical beans*."

"What's that about beans?" Aunt Brenda says.

"They're *unethical*," Uncle Owen repeats.

"What's unethical about them?"

"I dunno. What can be unethical about a bean?"

I look down at my plate, then glance up toward Laney.

She's watching me. And her parents are watching her watching me, which I notice, but she doesn't.

She lifts a fork and then both of her eyebrows.

Makes me smile.

Can't help it.

She cocks her head. *Do I need to come over there and force-feed you?* that gesture says.

Wouldn't object, princess. I would not object.

Her cheeks go a light pink as if she can hear my thoughts.

I pick up my fork, stab the fish, and dutifully take a bite.

She smiles. *Good boy.*

Fuck me.

I've never wanted to be a *good boy* in my life, but I would eat this entire plate and Uncle Owen's too if she'd purr that to me in bed tonight.

Doesn't hurt that it's delicious.

She jerks her head to the side like she's just realized someone's talking to her, and her face erupts in a deep red blush this time.

Her mother's frowning.

Her father looks confused.

And Uncle Owen and Aunt Brenda are still arguing over how a bean can have ethics and why that's such a big secret.

I put my head down and eat.

It's *good.* And I'm hungry.

I can work out more tomorrow. Cut back on my calories again when I get home.

Hell, the women who subscribe to my channel would relate to putting on a little vacation weight.

But what if it doesn't come off?

But what if they don't like it?

But what if this trip makes it all fall apart and you suddenly don't have a bigger purpose anymore?

I tell the voices to shut up and I get back to work cleaning my whole plate.

Like a *good boy.*

I am absolutely asking Laney to call me a *good boy* in bed tonight.

Zero. Question.

And that's what I'm fantasizing about when I realize something's wrong.

There's a commotion up near the head table.

"Whazzat?" Uncle Owen says.

"Someone fell," Aunt Brenda says.

"Out of their chair?"

"Oh, god, call 9-1-1!" Chandler's mom shrieks.

"Clear the room! I'm a doctor!" Lucky booms.

"You're a nurse, stud," Decker yells.

"Better than you," Lucky hollers.

Laney's out of her seat, bolting to the next table, where —*oh, fuck.*

It's her father.

Her father's on the floor.

Has to be.

No one else is missing from the table. Her mother's on her feet, sobbing and pointing.

And Lucky is diving into action.

I rise.

Everyone's rising.

Laney's hugging her mom, looking terrified, and I can't—I can't—

"EpiPen!" Lucky hollers. "Anyone have an EpiPen?"

"Me!" Chandler bellows. "Emma. *Emma.* Where's my EpiPen?"

"You don't have an EpiPen," my sister cries.

"I got mine!" Jack yells.

EpiPen.

EpiPen.

Fuck.

Fuck.

"You think he's allergic to something in the dinner?" Aunt Brenda says. "Who's allergic to bread crumbs and fish?"

"It's macadamia nuts," Addison says at the next table. "The fish has crushed macadamia nuts."

My fingers go cold. My head gets light. And I feel like someone punched me in the stomach.

"You think he's allergic to macadamia nuts?" Uncle Owen asks her. He's standing on a chair. "Might be right. Look. See? Already starting to breathe again with that EpiPen injection."

Gail drops to the ground next to Charles and cries.

Laney's holding the back of the chair with a death grip.

Everything's happening in slow motion and at warp speed all at once.

The kitchen staff has come running.

The resort staff has not.

The guests are all on edge, fidgeting and staying still and *this is not okay*.

"Back to eating, people." Jack and Decker move as one, clearing a space. "All's well."

"Still going to the hospital," I hear Lucky reply. "But they're right. All's well. And you're not gonna forget that little allergy the rest of the time here on the island. Right, Mr. K?"

"Didn't the kitchen staff get the allergy list?" Chandler says to Emma. "What the fuck's wrong with them?"

All's not well.

All is not well.

I look at Laney again.

She's not looking at me.

She's whispering furiously with her mom.

I want to hug her. I want to take her from here and never see that horrified, shell-shocked, grief-filled look on her face ever again.

But I did this.

I picked the menu.

I didn't see an allergy list.

And I almost killed someone who matters to the woman of my dreams.

So here the world goes again, reminding me that some dreams aren't meant to be.

30

LANEY

I AM GOING to throttle the crap out of Theo Monroe when I find him.

If I don't hug him to death first.

My father's fine. We get him to the hospital, where they treat him for an allergic reaction, and I help my mom hold it all together while he's admitted for observation overnight.

"Just forgot," he keeps saying to my mom. "You cut macadamia nuts out of our diet so long ago and always tell me what to order when we go out to eat. I *forgot*."

"You could've *died*," my mother keeps sobbing. "I didn't ask and *you could've died*."

"You didn't know there were macadamias all over this island."

"I told you three weeks ago I wasn't booking a tour of the macadamia nut factory across the island because you were allergic! I filled out the allergy information form on the wedding RSVP."

I flinch at that one.

Watching my dad go blue in the face while he gasped for

breath and then passed out was one of the scariest things I've ever seen in my life.

Terrifying doesn't even begin to describe it.

Definitely shifts some perspective.

Makes me think about what matters. About what's important. About hopes. Fears. Regrets.

And it reinforces how I want to live.

That's why I'm leaving my parents in the hospital while I catch a ride back to the resort now that I know my dad's stable and he's going to be fine.

Theo's not in our room.

He's not baking cookies in the bistro kitchen. Smells like he has been though.

Eventually, a very loud sneeze erupts from the general vicinity of the ocean, and it leads me to finding him sitting on the beach.

And shoveling his face full of cookies.

"Got enough to share?" I ask as I sit down next to him.

He lifts the bag and sets it far on his other side, well out of my reach. "No eating. I might kill you."

"Theo."

"Everything I touch turns to shit, Laney. Go away. You deserve not shit."

I ignore him, lift his arm, and settle under it. "It wasn't your fault."

"I picked the fucking menu."

So he heard through the grapevine that Dad's allergic to macadamia nuts.

Awesome.

Figured he would. It's why I kept texting him *this is not your fault.*

To no response.

"Don't even start with *you didn't know* and *this isn't your fault,*" he grumbles.

"How about *this is the universe's way of giving him a wake-up call that he's just as mortal as the next person?* Or maybe *this is the universe's way of reminding him to not be a judgmental ass?*"

"You shouldn't say things like that about your parents after they almost die. Believe me. That's a road to regrets."

I wrap my arms around him and hold him close.

He sighs heavily, like he's letting out all of the tension, and then wraps his other arm around me too.

A wave rolls to shore and covers our feet. It's cool but not cold. Just like it was this morning as we came down from parasailing.

"He *forgot* he was allergic because my mother's taken care of everything for him for the past too many decades," I say quietly. "And *she* didn't question dinner either."

"I should've asked."

"This wasn't your fault."

He grips me tighter like he's holding on to me since he can't hold on to the words and make himself believe them.

"I have a lot of secrets, Laney," he says quietly.

"Modeling is a cover and you're secretly a government assassin who just failed his last mission?"

"No." He doesn't laugh. Not even a little. "But I still don't want to tell you."

"Why?"

He doesn't answer.

Silence can say so many things. I want to hug him and kiss him enough to reassure both of us, but this silence—it's heavy.

Too heavy.

"Try me," I whisper. "Tell me a secret."

He shakes his head and drops one arm, then shoves half a cookie in his mouth.

The surf rolls over our feet again.

"Can we pretend I don't have secrets?" he asks quietly, smelling like chocolate chip cookies and paradise and everything right in my world. "For one more day? I don't want to ruin Emma's wedding by making you mad."

Whispering "sure" is one of the hardest things I've ever done.

I *want* to know his secrets. I want to know why he thinks they're so bad. I want to prove to him that I don't care, whatever it is.

Because this Theo?

The Theo who rescues cats and introduces me to parasailing and arranges meals on the fly so that his sister gets the wedding of her dreams even when he doesn't like the man she's marrying but respects her right to decide what she wants for herself?

I *cannot* believe this Theo has a secret so terrible that it would make me look at him any differently.

And it hurts that I haven't earned his trust enough for him to know that.

"Your dad's really okay?" he asks.

"Vitals are good. Benadryl's working. My mom's there to fuss, and the hospital staff is monitoring him too. He should be fine."

The surf rolls up to our ankles.

"You're my favorite part of paradise," he whispers. "Whatever happens, I just want you to know—you've been my favorite."

"Theo—"

He cuts me off with a searing kiss that takes me back over the ocean, to him telling me he wants love to be his purpose in life, that he wants loving someone to be all-consuming, all-encompassing, *everything*, the only thing that truly matters.

Like he chooses me.

He wants *me*.

And he desperately needs to know that I want him back. That I choose him back.

No matter his secrets. No matter our past. No matter what our relatives do or think or say.

I've never in my life felt more like I belong somewhere than I feel right now, with this man who had no reason to give me a chance at his heart kissing me like I'm his reason for living.

And I've never felt so inadequate as I do at wondering if I have it in me to love him as much as he deserves.

Everything in my life has always been so safe. Safe town. Safe family. Safe college. Safe job. Safe boyfriends. Safe sex.

Theo isn't *safe*.

He's *life*. Real life. *Big* life.

Can I be enough for him?

Can I?

"Awww, Laney and Theo, sitting in a tree…"

I flinch, and then I kick myself for flinching.

The Sullivan triplets. Where you hear one, you hear them all.

"I'm working on that reaction," I whisper to Theo as he releases me with a sigh.

"I know."

"I have a lot of work to do on me too. You don't embarrass me. *I* embarrass me."

He doesn't answer. Just watches me in the moonlight while the tide creeps farther up our legs.

"How's your dad, Laney?" Lucky asks.

"Better. Thank you. We're all so, so grateful that you were there and knew what to do."

"That was my brother."

Theo grunts softly. "Don't be a dick."

"Okay, yeah, that was me." Lucky's teeth flash in a grin in the moonlight. He apparently *is* alone. At least for the moment. "Welp. Gonna let you get back to what you were doing. Looked like fun. Need a third, you let me know."

I don't know what my face does, but it's enough to leave him laughing as he walks away.

I groan to myself. "It is *so hard* to get over decades of being a stick in the mud."

"Don't have to get over it," Theo says. "Just have to find where you're comfortable and where you're choosing for *you*."

I watch him in the moonlight too. He's resting his forearms on his knees, looking down like he's waiting for the next waves to roll in and he wants to know how close they'll get to his butt.

"You're very wise about the human experience."

"I'm very experienced in the human experience."

I nudge him softly with my shoulder. "Wanna come show me some of that experience after we play with some kittens? I'll help with chores."

"Not up for more fun in public?"

"Rather not risk the tide rolling in a jellyfish while you're naked."

He groans too.

And then he laughs. "Probably fucking right."

"Bring the cookies."

"Like I'd forget those."

He snags the cookies, then my hand.

And he grips it hard all the way back up to our room.

And then nothing else matters.

Nothing but that niggling fear in the back of my mind that this is all just a dream.

31

Theo

I'm so hot I'm roasting alive, but there's nothing in the universe that will make me move right now.

Not when Laney's bare ass is nestled against my morning wood, her arm trapping mine around her, her deep, even breaths pushing her back against my chest and then off again as light slowly filters into the bedroom.

Today, my sister marries a dick.

Tomorrow, I leave the island and head back home to *normal*.

And the day after—I don't know what happens the day after.

If Laney still wants to see me, I have to tell her. But not yet. Not today.

Tomorrow.

Or the day after.

Her phone buzzes on the nightstand.

She jerks awake and flails into a sitting position, tossing

off both me and the sheet covering her. "Custom cat claws," she gasps.

I angle back a little more in case she's not all the way awake yet. Stupid hand's asleep again. Starting to tingle.

And I'm starving.

Absolutely freaking *ravenous*.

"You always dream about work?" I ask her.

She blinks over her bare shoulder at me. "I...don't remember. Today, I mean. It definitely happens though. Once I even sent my parents a text in the middle of the night that we should offer custom-printed rocks. But I meant boulders. In my dream, they shrank to the size of—never mind. That's dumb."

I can't smile large enough at that. "No, it's adorable. I like how much you like your work. Not everyone does."

Her phone buzzes again—yep, that kills the smile—and she dives for it with a little squeak like she suddenly remembered it's probably important.

Most likely is.

Probably her parents.

Almost killed her dad last night. I can give her this one.

Especially since the reminder is very effectively killing my morning wood and I'd be pretty useless at making *her* smile anymore right now.

"Hey, Mom. Yeah. Yeah. How's Dad?"

Yep.

Morning wood all gone.

I climb out of bed, wincing as more tingles light up my arm. Laney's doing a lot of *mm-hmm*s and *uh-huh*s while I leave the bedroom and head into the bathroom.

Miss Doodles is perched atop the broken hide-a-bed, watching me. We let her out last night since she was clearly tired of having the kittens all over her.

Funny cat.

Can't blame her though. Seven kittens is a lot.

"Wanna see your babies?" I ask her.

She answers with a loud purr that I hear all the way across the room. And I take that as a yes.

"Yes, we're all helping Emma get ready in a couple hours," Laney says in the bedroom. "I'm glad he's feeling fine today. You two get some rest. No, really, go get rest. We'll do breakfast—and lunch—and dinner—when we're all home again. Just *rest*. I'll see you at the wedding."

I pick up Miss Doodles, who crawls onto my shoulder, lays her head down, and purrs like a freaking machine. "Good kitty."

She sighs happily and purrs more as I carry her into the room with her babies, who are all snuggled on top of each other in the bed.

Still sleepy time for them, apparently.

Miss Doodles leaps from my shoulder to join them on the bed like she missed them.

The kittens all rise and stretch and yawn and scramble for her with their big eyes and their oversize ears, making my heart melt into a puddle of utter love.

Speaking of fucking adorable.

And their little meows?

I could happily drown in those little meows.

The door opens behind me as I'm checking their food and litter, and Laney slips into the room wearing one of my T-shirts and nothing else. It covers her pussy, but just barely, as it touches her thighs.

Her hair's a disaster.

My fault.

No regrets.

Her cheeks are rosy, and her smile outshines even the best tropical sunrise. "Aww, look at them loving all over their mama. Oh my gosh! Even Fred's up there. Good boy, Fred. I won't get close." She turns that smile on me, and I swear it gets brighter. "Hand asleep?"

I'm flexing the troublesome one. "Warm-ups for when you're pissed and I have to jerk myself off."

She sputters out a laugh.

My stomach growls.

And she smiles even wider. "Wanna try some tropical smoothies for breakfast? I saw a place near that taco shop that looks like they'd have some pineapple mango something, with boba if we want to try it, and I'll bet they're even open."

"Shower first?"

Her eyes go dark in an instant. "You know I hate going out in public when I'm dirty."

And now I'm hard as a rock, remembering what she did in public yesterday.

I rush through finishing with the kittens, then toss Laney over my shoulder and haul her to the bathroom, where I teach her the fine art of the best kind of shower sex.

Means we have to rush through breakfast.

She doesn't order me to eat.

I eat all on my own. I'm starving.

Over breakfast, we talk about everything and nothing. Not our jobs. Not our families. But which TV shows we've watched. If skiing or snowboarding is better. Why she's only gone white water rafting once in her life and why it's been three years since she hit the slopes. Where I get my tattoos. What she'd have inked and where if she's brave enough.

And all too soon, we have to leave breakfast so she can help Emma get ready for her wedding.

Everything that felt so right at breakfast suddenly feels so wrong.

She grabs me by the cheeks before she slips out of the Jeep once we're back in the parking lot. "Are you okay?"

I could lie. Brush it off. Say I'm fine. I was ten minutes ago when we were having what felt like a totally normal breakfast date.

But I'm not.

At the end of today, my sister will be tied to Chandler Sullivan theoretically for life. He'll be at every holiday. I'll go to his kids' birthday parties. He'll be there every time I drop by to see Emma, and even if he's not, I'll know it's *his house* too now.

And tomorrow, we go back home and back to normal.

But *normal* is gone.

Bean & Nugget is in trouble and if Chandler's solution to the problem doesn't work, then I need to talk to Sabrina about how I can anonymously help her. Because I *want* to.

Laney might stick with me for a while but then get bored of me and move on after getting through her belated rebellion stage. *If* she takes it well when I tell her about my side hustle.

And I will never be the *me* that I was before this trip ever again.

"I don't want Emma to marry him, but I can't be the reason she doesn't," I confess to Laney after I've parked the Jeep when we get back to the resort. "And I'm—after the fire at the pool, and how he reacted to the gift the other night, and *all* of the other shit—she's waited so long for this, and I keep waiting for him to leave her and find a way to make it my fault so he doesn't have to deal with the consequences."

She studies me in a way that says I'm not crazy or paranoid, that she sees it too, and even if she doesn't, she understands why I do.

"It's so hard to watch someone you love do something that you understand but don't like," she says. "And even harder when you're afraid it'll hurt them."

Exactly. "That's how she's felt about me for all of our school years. That she loves me but I do shit she doesn't like."

She shakes her head. "The number of times I've heard her say *I wish I was more like Theo*... She admires you for living your life on your own terms."

"Now."

"No, then too. I remember because I didn't understand

then. But she did. She thought you were everything. I wish—"

"You could fix this," I finish for her.

She smiles. "I don't think I'll ever *fun* my way out of wanting to fix things."

"Fixing things is a superpower. Don't apologize for it." I nod past her. "Speaking of...looks like your getting-pretty bus is here."

She turns, and then she laughs.

Don't think it's at the sight of Emma and Claire talking to the driver of the limousine hired to take them to get their toes and fingers and faces and hair all done at a spa before the wedding.

Pretty sure the double take is at the sight of Sabrina in statement-making sparkly sunglasses, a pink boa, and a neon flashing necklace. She's carrying an oversize bag that appears to have more boas. Probably more sunglasses and necklaces too.

"I was just thinking, *I wish I could be more like Sabrina*," Laney says, "and then I remembered what you did in the shower this morning, and I'll bet Sabrina wants to be more like me without knowing why."

Now I'm half-hard. "Go on." I kiss her cheek, wanting to do more, but knowing the only place that will lead is to me tossing her into the back of the Jeep, where there's not enough coverage to keep her from exposing herself to the whole world. "Before I do something you'll regret later."

"Maybe we can sneak away from the reception and hide out in the kitchen again. I'll bring the ingredients. You be ready to take off your clothes."

If there's going to be a reception, I need to get the reception set up. She's not the only one with tasks today. "Killing me, Laney. Killing me."

"Save me a dance." She kisses me hard, and then she's off,

dashing across the parking lot to catch up with my sister and her other two bridesmaids.

I sit in the Jeep a minute longer, just watching, and when I turn, I almost jump out of my skin.

"Nice one," I say to Decker as I roll my window down. "Takes a lot to scare the shit out of me."

He frowns. "You hear what happened to Mr. K last night?"

Yep. My favorite thing to think about. "Was there. Lucky did a good job."

He looks across the parking lot to where the ladies are all hugging each other, frowning harder, which isn't a normal expression. "No, I mean, you hear that he's allergic to mac nuts?"

I wince. "Hard to miss."

"Me and my brothers got each other those DNA test kits for Christmas two years ago. Wanted to make sure we were related."

I open my mouth, and then I grin. "Can see where there'd be doubt."

"Our dad isn't our dad. We haven't told him."

Hello, left turn. "What?"

"And we're all allergic to macadamia nuts."

Oh, fuck. Oh, *fuck fuck fuck*. I could've killed my friends too. "You—you didn't eat dinner last night. Right? Tell me you didn't eat dinner last night."

"Oh, no way. We got our fish naked. Been asking about macadamias everywhere we've been this week. But...like... you're getting tight with Laney. We were wondering if you could ask her to, you know, take a test too. So we can see if we're right."

"That you're related?"

"Yeah."

"Decker. You're *identical triplets*."

"Not to *each other*. To *Laney*."

I blink at him.

Swipe a hand over my mouth.

Rewind the conversation and see where it veered after that left turn and where I lost track of what was going on, and why Laney needs to take a test to see if the triplets are related.

"You think...because you're allergic to macadamia nuts... and Charles Kingston is too...and a DNA test told you that your dad isn't your dad...that Charles is your dad," I say slowly.

"*Three* tests said our dad isn't our dad. Only reason Dad doesn't know is he hates computers and won't sign in to the account where you look to see if you have secret relatives. And I think Jack looks a little like Mr. K."

"*You're identical*," I repeat again.

He makes a face. "Only genetically. Otherwise, we look nothing alike. But genetically, we're all allergic to macadamia nuts. And my grandma never said a nice thing about the Kingstons, and she liked everyone."

I swipe a hand over my face.

And then something that's been quietly bothering me in a part of my brain I tend to ignore simmers to the surface.

Why didn't you ask Laney's family for money?

What did Sabrina say to that?

Why can't I remember?

Just remember the face she made. It said *because hell no*.

Not my business. Not my fucking business.

But it is if I want Laney to be my business. Can't keep secrets from her. Doesn't work like that.

And you're not keeping the biggest secret of all from her? that irritating worry center in my brain pokes and prods me.

But something else is suddenly bothering me too. "Allergies like that always get passed down?" I ask.

Is *Laney* allergic?

He shakes his head. "Not always. Guess Laney's lucky. Oh, shit. Unless Mr. K *isn't* her dad."

I squeeze my eyes shut.

Laney has too much of her father in her for that to be true.

"You'll ask her though? To take a test? And then hook up with us online so we can see if we're related?"

Wait.

Wait again.

"You've been fucking flirting with her."

He grins, but it's awkward. "Yeah, we didn't really suspect Mr. K was maybe our sperm donor until last night, and I kept it up last night so no one would suspect. No offense to Laney, but we made a lot of faces I won't repeat in front of you. Disappointing, really. Laney was hot in a bikini. But then, if we have the same genes, and we're all awesome, it makes sense."

"You—you—you're ridiculous."

"Yeah. Life's more fun that way. Until it's not. You know that. So you'll ask her? And like, if we flirt with her at the reception, just know we're all throwing up in our mouths for only genetic reasons and cover reasons while we do it."

"Yeah," I lie. "Yeah. I'll ask her."

"That'd be sick. Thanks." He looks over at the limo again as it pulls out of the parking lot.

"Sabrina know this?" I ask.

He grunts. "It's Sabrina." His frown gets deeper. "But I don't know if she knows just how much trouble the café's in. Chandler's kept that pretty close to the vest."

"She knows."

"You sure she knows?"

"Yep."

He eyes me. Then the spot where the limo used to be.

"Dunno, man. Seems like she'd be a lot more pissed if she knew. You know Sabrina doesn't get pissed without everyone knowing it."

I get the worst feeling in the pit of my gut.

The triplets' parents sold their share of the coffee shop to Chandler's family too, but Jack, Lucky, and Decker still had the option, just like Sabrina, to work at Bean & Nugget whenever they wanted to. None of them were interested though. They found their own path. Did their own thing.

But they're still in the family.

Still Chandler's cousins.

Sabrina's too.

Soon to be Emma's cousins-in-law.

I grab my friend by the collar and pull him down to face level with me. "Is this gonna hurt Emma?"

I expect him to brush it off. To tell me she knows, because they *don't keep secrets*.

But the grim set of his mouth is doing some talking for him. "She loves him, dude. She's been his wife in her heart for a long time. Today? This is just a formality. Bean & Nugget having some struggles won't change that."

Not the reassurance I was looking for.

"Hope it works out with you and Laney." He steps back from my door. "Wouldn't mind being related to both of you. Later."

I drop my head to the steering wheel while he walks away.

I have a wedding to set up. Final calls to make. Things to check on.

So that my sister can have all of her dreams come true.

But all I want is Laney. I want her to tell me this is the right thing to do.

She makes me feel okay. Valued for who I am. Understood. *Accepted*.

On a day when nothing feels right, I could go for a little reassurance.

But she has her own job today.

Time to get busy doing mine.

32

Laney

THE CHAMPAGNE IS FLOWING in the limo as we pull up in front of the spa where we're doing most of the pre-wedding prep. Hair. Makeup. Manicures. Pedicures.

Emma's getting a full-body massage and wrap.

We're all squealing that this is *finally* the day.

And I'm faking it.

Two weeks ago, I had no doubt this was what Emma was supposed to do with her life. Yes, Chandler took *forever* to propose. Yes, he's sometimes an arrogant jerk.

But she's said since they hooked back up after college that he's the one.

That she knows it.

That they're soulmates.

And she's been so happy since college, I never doubted it.

Two weeks ago, if you'd told me Theo and Chandler didn't get along great, I would've rolled my eyes and said *of course they don't*, and I would've blamed Theo for it.

But now—now, I'm so conflicted that smiling hurts.

"What is *wrong* with you?" Sabrina whispers to me while Claire helps Emma pick out aromatherapy scents for her treatments in the spa lobby.

"Do you really think Chandler's good for Emma?" I whisper back.

Her eye twitches.

My heart sinks. "That's not a yes."

"It's not fair to make Emma suffer because her beloved is on my shit list."

"If you'd tell me *why*—"

"Do you know what this week is missing?" she interrupts. "It's missing the kind of guys you hook up with for hot one-night stands."

I sigh at the obvious attempt at changing the subject. "Please tell me this wedding is a good idea."

She nods to Emma. "Tell me it's a bad idea. Look at her and tell me it's a bad idea."

I look.

I do.

I look at one of my best friends in the entire world, and *I don't know.*

She's smiling. But are those stress lines around her eyes or is it my imagination because I'm having doubts on Emma's behalf?

"Did you know that time Theo went to jail over the Snag-gletooth statue, it was Chandler's fault?" I whisper.

Sabrina purses her lips together.

"Does Emma know?" I press.

She presses her lips tighter, making them go white at the edges.

"*She doesn't know?*"

"Laney, Em's been living *for better or for worse, in good times and bad* with Chandler for *years.* I know she says they don't keep secrets, but I don't know if she knows. If she does, I'm the last person she'd tell."

I draw back. "I thought we were all best friends."

"We are. But she has *never* put herself in a position to find out if I know the worst things Chandler's ever done. I know she knows he cheated on every math test in high school. I know she knows he's the one who stole the stuffed mink from her dad's workshop not long after they started dating again after college. And I know she knows he's the one who trashed Bean & Nugget after Grandma died."

I gasp.

I gasp loudly enough that Em and Claire both look at us.

"Oh my god, whale penises are *not* that many times bigger than your dog," I spit out.

Sabrina briefly squeezes her eyes shut but then beams brightly at me. "Surprise!"

Em and Claire giggle and go back to the aromatherapy.

I lower my voice and lean closer to Sabrina again. "*I didn't know that was him.*"

"You didn't need to. She was upset enough that I knew and made me swear I'd never tell a soul because he was sorry and he was never, ever, *ever* going to do *anything* like that again. He swore it to me too. It wasn't just her sticking up for him. And that's the only time I've really thought he hated the café, and Em was just upset because it was…well, it was something Theo would do, and much as she loves him, she doesn't want to *marry* him, you know?"

"That's when they almost broke up three years ago," I whisper.

She nods. "There's a line, Laney. There's always been a line, and he's told her so much of the crappy stuff he's done that I think she probably knows. Did Theo tell you that jail stint turned his life around?"

"Yes, but *it still wasn't right.*"

"And it was over a decade ago. To you, it's a new injustice. To the rest of us…"

"*Everything* feels wrong though. Right now, everything feels wrong."

She doesn't argue. Not exactly. "So their wedding lines up with the bad times. All it does is make it official that she'll never leave him, no matter what he does. She knows men do stupid stuff. She'd say she does stupid stuff too."

I snort.

"*I know*, but *you know* that's what she'd say."

"Whoa, why so serious?" Emma asks as she and Claire turn to look at us.

We both jump.

"Laney was just making sure I have condoms on hand and I was giving her shit that she even had to ask," Sabrina says smoothly.

"Were you doing an art project?" Emma asks.

Sabrina gasps.

I crack up.

Claire smiles at all of us. "Did you find someone at the bar last night?" she asks Sabrina.

"No, but I have high hopes for tonight."

Claire and I giggle.

Emma wrinkles her nose. "But are you having enough fun?"

Sabrina mock gasps. "*Emma.* We're all having *loads* of fun."

"You're sure?"

"*Yes.*"

"I've been so worried that people aren't having enough fun this week. I just want *everyone* to be as happy as I am."

Sabrina links her arm through Emma's. "*No one* can be as happy as you. But we're definitely a close second this week."

We are *not* a close second.

Not by a long shot.

But it's what Emma needs to hear, and the reassurance makes her smile go soft and happy again.

I'm with Theo on this. I don't want to be the reason she doesn't get married. Not when this is all she's ever wanted.

And based on how quickly Sabrina's smile drops away when Emma looks away, I think she feels the same.

A woman in all black with a clipboard approaches us. "Ms. Monroe? We're ready for you and your party to get changed, and your massage therapist will be with you very, very soon."

"I can't believe it's finally *today*." Emma twirls with her robe, her smile bright and carefree.

"Worth the wait, hmm?" Claire says.

Emma smiles.

Sabrina forces a smile.

I force a smile.

She nudges me.

And rather than let myself get drawn into a scene that would make Emma ask what in the world is wrong with the two of us, I slip into one of the small dressing rooms. "Last one ready gets less-fancy tea and cookies in the serenity lounge," I say.

But even once we're in the serenity lounge—Sabrina, Claire, and I supposedly relaxing while Emma gets her massage—none of us are smiling.

Claire watches us mostly quietly.

Except for one small comment. "There's no drama like small-town drama, is there?"

Sabrina grimaces.

I wince.

She's not wrong.

And while part of me wishes I could've avoided it, the other part—

"So, you and Emma's brother, hmm?" Claire adds.

Yeah.

That other part.

No regrets.

Getting to know Theo—to understand what makes him tick, to look past who I thought he was in high school to who he truly is today, to *like* him, to have fun with him—has been worth every worry and irritation.

"He's a lot more than I ever gave him credit for," I tell her. "I just hope I'm good enough for him."

Sabrina smiles at me. "The very fact that you'd say you want to be good enough *for Theo* says everything you need to know about how much you two deserve each other."

"I can't believe I would've thought that was an insult two weeks ago."

She laughs.

I do too.

No matter what happens with Emma's wedding, Theo is the one part I will *never* regret.

"Did you know he's modeling?" I ask her.

She pins me with a look I can't interpret. "He...told you about that?"

"Not exactly. I figured it out. And then I dropped it. We're not talking about jobs. I'm not being boring."

She stares at me like I've grown a second head.

"What?" I ask. Creepy crawlies are dancing across my skin.

Something's wrong.

"I'm just really, really glad that you're finally finding the fun in your life, and really, really glad that you're fully out of that box you've been living in. Open-mindedness looks good on you."

"What aren't you saying?"

She grabs my hand. "Laney, I freaking adore you. I'm a little mad at Theo right now, but I will get over it, and in the meantime, I need you to know that I know that if this is real between you two that he will be the very, very, *very* best thing to ever happen to you, no matter the hurdles you're going to have to get over to get there."

"That's ominous," Claire says.

Sabrina doesn't flinch. "They're *very* different people. But see this? This glow all over Laney? That doesn't lie."

Claire gives me the *she's being cryptic* look while Sabrina gets up to refill her teacup.

"Your parents are gonna shit themselves when they find out you've been sleeping with Emma's brother, aren't they?" she finally says while Sabrina takes her time across the lounge.

I cringe. "Probably."

"You gonna let that fuck up a good thing?"

"Things worth having are worth fighting for."

She nods slowly. "Chandler's never had to fight for Emma. She just takes him as he is, even when the rest of us wonder if he's good enough for her. Everyone should have to fight a little for love. And everyone should be fought for."

I stop short. "I...never considered that before."

She grins. "You're welcome."

"I was really hoping at least one of us wasn't nervous about today."

"Emma made this choice a long time ago. But you— you've just found a good thing. Don't let fear of a fight get in the way."

"So your parents have unreasonably high expectations too?"

She laughs.

And then she cringes.

And then we're both laughing all over again.

I lift my teacup. "To a very memorable destination wedding," I say.

Claire clinks.

Sabrina lifts her own teacup across the room.

And when we all drink, I suspect we're all wishing our cups were spiked.

33

I'M SETTING up chairs on the lanai for Emma's wedding when Dad and Uncle Owen join me about an hour after Laney left with the bridesmaids.

"So this is where you've been hiding," Dad says.

"Don't think this is hiding," Uncle Owen says. "Looks more like he's doing the resort's work."

"Not what Emma was thinking it would be, is it?"

"Not compared to those pictures."

Dad claps me on the back, then heads to the cart of chairs and starts helping too. "Hawaii treating you good, son?"

"Yeah."

"Looks like it's not just Hawaii," Uncle Owen says while he, too, joins in to help.

Both men grin gleefully at me.

"Ready to see Em married off?" I ask, ignoring the questions they're not asking about Laney.

"All she's ever wanted." Dad hefts a chair under each arm. "Know it's tough on you, always wanting the best of the best for her and thinking nobody will ever live up to that, but it'll all work out. This time next year, we'll be fighting over who gets to hold her first baby, and nobody's gonna care what went down at this wedding."

"Hope it looks like Em," Uncle Owen interjects with a cackle.

"No worries then?" I ask.

Dad shakes his head. "Your mom would be so proud of everything she's done."

Not helpful.

One of us has blinders on, that's for sure.

Probably me.

And telling myself Laney's having doubts doesn't help. That's my fault too.

She wouldn't be if I wasn't influencing her.

"Sure would," I agree with Dad.

"You and Laney keep looking at each other the way you have been, and we'll be doing this again in another fourteen years," Uncle Owen says.

I don't laugh at the implication that Laney and I will be the next Chandler and Emma who date forever without getting married. Nothing about that is funny today.

Dad doesn't laugh either.

Just keeps setting up chairs.

Need to check on the catering staff in the bistro kitchen after a while. Won't have as many flowers as Emma wanted, but she has an arched trellis.

Don't know where Chandler is.

Glad he's not here. He'd probably tell me I'm setting up the chairs wrong.

"Funny, being at weddings," Uncle Owen says. "Wasn't it a wedding where Charles Kingston had an affair with Sherry Sullivan about the right number of months before the triplets were born?"

I choke on air.

"Funeral," Dad corrects.

I look at both of them.

Neither looks at me.

"Oh, that's right, that's right," Uncle Owen says.

"I'm not listening to any of this," I tell them both. "I don't want to know any of this."

"Probably should," Dad says.

"Gonna need your own ammunition if anyone tries to tell you you're not good enough for their daughter," Uncle Owen chimes in.

Dad nods. "Ugly, but true."

"Not interested," I tell them both. "But thank you."

"They're gonna hold a lot against you, son," Dad says. "Different world. Different rules."

Fuck.

Even if Laney will listen and hear me out when I tell her about my GrippaPeen channel, will her parents?

Will they cut her loose from the company if she picks me over them?

She *loves* her job. Works hard at it. *Dreams* about it.

"You two mind finishing this up?" I ask. "I gotta make sure the minister's on the way."

"We're trying to help," Uncle Owen says as I head off the lanai.

"Don't want you at a disadvantage," Dad chimes in.

It grates on me when they don't give me credit for turning my life around the past ten years.

But they usually do.

Which means—I turn back around. "You two have something more direct you want to say?"

"We were pretty direct," Uncle Owen says.

"Not what he's talking about, Owen," Dad mutters.

"Oh. He means the...other thing."

"Yes."

"The...*naked* thing."

Dad sighs.

"How—who—never mind."

"Emma was a little tipsy last night," Dad says.

"She didn't mean to slip," Uncle Owen adds. "And we're more tight-lipped than Sabrina."

"We just know that there are certain expectations of people in the business world that are different than—"

"I'm not going into the business world."

They share a look.

Then look back at me.

I know they mean well.

I know they do.

But right now, I feel like a teenage disappointment again.

"We've got your back, son," Dad says.

"But we know we might not be enough," Uncle Owen adds with a grimace.

I blow out a slow breath and head off the lanai again.

Liked yesterday a lot better.

This time yesterday, Laney was having an orgasm over bacon.

Now, the smoothie I had for breakfast is sitting wrong in my stomach. "When you're done with the chairs, go see if you can find some extra flowers in the open closet behind the bistro," I call over my shoulder.

I don't want to check on catering.

I don't want to check on the minister and the photographer and the music.

I don't want to check on the last-minute wedding cake that I almost had to offer sexual favors to get, and yes, I told Laney that story last night after I was feeling better about almost killing her dad, and yes, she laughed her ass off before kissing me until I forgot anything wrong has ever happened in the history of the world.

But I want my sister to have the best day of her life.

And I'm too up in my head as I head toward my rental car, which means I don't see what's coming until it's too late.

Chandler.

And the triplets.

Thought he'd be golfing.

"One of you want to make sure he doesn't light my clothes on fire?" Chandler asks while he steps to the far edge of the walkway.

He's carrying his bug zapper.

"Chand my man," Lucky says, "this is the time when you have to deal with it if Theo here does the obligatory pre-wedding *don't hurt my sister or I'll kill you* thing."

"It's a rule," Decker agrees.

"Even groomsmen can't stop it," Jack adds.

Chandler eyes me. "Gonna be like that?"

"Just looking for lunch."

"You turned pussy since you started getting paid to be naked," Chandler says.

"Whoa, man, we've got your back, but that might be too far," Lucky says.

"Do you *want* to get your wedding canceled?" Jack adds. "Even Em has limits."

Heat flashes across my face.

Not because Chandler jilting Emma is suddenly at the top of my brain.

More because none of the triplets look surprised. Or confused.

Dad and Uncle Owen know about GrippaPeen. The triplets know about GrippaPeen. Sabrina knows about GrippaPeen.

So who *doesn't* know?

And what happens when someone tells Laney first?

What happens when someone tells *her parents* first?

I like my life.

I make a difference in the world.

But that's not enough anymore. I want to make a difference in Laney's world.

"I'll handle this one for you, Chandler," Decker says. "Way better if I'm the one in a fight before your wedding." He grabs me by the collar and pulls me up the walk past his brothers and Chandler.

"I'm not going to fight you," I mutter.

"Dude's getting cold feet," he mutters back. "We're not letting him out this easy."

"Swear to god, if he hurts Emma—"

"We know."

I side-eye him.

"*We know*," he repeats. "And for what it's worth, we're rooting for you whenever you tell Laney. That's gonna be... well, even more awkward than successfully flirting with her would've been. Guess it's a good thing you're probably not her half-brother."

"Can I go check on the fucking wedding cake now?" I say through gritted teeth.

"Oh. Yeah. Good idea. Sorry about Chandler. He's allergic to weddings. He'll be better once he gets through the ceremony. More normal. Swear he will."

Doubt that.

Nothing will ever be *normal* again.

I like change.

But I don't know if I'll like the change that's coming from what this week has been.

34

LANEY

I HAVE no idea what to do.

Em's in her wedding dress. Everything starts in fifteen minutes. I haven't had a spare minute to check my phone since we left the spa, and we all promised Emma we'd be present in the moment instead of living on our phones today anyway.

Which means I don't know where Theo is.

Their dad is in here.

He's tearing up over Em in her gorgeous gown, hugging her and telling her that he wishes her mom could've been here to see her.

And I'm wishing Theo was in here right now too.

"He should be," Sabrina murmurs next to me.

I *know* I didn't say that out loud.

She shakes her head. "You're easy to read, Laney. And you're right. He should be in here. They're family. He shouldn't feel like he doesn't belong in his own family."

Fuck it.

Yes, *fuck it.*

I hand my bridesmaid bouquet to Sabrina and go digging in my purse for my phone.

I'm calling him.

But when I rescue my phone, I realize I should've done this *hours* ago.

Forty-nine missed text messages.

Four from my mom, updating me on my dad's continued avoidance of macadamia nuts and good health today.

Three from people at work, which I'll follow up on when I'm back in the office on Monday.

Which means the remaining forty-two are from Theo.

I open the text thread and start skimming.

Guessing you won't see this until after the wedding. But in case you're worried and check messages, everything's under control.

Wedding cake isn't quite what we hoped for, but it's a cake. Decker promised me he'll accidentally slip and fall into it before anyone realizes it says Chandler and Ella on it. Or Jack will push him. When I'm far, far away and can't be blamed for it.

Not that Em would care.

I know this is the day of her dreams.

If Chandler jilts her and I punch him and end up in jail, I just want you to know I'll have zero regrets.

But I hope he doesn't.

I think.

For her sake.

I just want her to be happy. Why does it feel so complicated?

I'm not asking you to fix this. I know it's not an easy fix. Just venting.

"Why does he think Chandler's going to jilt her?" Sabrina whispers over my shoulder.

"Because it took him way longer to propose than it should've?" I whisper back.

She flings a look over her shoulder at Emma, then back at

my phone. "Is he seriously setting up the whole wedding today?"

"There's no staff and nothing was ready. The wedding got deleted off the calendar."

She stares at me.

Back at my phone.

Then up at me. "He's a *very* good guy, Laney."

"I know."

"*No one* goes to this much trouble to help their sister get married to a prick." She shakes her head. "I'm going to get him."

"Theo?"

"Yes. *He should be here.*"

"Sabrina?" Emma says. "What's wrong?"

"Forgot something," she says. "Right back."

Before I can say that *I'll* go get him, she heads for the door.

"It's okay," I assure Emma. "Everything's okay."

She frowns.

Am I being the world's worst friend right now?

Or am I being the best?

I don't know.

I don't know.

Sabrina's right. Theo should be here, and I'm too up in my head over what he means to *me* to remember that he's Emma's *brother*.

And do you know what sucks?

What sucks is watching Theo bend over backward to make sure Emma gets the wedding of her dreams while Chandler's off playing golf or sitting by the pool all day.

Which would be fine—Chandler's the groom. This is his day too.

Except he'll give Theo *zero* credit.

He wasn't like this before.

He really wasn't.

Emma's eyes go huge. "Oh my god, did catering fall through for the reception?"

"No! No. I mean, it did, but Theo handled it, and he has the full list of guest allergies now that's been passed on to the new caterers, and—"

She blinks twice, her eyes going misty. "He's the best."

"And I wasn't supposed to tell you that," I finish. "Sabrina's going to get him."

"It hasn't been quite like I dreamed it would be," she says on a soft laugh. "But I'm getting married today. *Finally*."

"You worked hard and earned it."

Her nose wrinkles.

Honestly, mine does too.

You earned getting married? "That's not what I—"

"I know." She smiles. "I know what you meant."

"We're so glad all of your dreams are coming true today," Claire says, squeezing her in a gentle shoulder hug.

"Me too." She wipes her eyes delicately as she laughs. "*Finally*."

"Came with some glitches, didn't it?" Mr. Monroe says.

"It did."

"Like that time he almost broke up with you over a peanut butter pie."

Emma laughs again. "I can't believe he thought it was butterscotch. Who makes a butterscotch pie? And then calls it peanut butter for fun? Oh my gosh, do you remember the time he tried to convince me I was getting the wrong car?"

"And the time he thought my stuffed meerkat was a squirrel."

"And the time he got so sick when he didn't follow Mom's recipe closely enough and the eggs weren't fully cooked in that birthday cake the rest of us refused to eat for my birthday?"

Mr. Monroe chuckles. "Really shouldn't have made it two

days early. Remember when he took Theo's snow boots and thought his feet shrank because they were so loose?"

Emma's rolling now. "And the gloves! He got Theo's gloves too, and thought his hands shrank!"

"Good thing he never tried Theo's snow pants."

Emma cackles.

She absolutely cackles with glee, and then she sighs happily, wiping her eyes once more. "We've been through so much."

"*Gotten* through so much," her dad says. "Won't ever forget the way he sat up with you after Theo went to jail."

Emma sighs. "He was so understanding."

"He should've been, considering it was his fault," my mouth says.

She blinks. "What?"

Mr. Monroe frowns at me. "What?"

Oh, crap.

Oh, crap crap *crap*.

"How was that Chandler's fault?" she asks.

I open my mouth again, and this time, silence comes out.

Claire gapes at me.

No.

No no no.

I didn't say that. Tell me I didn't say that.

I look at Mr. Monroe, and I swear it's like looking at Theo's future. Tall. Slender. Wrinkles lining his face. Lots of laugh lines. Thinning hair, but not receding.

And utterly confused.

I look at Emma again, *praying* she'll be giving me the *my father didn't know, so come up with a cover story fast* look.

But instead, it's pure confusion. "What did Chandler have to do with Theo going to jail?" she whispers.

"I—I must've heard something wrong," I stammer.

"The Snaggletooth go-kart catastrophe," she says. "Is that what you're talking about?"

I gulp. "You—you know how I get details mixed up. I wasn't even there. Classes out late for the semester and all."

"What did you hear?"

"Ten years ago, wasn't it?" Mr. Monroe interjects. "Eleven, even?"

"Laney?" Emma says.

I swallow.

Then swallow again.

And wish Sabrina was here. "I heard Chandler was driving and Theo took the fall for him," I whisper.

Emma's lips part.

Mr. Monroe's face twists.

"But like I said, I'm sure I heard wrong. Other people would've known. It's not like they were the only two people there."

"Chandler wasn't there," Emma says slowly. "He told me he wasn't even there."

And *Theo doesn't lie.*

Not about stuff like this.

He owns it.

He owns it when he breaks the rules.

"Em, Theo wants you to be happy," I say, desperation creeping into my voice. "That's all he wants. For you to get the wedding of your dreams to the man of your dreams. Not to rehash history. He's *glad* he went to jail. He said it's the best thing that ever happened to him. It doesn't matter. It really doesn't. I'm sorry. It's stress. I've been so worried I'd screw something up or not fix the right thing, and—"

"Laney," she whispers, "it's okay."

It doesn't feel okay.

It feels like I've just crushed her favorite kitten.

She touches her dad's elbow. "You should go have a seat. It's almost time."

He looks between us, then nods and hugs her tight. "So beautiful," I hear him say. "You look just like your mama."

336

There's no fuss over her walking herself down the aisle. Mr. Monroe isn't the type to put himself in front of what his kids want.

And he's pretty quiet most of the time.

I think he'd prefer to *not* have the attention on him.

And when he's gone, Emma forces a smile at me. "Thank you," she whispers.

"Em—"

"No, Laney, I mean it. Thank you. For *everything*. I asked the most awful thing I could ever ask of anyone, and you didn't even hesitate. I know how much you're putting into making sure everything happens the way I want it to, and that's—that's so much more than I deserve or should expect of anyone. I didn't want to be a bridezilla—"

"*Emma Monroe, you are not a bridezilla.*"

"But I made everyone come here to Hawaii for this stupid fantasy I had about the perfect wedding—"

"You *invited* everyone, and *they chose to come* because *we all adore you.*"

"And everything's falling apart."

I crush her in a steady hug, knowing I can't fix everything. Not even close.

"Do you want to get married to Chandler today?" I ask her.

There's a slight hesitation that has my heart holding its breath.

And then— "Yes," she whispers.

"It's what you want?"

She hesitates again.

And then she nods. "It's what I want."

Dammit.

Dammit.

I pull away and nod back at her. "Okay. Okay. If this is what you want, then let's do this."

"We're here for whatever you need," Claire agrees.

Sabrina bursts into the room. "Oh my god, lost track of time. I can't grab Theo. I'm sorry, Em. I—what happened?"

"Bridal jitters," Claire says.

"I just can't believe it's here," Em agrees, but she looks more sick than excited.

"Us too," Sabrina chimes in.

"We're so happy for you," I say.

And I'm trying to be.

But it's so hard when your best friend is marrying a man that might've been good enough for her once upon a time, but who's looking less and less like anyone's Prince Charming by the minute.

35

THEO

SHE'S DOING IT.

She's fucking doing it.

Emma's getting married.

My suit's too tight. And damn this tie. I hate ties. They choke me.

And it's hot.

Why are we in formal wear for a wedding *at the beach*?

Why did I go out of my way to make this happen for her?

Quit being a selfish ass, Theo. This is what she wants.

Not what I want though.

What I *want* is for Laney to be holding my hand and assuring me all is fine. Instead, I can't even tell if she's read my messages because we're on different kinds of phones and hers doesn't send me read receipts.

The ocean's right there. *Right there*. I could walk out from behind this row of chairs on the beach, head straight to the water, and not stop walking until I'm swimming, and not come back to shore until it's done.

But I'm here because Laney's walking down the aisle in a fucking gorgeous pink-purple gown with her hair up fancy and her makeup all done, and I can't take my eyes off of her.

She slides me a half-hearted smile as she glances down my row when she passes, and yep.

I would sit in Hell itself watching and waiting for just a glimpse of that smile that's just for me.

Even the half-hearted kind.

Does that mean she read my messages?

Does it mean something happened today?

Does it mean she's just sending me a subliminal *I know this is hard, and I wish I could make it easier for you* like everything's the same as it was after breakfast?

Like no one told her my secret today and I can talk to her as soon as Emma leaves the reception and come clean and hope she takes it better than the Laney of a week ago would've?

Her mother makes a noise behind me.

I ignore it and focus on the fact that my front-row family-of-the-bride seat means that Laney's mere feet from me when she takes her spot to wait for Sabrina to come down the aisle as Emma's maid of honor.

She mouths something to me.

Looks like *I'm horny*.

But that can't be it.

Claire's already standing next to her, totally blank-faced.

I'm actively ignoring Chandler and his three groomsmen, who are standing on the other side of the arched trellis hung with tropical flowers that Dad and Uncle Owen finished after I left to get the cake.

Sabrina's next down the aisle.

I should look at her, but I can't stop looking at Laney, who's watching Sabrina and stifling a wince.

Why's she stifling a wince?

Why is Laney stifling a wince?

"I told her all bridesmaids should take a gas suppressant before the wedding," Gail says behind me. "Do you think she forgot?"

Charles grunts an answer.

Sabrina reaches the front and stops next to Laney.

The music changes, and then Emma's walking herself down the aisle in a fitted satin-and-lace number with a long train that'll have sand in it for the rest of its natural life, but it's what Emma wanted.

It makes her happy.

So that's what she got.

My dad sniffs with pride next to me.

The crying kind of sniffing with pride.

None of this *Oh, I'm so fancy that I sniff my approval* stuff. Not for my pops.

"She's such a lovely bride," Gail murmurs behind me. "She deserves every happiness."

On that, we agree.

All three of the Sullivan triplets keep looking behind me, to where Charles is sitting as well.

Uncle Owen twists like he wants to look behind us and see if Charles and the triplets have the same nose too.

This was supposed to be Emma's fantasy come to life, and instead it's a small-town shit show of secrets.

I train my eyes on Laney.

I want to have her over to my place at home. I want her to play with the kittens. Watch them grow into cats. Have snowball fights with her in the yard. Set a fire to warm her up.

Take her to bed and warm her up even more.

Taste the pancakes she teased me about over breakfast again today.

And I don't want to tell her what I need to tell her.

I don't want to know if she'll judge me.

If it'll change how she feels about me.

I can't just quit and sweep it under the rug like it never happened. She'll hear eventually.

She's not looking at me any differently right now, which I'm assuming means she hasn't heard.

Emma reaches us in the front row, which I only realize because Dad moves next to me. I tear my eyes away from Laney to watch my sister pause at the end of our row.

She pulls my dad into a hug, and as she does, she looks over his shoulder at me.

Fuuuuuck.

I know that look.

She's stressed.

She's stressed, and she wants me to crack a joke to relieve all of her tension and fix it.

"Love you, Daddy," she whispers to our old man, and then she steps up in front of the minister under the trellis, where Chandler's beaming at her and wiping his eyes.

Fucker hasn't bolted.

Is that a good sign?

I don't know.

"Holy shit, you're hot," he says to my sister while he looks her up and down. Not loudly. Just loudly enough for the front row to hear it.

His parents chuckle like they're so proud to have a son who recognizes he has a good thing.

We all sit.

All of us.

Me too, even though I'd rather go punch the guy who just told his bride she *looks hot*.

"Dearly beloved, we are gathered here today…" the minister starts.

The minister that I *fucking found*.

I did this.

This, too, is my fault.

Laney slides a glance at me, and I realize my knee's bouncing.

I stop it.

Her lips wobble like she's trying to send me a *good boy*, but she's sad.

Dammit.

She's sad because I told her I don't want Emma to marry a fuckaroni and cheese. Shouldn't have told her.

Shouldn't have made her deal with carrying that.

"Such a beautiful day to join two souls who have been in love since their youth, who have overcome trials and challenges and hardships to reach this day, today, when they proclaim their love before you, their closest family and friends…" the minister drones.

I got a talker.

Of course I did.

Couldn't have gotten a minister who'd just rip off the bandage and get it over with fast.

Had to pick the talker. One who doesn't even know them, but who's droning like he does.

Laney shifts another look at me.

I make my leg stop bouncing again.

But that's when it happens.

I feel the tickle.

Not the tickle of my hand waking up.

The tickle of *I need to sneeze*.

Nope. Nope nope nope. Not sneezing. Not doing it.

Emma hates it when I sneeze.

I sneeze loud.

Can't help it. I've tried. Even went to see a doctor about it once.

Breathe, dumbass. Just breathe.

"Before we proceed, is there anyone who knows of any reason why this man and this woman should not be wed?"

I twist my nose this way and that to try to stop the tickle. Also sit on my fucking hands.

The minister peers at me.

Laney looks at me too.

I duck my head and keep twitching my nose.

Will not sneeze. Will not sneeze. Will not sneeze.

The minister starts talking again.

It's getting stronger.

The tickle's getting stronger.

I don't sneeze a lot. But when I do, I fucking sneeze the shit out of sneezing. And this is not the time or the place to sneeze.

Why the *fuck* did I get a talker for a minister?

Shit.

Shit.

Gonna sneeze. Can't hold it back. I'm trying. *I'm trying.*

Need to stifle it.

Need to—

"*AAAAAAHHHHHH-CHHHHOOOOOOOOOOOOOOO!*"

—sneeze.

Uncle Owen startles so hard his chair wobbles and he almost goes down.

Someone behind me shrieks.

"Right now, son?" my dad whispers.

"Sick," one of the triplets says. The admiration kind of *sick*.

I look up.

The minister's watching me again. Chandler's staring at me with *you're such a dumbass* radiating out of him.

Really hope Emma lets me punch him one day.

My sister turns and looks at me, her face a conflicted mess of emotions.

Laney's eyes are bugging out of her head.

But more—her lips are wobbling.

"Allergies," I force out. I make a *go on* gesture.

Emma keeps staring at me.

Laney's pinching her lips together now, her eyes dancing. Not just with amusement, but with kindness. *Only you, Theo. Way to break the tension.*

The minister sucks in a deep breath. "Continuing on then. Emma. Chandler. In front of your family and friends and the beauty of this majestic world, I invite you to exchange your vows."

"Wait," Emma says.

I suck in a breath and almost levitate out of my chair.

Dad puts a hand on my shoulder and shoves me back down. This one comes with a frown bigger than the *really, son?* sneeze-frown.

Uncle Owen snickers. "Oooh, this is gonna get good," he whispers to me.

"Babe, he's fine," Chandler says. "Let's do this."

She looks over her shoulder at me one more time, and my heart sinks.

It sinks to the floor and keeps going through the sand underneath while she turns back to Chandler.

"This isn't about Theo sneezing, Chandler," she says. "It's about you letting my brother go to jail for you."

Every cell in my body freezes.

I freeze so hard that I'm actually cold, and I don't get cold. I can *feel* my blood leaving my body.

Laney makes a choked noise.

I would, but I can't move.

This is bad. *This is bad.*

"Babe, *what?*" Chandler says. "That's bullshit. Who told you that?"

"*Did you?*" my sister repeats.

No.

No.

This isn't happening. If she doesn't want to marry him, *fantastic.*

But don't let it be because of me.

"What did she say?" Charles murmurs behind me.

"Em, I love you, and I've tried really hard not to let that fuckup ruin things for us—" Chandler starts, only to be cut off.

Not by Emma, but by Laney clearing her throat.

Loudly.

"Who you callin' a fuckup, boy?" Uncle Owen says right on the heels of Laney's interruption.

I manage to make myself move to shove *him* back into his seat.

"Did. You. Let. My. Brother. Go. To. Jail. For. You?" Emma repeats.

This time, there's not a single person in the crowd who didn't hear her.

Probably not a single person in the crowd whose nuts aren't shriveling at the *you are in so much fucking trouble you will never climb back out of the pit of trouble in your entire life* tone that Emma uses about a fraction as often as I sneeze.

Which isn't often.

Chandler looks past her.

Straight at me.

If looks could incinerate a man on the spot, I'd be Ghost Theo hovering over this lanai for a brief minute before peacing out to see if souls can fly.

"What the *fuck* do you think you're doing, telling *my bride* shit about—"

"I told her," Laney interrupts.

Gail gasps.

I choke on my own tongue. *Why the fuck?*

"What did she say?" Charles says. "*What did she say?*"

Chandler gapes at Laney for a split second before a scowl takes over. "A guy gives you a good time for the first time in your life, and you believe any bullshit he spews?"

Uncle Owen and my dad both grab one of my arms and yank me back into my seat.

Those fuckers are strong for old guys.

"You never told her," Sabrina says to Chandler. "*You never told her?*"

"You knew?" Emma whispers. She looks back at Chandler. "What else? What else haven't you told me?"

"Nothing," Chandler says. "They're making shit up to wreck our day."

"*Dude*," Jack says quietly.

"What. Else?" Emma says. For the first time, her voice wobbles.

And it makes me want to leap out of my chair, toss her over my shoulder, and take her somewhere safe.

Decker coughs over something that sounds like *who paid for the wedding*.

I freeze again.

Chandler looks over his shoulder at his groomsmen. "So that's where we're going? You're going to take sides with a fucking *porn star* over your own *cousin*?"

He looks back at Emma, and the noise registers before my brain comprehends what I'm seeing.

My sister, the world's happiest person and largest pacifist, voted least likely to ever take part in a fight in high school and most likely to peacefully talk her way out of a hostage situation, just slapped her fiancé.

That's not a collective gasp of horror from the crowd.

It's *more*.

Bigger.

I finally succeed in jumping to my feet, my father and my uncle right beside me, ready to do what we need to do if he lifts so much as a fingernail in her direction, but the minister scrambles between us while the bridesmaids hover closer to Emma and the triplets angle closer to Chandler.

"Do. *Not*. Mock. My. Brother," Emma growls while Chandler rubs his jaw and gapes at her.

"*Especially* when he's paying for your fucking wedding," Sabrina adds.

Laney looks at me.

Back at Emma, who's now also gaping at me. Then at Sabrina, then back to me.

I squirm.

The minister pushes me back a half step.

"Who's a porn star?" Charles says behind me. And he's not the only one. I can hear Addison giggling somewhere behind me.

Fucking gossip.

Shit.

How many people are recording this?

Laney's not the only one looking at me.

Everyone is.

Everyone.

I can't look at Laney. I don't want to watch her realize she's been fucking around with a guy who lets his junk hang out for the whole world to see.

I don't want to see the horror. The embarrassment.

This isn't how I was supposed to tell her.

"Theo," Emma says. "You're paying for my wedding?"

I clear my throat and look down.

"*Theo.*"

"Theo?" Dad says. "You should've told me. I had money saved for this."

"I got it, Dad," I force out.

"How are you paying for this wedding?" Laney whispers.

"Oh my god, the press," Gail says behind me. "They'll eat her alive."

Heat flashes over the cold numbing my body.

She's not wrong.

Future CEO dating a porn star is a fucking awful headline.

348

Laney loves her job. She was *born* for this. It's her heritage, and she wears it well.

"You paid for my wedding," Emma repeats.

I finally find my voice along with my nuts, and I look up, aware that my face is flaming.

"He's not—" Chandler starts.

I cut him off. "I'm paying for your wedding, because I love you, and I want you to have your dreams."

Emma's breath is coming quick and fast as she turns on Chandler again. "*Why* is my *brother* paying for the wedding that *you insisted* you could afford?"

"Because Bean & Nugget is behind on taxes and he has no money," Sabrina answers for him.

Emma gasps. "Is *that* why you wouldn't let me do Bean & Nugget's returns? So I wouldn't know *you weren't paying taxes*?"

"They're not behind anymore," Addison says from the crowd while Chandler stutters that Sabrina's making stuff up. "He sold it to cover the debt and there's nothing left. My company handled the closing in Denver this morning."

Chandler goes ghost white.

The *caught* kind of ghost white.

I choke.

Several gasps go up in the crowd.

And Sabrina—oh, fuck.

Fuck fuck fuck.

Sabrina looks like *she's* been slapped. "No," she wrenches out on a sob.

"What the *fuck*?" Jack snarls.

"What the fuck?" Lucky echoes.

"You can't *sell Bean & Nugget,*" Decker says. "What if *my* kids wanted to work there someday?"

"You did not," someone on his side of the crowd says. "Chandler. Explain this."

Aunt Brenda's voice rises above all the others. "That better not be true, you little asswipe."

"*You sold it?*" Sabrina whispers. Laney grabs her elbow when she teeters on her heels. "I had a solution. *I had a solution.*"

"I'm not taking more porn star money from that dick," Chandler snaps.

"*Stop it*," Emma cries.

"*You sold it?*" Sabrina repeats once more. "That's *my life. I* should've had a chance to buy it. How—*no.*"

We were supposed to have two months.

I told her no.

I could've fixed this.

And I didn't.

Chandler reaches for Emma. "Babe. *Babe.* You know we'll work this out. Let's just get married—"

"*Seven years,*" Emma shrieks. "*Seven years*, you didn't want to get married, and now, when you've lied, cheated, and probably stolen from *everyone here*, pretending *everything's fine*, when *you let my brother go to jail for you and never thought to tell me*, when you *lied to me about what was wrong at work*, now that you've gotten caught, *now that you're hoping Theo will support us*, now you want to get married?"

"Think of our babies," he says.

She gasps.

Audibly, painfully gasps.

I'm clenching my fists and bouncing on the balls of my feet.

That's all she's ever wanted.

To get married, have babies, have a family. A *normal* family with a mom and a dad and a distinct lack of taxidermy animals lurking in every corner of her house.

"How. Dare. You?" Emma says.

"Babe. *Babe.* You know I don't want his money."

"I've known you for *fifteen fucking years*, Chandler," Emma shrieks. "You can't stand it that Theo's making money—"

"With his *penis*," Chandler says.

He angles back while Emma advances on him. "—and you're not," she finishes.

"Why are they calling you a porn star?" Laney asks me.

One more person I've let down today.

Emma's wedding is ruined. Sabrina's café is gone.

And Laney.

Laney's finding out in the worst possible way that I have a side hustle that's not the least bit respectable.

I square my shoulders and look her straight in the eye. "Because I am."

"Oh my god in heaven," Gail says.

"Shut *up*, Mom," Laney snaps.

"And I'm fucking good at it," I add.

"Theo, *stop*," Emma says.

I don't look at her. Instead, I stare straight at Laney. I want to see it.

I *need* to see it.

I need to see if she can live with me, *all* of me, even if this isn't how I wanted to tell her, or if she's one more person that I've let down today.

"I strip," I say. "I bare the goods. All of them. I put them on the internet. And I get paid a fuck ton of money. *That's* the kind of modeling I do."

Laney gasps so hard it's like she's in physical pain.

And I want to hug her.

I want to hug her and tell her I'll never do it again if she'll just give me a chance. A real chance. A chance at home, where everything's normal.

But I'm not giving up a good thing—a good thing where *I make a fucking difference*—to fit someone else's mold of *normal*.

That's not who I am.

"That's not what you do," Sabrina says.

"Isn't it?"

"Theo—"

"My penis pays my bills."

Laney's gaping.

She's gaping like I just broke her world, looking between me and her parents behind her.

And Emma—Emma makes a noise that's even worse.

"You done here?" I ask my sister gently. Have to be gentle. It's Em.

Her dreams are falling apart *right now*. I don't matter.

She matters.

Her eyes fill with tears.

My heart takes a punch to the nads.

"When you say *porn star*—" Laney starts.

"He's the top fucking dog on GrippaPeen.com, and that's not enough for him, the asshole," Chandler says. "Should've known I couldn't even ask him for a favor *for his sister*. He has to ruin everyone else's—hey. *Hey*. Let me go, you dickwad."

"Only doing this so Emma doesn't hit you again and get arrested," Lucky says as he hauls Chandler back from the trellis. "And the only reason I'm not hitting you for *selling the fucking shop* is because then I'd have to patch you up and that would piss me off."

The minister's standing there as a wall between the rest of the wedding party and Dad, Uncle Owen, and me, watching all of us like we're the best reality TV show he's ever seen.

Addison is cackling behind me, the fucking gossip.

I slowly become aware of the fact that there are phones pointed at me from all directions. Wedding guests. Family. Onlookers from the beach who stopped to see a wedding and got *so* much more.

And that's it.

Game over.

My face will be on the news within the next hour. If it's not Addison, it'll be someone else.

You don't get to be the highest-paid *faceless artist* on a site like GrippaPeen without the world wanting to know who you really are.

And they're all about to find out.

"You told me you were a model," Laney whispers. "I didn't think you meant—that's a lot different from—*oh my god.*"

It's not just my shame I'm feeling.

It's hers. Hers by association.

Date the bad boy in town? The *fun* guy who has his act together after struggles in school? Sure.

Date a porn star, even if he's a solo act?

There are some things Kingstons don't do.

And the absolute wrecked horror on her face while Sabrina stands next to her, tears streaming down her face over her own ruined dreams, is too much.

So I say the only thing I can think of. "Once a disappointment, always a disappointment. Can't say I didn't warn you."

"Oh my god, you *dick*," Sabrina says.

This time to me.

Probably well-deserved.

"Oh, god," Emma says, and then something even worse than tears in her eyes happens.

Emma, the sunshiniest sunshine in all of Snaggletooth Creek, starts sobbing.

Sabrina lunges for her.

Laney too.

Claire follows, almost plowing over Dad, who's also rushing to get to Emma.

And I don't.

I don't know how to fix this for her, and I can't stand the fact that she's losing her dreams because she stuck up for me.

I love my sister.

She's one of my favorite people in the world.

But I let her down.

353

She needs space.

I'll check on her soon. After everyone else smothers her. When she's alone.

"How *dare* you not tell our daughter—"

I spin and look Gail Kingston straight in the eye. "She's a grown-ass woman who's smart, kind, generous, and gorgeous, and she deserves way better than *all* of us."

The Kingstons gape at me.

"And don't fucking throw stones when you live in a goddamn glass house," I growl directly at Charles.

Both of the Kingstons go pale.

Uncle Owen claps.

Takes me a half-second to realize Aunt Brenda's clapping too.

Doesn't matter though.

When I look back at Emma, she's gone.

So are her bridesmaids.

So is Dad.

"This is all your fault, you fucking—"

Chandler doesn't finish yelling at me either.

Don't know if one of his disappointed family members got to him, or if I finally managed to train myself to not hear his voice.

All I know is that I'm done here.

Done.

It's time to pack up my cats and go home.

36

LANEY

THE VERY WORST sound in the world is Emma crying.

It's like if rainbows smelled like sulfur. Or if unicorns were assassins. Or if chocolate tasted like liver.

"I just wanted to get married and have babies and get dogs and live a normal life," she sobs. "But *he let Theo go to jail for him*. And *no one told me*."

"I'm so sorry, Em." Sabrina's crying too as we hustle Emma back to the resort and away from all of the prying eyes and the few guests who were clearly recording the meltdown on their phones. "I didn't mean—I shouldn't have—"

"Kept that from me for ten years?" Emma shrieks.

Okay.

This is worse.

This is *definitely* worse than Emma just crying.

I squeeze Emma's hand. "No one knew you didn't know."

"I would never date a man if I knew he sent my brother to jail."

Okay, in retrospect, I probably should've assumed that.

"We thought you'd forgiven him," Sabrina says.

"Because I'm *nice*? And *kind*? That makes me a *fool*?"

"No, it makes you the kind of person the rest of us wish we could be."

The last time I saw Sabrina cry, she was pulling Emma out of the creek that runs through downtown, convinced Em had drowned not long after we all sobbed our eyes out at Mrs. Monroe's funeral in middle school.

We've been through boyfriend breakups. Separation for college. Family funerals. All without the tears that Sabrina's crying right now too.

Her world is crumbling too.

"I'm so sorry, Em," she says.

"You always said you didn't have secrets," I say. "We thought you knew and just didn't want to tell us the things that—"

"Please. Give. Me. Space," Emma says.

Sabrina swallows another sob.

I don't know how I'm dry-eyed.

Probably shock.

A *porn star*?

Theo's *a porn star*.

And Emma's wedding is wrecked.

And Sabrina's family business is gone.

And *Theo's a porn star*.

"Okay," Sabrina says, her voice cracking like I've never heard it crack. "Okay. But if you need me, I'm here. And I'm sorry. I love you, Em."

"Can I get you—" I start, but Emma glares at me too.

"*Right before my wedding*?" she shrieks. "You tell me that *right before my wedding*?"

I cringe and swallow my own defense.

Doesn't matter if I've only known since yesterday.

Or that I thought she knew.

If I'd found out something that big about anybody else, any other time, I would've gone straight to Emma and

Sabrina and asked if they knew. If it mattered.

And I didn't.

"I'm sorry, Em," I whisper too.

"I want to be alone," she says.

Claire slips between us and takes her arm. "As soon as I get you to your room, I'll make sure you get time alone. Call me your bodyguard. Okay?"

Emma nods.

Her makeup's running down her face. Her hair's still perfect. Dress still pristine.

"I slapped him," she whispers.

"He deserved it for taking you for granted. You did the right thing, Em. I know it hurts now, but you've got an amazing support system behind you," Claire's saying as she leads Emma away from us.

"But I have to start *over*," Emma sobs. "It'll be at least three *years* before I have a baby now."

Claire looks back at us.

There's no judgment.

Feels more like she's promising she'll take care of everything and smooth things over with Emma.

I wrap my arms around Sabrina and pull her against me in a hug as they disappear into the building. "Are you okay?"

She buckles against me. "He *sold the café*, Laney. *My café.* It's *gone*."

"We'll fix this."

"*We can't*. And now Emma hates me and I hate knowing things and I am *never* going to know things again. I'm becoming a hermit. I'll forage for mushrooms and ice fish to feed myself, and I'll live in a secret cave that none of the rest of you know about."

"I'm sure you'll be very comfortable with the bears."

She doesn't laugh. "Please tell me you don't hate me too."

"Why would I hate you?"

"I knew about Theo and GrippaPeen. I knew he was paying for the wedding. And I knew he hadn't told you."

My heart twists. *Once a disappointment, always a disappointment.*

I told myself that as soon as Emma was okay, I'd go find him.

But I'm honestly terrified of what I'll find.

"It's not what it sounds like." She's sobbing, and she's trying to comfort *me*. "He's...a solo act. He doesn't screw women on video. And it's tasteful. It really is. Inspiring even. Don't—no, no, don't get mad that I've seen it. I found out by accident. And I quit watching as soon as I realized it was him."

I blow out a deep breath.

Definitely gonna need a minute for this one.

"Is that why you're mad at him?" I ask.

A sob wrenches out of her. "No."

"Why then?"

"I knew about Bean & Nugget's back taxes. I asked Theo for money, and he pretended like he was just an average construction worker even though I know his construction job is a cover."

"He...didn't help."

"Don't be mad at Theo, Laney. I get it. He wouldn't help because he didn't like that I knew he could. He doesn't want *anyone* to know he's loaded. And I get it. I do. He spent so much of our childhood being a disappointment that he didn't want people to suddenly like him because he's sitting on a half-billion dollars when he knew they'd be total assholes about the fact that he made it by stripping down on the internet. But it's *Bean & Nugget*. It's my *life*."

"*Sabrina*. Why didn't you come to me? You know I'd go to my parents, and we would've helped. We would've figured this out."

She pulls back and looks at me.

Really looks at me. "I couldn't."

"*Why?*"

"God, Laney, *I don't want to tell you*. Please don't make me tell you. It's not about you. You didn't do anything wrong. This is something older than all of us, and you and I can't fix it. It's done. Bean & Nugget is gone. And this is one more thing I *cannot* deal with today." She wipes her eyes. "You need to go. Go see Theo."

I flinch.

"Laney."

"He doesn't want me," I whisper.

"*Laney.*"

"I know. I know. We're not even dating, but you heard him. *You heard him.* I was a vacation fling, and he doesn't want *Plainy-Laney*. He doesn't want me to judge him. He doesn't want me to expect anything from him." My eyes are stinging. "He doesn't want me to hurt him."

She grabs me by the arm and tugs me down the walkway.

The one to my bungalow.

My bungalow with Theo.

"He saved a litter of kittens and their mama cat and that's why the other bedroom in his bungalow is blocked off," I whisper. "*He saved a litter of kittens*. He tried to save Emma's wedding. And *he's a porn star*. And Mom's right. The press— they'll care. *I don't want to care*. But *the entire world has seen him naked*. And I can't—I want—I can't—"

I can't let it go.

Every woman on the planet can see my boyfriend's naked penis.

Oh my god.

There are some who have probably seen it more than I have.

And he doesn't want to be my boyfriend.

"Go. Talk. To. Him." Sabrina shoves me softly as we reach the bungalow.

I dig my room key out of the secret pocket in my dress—I'll get my phone later from the bridal suite—and let myself inside.

The hide-a-bed is still sticking up weirdly in the living room.

But the open primary bedroom door makes me suck in a breath.

I scurry across the rug to peek in.

And when I get there, I have to stifle a sob.

Theo's here. He's taken off his suit jacket and has his white button-down half-open over the sleeveless white shirt beneath while he works his way around the room, putting the kittens in a cat carrier.

"What are you doing?"

He doesn't look up at me.

Doesn't answer.

Like he's waiting for me to reject him so he doesn't have to be the one to reject me again.

I can't do that.

I need answers, but I'm not going back to the life I used to live, and I want to believe there's a solid explanation for this. "*Theo*, what are you doing?"

"Vacation's over. Going home. Back to work."

I flinch.

And that's what he sees.

The first time he's looked at me since I walked in the room, and he sees me flinching at him going back to *work*.

Like he knew it would make me flinch, and I've just proven his point.

"Why?" I ask.

"Make more money. What it's all about, isn't it?"

"*Why* is this your…path?"

He snags Jellybean off the counter and drops her into the carrier with the rest of her brothers and sisters, who are all meowing like they're confused and worried. "Because I'm fucking good at it. That bother you?"

I swallow hard.

Yes.

Yes, it bothers me. But I'm trying very, *very* hard to separate my childhood lessons in *porn is for filthy sex addicts* from my grown-up knowledge that Theo Monroe is a good man with a big heart who's been overlooked by so many people his entire life.

"I like you," I whisper. "I like you a lot. And I want to understand so that—"

"So that what? You can convince me to quit? You can quietly judge me in your head while you're telling me to my face that you're not? So I can be the dirty little secret your parents don't talk about because they'd rather you date boring pricks who won't make the news but also don't know a g-spot from an asshole? I'm a big deal, Laney. I'm a big fucking deal, and those videos everyone was taking? They'll be all over the news in under an hour. You want that to be your next problem at work? You want to spend your days knowing that everyone around you is wondering if we had freaky sex or just normal sex? You want to know if they're wondering how many women I screw? If we made videos? You want that?"

I blink at the heat in my eyes and purse my lips together to make them stop trembling.

He's not wrong.

I've thought all of those things.

But I don't *want* to.

I want—

I want him to have a different job so this can be easier. And that's not fair.

Which means if I want *him*, I have to find a way to accept him for *all* of who he is.

But he won't let me.

"So that's it?" I finally force out as he scoops up the last kitten. "You've decided for me what I do and don't want?"

He sweeps past me with the cat carrier cradled gently in his arms. "Got a few bigger problems than you right now."

"Do you?"

"This was coming eventually, princess. Just ripping off the Band-Aid now before it gets stuck too hard and leaves that gross adhesive all over both of us."

"I still like you even when you're a dick who won't give me a chance to find a way forward for us."

His shoulders hitch.

"And I know you're being a dick because you're scared and you don't want to hurt, and you know what? I'm scared too. I don't want to hurt either. But *this isn't how we solve things*."

"Nothing to solve," he grunts.

"If you didn't care, you wouldn't be mean."

He freezes at that.

He knows.

He knows *exactly* what I'm calling him on.

I was mean because I liked you and I didn't know how to deal with it.

When he finally slowly turns to look me straight in the eye, dread blossoms so hard in my stomach that everything in my core clenches.

"Guess that's the answer then," he says. "I'm not good for you. Never have been. Never will be. Good luck, Laney. I hope you find whatever it is you're looking for. But it's not me. It was never going to be me."

And then he's gone, taking the cats and striding out the door so fast, I'd have no chance to keep up with him.

He doesn't pack his duffel bag. Grab his suitcase. Retrieve the ring light from under the bed that's no longer a point of curiosity, but instead a glaring *you should've seen this coming* piece of evidence about what he does for a *day job*.

But I guess when you're one of the biggest internet porn stars in the world, you don't care if you have to buy a new toothbrush or a new ring light.

"You're being a giant idiot," I hear Sabrina say outside the bungalow.

Theo grunts again.

And then she's catching the door and looking inside at me, her makeup running, her hair a mess, utter grief shimmering in her eyes in the very, very worst ways.

"Wanna go get drunk?" she whispers.

No, I don't want to go get drunk.

I want to *not hurt*.

But I nod to her anyway because what the *hell* else are we going to do?

"*Yes.*"

37

LANEY

SMELL THAT?

That's the smell of playing hooky on fresh powder under a brilliant winter-blue Colorado sky.

Sabrina couldn't come. She's busy trying to figure out how to get Bean & Nugget back. Emma went on her honeymoon solo. Or so Claire relayed to us. Em hasn't actually talked to any of us since the wedding that wasn't.

My parents are less horrified than I thought they'd be at the idea of me taking another day off work right after getting back from Hawaii.

So I convinced a neighbor to come with me, and I'm pretending I'm paying attention to her friendly chatter while we ride the lift up the slopes.

Theo's a dick.

My heart hurts.

And *I am not going back.*

Back to work, yes. Today or tomorrow. I still love my job,

no matter what questions I'll face when I set foot in the office again.

But back into the safe little box of joyless, day-in, day-out, same old same old repetition when I get home at night?

No.

Fuck Theo.

I'm going skiing.

It's been a few years, but my ski boots still fit. My helmet still fits. My ski pants still fit.

My absolute doozy of a hangover from my last night in Hawaii is almost gone.

And *I'm fucking going skiing*.

And, pardon my French, *fuck the bunny hill*.

I've been skiing most of my life.

I don't need the bunny hill.

I need *speed*.

I need *fun*.

I need to prove that I'm not a stick in the mud. My reaction to falling *hard* for someone who neglected to tell me that *he's a porn star*—and he's right, a big one at that, no pun intended, damn him—is a normal reaction for even the most adventurous women in the world.

Fuck Theo.

Fuck Theo and that fucking video of his that Sabrina made me watch while we were at the bar.

She showed me his penis on his GrippaPeen channel.

His glorious, beautiful penis, standing fully erect against the backdrop of the ink on his hard stomach while he knitted one of those hearts that were all over the resort just above it, his voice filling my ears. *People will tell you that you suck sometimes. Those people aren't the people who matter. Those people don't give a shit about you. They care that they feel better next to you. Fuck those people. Cut them out. You deserve people who love you unconditionally and forgive you unconditionally. And when you find those people, do the same for them. If you don't love them, if you don't want what they think is best for them, if you can't forgive them, then maybe you're not the friend they need either.*

I shake my head while wind chills my face on the lift up the mountain.

It was like he was talking directly to himself.

Emma gets to make her own mistakes. You can't coerce her to not marry Chandler just because you don't like him right now.

He didn't want her to get married.

But *he still paid for the wedding.* He *set the whole thing up.* He fixed all the problems at the resort that didn't even check us out on the last morning because it finally ran out of staff and shut down.

Because it was what *she* wanted.

He trusted her enough to let her live her life on her terms, and he made sure it wouldn't be an outside force that pushed her into making a decision she'd question the rest of her life.

I don't know if I could ever do that for someone.

I don't know how many people in my life would see what a gift that was from him to her.

But I know it's what I've never felt like I had from my own parents.

The gift of being able to make my own mistakes, no matter how big or small.

I always felt like I wasn't allowed to make mistakes at all.

And I know it's complicated.

I know it's because the people who love us don't want us to get hurt.

But how do we learn? How do we grow? How do we *live* if we can't fuck up on occasion?

I almost wipe out getting off the ski lift—definitely distraction because I'm thinking about Theo, *not* me being inept—but I recover and take the turn to head to the top of the run with my neighbor.

Feels good to be using my body again.

Flexing my muscles. Being cold at the start of the run, the skis and boots and poles familiar old friends.

Feeling.

Living.

Fuck the people who judge you for your body, he said in another one of the videos I watched through Sabrina's log-in late last night when I couldn't fall asleep. And yes, I donated what would've been the monthly fee to a cat shelter to get over the guilt that came with knowing I was breaking the rules and getting content that I didn't pay for. Fuck Theo.

Fuck Theo and his *your body is a powerful motherfucking treasure. It's your story. It's the children you've carried. It's the grief you've managed. It's the bones you've broken and the scars on your skin and the life you've lived. It's strong. It serves you while you're serving everyone around you who demands so much without remembering that you're a human being, and your body deserves for you to love it as much as it loves you.*

For a guy who refused to eat for fear he wouldn't look good on camera, he knows what to say to women with physical insecurities.

Fuck Theo again.

He doesn't get more room in my head.

Not today.

Today, it's about racing down this mountain slope, about feeling alive again.

Cold air rushing my face.

My skis pointing where I tell them to point.

My legs flexing the way I tell them to flex.

My body flying faster and faster and faster down this mountain.

You can soar. You can fucking soar. Anyone who tells you that you can't is either afraid or they're looking out for someone who's not you. I grew up in a world that told me I was supposed to be afraid. That there was danger on every corner. But I never saw it. I never saw it, and I didn't want to see it. I wanted to laugh. I wanted to race. I wanted to fly. I wanted fun. I wanted adventure. I wanted something more than just surviving. Still looking for it. I hope you are too. I hope you're flying high in your motherfucking dreams and that when people tell you no, you do it anyway. Might be shit. Or it might be the best fucking thing you've ever done for yourself. All kinds of fancy philosophers will put it more elegantly. Fuck elegant. Who has time to worry how it looks when it's time for us to fly?

I hate him so much.

I *hate* him.

All of that wisdom.

All of that wisdom born from years of experience. Years of feeling like a fuckup. Years of doing life his way anyway.

That's why they love him.

They signed up to see that glorious penis under a man knitting hearts, and they stay because *he gets it.*

He knows insecurities.

He knows fear.

He knows disappointment. *Being* a disappointment.

And he knows it gets better.

He knows you can *make* it better.

But not with me.

Never with me.

I'm not enough for him. He won't *let* me learn to be enough for him.

Fuck Theo.

Just fuck him.

Fuck him all to—"*Aaaaaahhhh!*"

Hell.

Fuck all of it all to hell.

Fuck Theo.

Fuck this mountain.

Fuck the person who should *not* be on this mountain who

just cut in front of me from out of nowhere, arms flailing, completely out of control.

Fuck falling.

Fuck my ski not coming off like it's supposed to.

And fuck the pain radiating out of my leg, which is most definitely *not* supposed to bend that way.

38

THEO

NOTHING like the distinct sound of tires crunching on packed snow over gravel to make a guy's entire body go on high alert.

I'm out back, behind my place, splitting wood. Without a shirt. In fifteen-degree weather. Surrounded by snow.

And I'm hot.

I'm always fucking hot.

But I grab a damn flannel and throw it on anyway. Together with the lumberjack hat, the work boots, and the baggy orange overalls, it should be enough to detract any more picture-takers.

Signs aren't working.

Gonna have to move.

Smash my phone.

Wish I had enough money to pay someone to take down the whole internet. Or that I'd listened to Emma when she told me I needed to *incorporate my business* and get a privacy shield.

Car stops out front.

For a split second, I hope it's Laney.

I hope she's coming to call me on my bullshit excuse to walk away from her.

But she already did that, didn't she? *You're being an asshole because you're scared, and I'm giving you a chance to meet me halfway.*

And I was the idiot who kept on leaving.

Because I like her.

I like her *too* much.

She's right.

I'm fucking terrified.

I found my reason for living in Hawaii. My purpose. What I want to do every day for the rest of my life.

I found *her*. And I watched her laugh. Squeal with utter joy. Try new things. Step outside of her comfort zone.

And all the while, I felt like she was finally seeing me.

Like she liked me back.

Fear isn't usually my thing.

But I'm terrified who I am and what I do would hurt her so badly that I'd break her.

And no matter how much I justify that what I did was right and necessary, I still hate myself for doing it.

There's a crunch of boots on old snow out front. I'm carrying so much tension in my back that I don't even know who I am anymore.

"Nice signs. They work?" Sabrina calls from somewhere around my cabin, completely deflating me. Not Laney. Not anyone from town either. Lots of them have been checking up on me. Well-meaning, every last one.

But I'm getting tired.

"If they don't, my giant axe usually does," I tell her.

She ignores the subtle threat and strolls around back and into view. Where I look like a lumberjack who's taken one too many hits to the head with the wrong side of his maul, she's close to picture-perfect in black leggings, black snow boots, a black wool coat, black gloves, and a black beanie—all of which have a dusting of dog fur—over her massive black sunglasses.

Or maybe she's just picture-perfect because she looks like a red-haired, pale-cheeked, dog-loving grim reaper and Death sounds like good company.

"Over yourself yet?" she asks me.

"Nothing to be over."

"I noticed you haven't posted anything new since we got back."

"It's been *three fucking days*. Thanks for subscribing. Always like taking my sister's friend's money."

The sound of helicopter blades beating the air drum overhead.

I flinch.

She looks up. "Wow. They're even coming from the sky to spy on you."

I head for my cabin's back door.

Not sitting out here waiting for more freaking reporters to get a picture of me, even dressed and looking like a loner mountain man.

Sabrina hustles behind me and slips into my cozy little kitchen as well before the door shuts behind her. Three of my kittens swarm immediately. Fred's hovering behind my empty coffee cup next to the sink. Left it there just for him. He likes cover, even if he's starting to like me a little more.

"Whoa. You really did take an entire litter of cats home from Hawaii."

"No idea what you're talking about."

She makes a frustrated noise. "Laney thinks you still live in that single-wide at the edge of your dad's property."

I don't take the bait to ask how Laney's doing.

Not my business.

My business is *not* hearing gossip about anyone else in

this town—*ever*—and chopping wood and stalking the internet for people who need a little cash thrown their way.

To pay for gas or groceries.

For medical expenses.

For someone to hire a naked polka band to interrupt their sister's wedding since she's marrying a douche canoe.

That one hit close to home.

And was my first random act of kindness when I decided my entire bank account needs to go, which is proving more difficult to accomplish than it should be.

"Hear from Emma?" Sabrina asks.

I shake my head and make myself look at her despite the hit of guilt that comes with the question.

I tried. Did my best to make sure she was getting what she wanted. And I still feel like I let her down.

Hard not to.

I snuck over to her bungalow to see her before I made all the arrangements for my cats and flew home, and she told me to go away. That she didn't want to do this with me right now, and we'd talk when she got home.

I know she'll forgive me. It's what she does.

And she won't do anything to imply her forgiveness is out of obligation, but I'll still feel like it is.

That's on me.

One more thing to work on.

Sabrina's body deflates. "When she gets home, can you— can you put in a good word for me?"

"Sure."

"I'm off gossip."

"Uh-huh."

"I am. Forever. I'm done."

I stare at her.

She crosses her arms and stares back while the kittens sniff around her boots.

Sabrina was born in the kitchen at the original Bean &

Nugget here in Snaggletooth Creek, and her soul will forever be there. She's been hearing gossip at that little café since before she was old enough to understand what it was, and she's been using it effectively since high school, when she finally found her own line of what she should and shouldn't cross.

Guess that line got blurry last week.

"I mean it," she says while she squats to stroke Jellybean's little head. "I'm done with the gossip. See? This is me *not* asking how many reporters you've seen up here and *not* telling you how many we've chased away down in town."

I lift a brow.

She makes a face. "And this is me *not* telling you that my new asshole boss has been sending messages through his secretary that we're to continue as normal until he arrives sometime next week if we want to stay employed. Which is *not* gossip. For the record. It's my reality. Also not gossip, because I thought you should know—that phone call you overheard Chandler having? *That* was with my new boss. Chandler actually wanted the asshole to *go to the wedding* incognito and spy on all of us so he'd know how best to handle all of us when he showed up and announced his new position while Chandler was supposed to be on his honeymoon. Can you believe that?"

"Chandler can suck a bag of dicks."

"Agreed. I don't care how much he's in the doghouse with everyone in town, it's not enough."

I stroll past her in the little kitchen to toss another log into the wood-burning stove. There's more than a little guilt popping up over not helping Sabrina when she asked me to.

Telling myself it was probably already too late doesn't help either.

Could've done it quietly. Not let myself get identified.

"And I'm not mad at you anymore," Sabrina adds softly.

"It wasn't right of me to ask you to help. I apologize for putting you in that position."

"Would've done the same in your shoes."

Miss Doodles looks up at me from the rug in front of the stove, where she's melted into the floor, her softly swishing tail the only other movement coming from her.

"Good kitty," I tell her while I bend down to scratch her behind her ears.

She blinks at me, then heaves a loud, contented purr and melts even deeper into the floor.

"I'm going to buy him out," Sabrina says, following me into the room with three kittens on her heels. "I want my café back. If you're feeling like investing in something worthwhile in your own hometown in addition to throwing all of your money at interesting charities here and there, I'd be happy to negotiate very fair profit-sharing terms with you."

I stare at her harder.

"I'm not gossiping. You're just predictable. And I'm not *asking* you to help. I'm telling you that I'm gathering investors, and I'd be honored if you'd consider Bean & Nugget worthy of your time and money."

I grunt and throw myself into my recliner, barely missing Snaggleclaw, who was hiding behind the quilt my mom made me when I was born. My recliner would be the only furniture I keep in the living room, except my dad stops by every now and then to visit. Uncle Owen too.

I'll get more eventually.

But I haven't lived here long—not easy to see a whole damn house and want it and know it's okay to spend your money on it when you've never had money like this before—and it cracked me up the first time the Sullivan triplets stopped by and told me I needed more furniture.

Haven't had a lot of other people out yet, but I want to.

And now that no one's gonna ask how I could afford my

dream cabin on fifteen acres in the mountains, it won't be so awkward.

Might be when I invite some of my construction buddies. Got fired from my cover story job when the owner realized his wife had been watching my videos. First message I had when I landed in Denver the other day.

Sabrina doesn't sit on a cat when she takes the extra recliner, but she does have those three kittens climb into her lap.

"I'll think about it," I grunt to her.

She grabs a knitted heart off the end table and teases the kittens with it. "I used a fraction of the ammunition I have against Chandler to get all of the books going back ten years. I know where they went wrong. I know how to fix it. I have a business plan. I know what I'm doing. I won't fail. And I won't ask again. You might have some of the deepest pockets in town, but I don't care if I have five investors or a hundred. I'm getting the money together to buy this fucker out."

"Asking Laney?" *Dammit*. Wasn't going to ask. Was *not* going to ask.

She shrugs. "Doesn't matter to me that the rest of my family's being dicks and holding grudges because they think her dad's the triplets' biological father. Which isn't gossip, again. I heard you heard. It's only gossip if you don't already know it."

"Look, Sabrina, I like you, but not right now. It's a me problem. Can you please go away?"

"I haven't answered your question yet."

"I take it back. I don't want to know."

"You want to know or you wouldn't have asked."

"Habit. I was being polite. You're friends. I felt guilty for not helping you when you asked in the first place."

"You're never polite for the sake of being polite, and you only feel guilty because it's residual guilt on top of the guilt you feel about how Emma's wedding ended, the fact that

Chandler secretly sold the café and blindsided all of us, and then what you did to Laney. Even though only what you did to Laney is your fault."

She's got me there. "Go away. Time to make more videos. I'm stripping and jerking off in three minutes whether you're still here or not."

"You don't jerk off on your videos and I know you know I know it." She rolls her eyes like she also knows I have permanently killed my boner factory. It's on strike.

Pissed at me.

Maybe I'm pissed at myself.

But this thing with Laney couldn't have happened any other way.

If I hadn't heard you could make a little side cash waving your willy on GrippaPeen.com, I wouldn't have tried it. If I hadn't unexpectedly shot to the top of the charts—who knew knitting and dicks would be such a hit?—I wouldn't have had the cash to pay for Emma's wedding, Chandler wouldn't have asked me to cover it, none of us would've gone to Hawaii, and the last week with Laney wouldn't have happened.

Ergo, if I wasn't an internet porn sensation, I would not have had an opportunity to fall so hard for Laney.

And Laney dating an internet porn sensation isn't happening.

It's just not. This is too far for her.

And now I'm being an extra-big dick to Sabrina because I can't deal.

She's right. I don't jerk off on camera.

"I'll ask her to invest," Sabrina says, "but not yet. She has enough going on right now."

Fuck me. When does it end? When does everyone else quit piling on the guilt too? Does she really think I don't feel anything about what I did on Saturday? "You want to say something, just say it and go away."

This time, I'm treated to a classic Sabrina Sullivan *you are an asshole* look. "When I say *enough going on,* I don't mean *she's crying into her pillow over how you were a total dick.* Please. Laney has enough self-respect to know when she deserves better than a guy who'll break her heart because he's terrified of having feelings for someone so awesome. I mean, you give someone a little bit of time to recover when they break their leg skiing. Self-centered much, Theo?"

I'm out of my chair like a firecracker went off in my butt, scaring all of the kittens and Miss Doodles too. They go flying back toward my bedroom. "She *what?*"

"She has enough self-respect—"

"The *broken leg* part," I force out through a clenched jaw.

"Oh, you didn't know?" She crosses one leg over the other and leans back in her seat. "Sorry. I'm off gossip. If you didn't know, it's gossip. My lips are sealed."

"*Sabrina.*"

"If you were family, that would be one thing, but you're just the guy without the balls to trust she'd listen to you explain why you like to make money baring the goods on the internet. You don't get the story about how she decided to skip work and go skiing and have fun and put her life ahead of her job, since you have to *do the things* to earn the inside story about people you want in your life instead of just *saying you're going to do the things.*"

Jesus. The café's new owner doesn't stand a chance if this is even a fraction of what she's about to throw his way. "Is Laney okay?"

"I mean, as okay as a person with a broken leg can be."

"Did she really break her leg, or are you fucking with me?"

"For your sake, I'm going to pretend you didn't ask me that."

"Where is she?"

Sabrina makes the *I'm zipping my lips and throwing away the key* motion.

Emma will—fuck.

Fuck.

Emma's not answering her phone while she's on her solo honeymoon. Hurting. And I can't fix it.

Just like—*fuck.*

Like I'm hurting. Like Laney was hurting Saturday.

I fist my hair and stifle a groan. "I don't want people judging her and treating her like shit for what I do, and they would. *They would.* I'm a fucking *porn star*, Sabrina. And she's *Laney fucking Kingston*. She deserves better than everyone thinking about her sex life every time they look at her, and *you fucking know they will.*"

"You're not a *porn star*. You're a naked inspirational speaker. But if you want to call yourself a porn star, fine. Put yourself in a box. Limit your possibilities with labels and assumptions. Have all the doubts in the world about one of my very, very best friends on this whole entire planet, who would *happily* love you with everything she has to give if you'd pull your head out of your ass because *she's not her fucking parents* and *she deserves some fucking credit.*" She rises. "And now you've made me mad. I take it back. I have no interest in letting you have any part of my hostile takeover bid to get Bean & Nugget back."

"You can't do a hostile takeover on a private company."

"Aww, look at Mr. Smartypants. And I thought all that time you spent playing on Reddit and tripling your money on that stock squeeze gamble was just for fun."

Is she serious? Is she serious right now? I didn't even tell *Emma* I was playing along in a little *screw the hedge fund managers* thing last year, and she hasn't gotten hold of my bank records to do my taxes for me yet this year.

And that's another thing I'll be in trouble for.

Lack of correct estimated taxes.

I hate the real world sometimes, even if I love a lot of people in it. "*How the fuck—*"

She waves a hand and flashes me a smile. "Oh, sorry. Forgot. I'm done gossiping. And now I'm mad that you tricked it out of me."

"Where's Laney?"

"Not tricking that out of me. That one, you have to earn." She dusts her hands. "Cute cats. I like them. Let me know if you're selling any. I feel like Bean & Nugget could use a feline upgrade. I mean, if my dog doesn't eat them. Which he probably won't. Probably."

"*I'm not selling my fucking cats.* They're my cats. Finders keepers, and I will fucking *destroy* anyone who hurts them or comes between us."

"Oof. Someone's in a mood. Better leave you alone."

"Where *the fuck* is Laney?"

"That's too many fucks, Theo. I don't like being *fuck*-ed at. You're on your own. Bye, kitties. Don't let him fuck at you too, okay?"

She strolls back through my kitchen, and a moment later, the back door clicks shut.

I lunge for my phone and pull up my Hey Neigh neighborhood app, which is the second-best source of information on Snaggletooth Creek gossip behind Sabrina.

Been avoiding it because—yep.

Theo Monroe is a porn star.

Here's Theo's GrippaPeen profile.

Is he really that big?

This isn't appropriate for us to discuss. There are CHILDREN on here.

Whoa, he's making like, OVER A MILLION DOLLARS A MONTH. You think he needs someone to run his appearances? Like an agent? I can learn to be an agent.

Saw three more reporters in town at Bean & Nugget this morn-

ing. Hoping for a Theo sighting. We have a CELEBRITY in our town! This is so exciting.

Do NOT, I repeat, do NOT give the reporters information about Theo. HE DIDN'T SHOW HIS FACE FOR A REASON. And he's one of ours. Protect him at all costs.

Yeah, protect him. He's OUR porn star. They don't get any part of him.

I put on blinders, pretend *Theo Monroe* and *GrippaPeen* are about someone else, and I search for Laney's name.

And there it is.

Sending hugs to Delaney Kingston. Poor thing. Did you all see her cast? I put together a meal train sign-up for anyone who wants to help her out.

She broke her leg.

She took a day off work, went skiing, and *broke her leg*.

Then told someone, who posted it for all of us to see, that if she'd known she was going to break a leg, she would've gone ahead and started on a double black diamond run so she'd have a better story than getting tangled up with a newbie on a warm-up run.

She was serious.

She wants to *live*. Have fun. Take chances.

And the first time she did it, she *broke her leg*.

Shit.

Shit.

She's probably sitting home telling herself she's not supposed to have fun. Not supposed to be adventurous. That this is a sign, and she needs to put herself back into the frumpty-dumpty fucking *box* labeled *Perfect Little Princess Plainy-Laney*.

I have to do something.

I have to.

Even if she doesn't want me, I need to make sure she still wants to *live*.

39

IF MY MOM doesn't quit fussing over if I have enough pillows under my cast, I'm going to scream. "Mom. Please. It's *fine*."

She and Dad flew home early from Hawaii when they caught wind of my accident on social media. I've already had an earful about how I should've called, and I've already given an earful back about how I can handle having a broken leg all on my own.

Which is maybe an exaggeration, but Sabrina's around, and our old middle school science teacher is recently retired and bored and has an entire crew lined up to check on me and bring me food at least three times a day, and my poor neighbor who was with me is checking up on me too.

Beauty of small-town living. Even when your blood relatives aren't around, the rest of your town family is.

"We've never had broken legs in the family before," Mom says. "This is terrifying."

"The doctor says it'll heal just fine. I can work remotely for a few weeks." And then, when I'm out of this damn cast, I can go hiking again. Take time off to maybe even do an overnight backpacking trip with Sabrina. Ask Emma to go on a hot-air balloon ride with me in Denver when she gets back, given that it'll almost be warm enough by the time I'm cleared for *fun* again.

Which I'm not telling my mom.

Not today, anyway.

"Are you hungry?" she asks. "Betty dropped off lentil stew for lunch. I can heat it up for you. She makes the best lentils."

"I'm fine, Mom. I really am." I'm not fine.

My leg itches, and it'll be six damn weeks before I can scratch it. The painkillers are working, but there's still some achiness in my shin. I slept like crap.

And I keep worrying over Emma on her solo honeymoon.

And then wondering what Theo's doing.

If he's in town or if he found a place to hide out while Snaggletooth Creek is crawling with reporters who are hoping for an exclusive photo of him.

Freaking Addison posting the video of Emma's wedding disaster on TikTok.

I hope she gets fleas in a place that she can't reach to scratch. That video exposed *all* of my best friends in our worst moments.

Mom purses her lips while she looks at me.

She's in linen pants and a silk blouse. Pearl earrings. Makeup. The upgraded diamond wedding ring Dad bought her the first year the company had over a million dollars in profits.

"Did Dad cheat on you when I was a baby?" I whisper.

Can't help it.

Sabrina was right. I didn't want to know. But I guilted it out of her last night while she dropped everything to sit with me in the emergency room.

Mom gasps and her chin wobbles. "Who told you that?"

"That's not really the important part, is it?"

She sighs and turns to the window. "Laney, sweetie, life's complicated, and you need your rest."

"I need a little more than that, Mom."

"Rest first."

"I don't *want* to rest. I want to go sledding. I want to go see a frozen waterfall. I want to race go-karts in the middle of town in the middle of the night. I want to drink too much and need Sabrina and Emma to carry me home. I want to learn to scuba dive and go back to Hawaii and dive with the turtles. I don't want to be *safe*. I don't want to be *smart*. I don't want to wake up when I'm seventy-four and realize my entire life has passed me by with no stories to tell about it beyond that time I had a really hot fling with a funny, adventurous, *rules don't exist* guy during the best-worst week of my best friend's life. And I want to know how many people in this town know that Dad cheated on you and just don't talk about it because *nobody* says bad things about us because we're the damn *Kingstons* and we fund too much around town to risk pissing us off."

She stares at me like I've lost my mind.

I probably have.

And I'm okay with that. I don't want my mind back.

I want my *heart* back.

I flop back against the uneven pillow behind my back and stifle a grimace of pain.

Probably shouldn't do that while my leg's in a cast. "Never mind. I'll take a damn nap."

"You're upset that we didn't offer to help Bean & Nugget," she says quietly.

"Did you know?"

She sighs. "You're upset that we weren't *asked* to help Bean & Nugget."

"And that's because...?"

She takes a long time to answer, and when she does, it's

on an even deeper sigh. "Christopher wouldn't have cheated on you."

So that's it.

She picks men for me that she thinks won't cheat.

Theo wouldn't have cheated.

Would he?

I don't know. *I don't know.*

Fuck Theo.

Just fuck Theo for making me fall in love with him and not having the balls to love me back.

I turn my head away and close my eyes. "I'd rather not get married at all than get married to someone who has the personality of a shoe insert. So if that's all you plan on introducing me to for the rest of my life, please don't waste your time."

"The gel inserts or the old-fashioned inserts?" she asks.

I glance back at her.

That's literally the funniest thing she's said in a decade. "We used to laugh all the time. Now it's all about work and responsibilities and what's right for *a family like us.* I know you and Dad worked hard to build all of this, and I love our mission and our purpose at work, but at home...at home, I want to be happy. I want to laugh. I want to love my life and know that when I'm seventy-four, I might have regrets, but I don't want them to be that I sat on my couch being boring and afraid of what may hurt me outside my doorstep. And that *includes* sex."

She wrinkles her nose and goes pink in the cheeks.

And my doorbell rings.

I sigh and pull up my phone to check and see who's there, and the minute I catch sight of what the doorbell camera is recording on my porch step, I gasp.

"What?" Mom lunges across the room like she's a freaking mountain lion. "What is it?"

It's Theo.

It's Theo, but it's not *just* Theo.

It's Theo, in baggy jeans and a thick Carhartt jacket and a black beanie, like he's in disguise, with what looks like a *cat carrier* hanging on his shoulder.

He shifts his weight and stares at the door for a minute, then looks down at the doorbell. An old beater truck sits in my driveway behind him.

That's so Theo.

Have half a billion dollars in the bank, still drive the truck that grounds him.

"What's he doing here?" Mom asks.

"*Shh.*"

He squats down in front of the doorbell camera and looks straight at it. "Hey. I don't know if you're in there," he says. "I don't know if you can hear me. But in case you can—I get it if you don't want to talk to me. I was an ass. I was a certifiable ass, and you deserve so much better than that. I'm sorry. I'm so sorry, Laney. So I brought the kittens. I don't have to stay. I'll go if you tell me to. But if the kittens would make you feel better, if they'd cheer you up—they're yours. For today. For tomorrow. For forever. You can have my kittens for as long as you want them. If you want them. If you're not here, and you see this later, the offer still stands. Send Sabrina to get them if you don't want to talk to me. I just—I just want to do something—anything—to help you get better. And this is the best thing I could think of."

"Kittens?" my mom says. "Kittens are—"

"Let him in." I swipe my eyes and cheeks. That *asshole.* He's bribing me with his kittens. And I *know* how much he loves his kittens. "*Let him in.* Or I'll do it myself."

I don't have to ask her twice.

"I'll hang out and wait for a few minutes in case you're seeing this," Theo says over the doorbell camera. "But if the kittens get cold, I'll—Gail. Hello."

My mom doesn't immediately answer, and when she does, I brace myself.

But there's nothing cool in her polite, "Please come in."

It's warm.

Kind, even.

I wouldn't know she didn't like him if I were a random fly on the wall. I *do* know she doesn't like him, and even I can't detect any lingering animosity.

I kill the stream on the video as Theo steps inside the door. My foyer is small, so it's only a moment before Mom leads him into the living room, where I'm propped on the couch.

His brown eyes land on me, and I'm so mad that I'm crying right now.

I don't want him to see me cry.

I don't want him to know he hurt me.

Fuck Theo.

But I love Theo.

No matter how much I don't want to.

He lowers his gaze and crosses the room to drop to one knee in front of me, setting the cat carrier gently on my rug. "Kittens?" he asks quietly.

"I will accept kittens."

"You feeling okay?"

"I am so mad at you."

He winces as he opens the carrier and lifts a gray kitten out. Jellybean.

It's Jellybean.

And she's meowing as he sets her carefully in my lap.

"I left Fred home with Miss Doodles, but the rest of them are here. Litter box is in the car. I'll come clean it. Or send someone else over if you don't want to see me."

"Why are you still being a dick?"

This is not me. It's not. I'm the polite woman my mother trained me to be.

But I'm *so angry* with him. And I'm *so glad* to see him. And he looks *so damn right* in here. Like he's the touch that's been missing against the sage green couches and the lavender walls and the ivory brick fireplace.

Like he's what makes it home.

His gaze wavers as he looks at me again. "I'm really bad at hope. Much better at action."

"And self-sabotage."

"Not mincing words today."

"Should I be?"

He drops another kitten in my lap. Jellybean's crawling up my chest to lick my chin. I close my eyes and let her while I order the tears to stop.

But Jellybean's licking them all away, and it's so sweet, and it's making my heart all kinds of soft and open and vulnerable.

I can *not* be vulnerable to this man again.

Not if he's only here out of guilt or obligation or anything other than because he wants to be here, with me, because I matter to him enough to have the hard conversations.

"I'm sorry, Laney," he whispers. "I'm an ass."

"You don't have to be."

Another kitten lands in my lap.

I know my mom's hovering. Watching all of this. But she's not saying anything.

And Theo's still here, dropping kittens into my lap.

He squeezes my thigh on my good leg. "Want me to leave them long enough that they'll need their litter boxes?"

"Yes." I do. I want them here, with me, crawling all over me and making their little meows and licking my chin and climbing on my shoulders to sniff my ear and tickle it with their little whiskers.

I want them *here*, so he has to come back and check on them.

"Okay. Right back."

The warmth from just being near him dissipates, and I peek my eyes open as I hear the front door shut.

Mom's watching me with her fingers to her lips.

"Please don't," I whisper while I stroke Widget, who turned three times in my lap and is now splayed across my thigh, purring like the world depends on the strength of his purr.

She blinks quickly. "I—I didn't know you were serious about wanting cats."

"There's so much about me that *I* don't even know right now."

The door opens again. Theo's back in the blink of an eye with a big box of litter and three pans. I point down the hall. "Powder room, please."

He nods and disappears.

Mom watches his retreating backside.

I close my eyes and lean back on the couch, six kittens all over me, and belatedly realize I have a kitten on my head, but there aren't any pinpricks.

Theo trimmed their claws.

He's a good kitten dad.

I pet Widget. I stroke Jellybean while she licks my chin, and then pull Snaggleclaw off my shoulder when she licks my neck and tickles me. Blinky and Panini attack each other on the blanket, spilling over my lap. Cream Puff's giving me a scalp massage, but he abandons me right before Theo walks back into the room.

"Nice form," he says to something over my head, "but wrong rocks. We'll work on that."

I look up as he pulls Cream Puff off of my curtains and sets him back on my lap.

Our eyes meet again, and if I didn't have to grab my crutches to get off this couch, I'd be tackling him in a hug.

The last time I saw that much grief and regret shining in a person's face was his mom's funeral.

I've lost grandparents. An uncle. A friend or two over the years in tragedies.

But the look of complete hopelessness and helplessness on Theo's face at his mom's funeral was something that quietly haunted me for years until I managed to make myself forget in high school because he was such a complete dick.

The memory's roaring back today though.

"Does it hurt?" he asks, dropping his gaze to the cast sticking out from under my blanket.

I shake my head. "Not much. Good drugs."

"The *you'll forget all of this by morning* kind of drugs?"

I shake my head again.

He nods once, and then he's gone again.

Tucking his hands into his pockets while he strolls back outside.

"He likes you," my mom says.

She sounds surprised. Like she didn't think he was capable of liking someone.

Or maybe like she didn't think he could like someone like me.

"He's a really good guy," I say quietly, "and I'm very, *very* mad at him."

She eyes me like she's afraid to ask the question.

The question. The *only* question.

Are you mad because he's a porn star?

I'm not, surprisingly enough. I want to know *why*. I want to know *how*. But I deeply believe that he has a good reason.

A guy doesn't get famous for having the internet's most inspirational penis without having a story.

And I want to hear it. From him.

With an open mind.

No matter where he's planning to go with his career from here.

"I'm mad at him because he didn't have enough faith in himself or in me to fight for me," I whisper to my mom.

She glances at the door as it opens again.

That's Theo again. Carrying another bag of supplies.

Quietly belonging everywhere he goes, whether he's causing chaos or setting up kittens with food and toys and litter.

Except I don't think he realizes how right he looks no matter where he is. Especially here.

Is that why he's quiet? I wouldn't think he'd do anything quietly.

But he does.

And right now, he's quietly hurting too.

I can *feel* it.

He disappears into my kitchen, and I hear the sounds of food bowls being laid out.

So do the cats.

All six of them perk up their ears and swivel their heads toward the kitchen.

"You are all so adorable," I whisper to them.

Cream Puff leaps off the couch first with a long jump that took an extra big butt wiggle for confidence, sniffing as he heads cautiously toward the kitchen, slinking like he knows *me* and the bubble around me is okay, but the rest of this house is suspicious.

Jellybean follows, then Widget, and then the other three all together as a group, tumbling over each other.

Theo pops his head out of his kitchen, spots the kittens, nods, and disappears again.

"He's odder than I thought," Mom murmurs.

He's nervous.

She makes him nervous.

He should be smiling. Cracking a joke. Relaxed.

He doesn't hide in the kitchen long. And when he returns after running the water in the sink a few times, he's holding a small brown lunch sack and a hair dryer.

He shoots a look at my mom, then crosses the room and

helps himself to the seat next to me, sitting close enough that I can feel his warmth but not close enough for our thighs to touch.

Without a word, he hands me the bag.

I smell what's inside before I open it. "You're cheating," I whisper.

"Expect any different?"

"No."

My mouth waters.

I *want* the cookies.

I want them *so badly*.

But I make myself set the bag aside.

He eyes me like he's waiting for the yelling to start.

I don't want to yell.

I just want him to tell me *why*. Why he's here. What he wants. What he's willing to do to get what he wants.

Not tricks. Not kittens and fresh-baked chocolate chip cookies.

Me.

I want to know what he wants with *me*.

He looks down at the hair dryer. "They'll tell you not to scratch down your cast. This one has a super low setting. Blow it down the cast if you itch. It'll help."

"Thank you."

"Yeah. Least I can—anyway. If I break one of my bones again, I might ask for it back."

"Again?"

He flexes his left arm. "Climbing accident. You were all in college."

We both fall silent.

It's the most comfortable *awkward* I've ever experienced.

Or maybe the most awkward comfortable.

I miss him.

I had three days of realizing I knew nothing about who

Theo truly is but enjoying every minute with him more and more and more.

I want to go on adventures. I want to see new places. Try new things.

Laugh.

Press boundaries.

Realize life goes on even when it's not perfect.

And I want to do it *with him*.

He lifts his gaze to mine again. Takes a deep breath.

And looks away.

I could ask my mom to leave.

But something Claire said is sticking with me. *I don't want to be easy. I want to know I'm worth fighting for.*

I love my parents. They drive me bonkers sometimes, but I love them.

And I am head over heels for Theo. I don't *want* to be.

Unfortunately, I can't help myself.

He's everything I've been missing in my life and so much more.

But I don't want to be *easy*. I don't want to bend over backward to make everyone else comfortable. I want to know I'm worth fighting for.

I want to know if he's willing to fight.

Will I fight for him?

Completely. Absolutely. Without hesitation.

But *he walked away*.

He walked away without giving me a chance to prove it to him.

If this is nothing more than neighborly guilt or neighborly kindness bringing him by, if he's not all in, then what's the point of fighting for him?

No matter how much it hurts?

You can't make someone love you.

"I started on a dare." His words come out so quietly that they almost don't register at first. "It—it was dumb. The dare.

The dare was dumb. And it got dumber the drunker I got. But I said I'd do it, so I signed up and posted a video of me knitting a heart, naked, while ripping off something I'd heard some radio deejay say about the double standard of having to be nice to extended family at the holidays while they insult your clothes and your car and your job."

I saw that video.

It made me mad.

Mostly because I grew up going to those family holiday dinners and hating them, and I felt like he was talking about me. About what my parents used to deal with anytime we'd see my mom's side of the family down in Denver.

"I didn't think I'd get five followers, but people started talking about it in some corners of the internet, and next thing I knew, I had two hundred. So I posted another video. Same setup. Knitting a heart, dick hanging out, talking about finding where you fit after years of being a perpetual disappointment."

My heart hurts.

I saw that video too.

Last night, actually.

I should've called *anyone* other than Sabrina to sit with me at the hospital.

She made me watch more of them.

I was just high enough on the painkillers to not fight her and just sober enough to remember.

"Then the comments started coming," he continues. "*You see me. Thank you. I needed to hear that today.* And for the first time in my life, I was doing something that mattered. Something *good*. There were women who told me they were leaving their husbands after years of abuse and neglect because *I* convinced them they deserved love. There were women who told me they were taking the leap and going back to school. Starting a new job. Setting boundaries with bosses and kids and parents. There were dudes who told me I'd inspired them to come out to their families and live their truth. And it kept growing. And growing. And then the money came, and then the paranoia came, and everything kept growing. I kept working construction so nobody would ask why I didn't have a job and Emma wouldn't worry about how I was supporting myself until I asked her to do my taxes and had to tell her. I quit knowing who to trust and how to act and if the women who hit on me in bars saw the real me and liked it, or if they somehow secretly knew about my GrippaPeen channel. If they recognized my tattoos or my voice. I was so fucking glad I didn't put my face on the screen and still paranoid that—"

"That they'd only like you for your money," my mom interjects.

Theo and I both jolt.

He eyes her.

I gape at her.

She's blinking quickly, like *she's* trying not to cry too.

"That," he says quietly. "Exactly that."

She nods.

Then she nods again.

Like she knows *she* is *exactly* who he didn't want to know.

He didn't want *her* approval because she suddenly found out he had a big bank account.

"I—I apologize if it seems that I'm one of those people," she says quietly. "I'll try to only think of you as a porn star."

I choke on a noise that might be a laugh, or it might be a sob.

I'm not entirely sure which.

"I'm not a porn star," he replies. "I'm a naked motivational knitter."

"Of course. I'll make sure to tell Charles."

"Are you two serious right now?" I ask them.

They both ignore me.

"I thought you'd take this worse," Theo says to her. "*You* don't need my money."

She glances at me but still leaves my question hanging. "It's quite the wake-up call to rewatch a video of your daughter yelling at you to *shut up* over your reactions to her, ah, favorite naked motivational knitter, and then to realize everything you've done to protect her has backfired the same way everything your own parents did to try to prepare you for the world made you resent them too."

Mom's face is going a mottled red.

Theo studies her for a minute, then nods. "I could probably get you a sound clip of some of my advice on the subject of parents respecting their kids' choices."

"That won't be necessary. But thank you."

"Offer stands."

"What's happening?" I point between them. "What's happening here?"

"I'm realizing I'm late to get dinner in the oven at home," Mom replies. "Laney, sweetheart, if you need *anything*, you know your father or I can be here in five minutes. Day or night. Anything. Theo, it was…lovely to see you again."

"Is this reverse psychology?" I ask her.

She shakes her head as she reaches the foyer. "Love you, sweetheart."

And then she's pulling the door open before she's even put on her coat and boots.

And it's just me and Theo.

Me, Theo, and three kittens who are peeking back in at us from the kitchen.

"Why are you here?" I ask him.

He holds my gaze for an eternity. An eternity when I want to hug him and kiss him and tell him I love him and I don't know if I can love him as big as he deserves to be loved, and an eternity when I want him to pull me into his arms and tell me that he wants me, *only* me, and that he'll do anything to get me back.

Which is ridiculous.

I'm *Plainy-Laney*.

What in the world can I offer to him that he can't find anywhere else?

He's here because he heard I got hurt having *an adventure* and he feels bad.

"Never mind." I twist in my seat, wishing I could get up.

"Because you're my purpose," he says quietly. "And even if you don't want me anymore, you deserve to know how special you are and how sorry I am that I was an ass."

My pulse goes on a breakaway. "If this is just a bunch of guilt—"

"My whole heart shattered into pieces when I heard you were hurt. Not because I wanted to be there keeping you safe. Because I missed out on being there to watch you fly. To watch you soar. To watch you do what I kept telling myself you wouldn't do so that I could lie to myself and say it was a *kindness* to you to be a dick on Saturday night instead of fighting for you like I should've. I don't want you to move on without me. I want you to move on *with* me. I lived in guilt for a lot of years before I found a way to accept myself for who I am, and it made me do a lot of shitty things. I don't want to go back to living in guilt for pushing you away when you're the only person I've ever wanted."

"But *why*? Why *me*?"

He leans over and scoops up two kittens that he keeps for himself. "Because you know all of the darkest, ugliest, worst parts of me. You have a million reasons to hate me. To never want to see me again. But you spent last week believing in me as one of the good guys. You. Laney Kingston. Accepting me. *Embracing* me. Living with me. There's nobody else in the world, Laney. No one else who could understand expectations and boxes and having to fight for the life you want to live. No one else who can challenge me the same. No one else who can make me feel like I'm on a bigger adventure than I am when I'm with you. I don't want easy. I don't want superficial. I meant it when I told you I don't want some half-ass love. I want it all. And I want it with you."

My heart is swelling outside of my chest. Tears drip down my nose. "For someone who's spent our whole lives calling me *Plainy-Laney*, you sure do know how to make a girl feel special."

He smiles softly and brushes a lock of hair out of my face. "Won't get that from some boring-ass banker."

"I don't care what you do for work," I whisper. "You're doing good in the world."

He shakes his head. "Time to move on."

"Theo—"

"Posted my last video already today."

"You're quitting because of me."

"Not quitting. Reconsidering my course. Penises are a dime a dozen. Got a pretty damn fine woody here, but they didn't come back for my dick. They came back for what I had to say. And as someone very wise reminded me last week...I like to eat."

My jaw won't quite close. "*Penises are a dime a dozen?*"

He grins.

And then grins bigger.

And then the butthead giggles.

And it's so cute that I drop my head to his shoulder and start laughing too.

"I was *so mad at you* ten minutes ago," I wheeze into his shoulder.

He wraps an arm around me and kisses my temple, heat radiating out of his body. He needs to lose the jacket. He's always too hot.

"I love making you laugh," he says. "Favorite sound in the world."

"No, it's not."

"It is. I've waited forever for this. I don't take it for granted."

Three more kittens poke their heads out of the kitchen.

Theo kisses my hair again.

My laughter subsides into a deep, contented sigh. "Sabrina told you about my leg, didn't she?"

"Yep."

"Was she a pain about it?"

"Yep."

"Good."

"She could've been a bigger pain. I deserved it."

"You are *so* lucky I'm in a cast right now, or I'd be putting you in a headlock until you said three nice things about yourself."

"Oh, look, the last kitten. Hey, did you see I brought you chocolate chip cookies?"

This man.

He's a little bit of a mess. But so am I. And our fun together is just starting.

I lean back a bit so I can look up at him. "I'm going to demand proper dates."

"Like the one with bacon?"

"Yes."

He smiles at me, and then he's kissing me.

Soft and slow and gentle, like he's afraid all of me is as damaged as my leg is.

"I missed you," I say against his lips.

"I'm still terrified this is a dream and you'll never forgive me."

"This isn't a dream."

"Are you sure?"

I kiss him again. "Nope. You're right. Feels like a dream."

He smiles at me. "A dream come true."

"I'm your dream?"

"You've always been my dream, Laney. Always."

"That must've been pretty awful."

"Worth it."

I smile back at him. The words slipped out so easily, but I fully believe him.

For all the years he annoyed me, I know exactly how he feels.

He starts chuckling again. "You're thinking it was way worse for you, aren't you?"

I shake my head. "Stay with me tonight?"

"Any night."

"I don't think I can make you pancakes for a few days."

"I don't want to stay for your pancakes."

"Not even *these* pancakes?" I move his hand to my breast.

He squeezes.

My clit tingles.

And I officially regret my skiing decision yesterday.

Except for the part that breaking my leg is what brought Theo back here.

"How about *I* be in charge of everything related to you and your pancakes for the next few weeks?" he murmurs.

"That doesn't seem fair to you."

"Consider it an extended apology that I'll enjoy very, very much."

"You know I forgive you, right? You don't have to keep making this up to me."

He lifts his gaze again and studies me.

And I don't think it's because I'm leaping to the wrong conclusions.

I think it's because he's surprised I leapt to exactly the right one.

"You know what's scariest right now?" he asks quietly.

"That you're scared at all?"

He shakes his head. "Just how easy it is to love you."

Just when I thought I was done with the tears for the day. "I think that means we're doing something right."

"*Right* and I have never been super tight."

"Don't worry. I've got you. We'll get you through."

He smiles at me again.

I kiss him again.

I can't seem to stop myself. And I don't want to. "I love you too," I whisper between kisses. "But I think I have the harder job of the two of us."

He outright laughs this time.

And then he shows me that it doesn't matter that my leg's in a cast.

He meant it when he said he'd take care of all of my pancakes.

EPILOGUE

Theo

Aﬀer a very succinct and honestly surprising press release from Kingston Photo Gifts announcing that Gail and Charles's daughter was dating a newly-retired GrippaPeen star, and they fully support her decision, and anyone with opinions about it can go to hell—I'm paraphrasing—the reporters have departed the Tooth for lack of juicy gossip.

Kinda nice that they're privately owned and don't have to make any board of directors or shareholders happy over their future CEO's private life.

But I'm still keeping myself scarce.

Mostly because I have nothing better to do with my time than spend all of it with Laney.

And today, I'm taking her out of her house for the first time since her accident.

We're going all the way across town, if you can believe it.

All the way to…

My house.

"Oh, look at your cabin," she squeals from the passenger

seat of her Volvo, which I will officially accidentally-on-purpose be calling her *vulva* the next time we talk about her car in front of her parents.

Gotta make sure they mean it when they say they accept me for who I am. And I'll only do it once.

Probably.

"Is that a good *look at your cabin*, or is that a subtle *I hate it, Theo, you have to move*?" I ask.

"It's *adorable*. I love it."

"All of my wallpaper inside is covered in boobs."

"Aww, you put your face on your wallpaper? That's adorable too."

I slam the brakes too hard as I jerk my head to look at her, not quite certain I heard her right.

And she doubles over laughing, nearly banging her head on the dash in the process. "Oh, your face," she gasps.

"Damn."

"You should see your face."

"Didn't think I'd rubbed off on you this fast."

"You rubbed off *all over me* in bed this morning."

And now I'm both intellectually impressed with that zinger and also sporting another hard-on at watching Laney push boundaries of her own.

Her cast sucks.

It's work-around-able, but it sucks. Especially when she gives me boners.

Giving her sponge baths does not suck though.

Not saying I want her in a cast forever, but there's a strong likelihood she'll be getting regular sponge baths for the rest of her life anyway. Eventually I'll find something to do with my time that resembles some form of a *day job* again, but for now?

For now, being Laney's personal manservant is all the purpose I need in life.

"Are we keeping score?" she asks. "Am I even close to you in smartass comments for the hour yet?"

Her eyes are twinkling. Her smile is as broad as I've ever seen it. And she's squeezing my thigh while I don't even try to resist smiling back at her. "You'd love wallpaper with my face all over it."

"We're doing tests with custom wallpaper at Kingston Photo Gifts. Here. Smile. I'll have an *accidentally* messed up roll sent to my parents' house."

"Get unbuckled, trouble. No garage. I'm carrying you inside."

Her eyes go smoky while her smile stays fixed. "That's my favorite."

I get her inside without slipping, and she squeals all over again. "It's Fred and Miss Doodles!"

I've been dashing back and forth between my house and Laney's to check on them. Sooner or later, we'll combine the litter again. Probably sooner.

We just have to decide whose house they live in or how often we want to transport them between our houses.

But that's not the bigger problem right now. "Shit."

"What? Was that a surprise? That couldn't be a surprise. I knew they existed, and you kept leaving me to check on them."

No, the *shit* is more about my shortsightedness. Two chairs in the living room.

No couch.

Huh.

Maybe all's not lost.

She'll have to sit in my lap.

Or we'll have to sit together in bed.

Did I make my bed?

Do I care?

"Nothing to prop your leg up on," I tell her.

She makes the squinty face that means she's debating if she believes me or not.

I'm not lying.

That is definitely one of the many thoughts flying through my head.

"To the kitchen with you," I tell her. "Best option right now for boring people with day jobs."

She ruffles my hair and kisses my cheek.

I love that she knows I'm teasing.

And I love that she's working from home for enough weeks that the gossip about us in her office will have probably died down by the time she makes it back there. And she says her parents have our backs. *You were working behind a paywall,* she keeps telling me. *Not walking around in public flashing everyone. Anyone who's seen your penis knew what they were signing up for, and that's on them. It takes two sides to make a naked inspirational knitter successful.*

"If you get your work done early," I tell her, "we'll go sledding."

"Meanie."

"I'm serious. Your leg's wrapped up tight. Probably safer today than it was last week. I'll pick a small hill."

"Tell me you didn't go sledding when you broke your arm."

"I did not go sledding when I broke my arm."

She lifts her brows at me while I settle her in at the table and slide a second chair over for her leg.

And I grin. "It was September. Hadn't snowed yet. Be right back. Fred might sniff you. He's getting braver. Treats are here if you want to try them."

I leave her with a bag of cat treats and head back out to her car to grab her crutches and the big-ass purse with her computer in it. I've barely retrieved them when once again, I'm cringing as I hear a noise.

Why are there tires crunching on my gravel?

Swear to fuck, if someone's coming out here to spy on Laney and me, even *after* I did that entire clothed, face-showing video telling my viewers I was closing up shop to save my body for one woman and one woman only, and *after* that press release—

Oh.

It's Sabrina.

Still annoying.

Except for the part where Laney and I haven't heard from her yet today.

We've all been checking in with each other to see if Emma's sent anyone messages from her solo honeymoon.

Laney's in touch with Claire too.

So far, all's radio silent.

I'm starting to not like it even more than I thought I wouldn't like it, even if Em's not scheduled to get home for another few days.

Sabrina screeches her car to a stop inches from Laney's bumper and jumps out.

And she is *not* happy. "Where's Laney?"

"Is it Emma?"

"No. *Where's Laney?*"

I point to the house.

Despite me having longer legs and being twice as close to the door as she is, and despite her heeled boots and the crap ton of snow on the ground, she beats me inside.

"Don't get up," I call to Laney as I hustle after her redheaded friend.

"*Sabrina.* Oh my god. What's wrong? *What's wrong?*"

I skid to a stop in the kitchen and find Sabrina digging through my cabinets.

"*Sabrina,*" Laney repeats. She flaps a hand at me. Silent request for her crutches.

"*Where do you keep the damn paper bags?*" Sabrina shrieks.

I reach over the fridge, pop open a cabinet that's too high for Sabrina to reach, and pull out a single paper sack.

She lunges and starts breathing into it as she uses the

lower cabinets along the back wall to support herself while she sinks to the floor.

"Emma?" Laney says.

Sabrina shakes her head. "*Me,*" she pants.

"*Oh my god, are you pregnant?*" Laney shrieks.

Fred yowls. Miss Doodles chimes in with a sharp *me-OW* of her own.

"Worse," Sabrina moans into the bag. "So. Much. Worse."

"Are you *dying?*" Laney whispers.

I'm feeling kind of useless, so I stand behind Laney's chair and settle my hands on her shoulders.

"Stand—Hawaii—boss," Sabrina says between puffs.

Laney stares at her. "Slower."

"Last night—in Hawaii—"

"The night I passed out drunk by like seven in the evening and you went out the rest of the night and didn't come home until the next morning?" Laney prompts. She glances at me. "Claire was there. I wasn't alone. Promise."

I nod.

Sabrina's bag crinkles as she sucks in air. "Hot guy—bar— slept with—"

Laney squeaks. "*You had a hot one night stand that night?*"

"So guilty—didn't mean to—too fun—but now—now—" Sabrina cuts herself off by gasping for breath inside the bag.

"Wait," Laney says. "Wait wait. Did you say *boss?*"

Sabrina nods fast and furious.

"He's—no."

Sabrina nods more while she puffs into the bag.

"*Your hot one-night stand is Bean & Nugget's new owner?*" Laney shrieks.

Sabrina moans. "*Yes.*"

And now that I know the world isn't exploding, there's not *bad* news about Emma, and Sabrina's probably about to ask us all for money again, which is fine, she can have it, I start to breathe a lot easier.

"Oh, god," Laney whispers.

Sabrina nods again. "Worse."

"*You're pregnant with your one-night stand-slash-boss's baby?*" Laney shrieks.

Sabrina throws the paper sack at her. "*I am not pregnant.* But I want him gone. And I don't—I can't—he won't—Laney. *Laney.* He's not like he was in Hawaii. Not at all. He won't sell to me. And I think he'll take the first opportunity to *fire* me. Bean & Nugget is a lost cause."

Oh, shit.

Shit shit *shit*.

Sabrina's gonna cry.

Cannot handle this.

Cannot handle this.

Laney crying? Yes. Please. I mean, not *please*, but like, if she has to cry, please let me be the one to put her back together.

Sabrina crying?

Get me the hell out of here.

Laney makes another noise. "Theo. Crutches. Please."

On the one hand, I'd like to go live in the woods to get away from Sabrina crying.

On the other, I get a boner every time Laney issues orders.

I bolt into action. Action's where it's at.

As soon as Laney has a single crutch in hand, she's pushing herself up.

Second crutch, and she's across the kitchen in four swings, including two to get around the table.

I'm right behind her because I'm basically her pet right now.

And I like it that way.

She swings her cast to one side and squats on her other leg so she's down at her friend's level.

Boner's getting bonier.

"Sabrina Sullivan, *you listen to me*," Laney says. "Are you listening?"

Sabrina nods.

"Bean & Nugget is *not* lost. Who are you?"

"You just said my name."

"*Who are you?*"

"Fine. *Fine.* I'm Sabrina Sullivan."

"No, you are *Sabrina fucking Sullivan*. And you are *not* going to let *some random man* that you've seen naked keep you from your dreams, because *we are the ugly heiresses and we let no men stand in our way*. Am I right?"

Sabrina nods, but she also starts breathing too hard again.

I grab her a new paper bag and hand it over.

"So you know what you have to do," Laney says to her.

Is it hot this winter, or is it just my girlfriend?

Also, I'm even more turned on every time she owns the nickname I gave her a couple decades ago.

"I can't, Laney," Sabrina whispers into the paper bag. "I quit. *I quit.* Theo. Tell her I quit."

"I'm gonna sit this one out," I say. "Just got back in her good graces," I add in a stage whisper. "Also, I don't think you'd be here if you didn't want her to fix this for you. I'd do what she says."

"You can't quit and you know it," Laney tells her. "It's in your blood. This is what you do. You know how to walk the line. So stand up. Get back in your car. Go back to work. And find out *all* of the gossip about him. This is what you've been training for your entire life. Find out the gossip. Use the gossip. *Get your fucking café back.* Am I clear?"

Sabrina takes a deep, shuddery breath. "But what if it makes Emma hate me even more?"

Laney sighs and reaches for Sabrina, then makes a strangled *ulp!* noise as she tumbles headfirst onto her friend.

Stupid fucking cast.

"Stupid fucking cast," she stutters.

"You are *seriously* rubbing off on her," Sabrina says darkly to me.

"It's awesome," I agree while I carefully lift Laney back up and get her back to her chair. "You okay?"

"I did that on purpose," Laney mutters.

I kiss her head. "Perfect avoidance of the question."

"Emma will *not* hate you for doing what you do best to get your café back," Laney says to Sabrina. "Pretend I'm hugging you while I'm reassuring you. And listen to me. *Listen to me*. She doesn't hate you now."

Sabrina winces.

Hell, I wince too.

Laney told me about what happened when I turned into an asshole and disappeared.

Only other time I know of that Emma's ever been that mad was the first time she dumped Chandler not long after they left for their respective colleges. She never told me why she dumped him, but it didn't matter.

Not when she was that furious.

Get the feeling this was worse.

And she might be over second chances.

"I'm rooting for you," I tell Sabrina.

"She'll forgive you," Laney insists. "But *I* won't if you don't go fight for what you want. And if you don't let me help you every step of the way."

"Okay." Sabrina sucks in a big breath. "But this is the last time I'm weaponizing gossip. I swear. *I swear*."

She takes a few more deep breaths, grabs both paper bags, hugs Laney, hugs me too, and heads for the door.

"Text me when you're ready to make a plan," Laney calls. "And go hug your dog. You'll feel better."

"You're too good for me," Sabrina calls back.

She sounds better.

Not quite there, but better.

Laney looks up at me.

I drop a kiss on her head. "Awkward. But maybe we won't be the biggest story in town for much longer."

She laughs a little.

And then she sighs. "Do you think I gave her the right advice?"

"Princess, you gave her the *only* advice. Don't worry. This is Sabrina. She has it. And she has you on her side. You've got me on your side. Emma gets home soon, and you'll be unstoppable once the three of you are reunited. This dickweed doesn't stand a chance."

She peers up at me.

I kiss her again.

Will it really work out for Sabrina?

No idea. Don't know what she's up against.

But I'm good with change.

Whatever happens, we're in for a ride, and I'm planning to enjoy the hell out of it with Laney by my side.

PIPPA GRANT BOOK LIST

The Girl Band Series

Mister McHottie

Stud in the Stacks

Rockaway Bride

The Hero and the Hacktivist

The Thrusters Hockey Series

The Pilot and the Puck-Up

Royally Pucked

Beauty and the Beefcake

Charming as Puck

I Pucking Love You

The Bro Code Series

Flirting with the Frenemy

America's Geekheart

Liar, Liar, Hearts on Fire

The Hot Mess and the Heartthrob

Copper Valley Fireballs Series

Jock Blocked

Real Fake Love

The Grumpy Player Next Door

Irresistible Trouble

The Tickled Pink Series

The One Who Loves You

Rich In Your Love

Standalones

The Worst Wedding Date

The Last Eligible Billionaire

Master Baker *(Bro Code Spin-Off)*

Hot Heir *(Royally Pucked Spin-Off)*

Exes and Ho Ho Hos

The Bluewater Billionaires Series

The Price of Scandal by Lucy Score

The Mogul and the Muscle by Claire Kingsley

Wild Open Hearts by Kathryn Nolan

Crazy for Loving You by Pippa Grant

Co-Written with Lili Valente

Hosed

Hammered

Hitched

Humbugged

Pippa Grant writing as Jamie Farrell:

The Misfit Brides Series

Blissed

Matched

Smittened

Sugared

Married

Spiced

Unhitched

The Officers' Ex-Wives Club Series

Her Rebel Heart

Southern Fried Blues

ABOUT THE AUTHOR

Pippa Grant wanted to write books, so she did.

Before she became a USA Today and #1 Amazon bestselling romantic comedy author, she was a young military spouse who got into writing as self-therapy. That happened around the time she discovered reading romance novels, and the two eventually merged into a career. Today, she has more than 30 knee-slapping Pippa Grant titles and nine published under the name Jamie Farrell.

When she's not writing romantic comedies, she's fumbling through being a mom, wife, and mountain woman, and sometimes tries to find hobbies. Her crowning achievement? Having impeccable timing for telling stories that will make people snort beverages out of their noses. Consider yourself warned.

Find Pippa at…
www.pippagrant.com
pippa@pippagrant.com